Prais

"*Genesis* leaves Left Behind in its hair-fraying, nerve-frying, blood-freezing apocalyptic dust!"

—WILLIAM MARTIN,
New York Times bestselling author of
The Lost Constitution

"*Genesis* reads like Left Behind on steroids!"

—DOUGLAS PRESTON,
New York Times bestselling author of
The Kraken Project

"If you liked the Left Behind series,
you'll love *Genesis*!"

—DAVID HAGBERG,
New York Times bestselling author of
Retribution

"*Genesis* may be the best apocalyptic thriller ever written. It makes Left Behind look like *Rebecca of Sunnybrook Farm*."

—JUNIUS PODRUG,
author of *Presumed Guilty*

TOR BOOKS BY KEN SHUFELDT

RAGE

KEN SHUFELDT

TOR®

A TOM DOHERTY ASSOCIATES BOOK
NEW YORK

This is a work of fiction. All of the characters, organizations, and events portrayed in this novel are either products of the author's imagination or are used fictitiously.

RAGE

A Tor Book
Published by Tom Doherty Associates, LLC
175 Fifth Avenue
New York, NY 10010

www.tor-forge.com

Tor® is a registered trademark of Tom Doherty Associates, LLC.

ISBN 978-0-7653-7595-7

Tor books may be purchased for educational, business, or promotional use. For information on bulk purchases, please contact the Macmillan Corporate and Premium Sales Department at 1-800-221-7945, extension 5442, or write to specialmarkets@macmillan.com.

First Edition: August 2015

Printed in the United States of America

0 9 8 7 6 5 4 3 2 1

To those men and women who have sacrificed and died to make this country what it is.

How can a man die better
Than facing fearful odds,
For the ashes of his fathers,
And the temples of his gods?

—THOMAS BABINGTON MACAULAY,
"Horatius at the Bridge"

RAGE

CHAPTER 1

His flight was the last to land, before the whiteout conditions forced them to close Dulles International. He'd intended to rent a car, but the counters were all closed. When he walked outside to hail a cab, he found one lone taxi that hadn't given up for the night.

When the cab stopped at the gate to the estate, Charles Goodwin found himself marveling at how quickly life could throw you curves. He was in D.C. to meet with Stevan Baldridge, the longtime chairman of the RNC.

Just the month before, Stevan and the committee had asked if he would accept the vice presidential nomination at the upcoming national convention. He'd made his fortune as an investment banker, and was a staunch Republican, so he'd been more than honored to accept a new challenge. At the time, he'd thought he could be a great partner to Peter Montblanc, the party's heir apparent.

After the security guard verified his identity, he opened the gate and allowed them to proceed down the tree-lined lane to the main house. When the cab stopped under the covered entryway to the majestic mansion, William, the family butler, walked out to greet Charles. William led him inside and said, "I'll take your overcoat, and you can go on back. Stevan is waiting for you in the downstairs library."

* * *

"Thank you for seeing me on such short notice," Charles Goodwin said.

"Never an issue, but what's the rush?" Stevan Baldridge asked. "The convention is still months away."

"True, but I wanted to discuss your plans for vice president."

"That's your job, my boy."

"Not if we want to regain the White House. The ticket needs someone who can pull in the minority vote, particularly the Hispanics."

"The latest polls I have show that we've made real progress with the minority voters."

"You mean the same assholes that kept telling us Romney was a shoo-in?"

Stevan shrugged.

"Have you gone through the data from the poll we commissioned?" Charles asked.

"No, I haven't. I assumed it would show the same splits we've been seeing from the national polls."

"You know what they say about assumptions. The data clearly points out what I view as a catastrophic shift in the demographics."

"You numbers guys give me a headache. I'm sure you're just overreacting?"

"Possibly, but if the numbers are anywhere close, it could be the beginning of the end for the GOP."

"That seems harsh, but even if you're right, where are we going to find someone that fits the bill?"

"That's why I'm here. I think we should vet out Victor Garcia."

"The mayor of Albuquerque? Have you lost your mind? He's not a politician; he's a war hero. I doubt he'd even be mayor if the Democratic candidate hadn't gotten caught with a hooker the week before the election."

"Probably true, but on paper he's got everything you'd

want in a candidate. He graduated top of his class at the Naval Academy and went on to be a Rhodes Scholar. He won a Silver Star for his actions against the insurgents that attacked the ambassador's gathering in Iraq."

"Was that when he lost his legs?"

"No that was from an RPG, a few months later in Afghanistan."

"Quite impressive, but I'm not sure the party is ready for a Mexican VP."

"There it is."

"What do you mean by that?"

"If you have to ask, you're part of the problem."

"I've got the utmost respect for you, but you can't come into my home and talk to me like that. I thought we could count on you to do what's best for the party."

You clueless bastard, Charles thought to himself. "That's what I'm trying to do. Let's face facts for a moment. We're at risk of losing a lot of seats in both houses, and if we don't make some real changes, we may never regain the presidency."

Stevan mulled over Charles's words before he said, "I guess it's worth taking a look. Fix yourself a drink while I make a few calls."

An hour later, the circular driveway in front of the mansion was filled with limousines. As Charles watched eight of the most powerful Republicans in the country sit down in the library, he found himself hoping that he hadn't overreacted to the situation.

"This had better be as urgent as you claimed. It's my fiftieth wedding anniversary, and my wife was mad as hell when I left the party," said John Steinberger, a multibillionaire and the most powerful donor in the party. "And what's this bullshit about needing a new VP candidate? We handpicked Charles."

"That's why we're here," Stevan told the group.

"Charles wants to bow out, and he wants us to vet Victor Garcia as our new candidate."

"Garcia? I've never heard of him," John declared.

"Me neither," Peter Montblanc said. "Seriously, you can't expect me to take on a running mate that no one's ever heard of. Besides, we can't have a VP that couldn't handle being president."

"We've had many that I wouldn't have wanted to run the country," Stevan said.

"We're all here, so let's get to it. I need to get back," John Steinberger said.

"Have any of you read the results from the poll you paid for?" Charles Goodwin asked.

"Yes, but they've got to be wrong," John Steinberger said.

"It's projecting that the next election could have a seventy percent Hispanic participation, and could compromise almost thirty percent of the total voters."

"Is that even possible?" Ty Pendleton asked.

"Possibly," Charles said. "No one seemed to notice the changes they slipped into the last budget that changed the EB-5 visa program."

"Never heard of it," Peter Montblanc said.

"Most people haven't. It was originally intended to foster foreign investment and job creation. If someone invested between five hundred thousand and a million dollars, depending on where the company is located, they were granted a fast path to a permanent green card status."

"So what, they still can't vote," Stevan said.

"That's where the changes come in. The program was amended to remove the cap on the number of visas, and to allow them to skip the green card and immediately become naturalized citizens."

"How the hell could that happen?" Peter asked.

"Same old shit. It was one paragraph buried in thousands of pages of legislation, which nobody read. Coupled with the Democratic get-out-to-vote campaigns, and the new amnesty programs, it's fueled a tremendous influx of newly minted citizens."

"What kind of numbers are we looking at?" Stevan asked.

"I double-checked the state's voter registrations, and the newly registered voters are in excess of eleven million."

"That doesn't bode well for us. We don't rate very highly with the illegals," said Mell Blanc, the next largest GOP contributor.

"Dear God," Charles murmured under his breath.

"This shouldn't be a surprise to any of us," said William McKinney, the GOP chief strategist. "This is just a continuation of what led to our failure in the last election. No offense, Peter, but I warned you we couldn't win with Charles on the ticket."

"So you think this guy can pull enough of the Mexican vote to make a difference?" John Steinberger asked.

"I do," Charles said.

"You must feel pretty strongly to turn down the VP role," Mell said.

"Trust me, it breaks my heart to do so, but yes, I do."

"Big whoop," Peter Montblanc said. "What the hell are you doing wasting my time on this unknown loser?"

"Given the circumstances, I think we should at least check him out," Stevan said.

"Whatever, but don't waste any more of my time until you have it put together. I'll need to see a comprehensive plan before I'll consider making any shift in our strategy."

"Understood," Stevan said.

"Charles, do you know Victor's full name?"

"Of course. It's Victor Delgado Garcia, and his wife's name is Melinda Esmeralda Santiago Garcia."

"Damn, that's a mouthful," Peter said as he walked out. "Thanks, Charles, I'll get my guys going on the background checks."

CHAPTER 2

Thirty days later, Stevan Baldridge reached out for an update. "What's taking so long?"

"Sorry, our normal investigators couldn't get anyone to talk with them. I finally had to pull in some guys from the CIA."

"I'm shocked that they wouldn't talk to a bunch of pushy white guys," Stevan said. "So what's the verdict?"

"Hell, I wish my background was as good. We couldn't find one person who had a bad word to say about him."

Stevan had his assistant call the mayor's office for an appointment and make the travel arrangements.

The flight from D.C. was uneventful, but as the G650 Gulfstream that John Steinberger had let him use was making its final approach into the Albuquerque airport, the turbulence from the winds off the nearby mountains was making it quite uncomfortable.

"Sorry about the rough ride, but we'll be on the ground shortly," the captain reported.

When they landed, they taxied over to the Cutter Aviation FBO. The copilot flipped the switch to open the door and lower the stairway as the limousine pulled up.

"I should be back by four P.M.," Stevan told the pilots.

Stevan hadn't wanted to call any attention to his visit,

so he'd had his assistant book a meeting room in the Hotel Albuquerque, a small boutique hotel in the historic Old Town district. The concierge greeted Stevan as he walked in.

"Good morning, Mr. Baldridge. My name is Hector, and if there's anything you need while you're with us, just let me know. Your meeting room is set up as you requested, and if you'll follow me, I'll show you to it."

There was a roaring fire going in the fireplace, and they'd removed the normal boardroom table and replaced it with a pair of heavy leather chairs and a small table covered with drinks and snacks.

"Mr. Garcia just called. He should be here shortly," Hector said.

A couple of minutes later, Stevan was surprised when Victor came ambling into the room.

"I know," Victor said when he saw the bemused look on Stevan's face. "Everyone is surprised to see me up and about."

As they shook hands, Stevan said, "Damn, you've got some grip."

"Sorry. It's the rehab. I was putting in twelve hours a day on my upper body strength while I was getting ready for my new legs."

When they took their seats in front of the fireplace, a waiter approached and asked, "Would you like something to eat or drink?"

"I'd take some coffee," Victor said.

"Same here," Stevan said.

"So what's up?" Victor asked. "We don't often get the chairman of the RNC in our neck of the woods."

"You're right, I don't get out this way very often, but if you don't mind, I'm going to skip the platitudes and get right to the point," Stevan said.

"Please do," Victor said as he shifted to a more comfortable position.

"We'd like you to be our vice presidential candidate."

Stunned, it took a few seconds for Victor to respond. "Really? There have to be hundreds, no, thousands of men better qualified."

"I'm not going to bullshit you; you wouldn't have even made my short list. It was actually Charles Goodwin who convinced us to take a look at you."

"So I'm to be the token Mexican?"

"I wouldn't have put it quite like that, but your ethnicity was a factor."

"If it were just me I'd say yes in a heartbeat, but I've got a family to consider. My kids have bounced around from base to base for most of their lives, and they've just gotten settled into their new school."

"One of our biggest contributors gives away millions in scholarships every year, and I'll see that your kids get full-ride scholarships to St. John's College High School."

"At least it's Catholic," Victor said.

Try as he might, Stevan couldn't get a read on what Victor was thinking as he sat pondering his answer.

After Victor had hesitated for several seconds, he said, "I'll do it, with one codicil. I don't want to be just a figurehead."

"That's not my call, but I'll do what I can."

"I guess that's better than nothing. So what's next?"

"The first week in July I'll send a team down to begin working with you. They'll brief you on the platform we'll be presenting at the convention, and begin laying out your role in the campaign. Oh, one other thing. I need you to resign once you're nominated, because we're going to have you on a very busy schedule."

"Anything else?"

"Please don't mention this to anyone. We want it to be a surprise announcement at the convention."

"Not even my wife?"

"You can tell her if she can keep her mouth shut."

"Not an issue."

When they got up to leave, Stevan said, "This is a great opportunity for you. Don't blow it."

"Understood."

On the way back to the airport, Stevan called Peter Montblanc.

"So how'd it go?" Peter asked.

"He'll do it."

"What a surprise. What did you think of him?"

"He seems like a fine young man. He's very articulate, and even on prosthetic legs he carries himself like a marine."

"He can walk?"

"Quite well actually."

"That's good. I wasn't looking forward to herding a cripple around. Come by when you land, and we'll have a quick drink and discuss our next moves."

Later that night, he knew he had to make the call, but he wasn't looking forward to it. He poured himself a tumbler of Scotch from the bar and sat down at a small table by the massive picture window. As he gazed out at the city's lights, he found himself wondering how he'd allowed it to go this far.

One of his college fraternity brothers ran Eldon Luxury Suites in downtown Washington, D.C., and he could always get him one of the penthouse suites when he needed a quiet location for a call or a rendezvous with his mistress.

He hit autodial on his encrypted satellite phone, but when the man answered he didn't give him a chance to speak. "Did you and your partner receive the packets I sent?"

"Yes, but why the drama? These phones are secure."

"They are, but just go with it. Golem was quite adamant about it. Everyone gets a code name. You're Jonathan, and your cohort is Fredericka."

"And you're to be Klaus?"

"A little humor is always good," Klaus said.

You don't have a humorous bone in your body, Jonathan thought to himself. "Who the hell is Golem?"

"Need to know, my boy," Klaus said.

"This must be important for you to call at this time of day."

"I think so. They're replacing Charles Goodwin with a Mexican by the name of Victor Garcia."

"Why?"

"They decided they couldn't carry the election unless they can capture more of the minority vote."

"What do we know of this Garcia fellow?"

"Top of his class Naval Academy graduate, ex-marine colonel, and a Silver Star recipient. He was just elected mayor of Albuquerque, but as far as I can tell, that's all the political experience he has."

"That's not necessarily a bad thing. How do we get leverage on him?"

"I haven't been able to find anything yet, but I'll stay on it."

"Keep me informed, and I'll pass this along."

CHAPTER 3

"How was your day?" Melinda Garcia asked.

"Pour me a stiff drink while I get cleaned up, and I'll tell you," Victor said.

"So, why the need for a drink?" Melinda asked when he sat down on the couch.

"I had a meeting with Stevan Baldridge this afternoon."

"The chairman of the RNC?"

"The same."

"There wasn't anything about him coming into town on the news last night."

"That's because he flew in to talk with me, and he left as soon as we finished."

"A special trip in to see you? That sounds exciting. What did he want? Did he invite you to speak at the convention? I'd love to go to New Orleans."

"Slow down, sweetie. The RNC wants me to be Peter Montblanc's vice president."

"Oh my God. You said yes, didn't you? I've got to tell my momma."

"You can't tell a soul, not even the kids. I promised that you'd be the only person I'd tell, and that you'd keep your mouth shut until the convention."

"Not fair."

"Melinda."

"OK, but it's going to be so hard. I can't believe it, vice president of the United States."

"We haven't won yet."

"Don't take this wrong, but why you?"

He knew why she was asking, so he addressed it head-on. "Because I'm a Mexican."

"Surely that's not all of it."

"Being a decorated, crippled veteran probably didn't hurt, but there's been such a shift in the election demographics that they've realized the Republican Party can't win without some sort of a minority representation."

Melinda could seem ditzy at times, but she'd graduated from the University of New Mexico, and had received her medical degree from the University of Maryland School of Medicine. "That's harsh, but who cares? How many people ever get this chance?" She gave him a big kiss.

"What's for supper, and where are the kids?" he asked.

"The kids are spending the night at my mother's, and I thought we'd go out."

"How about we order a pizza and stay in?" he asked as he kissed her neck.

"Good idea."

CHAPTER 4

The months had flown by, and before they knew it, they were boarding John Steinberger's Gulfstream for the flight to New Orleans. Peter Montblanc hadn't wanted them in town until Thursday, the final day of the convention.

"I'll be taking care of you today," the flight attendant told them as they came aboard. "Would you like something to drink before we take off?"

"I'd take a water," Victor said.

"Make mine a tea, if you have it," Melinda said.

"We have pretty much anything you'd like. Regular, jasmine, or green tea?"

"Green would be great."

"Sit anywhere you'd like, and there's a stateroom in the rear of the aircraft if you'd like to take a nap. We have a full in-flight entertainment system. If you'd like to watch a movie or listen to some music, just let me know what you like, and I'll put it on for you. We also have full Internet access, and I have laptops for you to use if you want to check your messages."

A couple of minutes later, the captain came back to speak with them. "I'm Captain Will Lomax, and the crew and I are honored to be taking care of you today. We'll be flying at forty-five thousand feet, and our flight time will be approximately one hour and fifty minutes to New

Orleans. It may be a little bumpy as we climb out, but the weather is supposed to be good the rest of the way, so we should have a smooth flight. Now make yourselves comfortable, and they should clear us for takeoff in a few minutes."

Melinda was reading the emergency instructions as they taxied. "This is some aircraft. I wonder what something like this costs?"

"North of sixty million," Victor said.

"No way."

"Way, I looked it up when Stevan e-mailed me the itinerary."

"I guess we're going to be moving in different circles than we're used to," Melinda said.

"For sure."

"Are you nervous?" Melinda asked.

"Hell, yes," Victor said. "I wasn't this scared the first time I went into combat."

"Please fasten your seat belts, we've been cleared to land," the first officer announced.

As they turned on final approach to New Orleans' Lakefront Airport, they were both getting excited. When they came to a stop in front of the Hawthorne Global Aviation FBO, they could see a limo coming across the tarmac to meet them.

"That must be our car," Victor said.

"I could get used to this," Melinda said.

By the time they reached the stretch limo, the ground crew had their bags loaded. As the driver helped them in, he said, "Help yourself to the bar. There's juice, water, or something stronger if you want."

The convention was being hosted at the Ernest N. Morial Convention Center, but Stevan Baldridge had asked them to meet him at their hotel, the Windsor Court. They had just walked into their room when the phone rang.

"Would you and Melinda mind meeting me in room 1152?" Stevan Baldridge asked.

"We'll be right down," Victor Garcia said.

When they walked in, Stevan introduced himself to Melinda, and said, "I hate to be so abrupt, but I wanted to brief you on what's going to take place tonight, before I have to take off. A car will pick you up at seven thirty. When you arrive at the convention center they'll escort you to a waiting room. They'll come and get you just before Peter goes on. He's scheduled to make his acceptance speech a little after eight. His speech is relatively short, and when he announces you as his running mate, you and Melinda will come on stage to be recognized. Peter will take care of introducing you to the delegates, and you won't have to speak. There will be a press conference afterward, and again we're not expecting you to have to answer any questions, but we do want you sitting at the table with Peter. Melinda, you'll be sitting with Peter's wife, Deborah, and I'll make sure that we make the introductions before then. Any questions?"

"Will I have a chance to visit with Peter before?"

"Unfortunately no, but I've scheduled a meeting for tomorrow morning. If you don't have any more questions, I need to get going."

When Victor and Melinda got back to their room, there was a huge vase of orchids and a box of expensive chocolates on the table.

"I wonder who this is from," Melinda asked.

"There's a card, open it and see."

"It's from Charles Goodwin, and it says: 'Best wishes, and many thanks for taking a chance and stepping up to help the party. If there's ever anything I can do for you, just give me a call on my cell.' Where do you know him from?"

"I've never met him, but he was their first choice for the VP slot. He stepped aside, and was the one that advocated that they pick me."

* * *

When the car dropped them off at the rear of the convention center, one of John's men led them inside to where they would be waiting. The room was not much more than a glorified storeroom. The only furniture were two metal folding chairs and a small table with two bottles of water on it.

A few minutes later there was a quick knock, and the door swung open. "Son of a bitch, it's true," Harold Winston said. Victor recognized him from his picture in a *New York Times* article he'd read on the plane. Harold was one of the leading contenders mentioned. "A dammed Mexican, I might have known. I'm going to kick Peter's ass for leading me on," Harold said with a snarl, and slammed the door shut.

"Well, that was special," Melinda said.

"Sorry, I'm not sure what that was supposed to prove, but that was Harold Winston, and by the sounds of it, he thought he was going to be the one they called on tonight."

"I don't know why I'm still shocked at racist assholes like that," Melinda said.

"There are a lot of good people in this country."

"I know, but it still pisses me off."

Five minutes later there was another knock on the door. "Come in," Victor called.

"They're ready for you," said Harry Mitchell, Stevan's personal assistant.

As they were walking up the ramp that led to the backstage area, Victor's heart was racing with the excitement of the moment.

"Welcome," Stevan Baldridge said. "You can wait right here, and we'll be ready for you in just a moment."

"I hope I don't pass out," Melinda said.

"You'll be fine," Victor said, as they stood listening to Peter Montblanc finish his acceptance speech.

"Thank you for the faith you've shown in me, and I promise you that with your help, we'll retake the White House and return our nation to its former greatness," Peter Montblanc said as he raised both hands and waved to the delegates. They gave him a standing ovation. "Now, I'd like to introduce a man that I have just as much faith in. Let's hear it for the next vice president of the United States, Victor Garcia."

"You're on," Stevan said as he pulled the curtain back so they could walk out.

Very few of the delegates had any idea of who Victor was, but they all stood and gave him a resounding roar of approval.

"Thank you," Peter said. "Standing to his right is his lovely wife, Melinda. We're running over on our time, so we're going to wrap it up, but we'll be handing out press kits so all of you can get to know Victor and his family. Now let's get to work, and thanks to all of you for making this the best convention ever."

Later that night, an encrypted satellite phone rang. "Yes?" Klaus said.

"It's official," Jonathan said.

"Damn, I was sure they'd make the last-minute substitution we suggested. I should have pledged more money."

"Money wasn't the issue. Montblanc has a burr up his ass about something."

"Why do you say that? He's always been one of our staunchest supporters."

"For the most part he still is, but he let slip that he has some personal agenda he intends to pursue."

"That can't be good. Have you made any headway on leverage on Garcia?"

"None."

"Keep at it, and keep me posted."

CHAPTER 5

A few weeks before the Republican convention, General Nikahd, the head of the Iranian military, had been summoned to an early morning meeting in Ayatollah Rostami's office, near the center of Tehran. The ayatollah had recently relocated his residence and offices to the parliament building in Baharestan Square, and the general hated going down there. A few years ago, he'd been tasked with quelling the riots in the square, and he still had nightmares about it.

As he made his way through the square, he caught sight of the parliament building. *That's still the ugliest building I've ever seen,* he thought to himself. After he'd cleared the security checkpoint and parked his car in the underground garage, he walked slowly toward the bank of elevators. The general had been a tall, good-looking man in his younger days, but the toll from the years of constant political turmoil and combat had worn him down. His dark brown hair had turned to gray, and the crevices in his face made him look twice his age.

The ayatollah's assistant met him when he stepped off the elevator and led him down the hall to the meeting. The room, like everything the ayatollah possessed, was bland and without any pretense of comfort or style. The ayatollah was sitting in a straight-backed chair, facing a couch and a small, plain, wooden table.

Even seated he was an imposing figure. A full beard cloaked his thin hawkish features, but his small, beady, dark brown eyes could burn a hole through your soul. He was above all the religious leader of the Islamic Republic, but he also possessed a keen intelligence and was, for the most part, a moderate in his thinking and actions.

"What's up?" General Nikahd asked as he took a seat on the couch.

"President Shirazi has just received the UN's latest demand," Ayatollah Rostami said.

"How bad?" General Nikahd asked.

"Bad enough. If we don't allow their inspectors unfettered access to any of our facilities, they're going to embargo the rest of our oil shipments," President Shirazi said.

President Shirazi was a bit of an enigma to the general. He knew he had to be in his fifties, but his boyish good looks, blond hair, and blue eyes still made him stand out in a crowd. Even after the council had promoted him to president, he was still prone to dressing like a Westerner, and his lifestyle often raised the hackles of the ayatollah and the other clerics.

"How is it that they can tell us we can't have nuclear aspirations, when Third World countries like North Korea have the bomb?" Ayatollah Rostami asked.

"You know the answer to that. It's those damned Jews," General Nikahd said. "They're scared to death we'll get nuclear weapons and use them to wipe them out."

"I'm afraid your last speech didn't help any," President Shirazi said.

"I'd watch what you say," Ayatollah Rostami said.

"I'll admit I might have gotten a little carried away, but we can't afford to show any weakness, and you know we can't allow those UN stooges to wander around wherever they chose."

"That's for sure," General Nikahd said. "If they were to find what we've got down south, the shit would hit the fan for sure."

"Don't give it a second thought," President Shirazi said. "I brought them in through Azerbaijan, and there's no way they'll be able to track them back to us."

"So you said. At the time I didn't feel like I could turn down the offer. However, in retrospect, I probably shouldn't have made the deal, but what's done is done."

"I know we've failed you. We still can't miniaturize the warheads," General Nikahd said.

"No shame there. The North Koreans have had the bomb for years, and they still can't do it either," President Shirazi said.

"I'm shocked the Chinese haven't helped them more than they have," Ayatollah Rostami said.

"They don't want those nut bags having delivery capability either," General Nikahd said.

"That's enough of this," Ayatollah Rostami said. "Did we get our money's worth?"

"Yes. They're everything they said. We should be able to take out anything within a thousand kilometers, and since they're solid fuel, there's no delay before launch."

"Excellent. I pray that we'll never have to use them, but it's comforting to know we can defend ourselves. Do either of you have any thoughts on how we should respond to their latest demands?"

"I think I should fly to New York and address the Security Council in person," President Shirazi said.

"What would you say?"

"I'd demand they loosen the new embargoes to allow the humanitarian aid to continue."

"It was an easier point to make before the Mossad ratted us out for using some of the oil shipments to acquire arms and munitions," General Nikahd said.

"That was unfortunate," President Shirazi said. "Did we ever find the traitor that tipped them off?"

"It was one of the Pakistanis we were using to launder the money, but he won't be an issue again," General Nikahd said.

"No matter," the ayatollah said. "It was a chance we had to take. Without the additional arms we wouldn't last a week against even those idiotic Afghans."

"I resent that," General Nikahd said. "Our forces are much better trained and organized than that rabble."

"Don't misunderstand. I wasn't criticizing your leadership, I was merely pointing out our obvious materials shortages due to the embargoes."

"Sorry, I guess I'm getting thin skinned in my old age."

The ayatollah looked over at President Shirazi and said, "I'm almost sure it's a fool's errand, but I suppose it can't hurt. While you're there I'd like for you to arrange a one-on-one with the secretary general."

"To what end?"

"I want you to convey my complete disgust at how they've treated us. They've not shown a shred of human decency toward our country, and their illegal actions have cause irreparable harm to Iran's economy."

"I can do that, but you can't believe he'll care."

"Of course not, but I don't want it said that I didn't try to bring it to his attention before we act to protect our interests."

"You want me to convey that message as well?"

The ayatollah pondered for a second or two, before he said, "Yes. Yes, I do."

"Very well, but he's likely to view it as just another empty threat."

"You're an impertinent bastard today," the ayatollah said. "General, would you see to the president's transportation needs?"

"Certainly. Is anyone else traveling with him?"

"Not this time."

When President Shirazi's plane landed at JFK, a representative from their embassy met him.

"I'm Major Khalid Yazdi, and I'll be taking care of you.

If you'll give Sergeant Masoud your claim check, he'll take care of your bags."

"Was your father General Yazdi?"

"Yes. Did you know him?"

"I was a member of his staff. He was a good man, and his death was a great loss."

"Murder would be a better word for it."

"If I remember correctly, that was never confirmed."

"Verified or not, I know damn well it was a Mossad hit."

"I'm not going to disagree, but we'll never know for sure," President Shirazi said. "What do they have you doing at the embassy?"

"I'm the military attaché, and I'm in charge of embassy security, among other duties."

"Then I'm in good hands. I need to go directly to the UN building. I've got a meeting with the secretary general at nineteen hundred."

"No problem. How long are you going to be in town?"

"Hopefully just a couple of days, but I'll stay until I complete my mission."

"If you have the time, I'd love to hear about my father," Major Yazdi said.

"If you're free, you could join me for dinner," President Shirazi said.

"That would be wonderful, and thank you for taking the time."

"No problem whatsoever. Your father was a great man. How old were you when he was killed?"

"Eleven months."

"Oh. I suppose your mother has told you quite a lot."

"Unfortunately she died giving birth to me."

"So you really never knew either of your parents?"

"Just what my mother's brother has told me, but unfortunately they weren't that close."

"I'd be honored to tell you what I know."

Major Yazdi opened the door to the embassy limo waiting at the curb.

"How long will it take?" President Shirazi asked.

"You never know for sure in this town, but at this time of day, I'd say a little over an hour," Major Yazdi said.

"That's going to be cutting it close. I thought I'd allowed plenty of time, but they kept us circling the airport for over thirty minutes before they let us land."

Luckily the traffic wasn't that bad, and they arrived with time to spare.

"I've been here many times, so I'll walk you in," Major Yazdi said.

"Thanks. I hope security doesn't take too long," President Shirazi said.

"Shouldn't be a problem, they know me. I forgot to ask, where are you meeting the secretary?"

"I'm meeting him in the Security Council chamber."

As they were going through security, one of the guards called the secretary general's office to tell them they'd arrived. By the time they'd gotten their identification badges, one of the secretary's staff was waiting.

"President Shirazi, I'm Margaret Thames, the secretary's assistant, and if you'll follow me, I'll show you the way."

"I'll wait here for you," Major Yazdi said.

"I don't know how long this will take," President Shirazi said.

"No matter, I'll be waiting."

CHAPTER 6

President Shirazi had attended a couple of Security Council meetings, so when they walked past the entrance, he asked, "I thought I was meeting the secretary in the main chamber?"

"He thought it might be more effective in one of the smaller rooms. Here we are. Go on in, he's expecting you," she said.

As he entered, he saw that the room wasn't much bigger than his office. It had two overstuffed leather chairs with end tables beside them, and a long table along the wall with snacks and drinks.

"President Shirazi. It's good to see you again," Secretary General Paul-Henri Archambault said.

"Thank you again for agreeing to meet with me," President Shirazi said.

"Would you care for something to eat or drink?" Secretary Archambault asked.

"A water would be nice."

"So, I think I know why you've come, but would you mind laying it out for me?" Secretary Archambault asked.

"Right to the point, I like that. I have two objectives. First I'd like to discuss how we could get you to loosen the embargoes so we can fulfill our need for food and medical supplies. Second, I want to see how we can reach a middle ground on the inspections you're demanding."

"Let's start with your first point. "Your country's lack of transparency and outright lies make it difficult to believe you wouldn't circumvent the rules again," Secretary Archambault said.

"I doubt there's anything I could say that would sway your opinion, but I give you my word that we won't bend the rules this time. We have far too many people who need medical care, and thousands that are near starvation."

"I apologize for being so blunt, but are you in a position to speak for the rest of your leadership?"

"I'm the president."

"Not what I asked."

After a short hesitation he said, "The best answer I can give is: it depends."

"On what?"

"The supreme leader can overrule me at any time, but I can tell you that on this subject, we're of the same mind."

"Fair enough. I thought you'd make the request so here's what I've arranged. The UN will handle the sale and transport for all oil shipments, and we'll use the proceeds to acquire the medical supplies and food you need."

"We can live with that," President Shirazi said.

"Good, let's talk about the inspections," Secretary Archambault said.

"In principle, we're not against allowing your inspectors into the country. As long as you'll agree to giving us prior notifications, and allow our scientists to accompany them, we'll consider your requests."

"That could work, with the understanding that you can't deny us reasonable access to any facility we request."

"I can't agree to that without seeing the locations you intend to inspect," President Shirazi said.

"That would defeat the whole concept of surprise inspections. There can be no exceptions."

"I understand, but I'll have to discuss it with the supreme leader before I can give you an answer."

"Fine. It's getting late, so why don't you make whatever calls you need to, and we'll meet back here at say, nine thirty tomorrow."

"That works. I'll see you in the morning," President Shirazi said.

"How'd it go?" Major Yazdi asked.

"Actually better than I'd expected. The secretary is a class act, but I need to get to my hotel because I've got to make some phone calls."

"Here we are," Major Yazdi said as they pulled up in front of the West Tower at One UN Plaza.

"This looks nice," President Shirazi said.

"It is. We've booked you a suite, and the view is magnificent."

"I assume the hotel has a restaurant, so if it's not too late for you, we could discuss your father over dinner."

"I'd appreciate that. What time?"

The president glanced at his watch and said, "My call shouldn't take very long, so let's say nine."

The major had already checked the president in, so they went directly to his room.

"This is President Shirazi for the ayatollah," he said when the ayatollah's assistant answered.

"How'd you do?" Ayatollah Rostami asked.

"They'll allow us to export enough oil to meet our needs, but we have to use their ships, and they'll control the purchases, including the transportation."

"Inconvenient, but acceptable for the time being. What about the inspectors?"

"They aren't backing down on the unlimited access to any location, but they will allow our people to accompany the inspectors."

"You know we can't allow that. What do you recommend?"

"We could agree to their demands, and hope they don't ferret out the facilities in the south."

"That might hold up for a little while, but if they do figure it out, and we don't comply, it will tell them we're hiding something. I know it's not what you want to hear, but I need you to tell him we simply can't agree to his conditions."

"Okay, but if I do, sooner or later they're going to escalate the sanctions. The secretary has the backing of the Security Council, and I'm afraid they might even authorize the use of force against us."

"I understand, but we'll deal with that when we have to. When do you intend to return?"

"I've got a meeting with the secretary in the morning, and when I'm done, I'll head back."

"Have you been waiting long?" President Shirazi asked.

"No, and I can't tell you what this means to me," Major Yazdi said.

After the waiter brought their meals, the president said, "For some reason, your father took a liking to me, and his mentoring was a huge part of why I've had a successful career. I can remember when you were born, and he used to talk about you all the time."

"Did he ever talk about my mother?"

"Once, after he'd had a couple of drinks. He said she was the love of his life, and that he could never love another woman like he loved her. He said her brother's family were taking care of you, but that he intended to retire when his tour was up, so he could take care of you."

"I never knew that. Do you remember anything else?"

"He was a true professional, and he did his best to balance his duties against his natural empathy for people.

I got out shortly after that to go back to school, and a couple of months later he was killed while he was in Jericho for a meeting with the Hamas leadership."

"It's driven me half-crazy not knowing who was behind his death. I've read the reports a hundred times, and even though they said it was a suicide attack by a Fatah extremist, I don't believe it for a second," Major Yazdi said.

"If I knew the answer I'd tell you, but I will do this for you. I'll have our head of intelligence review everything they've got on it."

"I appreciate that. After all this time I don't know why I'm so hung up on knowing, but I am."

"I'd feel the same if it was my father."

President Shirazi spent almost thirty minutes recounting every anecdote about the general he could remember before he said, "I'm sorry to cut this short, but I'm exhausted."

"No problem. I can't tell you how much I appreciate your taking the time. I'll be back to pick you up in the morning."

The next morning, Secretary General Archambault got up to greet President Shirazi when he arrived for their meeting.

"How was your evening?"

"Short. I'm afraid I'm not a very good traveler," President Shirazi said.

"I have the same problem. I can never sleep properly until I've been somewhere for several days. How about some coffee?"

"That sounds good."

"So, have you got your answer?"

"I do. Here is a list of all of our nuclear facilities, and we'll allow your inspectors into any of them, with twenty-four-hours' notice."

"That's a start, but as I said before, we're going to need

to inspect a wider range of locations, so we can follow up on any leads we develop."

"At this time, we're not prepared to allow that kind of freedom."

"What if I tell you it's an absolute requirement?"

"It's simply not possible."

"I'm sorry you feel that way, because you don't have a lot of friends left on the Security Council. I'm afraid that they're going to want to take more drastic measures when I tell them your country isn't willing to be completely transparent."

"Are you threatening me?" President Shirazi asked as he stood up.

"No, I'm simply trying to explain what I think will happen if you don't face the gravity of your situation."

"I've told you what I'm empowered to offer; the rest is up to you. I'd hoped we could keep the situation from escalating, but I see that's not going to happen. Will you at least allow my first request?"

"I can't promise anything, but I think I can get the council to allow the humanitarian aid. I would ask that you try to talk some sense into the supreme leader, before this gets out of hand."

"I'll do what I can," President Shirazi said.

When President Shirazi's plane landed he went straight to the ayatollah's office.

"Good to have you back," Ayatollah Rostami said.

"I'm sorry, I couldn't convince the secretary to back off on the inspectors," President Shirazi said.

"I never thought you could, but at least you got the oil spigot turned back on."

"Partially, but it'll provide some relief. You do realize that this is going to escalate?"

"I know. I just wish I knew who was keeping this stirred up."

CHAPTER 7

It had been a long night for Victor and Melinda, as they'd made appearances at several of the larger parties celebrating their nominations, but Peter Montblanc had scheduled their first face-to-face meeting for early the next morning.

"That was a great speech you gave last night," Victor said as they shook hands.

"Thanks, and let me begin by apologizing that we didn't do this months ago."

"Not a problem, I know you've been very busy. I just hope I can hold up my end of the deal."

"I've studied your background, and I have no doubt you'll be a tremendous asset. I'm going to speak plainly, if that's alright," Peter said. "The Republican Party is seen as elitist, and out of touch with the demographics of the country. When we saw the projected shift in the makeup of this year's voter, it scared the shit out of all of us. I know you don't know much about politics, but you're a bright man, and I need you to help us connect with the minority voters."

"I understand, and I'll help in any way I can."

"Great. Stevan told me about your one request, and I promise that if we're successful, I'll make sure you have something that you can sink your teeth into. Are you familiar with the top three focus points of my platform?"

"I've studied the materials Stevan sent."

"I want you to focus on the Afghanistan, Iraq situations, and the need to get all of our troops back home."

"I can definitely speak to that. I know it's not in your top three, but how about adding something in about job creation?"

"I'm fine with that in principle," Peter said. "However, I'd need to see the specifics before you work it into your speeches. While we're on that subject, have you met Charles Goodwin yet?"

"No, but I'd like to."

"Great, he's volunteered to act as your speech writer and mentor. If you're open to the idea?"

"I'd be honored."

The meeting was scheduled to run until noon, but they'd lost track of time until Peter's assistant interrupted. "You've got to get going," John Jacobs said.

"Sorry to break this up, but duty calls," Peter said. "I should have mentioned it earlier, but the Secret Service would like to talk with you before you go back to the hotel."

"Secret Service?"

"Yes. They're going to be providing you with a detail of your own. I doubt you noticed, but they've been shadowing you and your family since the announcement."

"OK, but do you really think that's necessary? I don't have any enemies."

"You do now."

The Secret Service briefing took longer than he'd expected, and it was almost 5 P.M. by the time Victor got back to the hotel.

"How'd your meeting go?" Melinda asked. "I was expecting you back hours ago."

"Sorry, Peter and I talked longer than we'd planned, and then I had to meet with the head of our Secret Service detail."

"Really?"

"Yes, they'll be with us from now on."

"That's a little scary."

"In a way yes, but comforting too. You need to give your mom a call, and let her know they're already outside the house, and not to worry."

"I'll call her right now."

"They'd like to brief her on the protocol, so have her call this number, and tell them it's alright to come up to the house."

"You know this is going to freak her out."

"That's why I want you to talk to her. Just be sure and tell her it's all precautionary."

"How'd it go?" Victor asked when she got off the phone.

"It took her a minute, but she's fine," Melinda said. "You never told me how your meeting went."

"Much better than I expected. He seems like a fairly nice guy, for a white guy."

"Stop that."

"I was just kidding. He came right out and admitted that's why they picked me. We talked about a lot of things, and I actually agree with many of his viewpoints, so I don't think I'll have any issues speaking up for him."

"Did he give you any idea what they want you to do?"

"Definitely. I need to go ahead and step down from mayor. I think I'll do that tomorrow morning, and then I'll have my first working meeting with Charles Goodwin."

"The guy that sent the flowers and candy?"

"The same. He's volunteered to be my speech writer and mentor me through the entire campaign."

"That's wonderful. I Googled him after he sent the gifts, and he's quite a guy. He was an investment banker before he retired, and even though he's a leader in the Republican Party, he's got the reputation of a consensus builder for both parties."

"Sounds like a good guy to have on our side."

"I hope I can meet him someday."

"Your wish is granted, because he's meeting us for dinner at Antoine's at eight."

"I'd better start getting ready," Melinda said.

A little before eight, the Secret Service limo dropped them off at the restaurant. Built in 1795, it was located in the heart of the historic French Quarter.

"This looks nice," Melinda said.

"It's supposed to be one of the finest restaurants in town," Victor said.

When they walked in, the maître d'hôtel asked, "May I have your name, and do you have a reservation?"

"Victor Garcia."

"Mr. Garcia. Mr. Goodwin is already here. Just a moment, and I'll have one of my staff escort you."

The restaurant had fourteen dining rooms, and Charles had reserved one of them for their meeting. It overlooked the lush courtyard below and was quite impressive.

"I'm so glad to finally meet you in person," Charles said as he shook Victor's hand. "And this must be your lovely wife, Melinda."

"Thank you, kind sir," Melinda said. "The flowers and candy were very thoughtful."

"You're more than welcome, my dear. Please have a seat. Would you like some wine?"

"That sounds nice."

"Do you have a favorite?"

"We're not big drinkers, so we'll trust your judgment."

When the waiter handed them the menus, Victor asked, "What would you recommend?"

"Any of it will be great, but have you ever tried authentic New Orleans cooking?" Charles asked.

"No, we haven't."

"Personally I love the blackened dishes, but I've got to warn you, some of them can be pretty spicy."

Melinda laughed and said, "We're Mexican, our baby food was spicy."

Charles motioned their waiter over. "Would it be possible for you to set up a small buffet for us?"

"Chef Randolph has instructed us to give you whatever you request," the waiter said.

"Just bring us a sampling of everything on the menu. Also, I'd like a wine bar with the recommended wines from the menu."

"It'll take us a few minutes. Would you like some wine and a salad while you wait?"

"Skip the salads, but bring us three glasses of the pinot noir from the Schindler vineyard."

"Very good, sir."

The dinner was excellent, and they'd gotten a chance to talk at length about what lay ahead.

As they got up to leave, Charles handed Victor a room key and said, "I've arranged for a private room at your hotel for our meeting. How does eight A.M. sound?"

"Works for me, and thank you so much for dinner and the conversation."

CHAPTER 8

"So what's on the agenda for today?" Victor Garcia asked.

"We should have been doing this weeks ago, so we're going to have to hit it pretty hard for the next week or two," Charles Goodwin said.

"No problem. I've resigned my position with the city, and Melinda's mom has our two children under control."

"Peter said you had a good meeting yesterday. I was afraid you might be put off by his style; he's very direct."

"Not a problem. You don't need to sugarcoat anything for me."

"I'm going to put you on the spot, and ask you to give me your version of your life from high school on."

"I grew up in San Jon, New Mexico, a tiny village just off of I-40. School always came easy to me, and I was a straight-A, honors society student from the very beginning. I enjoyed athletics, but the only sport I excelled in was track. I won the state meet three straight years in the hundred meters and the long jump. I'd've won four times if it hadn't been for the accident."

"Is that the one that killed your family?"

"Yes, worst day of my entire life. I was the only one from our school that qualified for the state meet, so the coach had taken me to Albuquerque in his car. We'd gone down the night before the meet, and my folks were going to drive down the next day. A drunk driver was going the wrong way on I-40 and hit them head-on. My mom and dad were killed instantly, and my little sister died on the way to the hospital."

"Horrible."

"The coach's family took me in so I could finish what was left of my senior year. You never know the twists and turns to your life. They ran an article about the accident in the *Albuquerque Journal* that caught our congressman's attention, and he nominated me for admission to the Naval Academy. I did well there, and received a Rhodes Scholarship to Oxford.

"After I completed the two-year program with honors, I entered the Marine Corps as a second lieutenant. After the twenty-six-week officer course at Quantico, Virginia, I served my first tour in Iraq. From there I went to the Naval War College, where I received a degree in national security and strategic studies. After that I did two more tours in Iraq, followed by a tour in Afghanistan."

"Was Afghanistan where you earned your Silver Star?"

"No, that was during my last tour in Iraq."

"Tell me about that," Charles said.

"The ambassador had called for extra security at an off-site event he was hosting, and we drew the short straw."

"I would have thought that guarding the ambassador's party would have been a primo assignment."

"Milford Astor liked everything his way, and if you spoke up, he'd make your life hell. He's ended more than one career in his time, and we all cringed whenever we drew a security assignment for him.

"The event was being held at a golf course, and we really didn't have enough men to do the job properly, but he was adamant that we keep a low profile. The insurgents attacked in force, and they blew through the small team I had guarding the main entrance in seconds. I would have died with them if the ambassador hadn't summoned me to chew my ass for my men being so visible.

"I was standing with the ambassador, and the Iraqi prime minister, Nouri al-Maliki, when they busted in. Al-Maliki's bodyguards and I took them on, and we managed to kill the first six. Unfortunately, one of them managed to detonate a suicide vest, killing both bodyguards and wounding me. All I had was a M9 Beretta, but it was empty. So I grabbed one of the guard's MPX machine guns, and moved to meet the second wave of attackers."

"By yourself?"

"Yes, but luckily there were only four of them, and I was able to neutralize them."

"I imagine the ambassador was quite grateful," Charles said.

"Hardly, he chewed my ass for my lax security practices, and threatened to have me drummed out of the service."

"Astor's well connected. How did you manage to turn it around?"

"I didn't. Prime Minister Maliki interceded on my behalf."

"You were fortunate. He's usually not a fan of Americans, but please, go on."

"After a short stay in the hospital, they awarded me the Silver Star and a Purple Heart, and shipped me to Afghanistan."

"How'd that go?"

"Someone had a perverse sense of humor, because they put me in charge of the embassy's security detail. Luckily for me, Ambassador Quentin took a liking to me, and it turned out to be a pretty cushy gig. I only had thirty-one days left when it all went to Hell.

"The ambassador was on his way back to Washington for a meeting, and we were escorting his armored limo to the airport. He'd asked me to ride along with him so he could lay out what he wanted done while he was out of the country. We'd just made the last turn before the airport entrance, when a pair of massive explosions took out the front and rear MRAPS we were using for security. I was yelling at the driver to floor it, when we got hit with an RPG. The car was armored, but it blew the driver's side wheel off and wounded him. I put a call in for a rapid response team, and jumped out to try to hold them off until they could reach us. I was using the car for cover, and was doing pretty well until the next RPG round hit and blew off my right foot just above the ankle and shattered my left leg.

"When the rapid response team arrived they took out the Taliban insurgents and rerouted a passing medevac to our location. It couldn't have been more than a few minutes before they had me stabilized and in the air back to a field hospital. They couldn't save my left leg, and had to amputate it just below the knee. I was fortunate that neither injury got above the knee, because it made it much easier to learn to walk again. I got another Purple Heart and a Bronze Star out of that one.

"After rehab I considered staying in, but I didn't think I should put Melinda through any more."

"Impressive. I believe both of your families were originally from Mexico."

"That's right, although it was several generations ago."

"Doesn't matter, the voters we're targeting will still see you as one of their own," Charles said. "I've got a handle on the whole bring our troops home angle, but Peter mentioned that you wanted to include something about jobs. Did you have anything specific in mind?"

"Ever since the recession of 2008, the government has wasted trillions of dollars buying bonds, extending unemployment, and subsidizing green energy projects. I know some would say the Federal Reserve saved the financial system, but from my point of view, all they did was line the pockets of the now infamous one per-centers."

"I actually agree with you on that, but what would you propose?"

"I'd launch a two-pronged attack to address the rampant destruction of the middle class, and if you believe the government's own figures, the twenty-two percent of all Americans who are living in abject poverty. Instead of allowing our jobs to be moved offshore, we need to ensure every available job is filled by an American citizen. Unfortunately, the H1B programs are actually filling a desperate shortfall in high-tech workers. In order to rectify the situation, we've got to convince our young people to pursue a college degree, or at least the technical training needed to fill these positions. We've got to change the college loan programs that have put many of our students in such a financial hole that they'll never recover."

"College loans are big business, and the banking lobbyists will fight anything we try to do."

"Probably true, but instead of loans, we need to issue Pell Grants to cover the entire tuition bill for anyone that participates in a program that fits the needs we're currently filling with high-tech visas. Then for every student that completes the necessary college coursework, or an appropriate technical school, we'll remove a visa authorization on a one-for-one basis. To make it more attractive to the employers, we'll provide hiring incentives to cover half of the newly hired workers' wages for the first three years."

"That's going to cost a fortune," Charles said.

"True, it's not without a cost, but if you factor in the taxes the workers will pay, and that they'll be off the unemployment and welfare rolls, it will be money well spent."

"What's to stop the companies from just moving the jobs overseas?"

"We'll impose a hefty surcharge for any job or plant that's moved overseas, and we'll implement additional taxes on any finished goods that a U.S. company imports."

"That's going to piss off a lot of very powerful people," Charles said.

"Undoubtedly true, however, the groups of people that we're trying to garner support from will see that as a real plus."

"You do realize that's the same group of people that are our biggest benefactors?"

"I do, but if we want to win the election, they're not the ones that will swing it our way."

"You've got a point. I can see where your approach could work with the more skilled labor, but that's not where the bulk of the unemployment is."

"Agreed. To address that issue, we'll have to institute programs of a similar scale to the ones the fed used to prop up the banks and the bond markets."

"To what end?"

"If we make low or no-cost loans to rebuild our manufacturing industries, we should be able to create millions of jobs. Couple that with subsidies, and we can make our goods competitive in the world's markets."

"The WTO will be all over our asses," Charles said.

"Who cares? What have they ever done for us? Next, we'll try to address our country's infrastructure problems. The power grid, waterways, dams, railroads, highways, and bridges have been allowed to deteriorate to the point that they're close to becoming unstable. Even our air traffic control is thirty years behind the rest of the world."

"That's an awful lot to bite off. We'll have to beef up several agencies to deal with that many projects."

"The federal government would just screw it up, but if we make the funds available to the states, they'll be able to address their individual needs."

"That could cost billions."

"Could be a trillion or more, but so what? It will generate millions of new jobs, which will put the money directly back into the economy. Unlike the Federal Reserve schemes."

"I take it you've haven't detailed your thoughts for Peter, and his staff."

"No, I haven't."

"If you don't mind, I'll take a copy of your notes with me, and I'll see if I can craft a proposal that Peter and his team might accept."

"They're not much more than talking points."

"Not a worry. I actually get off on this sort of thing. Moving on, I'd like you to look over this rough draft of your first speech."

"Who's the audience?" Victor asked.

"You're scheduled to be the featured speaker at the United Farm Workers convention in Los Angeles."

"I'll look it over tonight."

"I'd like to go through the platform with you in detail, so that I can assess your pros and cons."

It took several hours to get through the seventy pages of the GOP platform.

"That was agonizing," Victor said.

"It was at that," Charles said. "The sad thing is that we may be the only two people who have ever read that mess in its entirety."

They spent the rest of the day talking through the makeup of the support team they'd need and tentative travel arrangements.

"Great, I think we're off to a good start," Charles said. "Let's call it good for today. If you'll read over the speech, I'll take a stab at your notes, and we'll go at it again tomorrow."

CHAPTER 9

When they got back together, Charles Goodwin asked, "What did you think of the speech?"

"I liked the message, but I took the liberty of reworking it for the audience. The language would have been fine for Peter's crowd, but it's not suitable for farm workers."

"I'll take a look at it so that I can get a feel for what you're going to need. I started fleshing out your notes, but I think you're trying to sell too much too soon. I'd like to see you approach Peter in stages."

"What would you suggest?"

"Which initiative do you feel the strongest about?"

"The infrastructure refresh would definitely resonate with demographics you're wanting me to focus on."

"Take a look at this, and make sure I got it right."

Victor spent several minutes reading through Charles's work. "I like the way you summarized each initiative's intent and then detailed the projected costs and benefits, as well as any known dependencies or risks. What's next?"

"If it's alright with you I'll send it over to get Peter's feedback." Charles took a moment to craft a quick e-mail, and sent it on its way. "We won't go as late as yesterday, but I'd like to have you spend the rest of the morning practicing giving the speech. I had them bring in a podium so I could see how you come across. Some like working behind a podium, but some people do better without one."

"I've never used a podium, so I'm not sure," Victor said.

Charles had him go through it several times. He tried to throw as many curves at him as he could so he could see how he reacted.

"Good job. I think you do better without a podium," Charles said. "Which foreign languages do you speak?"

"I'm fluent in Spanish, French, and several dialects of Arabic, and I can get by in Pashto and Dari."

"Impressive. I've worked you pretty hard, so I'm going to let you have the rest of the day off."

"Thanks, Melinda has been cooped up in the hotel, and I'm sure she's ready to see the sights. What happens next?"

"John Steinberger is going to let us use one of his Gulf-streams, so I'll swing by and pick you up next Monday. You've got at least three speaking engagements a week from now until Election Day. The last thirty days are going to be particularly challenging, because you've got two vice presidential debates to do as well."

"Debates? I've never been much of a debater."

"Not to worry, we'll work on it."

"You're back early," Melinda said.

"Charles gave me the rest of the day off," Victor said.

After they'd talked it over, Victor called Scott Stubbs, the agent in charge of their security. "We'd like to see some of the sights."

"No problem. I'm a New Orleans native, so I'll make sure you see the best parts."

As evening approached, Victor asked, "We're getting hungry. Do you have a favorite restaurant?"

"Depends, you want something Cajun?" Special Agent Stubbs asked.

"We had that last night. How about a nice seafood res-taurant?"

"The Bourbon House has the best seafood in the city. The only caveat is that if it's not in season they won't have it, because they serve only fresh caught."

When they dropped them off at the restaurant, Victor said, "Come in and eat with us."

"Thank you, but no," Special Agent Stubbs said.

"Why not?" Melinda asked.

"Because it would distract us from why we're here."

"And what would that be?" she asked.

"To ensure your safety."

"Oh!"

They had a wonderful meal, but as they were eating dessert, a group of drunks wandered by their table on their way out.

"What the hell? This is that Mexican they picked for vice president," Richard Booker, the leader of the group, said with a sneer. "How's it feel to be the token Mexican?" he asked.

Victor just ignored him.

"I'm talking to you, wetback."

"That's enough of that," Victor muttered under his breath.

But as he braced himself to stand, one of Scott's agents grabbed the man's arm and said quietly, "You need to come with me, sir."

"Get your damn hands off of me," he bellowed.

The agent bent his wrist back until he went to his knees.

"Shit, that hurts."

"Tough. I'll let you up if you'll shut your mouth and be on your way, otherwise you're going to jail."

"You can't threaten me."

"Just telling you the way it's going to go down. Now, what's it going to be?"

"Come on, Dick, let's get out of here," one of the group said.

"OK, but this asshole has to let me up."

The agent, accidentally, applied a little extra pressure as he pulled Richard back to his feet.

"That hurt."

"Be on your way, asshole."

On the way back to the hotel, Victor said, "Thanks for taking care of that guy back there."

"No problem, sir. I'm sorry we didn't get to him before he ruined your dinner."

"It's not the first time we've had to put up with racist assholes."

They spent most of the next day with Stevan and his staff so they could brief them on the calendar of events they had planned. They didn't get home until almost midnight the next day, but Esmeralda, Melinda's mom, was still up.

"I watched the entire convention in hopes of seeing you two, but the only time I saw you was when Mr. Montblanc introduced you."

"They kept us out of sight until just before we were scheduled to go on," Melinda said.

"That doesn't seem fair."

"It wasn't about fair, they simply wanted to keep Victor's nomination as a surprise."

"They definitely succeeded. I don't suppose you could tell from your vantage point, but even though they were clapping, there were a whole bunch of them that didn't look that pleased."

"No surprise there," Victor said. "As nice as he was to me, even Peter Montblanc wasn't overjoyed."

"Mother, it's late. Why don't you spend the night?" Melinda said.

* * *

The next morning, Melinda was sleeping late, and Esmeralda and Victor were drinking coffee on the patio.

"Thank you for asking me to come and stay with the kids," Esmeralda said. "It was nice having them around. It gets lonely at my house since Hector passed away."

"I know you miss him. I can't believe it's been a year since he passed away."

"I know. At first I was busy sorting things out, but now I'm not sure what to do with myself."

Her comment got Victor to thinking. "I haven't discussed this with Melinda, but what would you think of moving in with us?"

"Why? Do you think I'm getting senile?"

"Not at all. It's just that I'm going to be on the road a lot, and I'm going to need to take Melinda along on at least some of the trips."

"What happens if you win the election?"

"Obviously we'd have to move to D.C., but I'd want you to come with us."

"This is a big decision for me, and you'd better discuss it with Melinda."

"Discuss what?" Melinda asked as she sat down at the table.

"I asked your mom if she'd consider moving in with us. We're going to need someone to look after the kids, and they both love her to death."

"That's a great idea," Melinda said.

"Okay, we can try it, but you have to promise you'll tell me if it becomes a problem."

School was letting out early that day, and Alejandro was sitting in the car waiting on Juanita to get done talking with her friends. "Come on. I've got things to do," Alejandro yelled out the window.

"Hold your horses," Juanita said. "What's the rush?" she asked as she got in.

"I've got a lot of homework for tomorrow."

"Whatever. I'm betting it's call of duty with your buddies."

Alejandro hadn't been driving for very long, but he was an excellent driver. As he merged onto the expressway he checked his mirrors. "That asshole won't get off my ass," he said. As he moved over to the center lane, the pickup pulled even closer. "What the hell?" he said. As the pickup came closer Alejandro sped up.

"Slow down, you're going to get a ticket," Juanita said.

"This jerk won't get off my ass." He checked his mirror to see where the pickup was, and saw that it was starting to drop back. "That's better."

When the Ford 350 had retreated to about a hundred feet behind them, the driver floored it. As the black diesel smoke boiled out of the twin stacks behind the cab, it vaulted forward toward their car.

"Shit," Alejandro said when he saw it coming at them.

The pickup was outfitted with what the locals called a cow catcher bumper, and when it hit their car, it crushed the whole back end of their car and sent them spinning toward the cement divider in the center of the expressway. Juanita was screaming in terror as Alejandro fought for control. He managed to straighten it out enough so that they only sideswiped the cement barrier. As he braked, the pickup swerved into the side of their car and drove it into the barrier.

"You damn fool, we're supposed to kidnap them, not kill them," the leader of the four-man team said. "You'd better hope to God they're not dead."

As the four heavily armed thugs got out of the truck, a black SUV slid to a stop beside the pickup. The driver lowered his window, and opened fire with his 357 P229 Sig Sauer pistol. His partner stepped out on the running board, and began firing over the roof with his 9mm Heckler & Koch MP5 machine gun.

"Cease fire," said the driver, Special Agent Guthrie.

As the agents ran across the freeway to make sure the thugs were no longer a threat, cars and trucks were slamming on their brakes to avoid the accident. After they'd made sure the attackers were all dead, Special Agent Guthrie said, "Roberts, check on the kids while I get us some help out here. Control, we're northbound on I-25 near exit 224B, and we need backup and an air ambulance ASAP."

"Roger that. What's the status of Roughshod and Diamond?"

"Unknown at this time. They were attacked by four hostiles, and Agent Roberts is checking on them."

"They're both alive, but unconscious," Agent Roberts said.

"Control, both subjects are alive but unconscious."

"Understood. Help is on the way."

"Were you expecting visitors?" Victor asked when the doorbell rang.

"No," Melinda said.

"Oh God no," Melinda said.

"What's wrong?" Victor asked.

"The kids have been in an accident."

"What's going on, and who are you?" Victor asked.

"I'm Special Agent Chaffee, and your children have been in a car wreck on I-25. If you'll come with me, we'll get you to the hospital."

As they walked outside to the SUV waiting at the curb, Victor asked, "What's with all the guns?"

"It's protocol for this type of situation."

"What does that mean?"

"It's our normal escalation when there's been an attack."

"Attack? I thought they were in a car wreck."

"I don't have the specifics, but they'll brief you at the hospital."

The local police provided a lights-and-siren escort to University of New Mexico Hospital. Four more Secret Service agents met them when they pulled up to the entrance of the hospital.

"Mr. Garcia, I'm Special Agent Loomis. Please follow me, I'll take you to your children."

"What the hell happened?" Victor asked as they walked inside.

"I don't have that information, but I'm sure the agent in charge will brief you."

"Where are my kids?" Victor asked.

"The trauma team is still evaluating them," Special Agent Stubbs said.

"Quit the bullshit, I want a straight answer," Victor said. "What happened to our children?"

"They were attacked by four men on their way home from school."

"Why would someone try to hurt our children?" Melinda asked.

"I don't have that answer yet, but that's why I had a protection detail following them."

"Some protection," Esmeralda said.

"I understand your frustration, but the agents did kill all four of the assailants. Here's one of the doctors now. Maybe he's got an update for you."

"I'm Dr. Stevens, and I've got good news. We were afraid Juanita might have a minor concussion, so we ran an MRI on her but it came back negative. They are pretty banged up, but I don't think there's anything to worry about."

"That's great news," Victor Garcia said. "When can we take them home?"

"We'd like to keep them overnight, but you should be able to take them home in the morning."

"When can we see them?" Melinda asked.

"You can go on back. They're down the hall to your left, in rooms 101 and 102. Any questions for me before I go?"

"No, and thanks for taking care of them," Victor said.

When the kids checked out the next morning, Special Agents Stubbs had a limo waiting out front.

"What's this?" Victor Garcia asked.

"We'll be handling all of your transportation needs from now on," Special Agent Stubbs said.

"Is this armored?" Alejandro asked.

"Yes, it is, level A9/B6."

"Cool."

When they got home, Agent Stubbs followed them inside.

"I know you've just been through a very traumatic situation, but I need to lay out some ground rules for you and your family," Agent Stubbs said.

"Can't it wait?" Melinda asked.

"I'm afraid not."

"Okay, we're all yours," Victor said.

Agent Stubbs handed them each a packet and said, "This covers what we'll be doing in the future. It covers everything from your use of social media, to the protocol we'll be following whenever you go out. Take a few minutes to read the information in your packets, and then I'll answer any questions you might have."

"Why does it have 'Roughshod' on the top of my sheet?" Alejandro asked.

"That's the code name we're using for you. Your mother's is Bella, Juanita's is Diamond, and your dad's is Quicksilver. I know you may think that they're silly, but it's a tradition."

"I guess it could be worse," Alejandro said. "It could have been fluffy."

"I could change it if you'd like."

"Don't you dare."

"Do any of you have any more comments or questions?" Agent Stubbs asked.

"Agents Stubbs, thank you for what your team did, and we'll get back to you if we think of anything," Victor said.

"No problem, that's our job."

As the kids got up to leave, Victor said, "Sit back down for a minute. I've got something else that I need to say. I want to apologize to all of you for putting our family through this. I hate that I've put you all in danger, but I feel like this is something I've got to do."

"Dad, it's alright," Juanita said.

"It sure is," Alejandro agreed. "We'd be mad if you didn't do this. Our country needs you, and it's taken far too long for our country to have a Hispanic candidate."

That night, after they'd turned out the lights, Victor rolled over and said, "I'm so sorry. I promised you when I got out that I'd never put anything ahead of you again, and I've done it again."

"Quit that. We talked about this, and it was our decision this time. I know they're using you, but I just know in my heart that God has put you on this path for a reason."

"I'd swear you were in confession with me. That's almost word for word what Father Mendoza told me."

"Well, there you go. Now how about you start making it up to me?" she said as she pulled him on top of her.

"You swore you had it handled," Klaus said.

"I screwed up," Jonathan said. "I didn't have much time, so I used some hired muscle, and they blew it. The only positive was that they managed to get themselves killed before they could talk."

"They'll have upgraded their security, so there's no use trying that again. How did you do with your other task?"

"It's turned out to be more difficult than I'd anticipated," Jonathan said. "After Goodwin stepped aside, he threw his weight behind Victor, and convinced them that they couldn't retake the presidency without him."

"Damn it. I thought for sure we could get our man in. It's too late to do anything about it before the election. We can always take care of it later if we have to, but don't ever fail me again."

"You can't threaten me."

"You know me better than that," Klaus said.

As the hair on the back of his neck stood up, Jonathan said, "It won't happen again."

CHAPTER 10

Peter and Victor hadn't talked face-to-face since their initial conversation, but Peter had made a point to call Victor at least once a week. They had a lot riding on the voters' acceptance of Victor, so Stevan had commissioned three different research firms to try to gauge the impact he was having.

"How do the numbers look?" Peter Montblanc asked.

"Outstanding. Whatever Victor is doing is working. Depending on the demographic, the numbers are showing a five to eight percentage points' uptick since our last look. If he can keep up the pace, I think we've got a real shot."

"I've got a call with him in ten minutes, and I'll make sure to mention it. How about my approval ratings?"

"Still growing. Your last debate may have sealed the election. When you put her on the spot for all their foreign affairs gaffes, it drove home your commitment to a new foreign policy."

"It wasn't a political ploy. If we don't manage to tone down the rhetoric on both sides, the entire Middle East could go up in flames."

"Before you get on your call with Victor, there's a weather front coming in, and they've moved your departure up by thirty minutes."

* * *

"How are you holding up?" Peter Montblanc asked.

"Good most days," Victor Garcia said.

"Something happen?"

"No. I still have some issues if I spend too much time on my feet."

"I can't even imagine how you get by. I've got to cut the call short, but I wanted to make sure that I thanked you for all of your hard work. I've just gone over the latest election projections, and you've really moved the needle."

"Thanks, but I'm sure glad we've only got two more weeks."

"Do you think you'll be able to keep the pace up?"

"Absolutely."

After they'd talked for another five minutes, Peter said, "One last thing. Stevan Baldridge is hosting an election night party at his house, and we'd like for you and Melinda to be there."

"I'm speaking in Phoenix that day, but we shouldn't have any trouble getting back in time."

As their plane was landing at Dulles International, Melinda said, "I can't believe it's finally over. Flying in a Gulfstream was neat at first, but the new has worn off."

"It's funny how a couple of hundred hours in the air can change your perspective," Victor said.

"Your car is waiting," the stewardess said. "We're two hours behind schedule, so you'll need to go straight to the reception. Don't worry about your luggage, we'll make sure it gets to your hotel, and good luck tonight."

"Thanks," Victor said. "Did you guys ever get a chance to vote?"

"Of course. We all voted absentee, weeks ago."

Stevan's butler met them as they stepped out of the limo. "Please follow me, they're all gathered in the ballroom."

"We were afraid you weren't going to make it," Stevan Baldridge said.

"We ran into some weather," Victor said. "How are we doing?"

"Not too bad, Mr. Vice President."

Melinda squealed with joy, and blurted out, "Oh my God! . . . Sorry."

"Nothing to be sorry about. We're all excited," Stevan Baldridge said. "Harry just talked with their campaign manager, and I'm expecting a call conceding the election at any time."

"I still can't believe it," Victor said.

"Believe, because you're a big part of why we won. I have to admit that I had my doubts when Charles approached me, but he was dead on."

"I have her on the phone," Stevan's assistant said.

"Why don't we all go to the library," Peter Montblanc said.

While Peter took the call, Charles Goodwin flashed back to the night they'd all met in that very room to begin the journey.

When Peter hung up, he said, "Break out the champagne."

When everyone had a glass, Peter addressed the small group gathered in the study. "Before we go out to meet with the press, I'd like to say a few words. You've all given so much. Without your money, time, and most important, your steadfast belief in me, none of this would have been possible. Salute."

"Money well spent," John Steinberger said.

"I'd also like to recognize the sacrifices that Victor and Melinda have made to make this all possible," Peter said.

"Thank you for giving me the opportunity," Victor said.

"Victor, why don't you and Melinda go on out and start mingling? I need to spend a few minutes with Stevan and John."

*   *   *

"Stevan said you needed to run something by me," Peter Montblanc said.

"I know you're going to be swamped for the next few weeks, but I've got a couple of things that can't wait," John Steinberger said.

He really is a presumptuous bastard, Peter Montblanc thought to himself. "Sure, what have you got?"

"You're about to be presented with a unique opportunity, and we wanted to make sure that you didn't waste it," John Steinberger said. "This is a list of the three candidates we'd like you to nominate to fill the upcoming vacancies on the Supreme Court."

"Three? LeMasters was the only one I was aware of," Peter Montblanc said.

"Trust me, there are going to be two more openings."

Peter folded the list, and slid it into his jacket pocket. "I'll definitely look them over."

"You misunderstand me. I don't want you to look them over, I expect you to nominate them."

"I think he gets it," Stevan Baldridge said when he saw the look on Peter's face. "Peter, we've kept you long enough. Get out there and enjoy the moment."

I guess this is why I've heard all the stories about the king makers, Peter thought to himself.

The anchors from every major network were seated in the first row, and the camera crews flanked the temporary stage they'd set up. When he'd finished his victory speech, he and Victor moved to the back of the room so they could take a few questions.

After almost an hour of nonstop questions, Peter said, "OK, that's enough for tonight. Get yourselves a drink, and enjoy the rest of the evening."

They rejoined the rest of the group when the reporters left.

"How are you two holding up?" Stevan Baldridge asked.

"Not too bad, but do you have somewhere quiet I can go? We need to check on our kids," Victor Garcia said.

"I meant to say something earlier," Stevan Baldridge said. "I'd like for you to spend the night."

"We'd love to, but our luggage is at the hotel," Victor Garcia said.

"I hope you don't mind, but I took the liberty of having it moved."

"That was very thoughtful, and we'd love to spend the night," Melinda said.

"Excellent."

"It's been a long day, so if you don't mind, we probably won't come back down," Victor said.

"I've got one more interview to do, and then I'm going to turn in myself," Peter Montblanc said.

"We'll be serving brunch starting at ten, but if you need anything, the staff is available around the clock, so don't hesitate to ask."

They were usually early risers, but Victor and Melinda didn't get up until almost noon.

"Good morning, sweetie," Victor said.

"Good morning to you, Mr. Vice President, sir. It looks like you get to start ordering people around again."

"Smart-ass. But that's not a bad idea. Get that nightgown off."

"Yes, sir," she purred.

D.C. was experiencing record highs for November, so everyone was gathered on the massive veranda, enjoying the Indian summer.

"You two look refreshed," Stevan Baldridge said.

"Sorry we missed brunch," Melinda said as they sat down at the table with Stevan and Peter.

"Not a problem. Just tell them what you'd like, and they'll bring it out here," Stevan Baldridge said.

"When you're finished, I'd like to spend a little one-on-one time with you," Peter Montblanc said.

"We can do it now if you'd like," Victor Garcia said. "I can eat later."

"Nonsense, take your time. I need to make some phone calls, so just let one of the staff know when you're done, and I'll meet you in the library."

Stevan Baldridge stayed and visited with them while they ate, and when they finished, he asked Melinda, "Peter and Victor could be at it for hours, do you have any plans for the afternoon?"

"No, I don't."

"The vice president's wife is a friend of mine, and she called last night to see if you'd like to come over and take a look at where you'll be living for the next four years."

"How nice. I'd love to."

"This is certainly a beautiful part of the city," Melinda said. "Isn't that Georgetown University over there?"

"Yes, it is. Are you familiar with it?"

"A little, I attended a lecture there a few years ago. That's an impressive house," Melinda said when the residence came into view.

"This entire area is the United States Naval Observatory. The residence was built in 1893, but don't worry, it's been updated several times over the years."

Stevan made the introductions, and the vice president's wife took them on a tour of the house.

"I can't thank you enough for taking the time to show me around," Melinda said.

"My pleasure," she said. "We're going to move out in a

couple of weeks before the inauguration. I'll schedule a cleaning crew, so you won't have to worry with that. If you haven't hired your staff yet, I'd recommend that you keep the current crew, they've been great."

"I'll do that, thanks."

"What did you think of the place?" Stevan asked as they drove off.

"I don't have the words. Neither one of us comes from money, so this is going to be quite a shock to our family."

"When we get back I've got a young lady I'd like for you to interview for your assistant."

"Assistant?"

"You're going to need one. Even though you won't have any official duties, there's a lot that goes on that you'll want help with."

They had dinner with Peter and Stevan, and then they excused themselves for the night.

"How was your day?" Melinda asked.

"He's a dynamo," Victor said. "We must have talked about hundreds of things, but I couldn't believe how passionate he is. I'd assumed most of the rhetoric in his speeches was for show, but he really believes in what he wants to achieve."

"Did you talk about your role?"

"At length. I'm going to take point on getting the rest of our troops back home."

"That should keep you busy. What's he going to tackle?"

"Iran. He feels, and I agree, that a nuclear Iran is a danger to the entire world."

"Well, I'd agree with him on that one."

"On a lighter note, we can go home in the morning," Victor said.

"Great, let's give my mother and the kids a call before we turn in."

"What have you found out?" Klaus asked.

"He's going to focus Garcia on extracting the rest of our troops," Fredericka said.

"What's he going after?"

"His first priority is going to be Iran."

"That's good news. I'll make sure he receives all the support he needs. Have they shared our list yet?"

"Definitely, but they weren't sure how open to it he was. I think he was a little shocked by the approach."

"He'll just have to get used to how business is done in the Beltway. Anything else?"

"Nothing specific, but I still feel like he has some other big agenda in mind."

"You've said that before, but until we have something tangible, there's not much I can do. If anything changes, you need to contact me immediately."

"Understood."

CHAPTER 11

The weeks leading up to inauguration day were almost manic, as they tried to coordinate moving to a strange city, enrolling the kids in new schools, and helping Melinda's mother get her affairs in order.

"I think that's the last of it," Melinda said.

"I didn't think we'd ever get done," Esmeralda said as the mover took the last of their stuff away.

"I'm sorry that we're going to have to live in a hotel for ten days, but at least we can rest up a little before we have to start moving in," Melinda said.

"I still wish we were taking the cars," Esmeralda said. "You know how much I hate having to depend on someone else."

"It would be a wasted effort. After what happened to the kids, the Secret Service isn't going to allow any of us to go anywhere without a security team, and they'll be providing the transportation."

"Thanks for the link you sent me," Esmeralda said. "The picture of the area and the house are amazing, but how are you going to afford it all?"

"The government covers almost everything."

"No wonder our taxes are so damned high."

* * *

"We'd better get going, we're scheduled to take off in fifty minutes," Melinda said.

"I hate going through security," Esmeralda said. When their car pulled up alongside the Gulfstream, she said, "I could get used to this."

The outgoing VP's family had moved out on schedule, and when the cleaning crew was finished, they started moving in. "Your rooms are on the third floor," Melinda told the kids.

"I'm the oldest, so I get first pick," Juanita declared.

"By one minute, but it's fine, because I really don't care," Alejandro said.

When the moving vans pulled up, Melinda went out to line them out. "Don't worry about it, Mrs. Garcia," the butler Larry Thompson told her. "We've got it."

She was about to protest, when he said, "This is why we're here, so let us do our jobs. Why don't you take your family and tour the city for a few hours? We should be done by the time you get back."

"Are you sure?"

"Absolutely."

When Victor got home that night, dinner was on the dining room table, and the rest of the family was just sitting down to eat.

"Looks like I got here just in time," Victor said. "This looks great, but I was expecting you all to be worn out from getting settled in. Didn't the movers show up?"

"They came, but Larry Thompson and his staff took care of it. I was going to cook dinner, but Margaret Webster and the rest of the kitchen staff took care of that too."

"So what did you do?"

"We drove by St. John's so the kids could get a look

at the campus, and then we hit a couple of malls," Melinda said.

"Where's your mom?"

"They took her a plate. She had one of her headaches, and asked if she could eat in her room."

"Is she alright?"

"Yes, I think she's just a little overwhelmed by all of this."

"Who isn't?" Victor said. "I spent the morning with the president in a top secret intelligence briefing, and the afternoon with the head of the Joint Chiefs, discussing strategy and manpower allocations."

"Well, aren't you the important one?" Melinda said.

"I'm sure it will sink in after a while, but at this moment, I just feel overwhelmed. What did you think of St. John's?" Victor asked.

"We didn't get to see very much, but we're scheduled to go back on Monday," Juanita said. "They set us up in their ambassador program, so we could get a real feel for it."

"What we did see looked pretty neat," Alejandro said.

Victor was very busy as inauguration day approached, but the week before the big day, he took a couple of hours off to meet with Charles Goodwin.

"Thank you for taking the time to meet with me," Victor Garcia said.

"Never a problem, my friend," Charles said. And for the first time, he realized he really meant it.

"I know Peter has you doing a million things, but I'd like you to administer the Oath of Office to me."

"I don't know what to say, other than it would be my honor."

"Thank you. You've helped me more than you can ever know," Victor said. "I've got one other thing to ask you, and please don't feel you'll offend me if you decline."

"Shoot."

"Would you consider being my chief of staff? I know you don't need the hassle, but it would mean the world to me."

"Again, it would be my honor. I think we'll make a great team."

The whirlwind of activities never let up, but finally inauguration day arrived.

"How do I look?" Melinda asked.

"Beautiful as always, my dear," Victor said.

"Are you kids ready?" she asked.

"Yes, Mom," Juanita said.

"Are you sure you want me to sit with you?" Esmeralda asked.

"For the thousandth time, yes," Melinda said.

"It's time," Special Agent Stubbs said.

This time they were traveling in an armored stretch limo, flanked by Secret Service SUVs in front and back.

"Why the extra security?" Victor asked.

"Nothing special, we're just being extra careful since we received that last batch of threats."

"What threats?" Melinda asked.

"Nothing to worry about, Mrs. Garcia. We've already tracked down the crackpot that sent them, and he was no real threat."

As Victor Garcia stepped onto the inaugural platform to join Charles Goodwin, he was hoping he wouldn't screw it up.

Charles shook his hand, and whispered, "You'll be fine, now repeat after me. I, Victor Delgado Garcia, do solemnly affirm that I will support and defend the Constitution of the United States against all enemies, foreign and domestic; that I will bear true faith and allegiance to the same; that I take this obligation freely, without any mental reservation or purpose of evasion; and that I will well and faithfully discharge the duties of the office on which I am about to enter; so help me God."

They shook hands, and then Charles embraced Victor, and said, "You're going to do a great job."

After Victor shook hands with Peter Montblanc, he sat down beside Melinda, while James Avery, the chief justice of the Supreme Court, swore in Peter.

After the ceremony, the Secret Service took Esmeralda and the kids back to the house, while Victor and Melinda spent the rest of the day and most of the night making rounds of the inauguration day events. When they finally got home around 2 A.M., everyone except Larry Thompson was already in bed.

"You didn't have to wait up," Victor said.

"Of course I did, it's my job. Congratulations, you'll make a fine president."

"Vice president, but thanks for the vote of confidence."

"Sorry, Freudian slip. Although I personally believe you'd be better at it than Montblanc."

As they lay in bed trying to wind down from the day's events, Melinda said, "You know what, I agree with Larry."

"About what?"

"That you'd make a better president."

"You're just biased."

"You think? Come here, you, we need to celebrate."

"Do you know what time it is?" Fredericka asked when she retrieved the satellite phone from the hidden compartment in the nightstand.

"I need the two of you to give me an assessment of your abilities to implement stage one of our plan," Klaus said.

"We're in great shape as long as you-know-who doesn't get in the way."

"I understand, but I won't tolerate any interference from him."

"What do you mean by that?" she asked.

"Never mind, it's far too early to contemplate anything drastic."

"I know he's out of reach until Friday, but I'll touch base with him as soon as he returns."

"OK, but I need your answers before next week, because I've got to do something about the current situation before they complete their plans."

CHAPTER 12

President Montblanc had scheduled their first working meeting for the following Tuesday. It was scheduled for 6 A.M. in the Oval Office, but Vice President Garcia was sitting in his new office in the West Wing of the White House by five.

At 5:45 Victor braced himself, and lurched to his feet as the chair rolled back into the desk. He'd progressed to where he didn't have any trouble getting around, but the rollers on the plush leather chair made it difficult for him to get to his feet.

As he was walking out, he ran into his new secretary, Mildred Jenkins. "Good morning, Mildred," Victor said.

"You're out kind of early," Mildred remarked. "Do I need to come in earlier?"

"No, you're fine. I have a six o'clock meeting with the president, so I wanted to give myself a little extra time in case I got lost."

"I'd be happy to show you the way. Do you need anything for your meeting?"

"Not that I know of. Before I forget, would you see if they can bring me another chair?"

"Sorry, I tried to pick out a nice one."

"It's very nice, but I need something that doesn't move around so easily. If it has rollers, I need to be able to lock them, otherwise I have a difficult time standing."

"Right on time," Peter said. "Would you like some coffee?"

"Sure, and black is fine."

"Thanks for coming in so early, although I saw you arrived at five."

"A little overanxious, I suppose," Victor said.

"We've got a lot of work ahead of us, and I wanted to lay out what I need you to do first."

"Good, I'm ready to get back to work," Victor said.

"How did your meeting with Stewart Appleby go?"

"For the chairman of the Joint Chiefs, he was very open and blunt with his assessment of our current situations."

"He sent me a folder of his recommendations, but I haven't read it yet," Peter said. "Did you have time to get to that when you met?"

"We did, and I liked what I saw."

"Great. Would you mind netting it out for me?"

"We're down to eight thousand troops in Iraq, and he's recommending we pull that back to six hundred, and that they only be used for embassy security."

"I can live with that. How about Afghanistan?"

"The situation is still very convoluted, and he admitted that he really didn't have a clear vision for a path forward."

"Damn. I know it's been a while, and that you weren't in the top command echelon, but I'd like to hear your thoughts."

"I'd get the hell out of there. No matter what we do, the Taliban is going to regain control at some point, and all we're doing is wasting lives trying to forestall a forgone conclusion."

Peter handed Victor a sheet of paper. "I couldn't agree more. Read this and let me know what you think."

When he finished, Victor said, "Perfect. Do you think the UN will go along?"

"They've already signed off on it. We're going to coordinate the opening with the departure of the last of our troops. We're going to operate it as a UN enclave, with multiple embassy staffs housed there. The UN will be responsible for security, and all of the countries involved will split the cost."

"I like it, but we need to make sure they don't cut corners on security."

"I need you to work with Harry on the exit plans, and so we can have everything wrapped up by the end of next year."

"We'll have to hustle, but we'll do our best."

"Good. Once you have that lined out, I want you to work with Matthew Summerville, the secretary of transportation, on how we can begin implementing your vision for the infrastructure refresh."

"I know you said you'd think about it, but I never really believed you'd try to move it forward," Victor said.

"I can't promise you we'll get it done, but this country needs something to jump-start the economy. While you're working on that, I'm going to attempt to broker a deal between the Palestinians and the Israelis."

"It's long overdue, but neither side has shown that they're willing to make the necessary concessions."

"I know it's a long shot, but I'm going to get this done or die trying," the president said.

Victor almost asked why he was so hell-bent on forcing a solution, but he decided to let it pass.

"Once that's done, I'll try to rein in the Iranians."

"Good luck with that."

"I know it's going to be a challenge, but I'm hoping their new leader is going to be more reasonable than the previous regime."

"Why the urgency? They've been a pain in our ass for decades."

"The CIA is convinced Iran could have a deliverable nuclear weapon within two years."

"I thought they'd backed off trying to develop nukes," Victor said.

"They did, but the CIA thinks they're trying to buy them on the black market."

"Is that even possible?"

"Unfortunately, yes. I talked to our Russian ambassador last night, and the Russians are willing to strong-arm them into meeting with me when I'm ready."

"What are you trying to achieve?"

"I'm going to try to get them to allow UN oversight of their nuclear programs."

"The UN has been attempting that for years. What's changed?" Victor asked.

"Their economy is in shambles from the sanctions, and we've had reports that the Iranian clerics are afraid that the Arab Spring phenomena could happen to them if they don't act."

"Where would you hold the meeting?"

"The Russians are recommending Egypt."

"Why Egypt? It's not exactly the poster child of stability."

"Not sure, but the Russians were adamant about it."

"I wouldn't trust any of them."

"I don't, but I don't have much choice if I want to move this forward. Sorry to cut you short, but I've got a press conference at eight to announce the upcoming negotiations with the Israelis and the Palestinians, but if you need anything, just let John Jacobs know."

When Victor got home that night, Melinda asked, "How was your first day?"

"Busy. I had an early meeting with Peter, and then I spent the rest of the day organizing my office. You wouldn't believe how big the White House complex is."

"Actually I would. I got to tour it during my high school graduation trip."

"It's awfully quiet in here. Where is everyone?"

"The kids have decided to live on campus, at least for a while, and my mother has gone back home."

"Damn! What brought all that on?"

"The kids decided it was too big of a hassle to make the trek back and forth every day. However, if the truth be told, I think they wanted to be around the other kids."

"Was Agent Stubbs alright with it?"

"He had some reservations, but he worked through them."

"How about your mother?"

"I think she was already homesick, and the only reason she came was for the kids."

"When's she leaving?"

"Already gone. She should be landing in a couple of hours."

"So we've got the whole place to ourselves?"

"During the week; the kids will come home on weekends."

"I wouldn't bet that lasts very long," Victor said.

"What's up?" Klaus asked when he answered the phone.

"I've found out the first part of what the president's plan is," Fredericka said.

"Let's hear it."

"He' going to broker a treaty between the Israelis and the Palestinians. He wants to roll the Israeli borders back to the pre-1967 lines, and in return, he's going get the Palestinians to cease their attacks and allow the UN peacekeepers in to monitor their compliance."

"There's not a chance in hell of either one of those things getting done."

"Whatever, I'm just letting you know what he's got in mind," she said.

"Changing subjects," Klaus said. "Have you gotten your counterpart under control?"

"It's hard to tell with him. Some days I'm not sure he's really that committed to our cause."

"Leave that to me. I know how to get him refocused. Call me if you find out any specifics."

"Has he come around on the nominations?"

"He has. He had them independently vetted, and of course they passed with flying colors."

"They'd better, we've paid a fortune to have them groomed."

CHAPTER 13

Shortly after the press conference announcing the negotiations, the secretary general of the UN, Paul-Henri Archambault, called the president.

"Mr. Secretary, it's good to hear from you," President Montblanc said.

"Congratulations on the summit, but how in the world did you convince Saeed Jabra to sit down with Ben Weizmann?"

"Saeed agreed right away, when I assured him they were willing to discuss returning the border to the 1967 positions."

"You got the Israelis to agree to that?"

"Not yet. But if Prime Minister Weizmann doesn't agree to the rollback, I'll make sure the U.S. cuts them off from all aid."

"I don't mean to tell you your business, but there's no way in hell you can get that done. Their lobbyists are world famous for their ability to manipulate Congress."

"Not this time."

"I like your enthusiasm, but you'd better cover all of your bases, because they've got more influence than you could ever believe."

* * *

The summit was taking place in Bonn, Germany, and when *Air Force One* landed the Secret Service agents were already waiting on the tarmac.

"We'll be in the limo on the left, Mr. President," said Special Agent Sam Jacobi, the head of the president's Secret Service detail.

"There's no rush. Prime Minister Weizmann's plane had mechanical problems, and he's not landing for a couple of hours."

They were meeting at the Kameha Grand hotel, just minutes from the airport, and when they arrived, the concierge rushed out to meet them.

"Welcome to the Kameha Grand, President Montblanc. My name is Randolph Gruber, the hotel's concierge. Your meeting room is all set up, and we have you in our finest suite. If there's anything that I, or any of my staff, can do for you during your stay, all you have to do is ask."

President Montblanc spent the afternoon working through his e-mails and reading status updates. They'd rescheduled the meeting for eight o'clock that evening, and after the president had eaten dinner, he sat down to go over his notes one more time. He realized the meeting was going to be difficult, but he'd made up his mind to do whatever it took to get the Israeli government to put an end to the needless bloodshed. When Victor had asked him why he was so passionate about getting it done he hadn't told him the truth. Because even after all these years, the real reason was still too painful to recount.

Several years before he'd met his wife, Deborah, he'd had a passionate love affair with a young Palestinian girl he'd met while attending a summer session at Cambridge University. Adliya Batatu had been her name, and if he was honest with himself, the only woman he'd ever known that had touched his very soul. When they'd made love, her dark brown eyes had burned with a passion that he'd never experienced again. When the summer had ended, he vowed that he'd return to bring her to America as his wife.

Excited to share the news, she'd returned to Jerusalem to get her father's blessing. Unfortunately, her father was a leader in Hamas, and was on the top of the Israeli's hit list. On her first day back, they'd been on their way to the countryside for a picnic, when an Israeli aircraft had destroyed their Land Rover with a missile.

Their deaths hadn't been reported, so Peter had no way of knowing why she'd disappeared. He'd tried in vain for months to contact Adliya, and it wasn't until he'd convinced his father to pull some strings in the State Department, that he'd finally discovered what happened.

Unable to cope with the loss, he'd become so depressed that he'd dropped out of school. His dad had finally sat him down, and threatened to disown him if he didn't get his act together, and reenter college. He'd gone on to become a powerhouse in American politics, but he'd never forgotten Adliya.

"I'm so sorry. The damn plane was being difficult," Prime Minister Weizmann said when he arrived.

"Not an issue. Have you eaten?" President Montblanc asked.

"I had something on the plane. It's late, so let's get to it."

"I'm not going to insult you by pretending that I intend to give you a choice in this matter," President Montblanc said. "I expect Israel to agree to pull all of your settlements out of the West Bank, and return the border to the pre-1967 boundaries."

"Are you insane?! Even if I wanted to, which I don't, I could never convince my government to even consider it."

"Your problem. The fact remains that you will do it, or I'll make sure you never get another dime, or any other form of assistance from the United States."

"You're delusional. We've got lots of friends on Capitol

Hill, and even with your mandates, you couldn't ram something like that through," Prime Minister Weizmann said as he leaned back and lit a cigar.

"Times have changed," President Montblanc said.

The prime minister wasn't used to being talked to like that, but when he looked into Montblanc's eyes, he realized he was being deadly serious.

"We're reasonable men, can't we negotiate this?" Prime Minister Weizmann asked.

"We can negotiate anything else you'd like, but this is a nonnegotiable point with me."

The prime minister stubbed out his cigar, and closed his eyes to try to gather his thoughts. "You're placing me in a very difficult position. If I were to agree to this, and I'm not saying I'm ready to do that, I'd need something in return."

"Name it."

He hadn't expected such a quick response, but the prime minister was quick-witted, and a pretty good horse trader himself. "I'd say, at least five hundred of the Ground Combat Vehicles, another hundred F-35 Joint Strike Fighters, the plans for your new GMD antimissile systems, and twenty of your new frigates, equipped with the next generation Aegis combat systems."

"Whoa. You could be talking a trillion dollars or more," President Montblanc said.

"And you're talking political suicide if I don't get something of that scope in return."

The president pondered his chances of pushing that kind of commitment through Congress, and said, "Done."

"I can't believe you can pull it off, but once I see it in writing, I'll follow through with the Palestinians. I do have to ask. Why would you put your presidency on the line for those animals?"

"It's time for the violence to end," President Montblanc said.

"We have a deal then," Prime Minister Weizmann said. "I must say you're not what I expected from your dossier."

"I'm not sure whether that's a slam or a compliment, but you have my word that you'll get your weapons," President Montblanc said as they shook hands to leave.

"We'll see."

But don't fool yourself that I'll soon forget this, Prime Minister Weizmann thought to himself.

Jonathan had been working late to prepare for a 0800 meeting and was just about to call it a night when the front doorbell rang. He minimized the application screen he was in and clicked the icon to activate the front door camera. When he saw the Washington courier waiting on his front porch, he went to see what he had for him.

"Good evening, sir. I've got a rush package for you," the courier said as he handed him a letter-sized padded envelope. When Jonathan took it from the courier, he turned to leave.

"Don't I need to sign for it?"

"No, sir. Have a great night." The courier returned to his truck, but before he left for his next stop, he took a moment to erase the address from his onboard computer.

Jonathan pitched the package onto his desk and turned out the light. "Hell, I'd better see what's in it," he said as he turned the light back on. He pulled the tab to open the envelope and read the sticky note on the front of the sheets. He sighed and started reading through the rest of the material. There were only six pages, but he spent almost an hour reading them over and over. He'd always known it might come down to this, but the reality of what he was being asked to do made him want to puke.

He walked over to open his wall safe and put the instructions inside. He took a minute to leave his assistant a voice mail, asking her to reschedule his first meeting, and called his car service to reschedule his pickup. When he finished, he went upstairs to try to get some sleep.

He had several vivid dreams about what might lie ahead of them, and by the time his alarm went off at 0445, he was soaked in a cold sweat. He quickly showered and went downstairs to meet the car service.

"You're up awfully early, sir," his driver said.

"I need to make a stop before I go in," he said as he handed the driver the address.

When they arrived at his destination, the door opened immediately when he knocked. "Come in, and have a seat," Fredericka said. "I've got to go pee, but help yourself to the coffee and sweet roll."

When she returned, she fixed her coffee and grabbed a cinnamon bun. "Now what the hell was so urgent?" she asked as she took a bite.

"I made you a copy, but make damn sure you don't let it fall into the wrong hands," Jonathan said. "You'll want to spend some time with it, but I'll give you a brief overview of what they're planning, and what we're going to be expected to do."

When he finished, she said, "Shit. I know we've been preparing for this day, but I'd prayed it would never come."

"Me too, but we'd better get to work."

"Yes, time is short, but we've got to be very discreet."

"You think?"

CHAPTER 14

When President Montblanc got back to Washington, he called Senator Miller, the president pro tempore of the Senate, in for a meeting.

"I heard you met with Ben," Senator Miller said. "How is the old scoundrel?"

"That's why I asked you to come over. We worked out a deal for some additional arms shipments," President Montblanc said as he slid the list across the table.

"Good lord," Senator Miller said. "No disrespect, but have you lost your frigging mind?"

"Probably, but this is what I need you to get done."

"This will take some time."

"Unacceptable. I'm going on national TV tonight to announce that we are coming to the aid of our best ally, and that this initiative will help jump-start the economy. If you're worried about support, I've already spoken to the various defense contractors that stand to make a bundle off of this, and they're going to join me in saying that this will create a lot of new jobs."

"Whatever. Even if we ram this through, how are we supposed to come up with the money?"

"I've already submitted a resolution to remove the defense spending limits for the next ten years."

"Surely you don't think that's going to fool the opposition? They'll be all over this in a heartbeat."

"No, they won't. After the ass kicking we just gave them, they're going to wait and see how it plays out."

"Have it your way, it's your funeral. I'll get with Shelby Cohen first thing this morning, and we'll get it done."

The legislation set off a firestorm of criticism in the press, but to the surprise of everyone, including the president, it really did create a major surge in the economy. Three months later, John Jacobs came strolling into Victor Garcia's office and sat down.

"What's up, John?" Victor asked.

"The president has spent the last three days in meetings with the UN Security Council."

"Did he get them to listen for a change?"

"The council just passed a resolution that authorizes the use of force if the Iranians don't allow the IAEA (International Atomic Energy Agency) inspectors immediate and unfettered access to all of their nuclear facilities."

"It's about time," Victor said. "I know Peter has really been pushing them to move forward with this."

"He has, and that's why he's volunteered to present the UN's demand to the Iranians."

"Damn, that'll get them stirred up, but what are the odds of them agreeing to meet with him?"

"Surprisingly, the Russians stepped up, and bullied them into taking the meeting."

"When do you expect to hear back?"

"That's why I'm here. We've just received the meeting confirmation, and President Montblanc is leaving in the morning."

"I know in the past the Egyptians had offered to provide the venue. Is that where they're meeting?" Victor Garcia asked.

"Yes, but not in Cairo as we expected. They're holding it in Hurghada."

"I've heard of it. Resort area on the Red Sea?"

"I'm impressed. The meeting site is actually about forty-five minutes from the airport, at the five-star Ibero-tel Makadi Beach Hotel, and it's supposed to be quite spectacular."

"That sounds nice, too bad it's not a vacation."

"Certainly not a vacation, but since the Russians rented the entire hotel for the meeting, Deborah is going along."

"Anything you need me to do?"

"No, we're good. The president just wanted me to give you a heads-up."

As the Boeing 747-200B lifted off from Andrews Air Force Base, President Montblanc turned to John Jacobs and asked, "I forgot to check, did Gemal make it?" Gemal Helal wasn't a well-known public figure, but he was very shrewd and a much sought after interpreter/negotiator.

"Yes. I put him up in one of the staterooms. Would you like me to bring him back?"

"Definitely."

"Gemal, I apologize for the drama and lack of notice," President Montblanc said.

"Not an issue, but I have to admit, I was more than a little concerned when the Secret Service showed up on my doorstep and told me I had to come with them."

"Sorry, they can be a little over the top at times, but in this case we couldn't chance telling you ahead of time. I hope I haven't caused you too much of an inconvenience."

"Not too much, but I would be interested to know what precipitated the need for this much secrecy."

"We're meeting the Iranian president in Egypt, to see if we can reach common ground on their nuclear ambi-tions."

"I think you know I was born in Egypt, but it's the last place on earth I'd use," Gemal Helal said.

"The Russians insisted."

"Russians! Don't tell me they're in the middle of this."

"Afraid so. I couldn't get President Shirazi to take the meeting, so I asked for their assistance. Have you ever met Shirazi?"

"I've met with Saeed many times when he was the oil minister. I worked with him on a deal for Chevron for almost a year, and just before we were supposed to sign, the conniving bastard welched on it and signed a twenty-year lease with BP."

"I know he doesn't have a great track record, but he's running the show now, so I don't have any choice."

When *Air Force One* neared the coastline, a squadron of F-35s out of Germany met them.

"Why are there aircraft following us?" Gemal Helal asked when he noticed the fighter jets.

"They're going to escort us the rest of the way," John Jacobs said.

"You expecting trouble?"

"We're not sure. The director of the NSA said they've seen a tremendous surge of encrypted traffic in the last week, but they haven't been able to crack it yet. He wanted the president to postpone, but he wouldn't hear of it."

"His dogged determination is why he's president, but these are dangerous people."

When the aircraft came to a stop at the hangar, they could see people rushing out to meet them.

"Mr. President, your car is ready," said Special Agent Sam Jacobi, the head of his Secret Service detail. They'd sent a C5A Galaxy on ahead with their support vehicles, and twenty additional Secret Service agents.

"Thanks, Sam. If it's alright, I'd like Mr. Helal to ride with us," President Montblanc said.

"No problem. Before I forget, this is Major Jameson, he'll be carrying the football on this trip."

"What happened to Lieutenant Commander Carrolton?"

"He had an appendix attack, and we had to replace him. Everyone should visit the bathroom before we leave, because it's going to take at least an hour due to the traffic, and we won't be making any stops," Special Agent Jacobi said.

"That sounds ominous," Deborah Montblanc said.

"Nothing to worry about, it's just protocol," Special Agent Jacobi said. "Besides, I doubt you'd want to use any of the facilities along the way."

The Egyptians had provided twelve motorcycle policemen to escort them to the resort, and the Secret Service had armored SUVs in front and back of the president's vehicle.

"Damn, Sam, are you expecting trouble?" President Montblanc asked.

"Better safe than sorry, Mr. President. I'm going to ride up front, but if you need anything, just ask one of the other agents and they'll take care of you."

With the motorcycle cops clearing the way, they made it to their hotel in thirty-five minutes.

"What a beautiful hotel," Deborah said. "But where is everyone?"

"It's the top five-star hotel in the area, but the Russians bought out the entire facility for our meeting," Peter said.

When their convoy stopped at the entrance to the hotel, the hotel manager met them. "Greetings, President Montblanc. My name is Abdul Assam, and I'm the hotel manager. I know you've come a long way, so if you'll follow me, I'll show you to your rooms.

"Here we are," Mr. Assam said as he opened the double doors to their suite of rooms.

"Very nice," Deborah said.

"Dinner will be served at eight in the main dining room, but if you require anything before then, just ask."

"My team is on this floor as well, and we'll have two men on duty in the hallway at all times," Special Agent Jacobi said.

After they'd freshened up, Peter and Deborah went out on the balcony to enjoy a moment alone.

"My, what a view," Peter said as he looked out at the pristine private beach and the waters of the bay.

"Truly idyllic," Deborah said. "I just wish we could take a little time for ourselves."

"Me, too, but that's not why we're here. I'll have to check with Sam, but I bet you could lay out on the beach if you'd like."

"That would be wonderful."

"Remember, you can't leave the room, or go anywhere without one of the agents."

"I remember, but it seems pretty silly since we're the only ones here."

After they'd finished their drinks, Deborah said, "I think I'll take a quick nap."

"Go ahead, I've got to check my messages," Peter said.

"It never stops, does it?"

"Afraid not, but it's what I wanted, so I've got no reason to whine about it."

That night they got dressed, and went down to dinner. When President Shirazi saw them come in, he stood up and waved them over.

"President Montblanc, it's good to finally meet you in person," Saeed Shirazi said.

"Thank you, President Shirazi. I'd like to introduce my wife, Deborah, and I believe you know Gemal Helal."

"It's my pleasure to meet you, Mrs. Montblanc."

"The honor is mine, Mr. Shirazi."

"Gemal, how long has it been?"

"Too long, Saeed," Gemal Helal said. "You've come a long way since we last met."

"Not so far. I'm still trying to keep Iran afloat, just in a different capacity. It's just as well our deal fell through, BP lost a fortune when the sanctions took effect."

"It was fortuitous, but I have to admit I was bummed at the time."

"I know. I wish I could have explained what was going down, but when the ayatollahs pulled the plug, they swore me to secrecy."

"Water under the bridge as they say," Gemal said. "Hopefully we can be more successful this time."

"Have a seat, my friends," President Shirazi said. "The food here is unbelievable, so I think you'll be pleased with whatever you order."

After they'd finished eating, President Shirazi said, "We could get started, if you're not too tired."

"That would be fine. Dear, why don't you go on up, I'll be there when we're finished."

After she'd gone, President Shirazi said, "It's a lovely night. Let's take our drinks out by the pool."

On the way out, President Shirazi waved one of his bodyguards over and instructed, "Please go up and escort the ayatollah down to where we're sitting.

"I apologize for not telling you earlier, but I'm not the one you're going to have to deal with," President Shirazi said.

"Why not?"

"I'm afraid the senior clerics don't yet trust me to handle something of this importance, so the supreme leader, Ayatollah Mohammad Rostami, is here to handle the negotiations. He doesn't speak or understand any English, so it's a good thing you brought Gemal along."

"Excuse us, we need a moment alone," President Montblanc said. Gemal and the president got up and walked to the other side of the pool. "This is total bullshit," President Montblanc said. "What do you think he's up to?"

"Saeed is never that forthright, and I'm going to guess that you're in for some tough discussions."

When they'd finished discussing their approach, they went back and sat down with President Shirazi.

"I'll make the introductions when he arrives, but he may ask me to leave," President Shirazi said.

"How does that work?" President Montblanc asked. "I thought you were in charge?"

"Only when it fits into their plans. In truth, I'm little more than a puppet."

When the ayatollah arrived, President Shirazi made the introductions, and as he'd feared, the ayatollah said, "That will be all for tonight, President Shirazi."

Since he spoke no English, his interpreter had to translate back and forth.

"Let me know if his translator changes anything," President Montblanc said.

"He's struggling with some of it," Gemal Helal said. "I had the same problem with English when I first learned it. Why don't you ask him if it's alright if I take over?"

"Mr. Rostami, would it be alright if Mr. Helal takes over?"

"He says that's acceptable," his interpreter said.

"Why does your country feel that it has the right to dictate how we run our affairs?" Ayatollah Rostami asked. "We've been on record for years that our nuclear ambitions are strictly peaceful."

"Just to be clear, I'm speaking on behalf of the entire UN Security Council, not just the United States," President Montblanc said.

"Understood, but that doesn't change the facts."

"We've repeatedly heard your version of the truth," President Montblanc said. "However, your continued denial doesn't alter the UN's intent to verify your claims."

"Are you threatening us?"

"The Security Council has given your country a very clear expectation of what's required, and if you allow the deadline to expire without making some sort of arrangements, they will take action."

"We'll not be threatened. We're done here," the ayatollah said as he got up to leave.

President Montblanc stood, and said, "Don't be hasty, we need to work through this."

"I'll not listen to another word tonight."

"Before you go, let's at least set a time to get back together," President Montblanc said.

"I'll need to discuss this with my advisors before I can set another meeting. However, it will be a total waste of time if you keep making the same silly demands. We're a sovereign nation, and we will not be threatened by infidels."

"That went well," President Montblanc said.

"I knew you were in trouble when he didn't even let Shirazi sit in. I wouldn't give you a nickel for Saeed's chances of living out the year."

"Really," the president said.

"Beyond a doubt, he's done. I don't know whether it will be an accident, or they'll just have him executed, but he's finished."

"I'll see you first thing in the morning, but I'd better get on the horn and give the secretary general an update," President Montblanc said.

The next morning, President Montblanc and Deborah were sitting on their balcony overlooking the deserted beach.

"This is a little scary," Deborah said.

"How so?" Peter asked.

"Such a beautiful beach, and it's totally deserted.

Almost like one of those end-of-the-world movies you're
so fond of.

"Do you want me to get that?" Deborah asked when
the phone rang.

"No, I'll get it, I'm sure it's for me."

"President Shirazi would like you to have lunch with him
by the pool," Abdul Assam said.

"What time?"

"Twelve thirty."

"I'll be there."

"I almost forgot. He asked that you bring Mr. Helal."

"Sure, no problem."

"Thank you for coming," President Shirazi said.

"It's why we're here," President Montblanc said. "Will
the ayatollah be joining us?"

"No, he's on a video conference with the council."

"So he's authorized you to take the lead?" Gemal Helal
asked.

"Hardly, but he was certain that he couldn't get anything done by the five P.M. deadline, so he asked me to try
to work out a twenty-four-hour extension."

"Why bother with the charade? You have no intention
of allowing IAEA to carry out the required inspections,"
President Montblanc said.

"Up to now that's been true, but our people are suffering, and the council thinks that large-scale unrest could
be a possibility."

"That's never concerned them in the past."

"True, but in the last month we've had to execute two
highly placed members of the military, and a military in-
surrection isn't something they want to deal with."

"I wasn't aware of that, but why should I believe you
this time?"

"I doubt there's anything I could say to change your mind, but could you at least grant us this small reprieve?"

"I'll need to touch base with Mr. Archambault before I could commit to that. Why don't you and Gemal visit while I give him a call?" The president walked over to another table out of earshot and placed his call.

"We're talking with President Shirazi right now, and he's requested a twenty-four-hour extension," President Montblanc said.

"What's your gut tell you?" Paul-Henri Archambault asked.

"That they're stalling, but another day won't matter."

"Then go ahead, but this is the end of it."

"What did the secretary general have to say?" President Shirazi asked.

"He granted the extension, but he said that there won't be another."

"Understood, and thank you for making the effort."

When they finished lunch, President Shirazi excused himself and left.

"Have you changed your mind on President Shirazi?" President Montblanc asked.

"I'm afraid not," Gemal Helal said.

"I didn't sense any nervousness from him."

"He doesn't have any family, and I know he's deeply religious, so he's probably resigned to his fate."

"How'd lunch go?" Deborah asked as she was drying her hair.

"The food was excellent, but other than that we didn't achieve anything. It looks like you've been swimming?"

"Yes, Mr. Jacobi said it would be alright, as long as his men went along. The water was wonderful, but it wasn't much fun by myself."

"Sorry, but I doubt I'll get much time for swimming."

"There's the phone again," Deborah said.

"This is President Shirazi, and Ayatollah Rostami would like to meet with you tonight after dinner."

"What time?" President Montblanc asked.

"Around nine."

"That should work. Is it alright to bring Mr. Helal?"

"Of course," President Shirazi said. "I'm about to leave for the airport, so I won't be attending, but I'd like to thank you for your courtesy and professionalism."

"It was my pleasure," President Montblanc said. "I hope we can work together again in the future."

"I doubt that will be possible, but thank you for the thought."

President Montblanc's security team and Major Jameson were following at a discreet distance as he and Mr. Helal walked out to the pool to meet with Ayatollah Rostami.

"Stay alert, the ayatollah has brought seven body-guards with him," Special Agent Jacobi said.

"Good evening, Mr. Rostami," President Montblanc said.

"Thank you for taking such a late meeting, but I had some details to attend to before I could meet with you," Ayatollah Rostami said.

"Not a problem. I hope that we can have a more productive session tonight."

The ayatollah closed his eyes for a second or two before he answered. "If only that were possible. As I told you last night, we'll not be threatened, or intimidated. In the last twenty-four hours, your navy's ships have entered the Gulf of Oman, and the French have moved several squadrons of Mirages within striking distance of our territory."

"That's true, but we'll stand by our word to not take any action before the deadline."

"It doesn't really matter. We have no intention of acceding to the United States', or the so-called United Nations', unlawful demands."

The president had known it was going to be a difficult negotiation, but he couldn't believe that they weren't even going to make an attempt at a compromise. "Then why bother with all of this?"

"I'd hoped the council would grant me more leeway, but unfortunately that wasn't the case," the ayatollah said as he got up to leave.

"That's it?"

"I'm afraid so," he said as his men surrounded him and led him away.

CHAPTER 15

"That's right, Mr. Secretary, we didn't talk for more than five minutes, and when I asked him why he'd bothered, he gave me a bullshit excuse about the council not allowing him any discretion in the matter."

"Unbelievable," Paul-Henri Archambault said. "Are you going to be speaking with him again?"

"No. In fact I got the impression he was leaving," President Montblanc said.

"I'll convene an emergency session of the Security Council to update them. We'll hold to the extension unless they do something stupid, but if I don't hear something new from you, we'll initiate the operation on schedule."

"I understand, and I'll let you know if the situation changes. Mr. Secretary, I hate to cut this short, but I've got to take this call," President Montblanc said as Sam Jacobi held up a secure satellite phone, and whispered, "You need to take this, right now."

"This had better be important," President Montblanc said.

"I've got the director of national intelligence on the line, and he said to get you on the horn no matter what you were doing."

"What's so damn urgent?"

"You need to get the hell out of there, and I mean right now," Gregory Kellogg said.

"Slow down, and tell me what's going on."

"The Iranians have begun large-scale movements of their ground and naval forces, and it looks like the shit's about to hit the fan. We've contacted *Air Force One,* and they'll be ready to lift off as soon as you arrive. I've also contacted Paul Boothby, the secretary of defense, and Stewart Appleby, the chairman of the Joint Chiefs of Staff, to let them know what we're seeing."

"Alright, I got it. We'll leave as soon as we can get packed up."

"No, just leave it, and put Special Agent Jacobi back on."

"Deborah, wake up, we've got to go," the president said, and he gently shook her.

"What?"

"Get up, we're leaving."

"Is it morning already?" she asked sleepily.

"No, but we have a situation, and we've got to leave."

"It'll take me a few minutes to get packed."

"Just get dressed, we're leaving everything."

"Oh. Are we going to be alright?" she asked as she started dressing.

"I'm sure we will, but you need to hurry."

They were just starting to prep the president's plane for takeoff, when the next call came in.

"Yes, sir, I understand," said Colonel Swartz, the chief pilot on *Air Force One.* "Ed, get everyone to their stations, and have Agent Lawrence come up here."

"Yes, sir, what can I do for you?" Special Agent Lawrence asked.

"I need you and your team to deploy into defensive positions around the aircraft and prepare for an attack."

"Oh, hell. Anything you can tell me about what to expect?"

"Supposedly there's a force of armed men, numbering at least a hundred, shooting the hell out of the Egyptians guarding the airport, and I'm going to take a wild guess that they're here for us."

"You should go ahead and take off," Special Agent Lawrence advised.

"Can't, the president is on his way, and I've been ordered to wait on him."

"Understood. We'll do what we can, but we won't be able to handle a force of that size for long."

When Special Agent Lawrence reached their command center at the back of the aircraft, he gathered his twenty-man team around him. "Listen up. I need you to break up into two-man teams. Herbert, open the weapons locker, and issue one of the Javelins to each team. Make sure you get some extra magazines as well. Dillon, you and Rogers pull the SUV around to the front of the aircraft."

"What's up, boss?" Agent Dillon asked.

"We've got a large number of hostiles headed our way."

It only took the attackers a few minutes to clear out the Egyptian security forces, but it gave the agents enough time to get into position. The attackers had commandeered civilian vehicles when they'd come ashore, so they were in everything from pickup trucks to limousines. As Agent Lawrence watched the ragtag collection of vehicles speeding toward them, he waited until the last moment before he ordered, "Fire."

The SUV had a roof-mounted M134 Gatling gun, and when Agent Rogers opened fire, he was spraying four thousand rounds a minute at the onrushing vehicles. They only had ten Javelins onboard, but the antitank missiles were deadly, and as Agent Lawrence watched the first wave of the onrushing vehicles turn into burning junk, he allowed himself a glimmer of hope that they might be able to hold them off until the president arrived.

When they'd expended their missiles, the rest of the teams opened fire with their FN P90 submachine guns. The Americans were throwing up a formidable defense, and when Major Hamdi, the commandos' commander, saw his first wave cut down, he had his RPG teams stop and open fire. They took the SUV out first, and as it was blown to bits, the concussion blew out *Air Force One*'s front windshield.

"Ramstein, we're under attack, and the aircraft is no longer airworthy," Colonel Swartz radioed. "You'll need to arrange an alternate pickup for Megatron," he continued, indicating the code name for the president.

"Understood, and good luck. Ramstein out."

"Let's get something to fight with, and see if we can help out," Colonel Swartz told his aircrew.

Colonel Swartz and his men joined the agents, and they were putting up a ferocious defense, but as the attackers closed on their position, the number of defenders was dwindling quickly. They were down to six agents and a couple of the aircrew left alive, when a volley of RPGs ruptured *Air Force One*'s fuel tanks and it exploded into a gigantic fireball.

The ensuing inferno wiped out the last of the American defenders, and Major Hamdi ordered, "Cease fire, and make sure they're all dead. We've taken care of the aircraft."

"Excellent, we'll be landing in five," Colonel Tavaazo ordered.

A couple of minutes later, the Antonov An-225 Mriya landed with Colonel Tavaazo and his team.

Forty-five minutes before the attack on the airport, Special Agent in Charge Sam Jacobi had just finished getting a sit-rep from the director of national intelligence.

"Alpha team, bring the vehicles around to the front,

and we'll be right down. Baker team, destroy everything but the weapons and form up with Alpha."

"I haven't been able to contact the aircraft, but the director said they're expecting us," Special Agent Jacobi said as he helped President Montblanc and his wife into the vehicle. "Alpha team, you take the lead, and we're not stopping for anything," Special Agent Jacobi said.

There was almost no traffic at that time of night, so the armored SUVs were able to speed throughout the night at over 100 mph. They slowed as they reached the entrance to the airfield, and Special Agent Jacobi said, "This looks bad."

As they weaved in and out of the debris and dead bodies, no one said a word.

Agent Jacobi opened the window to the rear, and said, "Ramstein received word that the aircraft had been damaged, and was no longer airworthy, before they lost contact with the crew."

"What do we do now?" President Montblanc asked.

"We've been diverted to an alternate location."

"How about our men?" President Montblanc asked.

"No word."

"Let's take a quick look."

"That's not a good idea, and my only priority is your safety."

"Understood, but what can it hurt if we do a quick drive-by?"

"Sorry, and you'd better buckle up, because we're getting the hell out of here."

As the small convoy made a high-speed turn to leave, Agent Jacobi observed, "That's a hell of a fire," as the flames from *Air Force One* boiled above the tops of the hangars. They'd just gotten turned around when the commandos cut them off.

As they slid to a stop, President Montblanc said, "Get us out of here."

"No can do," Special Agent Jacobi said. "They've got

us surrounded, and there are far too many of them for us to shoot our way out."

"I'm going to destroy the football," Major Jameson said.

"Yes, of course," President Montblanc said.

CHAPTER 16

Victor was sleeping peacefully when he heard a knock on their bedroom door. He didn't want to wake Melinda, so he put his legs on, threw on a robe, and stepped out into the hall.

"I'm sorry to disturb you, but you need to get dressed, and come with me," Special Agent Scott Stubbs said.

"What's up?"

"There has been some sort of incident with the president."

"What sort of incident?"

"I really can't say. Mr. Boothby didn't provide any details. However, they need you at the White House situation room ASAP."

Victor knew the secretary of defense wasn't prone to hyperbole, so he knew the shit had hit the fan. "Would you call for the car while I get dressed?"

"There's one waiting outside."

"It's the middle of the night, what are you doing up?" Melinda asked.

"I'm headed to the White House for a briefing. Go back to sleep, I'll be back as soon as I can," Victor said.

"You be careful," she said as she rolled over to go back to sleep.

Special Agent Stubbs and three other agents flanked

Victor as he made his way to the armored SUV waiting in the driveway. "Where's the car?" Victor asked.

"We'll be using this for the time being," Special Agent Stubbs said.

As they were pulling away, armored SUVs took up positions in front and back to provide an escort. "Is that a mini-gun?" Victor asked as he was studying the SUV in front.

"It is, and all of the vehicles have B7/NIJ VI-class armor."

"Expecting a war?" Victor asked.

Their min-convoy had a police escort, so they arrived at the White House in record time. The SUV had barely come to a stop when they were surrounded by twenty heavily armed soldiers who hustled them inside the entrance to the West Wing. Once inside, they went directly to the elevator that would take them to the basement, where the White House situation room was located. When they got off of the elevator, they stopped at the guard station to get the vice president an RFID badge, so he would be able to move freely around the basement levels. Normally it wouldn't have been necessary, but when they'd activated the level one security protocol, every entrance in the facility was locked down and secured by a RFID reader. While they were encoding it with his information, he could hear some of the conversations going on inside the room.

"I can't believe we could end up with this bozo as president. The only reason they let him on the ticket was to win the immigrant vote."

Victor felt his blood pressure rising, but before he could figure out who was talking, the marine sergeant said, "Here you go, sir. This will let you into any room in the building."

The room fell silent when Vice President Garcia entered. He'd been in the situation room a couple of times, but never when there was an actual incident going on. There were twenty two-hundred-inch, ultra-hi-def flat-screen TVs lining the walls, and a six-hundred-inch, ultra-hi-def projector screen at the far end of the room. They were showing real-time footage from several different locations, and the effect was almost overwhelming.

General Appleby, the chairman of the Joint Chiefs of Staff, was sitting at the head of the table, but as soon as he saw the vice president enter, he got up and said, "Sit here."

As they all rose to their feet to recognize him, he took a quick mental roll call. On the left side of the table there was Tom DeMarco, the secretary of state; Paul Boothby, the secretary of defense; Mary Beth Greider, the secretary of Homeland Security; Margret Grissom, the director of the CIA; and Gregory Kellogg, the director of national intelligence. Seated across from them were Harold Crowe, the secretary of energy; Walter Middleton, the secretary of the Treasury; Jerry Burns, the national security advisor; and Roberto Diaz, the United States ambassador to the UN.

"This looks serious," Vice President Garcia said.

"That's putting it mildly," General Appleby said.

"Would one of you bring me up to speed, and shouldn't we get the president in with us?" Vice President Garcia asked.

"I'll brief you, but we've lost touch with the president," said Gregory Kellogg, the director of national intelligence.

"Lost touch? What the hell happened?"

"We don't have a clear picture yet, but I can walk you through the events that preceded his disappearance. At oh-nine-hundred local time, the Israeli Air Force carried out a series of preemptive airstrikes against the Syrian's chemical weapons depots."

"I thought that that shit had all been destroyed," Victor Garcia said.

"That was the story, but evidently they had some they didn't divulge."

"Sorry, continue."

"A short time later, three Israeli armored division crossed the border at Quneitra."

"The Israelis are invading Syria?" Vice President Garcia asked.

"We're not sure of their intent. In response, the Iranians started moving large numbers of troops and equipment into position for a possible counterstrike. Shortly after, Jordan's and Lebanon's armed forces began mobilizing. As the situation continued to escalate we became concerned for the president's safety and strongly suggested that they leave the country. His motorcade was on the way to the airport in Hurghada when we received word that *Air Force One* was under attack. We were able to contact Sam Jacobi, the agent in charge, just as they were entering the airport, and diverted them to an alternate location, but we haven't heard from them since."

"I thought we had the best technology in the world to stay in touch with the president."

"We do, and we've never had any issues before."

"Let's go around the room so I can hear from the rest of the team," Vice President Garcia said. "Jerry, let's start with you."

"I've had NSA reposition one of their satellites over their last known position, and we've confirmed that *Air Force One* has been destroyed, and that much of the airport is in ruins."

"Why didn't we have one over the president's location?" Vice President Garcia asked.

"We weren't worried about it because we normally have two over the area, but some nitwitted technician took them both offline for maintenance."

"I assume we've dispatched a rapid response team," Vice President Garcia said.

"SEAL team ten has just arrived on scene, but until we hear from them, we're not going to know much else."

They continued around the room, but none of them had anything to add.

"Finally," General Appleby said as he read the dispatch that Major Turner had just handed him. "SEAL team ten just sent their first sit-rep. The situation is still extremely chaotic, but I'll run down what they have so far. As we already knew, *Air Force One* has been destroyed, and they've verified twenty-nine casualties so far."

"President Montblanc?"

"They haven't been able to locate him or his wife, but many of the bodies are badly charred."

"Iranians?"

"Too early to say. Colonel Billups is the SEAL team commander, and he's currently interrogating the survivors of the attack."

"So some of our people survived?" Secretary of State DeMarco asked.

"Sorry, I should have been more specific. They're all Egyptian."

"So we still don't know where the president is, or whether he's even alive," Vice President Garcia said.

"Correct."

"How long has he been unaccounted for?" Vice President Garcia asked.

"A little over eight hours," Director of National Intelligence Kellogg said.

"Damn. What about the Iranians? Have they made any moves on the Israelis?"

"No. In fact, several of their units have returned to their original positions," National Security Advisor Burns said.

"What the hell are they up to?" Secretary of State DeMarco asked. "They can be unpredictable, but they rarely do anything without some sort of objective in mind."

"In this case I'm far more concerned with the Israelis," Vice President Garcia said. "Did we have any warning they were going to attack Syria?"

"They've been threatening for months, but we never thought they'd do it without giving us a heads-up," Secretary of State DeMarco said. "In fact, just before he left, the president warned Prime Minister Weizmann against provoking any incidents during the peace conference."

"General Appleby, I've got Colonel Billups for you," Major Turner said.

"What have you got for us, Colonel?" General Appleby asked.

"We're not even close to being done, but I wanted to give you an update. The group that carried out the attack swam ashore at a location about twenty minutes from the airport. Once on shore, they commandeered several civilian vehicles, and made their way into Hurghada."

"Where were the dammed Egyptians?" Secretary of State DeMarco asked.

"A few hours before the attack, several large-scale riots broke out around the city, which drew a significant number of troops away from the airport."

"This is sounding more and more like a setup," General Appleby said. "Continue."

"With most of the army units off trying to quell the riots, all that was left was the normal airport security, and one understrength rifle company. Once the terrorists cleared the Egyptians out of the way, they attacked *Air Force One*. From the looks of it, the agents on board put up a spirited defense, but they were vastly outnumbered and outgunned. Shortly after the attack, a Russian Antonov An-225 landed at the airport, carrying another group of commandos. We know that the first group destroyed *Air Force One*, but we're not sure what the purpose of the second group was, and both groups left on the Antonov."

"Russians?" Vice President Garcia asked.

"No, the Antonov is registered to the National Iranian Oil Company. They took their casualities with them, so I have no way of proving it, but judging by the tactics they used, I'd say it was one of the Takavar units."

"Iranian Special Forces?" Secretary of State DeMarco asked.

"Yes. The Takavar units are roughly equivalent to our SEALs," General Appleby said. "A mission like that would be right up their alley. Any sign of the president?"

"We haven't been able to identify the type of device they used, but there's a huge crater about a thousand yards from where *Air Force One* was parked. So far all we've found are bits and pieces, from what looks like the type of vehicles the president's convoy was using. There's also a lot of biologic material mixed in with the debris, but it's going to require DNA identification."

"Thank you, Colonel. If you find out anything else, give us a call immediately."

"What the hell do we do now?" Secretary of Defense Boothby asked.

"We've got to ascertain the president's status before we do anything else," Vice President Garcia said. "Roberto, you know Paul-Henri pretty well, don't you?"

"I've worked with him for years," Ambassador Roberto Diaz said.

"I need you to give him a call, and get him to postpone the UN operation until we can get a better handle on the situation."

"I can do that. How much can I tell him?"

"Can he keep his mouth shut?"

"He will if I ask him to."

"Fine, tell him whatever you need to."

"I think we should get Harry Miller over here immediately," Secretary of State DeMarco said.

"What do we need him for?" Vice President Garcia asked.

"We need the president pro tempore of the Senate to

invoke section four of the Twenty-fifth Amendment to the Constitution."

"Do you really think that's necessary?" Vice President Garcia asked.

"Most definitely," Paul Boothby said.

"It's about time you called. I was getting worried," Klaus said.

"The operation was a complete success," Fredericka said.

"Excellent. How about the cleanup?"

"Everything is in place. Once they've delivered the package, it will be taken care of."

"What about the cleanup team?"

"Their aircraft will blow up shortly after takeoff, and the rugged terrain should be enough to ensure they're never found."

"Good work, my dear. Keep me posted if anything changes."

CHAPTER 17

"How was your meeting with President Montblanc?" Mustafa Jaborandi, the ayatollah's personal assistant, asked when he arrived for his early morning meeting.

"It was a waste of time. I'm expecting General Nikahd, so show him in as soon as he arrives," Ayatollah Rostami said as he went into his office and closed the door.

When the general arrived, the ayatollah got right to the point. "How did the Israelis respond to our units pulling back?" Ayatollah Rostami asked.

"They've stopped their advances, but it looks like they are digging in," General Nikahd said.

"I never expected them to attack the Syrians."

"One of our sources said that they found out they'd hidden a large cache of chemical weapons."

"Damn it. I warned them to get rid of all of that shit. Oh well, it's his ass for sure this time, because we're sure as hell not going to bail him out again. Do you think we should put the military on full war alert?"

"We've been there since four this morning."

"Who authorized that?" Ayatollah Rostami asked.

"I did, as soon as the American fleet entered the Gulf of Oman, as per our conversation last week."

"My apologies, this turmoil is starting to wear on my nerves."

General Nikahd had never seen the ayatollah like this. When he'd first taken power, the general had been afraid he was going to be another hardliner, but as he'd gotten to know him better, he'd discovered he was a thoughtful man. Brilliant in many ways, but the general was still amazed at how naive he could be at times.

"I haven't seen you since your return. How did your meeting with President Montblanc go?" General Nikahd asked.

"It went as planned, but in retrospect, it may have been a mistake," Supreme Leader Ayatollah Rostami said.

"How so?"

"As we were breaking up the meeting, he asked why I'd taken the meeting, and I told him that the council hadn't allowed me any latitude in the matter. I have no idea what I was thinking. I'm afraid he's going to construe my remark to mean that I've lost control, and that's the last thing we need right now."

"I'm sure it will be fine," General Nikahd said. "I've got several things I need to pass by you, if you have the time."

"I slept on the plane, so I'm fine. Would you like some breakfast?" Ayatollah Rostami asked.

"That sounds great."

They ate a leisurely breakfast as they worked, but just before eight o'clock, General Nikahd's aide interrupted them.

"I asked you not to interrupt us unless it was something urgent," General Nikahd said.

"The Americans just attacked our southern command with cruise missiles, and Colonel Javari is demanding to speak with you."

"You assured me that they weren't aware of the Chah Bahar facility," Ayatollah Rostami said.

"I did, but I guess the dammed Jews found us out. Let me see what the colonel has to say."

The general spent a few minutes quizzing the commander of the Chah Bahar missile installation. When he was satisfied he understood the situation, he muted the call and said, "The Americans hit them with at least a dozen cruise missiles. They've lost over a third of their missiles, but the nuclear missiles are intact. What are your orders?"

The ayatollah closed his eyes for a few seconds before he ordered, "Tell the colonel to launch everything he has left."

"Nukes too?" the general asked.

"No, get them out of there."

"Colonel, load the nukes on trucks, and bring them to the Isfahan facility. Give the trucks three hours to get clear, and then fire everything you have left," General Nikahd said.

"They're on the way," Colonel Javari said.

Golem had been sitting lost in his thoughts when the satellite phone's strident ringing jolted him back to reality.

"Yes?"

"It's done," Klaus said.

"Excellent. Did anyone spot them?" Golem asked.

"We were monitoring all forms of communications, and it looks like they got in and out without being spotted."

"They said the new models were virtually undetectable. Excellent news. Keep me informed. Wait, I need an update on our other operation."

"They've been delivered, and they're in good shape, considering."

"Make damn sure they stay that way. They may be the only leverage we have when it's all said and done."

When Golem hung up, he picked up his glass of wine and swiveled his chair to gaze out the floor-to-ceiling windows of his chalet. It was a moonless night, but the city lights of Bern, Switzerland, glimmered below. The scene was idyllic, but he longed for his homeland. A pervasive melancholy swept over him as he recalled the events that had led to this moment.

He'd often wondered why, but his life had been blessed since he'd been forced to flee for his life during the Yom Kippur War. He'd just started his mandatory military career when he got out of grad school. He'd been a newly minted lieutenant assigned to a detachment in the Golan Heights, and he'd been the only survivor when the Egyptian and Syrian forces overran their position.

He hadn't realized it at the time but he'd been suffering from PTSD and survivor's guilt.

Overcome by his shame, he'd changed his name and relocated to Germany. He'd made his first million working for Deutsche Bank AG, and from there he'd branched out on his own. Buchman LTD had grown into the largest privately held company in the world, and Ravi felt great pride in that. His almost unlimited wealth had allowed him to try to rectify the one failure he'd had in life. He closed his eyes and prayed to God that He would grant him the power to protect Israel from her many enemies.

CHAPTER 18

The Senate was just getting started for the day when Special Agent Scott Stubbs approached Senator Harry Miller, president pro tempore of the Senate. He held out his identification and said. "Senator Miller, I need you to come with me."

"Excuse me, who are you?" Senator Miller asked.

"I'm Special Agent Scott Stubs, with the United States Secret Service, and I'm here to escort you to a meeting of the National Security Council."

"The NSC! Okay, sure. Just let me get Senator Bullard to take over for me."

When they reached the briefing room, Special Agent Stubbs said, "Go on in, they're expecting you." They were just wrapping up when the senator entered, so he slid into an empty chair.

Whey they finished, they disconnected the videoconference, and Secretary of State Tom DeMarco said, "Senator Miller, thanks for coming."

"Happy to, but it must be something big, to send the Secret Service after me."

"The president is missing, and we need you to help us invoke section four of the Twenty-fifth Amendment to the Constitution."

"Oh my God!" Senator Miller said. "I'm happy to help in any way I can, but that section has never been used."

"You're right, but the situation we're facing is why it was added."

"I'm sorry, but would one of you mind explaining what you're contemplating?" General Appleby asked.

"Sorry, I forget not everyone studies constitutional law for light relaxation," Tom DeMarco said.

"To summarize, the Twenty-fifth Amendment deals with either the permanent or temporary replacement of the president or vice president. Section four lays out the procedure required for the vice president to be named as the acting president of the United States, in the event of the president being unable to fulfill the duties of the office. The NSC will draft the declaration, and then we'll submit it to the president pro tempore of the Senate, and to the Speaker of the House of Representatives. We need to get this done as quickly as possible, but the procedures for invoking it have never been formally addressed. When the Speaker of the House gets here, we're all going to sit down and work through the language needed for the declaration."

As Speaker of the House, Shelby Cohen was the most powerful woman on the hill, and could at times be very difficult to work with, but when they explained the situation, she said, "Let me take the first cut at it, and then we can make whatever changes we need to. Does anyone have a laptop I can use?"

"Here you go," Major Turner said, as he handed her his MacBook Pro.

She never slowed once she started typing, and in less than thirty minutes she asked, "Which printer do you want me to use?"

"Situation-one is the printer in here," Major Turner said.

When he came back with the printouts she asked, "Would you mind handing those out?" She gave them a few minutes to read the document, before she asked, "What do you think?"

"It's perfect," Tom DeMarco said. "I'm a real student of this kind of crap, but I couldn't have done half as well."

"Great. The next step is to present this to a joint session of Congress for ratification. I'd recommend that it be a closed meeting, because I don't think we're ready to go public with this," Shelby Cohen said.

"Agreed," Harry Miller said.

"How long do you think it'll take to get it ratified?" Tom DeMarco asked. "I left before roll call, but I'm almost certain I've got enough senators in town to hit the two-thirds threshold."

"I'd already taken roll call so I know I'm in good shape as well. I'll have the sergeant at arms escort the representatives to the Senate chamber, and we'll get this taken care of," Shelby Cohen said.

"I'll give you a call when it's done," Harry Miller said.

"While they're taking care of that, I want to discuss our next moves," Vice President Garcia said.

"We need to move to at least a DEFCON 2 status," General Appleby said.

"I agree," Paul Boothby said.

"I think you should consider DEFCON 1," Gregory Kellogg said.

"I'd be uncomfortable going straight to DEFCON 1," Vice President Garcia said. "We've got most of our naval assets in close proximity to the Iranians, and I'm afraid someone will get trigger happy."

"I concur," General Appleby said. "DEFCON 2 is going to make a lot of people very nervous, but I do think it's a necessary step."

"Good," Vice President Garcia said. "Is there anything we need to take into account before we do?"

"We should reach out to the Israelis and see what they're up to," Secretary DeMarco said.

"Good idea," Vice President Garcia said. "How about the Chinese and the Russians?"

"Definitely," General Appleby said. "We don't need to spook them into doing something rash."

"No problem, is the presidential hotline in the Oval Office the best way to contact them?" Vice President Garcia asked.

"It is, but you can do it from here," Major Turner said. "We just upgraded the equipment in here to be compatible, but I'll need to call upstairs to get the IP addresses."

"Would you like for us to clear out?" General Appleby asked.

"It's probably better if you do, but I'd like Secretary DeMarco to sit in, since he knows them all," Vice President Garcia said.

"No problem, we'll be next door. Just let us know when you're finished."

"I hope you don't mind my putting you on the spot," Vice President Garcia said.

"Not at all," Secretary DeMarco said.

"What sort of man is Prime Minister Weizmann?"

"Don't let his diminutive size fool you. He's a vicious adversary, and a real hardliner, but he's also a survivor. They've pushed him out three times over the last two decades, but he's always managed to bully his way back into the top job. He's got powerful friends throughout the international business community, and an especially close relationship with Harry Miller and Shelby Cohen."

"Good to know."

"We're ready," Major Turner said. "Who would you like to contact first?"

"Let's start with the Israelis," Vice President Garcia said.

The video conference system was set up to identify the caller and required a positive confirmation before it would establish the connection.

"What can I do for the president of the United States today?" Prime Minister Weizmann asked. "Oh, it's you,

Mr. DeMarco. I was expecting the president. Is that Vice President Garcia with you?"

"Yes, it is. You've done your homework, as usual," Secretary DeMarco said. "I'm going to let Mr. Garcia take over, but I'll be here if either of you need me."

"I assume you've called to talk about the recent events?" Prime Minister Weizmann said.

"I know President Montblanc discussed this issue with you, but I need to know what the hell you were thinking when you precipitated this crisis," Vice President Garcia said.

"I don't appreciate your tone, but I'll give it to you straight up. We've grown tired of the United States' promises for a peace accord, and we're going to do whatever it takes to protect our interests. If President Montblanc had bothered to discuss it with me, I'd have advised him not to take the meeting, but once again your country ran off on their own, trying to exercise a leadership role that quite honestly, no one ever asked you assume."

"I'm sorry you feel that way, but don't think that we're going to bail you out when the rest of the Arab world unites against you."

"As a matter of fact, we will expect you to come to our aid if necessary."

"The president warned you not to do anything that might jeopardize the status quo, so you're going to have to live with the repercussions."

"If I were you, I wouldn't be making idle threats. My country has powerful supporters within your government, and they won't let us down."

"I'm sorry to interrupt," Secretary DeMarco said, "but I'm going to have to agree with Vice President Garcia on this. President Montblanc was very clear with you on this point, and our government will not come to your assistance if you're the aggressor."

"We'll see, and I don't think there's any need to continue this," Prime Minister Weizmann said as he broke the connection.

"What the hell is up with him?" Vice President Garcia asked.

"I'm not really sure, but we'll need to proceed carefully, because they do have friends in high places, as the old saying goes."

"I hope the rest of our calls go better than that," Vice President Garcia said.

Next they called Xi Zhang, China's general secretary of the central committee.

"I've been expecting your call, Mr. President," Xi Zhang said. "Sorry, Mr. DeMarco, I was expecting President Montblanc."

"It's my fault, we should have edited the identification, but we're in kind of a hurry," Secretary DeMarco said. "I'd like to introduce Vice President Garcia."

"Has something happened to President Montblanc?"

"There was an incident during his trip to Egypt, and we've been unable to locate him since."

"I just finished reading an internal report on the incident, although it didn't make mention of the president being missing," Secretary Zhang said.

"We've managed to keep it quiet so far," Secretary DeMarco said. "However, in the next few hours we're going to announce that President Montblanc has been incapacitated by a sudden illness, and that Vice President Garcia is assuming the role of acting president."

"What's an acting president?" Secretary Zhang asked.

"It's the term used in the Constitution for when the president is temporarily unable to fulfill the duties of his office. It's never been used under these circumstances, and it's one of the reasons we wanted to inform you first."

"It speaks to your commitment to peace, and I give you my personal pledge that my country will assist you in any way we can. We've been monitoring the Middle East situation closely, and we have grave concerns that this could inadvertently escalate into a worldwide nuclear conflict."

"I share your concerns," Vice President Garcia said. "Which is my other reason for the call. I'm changing our readiness status to DEFCON 2, and I didn't want you to think it was any threat to your country."

"A prudent action in my estimation. I'll make sure our military is informed, and it won't be an issue. I know a little of your background, and to be honest, I was afraid the warrior in you might overwhelm the statesman in you, but let's both work to keep the situation under control if we can."

"You have my word on it. My apologies for needing to cut our first conversation short, but I need to have this same call with President Baryshev."

"Not an issue, and again, I appreciate the call. Good luck in your new role, and don't hesitate to reach out if I can be of any assistance."

"He seemed cordial enough," Vice President Garcia said.

"He can be when he wants, but he can be a cold, calculating, son of a bitch when it suits him. I will say this about him. If he tells you he'll do something, it's money in the bank."

"How about President Baryshev?"

"I don't know him as well. He's a consummate politician, but I wouldn't trust him as far as I could throw him, and he's a big bastard. If we're going to get this done today, we're going to have to pick up the pace," Secretary DeMarco said. "If you don't mind, I'll try to move this along."

They placed their next call, and when President Baryshev answered, he almost filled the screen. At six foot ten and almost four hundred pounds, he was a bear of a man.

"Secretary DeMarco, I was expecting President Montblanc," President Baryshev said.

"Sorry about that, but we didn't have time to change the caller ID. I'm sorry to be abrupt, but our time is short," Secretary DeMarco said. "I would like to introduce Vice President Victor Garcia, and he's about to become the acting president of the United States."

"Is President Montblanc ill?"

"Missing. There was an incident during his trip to Egypt, and we honestly don't know his status. We're going to use a cover story that President Montblanc has experienced a sudden illness as the reason for naming Vice President Garcia the acting president, but we wanted to make sure you were aware of the truth."

"Unfortunate. I've never met him in person, but he and I talked briefly, shortly after he took office. It's good to meet you, President Garcia, but I wish it could have been under better circumstances."

"Thanks," Vice President Garcia said. "The other reason for the call is that I wanted to give you a heads-up that I'm taking our alert status to DEFCON 2. I wanted to let you know the reason for it before we did, and assure you that it's not a threat to your country."

"I'd do the same in your position. Is there anything we can do to help?"

"I may need to ask for your help in controlling the Iranians."

"I'll do what I can, but they're growing more difficult to reason with. As I'm sure you know, we have a mutual defense treaty with them, but if they strike first, I give you my word that we'll stay out of it."

"I'm still holding out hope it won't come to that," Vice President Garcia said.

"Me too, but while we're on the subject of controlling, have the Israelis lost their minds?" President Baryshev asked.

"I just had a brief conversation with Prime Minister Weizmann, but I still couldn't tell you what they're trying to achieve. I did demand that they cease all hostilities, and told him that we wouldn't defend them if they were being the aggressors."

"Knowing that little bastard, he probably told you to piss off," President Baryshev said.

"You've got him pegged pretty well."

"For a supposedly religious man, he's a ruthless bastard, and far more devious than they accuse me of being."

"There's been a hell of a lot of people killed in the name of religion, that's for sure. I don't mean to cut you off, but unless you have something else you'd like to discuss, I've got several other issues to attend to."

"Well, what do you think?" Vice President Garcia asked.

"He knows more than he's admitting, but at least he said they'd stay out of it," Secretary DeMarco said.

"I'm sorry to interrupt," Major Turner said. "There's been another incident, and the general wants to reconvene the council immediately."

CHAPTER 19

Fourteen hours after the attack on their convoy, President Montblanc and his wife regained consciousness. The only light in the windowless room was a tiny night-light on the far wall. When President Montblanc regained consciousness, he was struggling to figure out where he was, and what had happened. His drug-induced dreams had been laced with a vivid kaleidoscope of events.

"Damn, I hope that was just a bad dream," he muttered.

He sat up on the edge of the king-size bed, and looked around the room. *Where the hell am I?* he thought to himself. He glanced over at the other side of the bed, and saw that Deborah was starting to stir.

"You okay?" he asked.

"I think so. Where the hell are we?"

"I've got no idea." He got up and walked over to the doorway dimly outlined by the night-light. He felt around for a light switch. When the light came on he saw that the door led to a nice-size bathroom. He flipped the other switch, and the light in the center of the room came on. He didn't recognize anything, but the room looked to be about thirty-by-thirty. There was a kitchen table and four chairs on one side of the room, with a large metal door behind it. There was a hundred-inch flat-screen TV on one wall, and facing it was a large leather couch with two overstuffed leather recliners on either end.

"What's the last thing you remember?" Peter asked.

Deborah didn't say anything for several seconds as she struggled to remember. "It all seems like some sort of dream, but I seem to remember that we were attacked as we entered the airport, and then some really nasty people dragging us out of the car. After that, not much."

Her comments triggered his memory. "We were attacked, and I remember someone telling us that we weren't going to be harmed, and a sharp prick in my neck, then nothing."

She rubbed a sore spot on her neck and said, "I don't remember any of that, but my neck hurts. Do you think we've been taken hostage?"

"Could be, and if we have, they should be coming to talk with us before long."

They'd taken all of their personal effects, and there wasn't a clock in the room, so as they sat and talked, they only had a vague sense of how much time was passing.

"I'm going to see if the TV works," Deborah said.

"Might as well," Peter said. "I'm really surprised that someone hasn't come to check on us."

"This TV is screwed up, all I can get is a menu of movies," Deborah said.

"Let me try it." She handed him the remote, but after a few minutes he said, "You're right, but I guess it's better than nothing."

They had no way of knowing, but the room was fitted with hidden cameras so their captors could watch their every move.

"How are they doing?" asked Richard Ellis, the leader of the group.

"They seemed a little dazed at first, but I think they're coming around," Larry Roberts said. "The president has checked out every inch of the room, and he must've beat on the outside door for twenty minutes before he gave up, but they're watching a movie right now."

"Understandable, we kept them sedated for quite a while. Have they had dinner yet?"

"No, but they're going to deliver their meals in a few minutes."

"Make sure everyone stays in character."

"Will do. Boss, what the hell are we doing?"

"We're making a buttload of money, that's what."

"I know that, but who's pulling the strings?"

"It's better you don't know."

"That sounds rather ominous."

"Think about it. They just had the team that captured them offed. What the hell do you think will happen if we screw up?"

"Point taken."

When the door to their room opened, a swarthy, roughly dressed man pushed a food cart through the door, followed by a huge, heavily armed guard. As he started placing their meals on the table, Chris Collins, the burly guard growled, "Hurry, up, my dinner is getting cold."

"Shut up, and it wouldn't hurt you to miss a meal or two," Larry Roberts said. "I've brought you some bottled waters, but we have tea and coffee if you'd rather have that," Larry told them in heavily accented English.

"Water is fine," President Montblanc said. "Tell your boss I'd like to talk with him."

"That's not possible."

"And why not?"

"He's not here at the moment, but I'll pass along your request."

"Sit down and eat before it gets cold," Deborah said. "Did you recognize the language they were speaking?"

"Farsi," Peter said.

"Damned Arabs," she said. "What the hell do they want with us?"

"Leverage. Our forces are providing most of the muscle for the UN task force, and they probably think that taking us hostage gives them an edge in the negotiations."

"What does that mean for us?"

"We should be fine. At some point they'll trade us for some sort of concession from the UN Security Council."

"Are you sure?" she asked tearfully.

He put his arm around her and said, "I'm so sorry you've gotten caught up in this, but trust me it's going to be fine. They know that hell would rain down on them if anything happens to us."

"The president seems awfully sure of himself," Larry Roberts said.

"He didn't get to be president by being indecisive," Richard Ellis said. "I want you to remind those two nitwits that the president can speak Farsi, so they can't be spouting off."

"I know. Chris is a smart-ass, but trust me you'd want him on your side in a fight."

"I remember. You forget we've done some previous jobs together, but he's a sick bastard."

"A complete sociopath."

"Just keep an eye on him, I don't need him screwing this up on us."

CHAPTER 20

"Sorry if I messed up your call, but the Iranians have launched an attack against the CVN-69 battle group," Major Turner said.

"What happened?"

"We're still waiting on the details, but it looks like they launched a salvo of surface-to-surface missiles from some previously undetected shore batteries, outside of Chah Bahar."

"Where the hell is that?" Secretary DeMarco asked.

"It's near the southernmost tip of the country."

"How bad?" Vice President Garcia asked.

"It's bad, but not catastrophic."

"Is that the Dwight D. Eisenhower battle group?"

"Yes, sir, it is."

"Recommendations?" Vice President Garcia asked.

"Admiral Kenyan has removed the immediate threat with airstrikes from the other battle group, but we need to impress on them that there's a price to be paid for screwing with us," General Appleby said.

"Do you have a target package in mind?"

"To start, I'd recommend an airstrike on Bandar-e Abbas. It's a naval airbase and their naval headquarters."

"Do it," Vice President Garcia said.

"I'd like to let Secretary General Archambault know what's going on," Roberto Diaz said.

"Fine. Just make sure he knows it hasn't happened yet. You undoubtedly already have this, but I'd like to see a list of strategic targets, in priority order," Vice President Garcia said.

"Not a problem," General Appleby said. "Major, would you print out a copy for the president?"

"Not there yet," Vice President Garcia said.

"Actually you are," Shelby Cohen said as she and Harry Miller walked in.

"It's official, you're the president, until such time that President Montblanc is deemed fit to resume his duties," Harry Miller said.

"Please don't congratulate me," President Garcia said. "While I'm honored to do it, it's a sad day for our country."

"We've got a lot to cover, so let's get back to it," General Appleby said.

"These sort of events rarely take place in a vacuum. What else is going on?" President Garcia asked.

"You must be a mind reader, because the NSA just issued an alert to the coast guard commander in Portland," Gregory Kellogg said.

"What sort of threat?"

"They've intercepted a series of encrypted communications from a Middle Eastern terrorist group, and they believe there's some sort of a WMD onboard a cargo ship headed to the West Coast."

"Credible?" General Appleby asked.

"Very."

"Anything else?" President Garcia asked.

"The Pakistani army has moved seven of their eleven corps near the Afghanistan border."

"I know there's no love lost there, but I would have expected them to go after India if they were going to start a war," President Garcia said.

"I think they know they can't handle the Indian army,

and besides that the Afghans don't have any nukes," General Appleby said.

"How many men do we have left in Afghanistan?"

"Give me a second to look it up," General Appleby said. "We've got eight hundred, and if you include the UN troops, there's just over two thousand."

"That's not enough to make any difference if they launch an all-out attack," President Garcia said. "Does anyone have any intelligence on what they might be up to?"

"We've feared they were in bed with the Taliban for some time, so they could be trying to return them to power," Gregory Kellogg said.

"I know we're stretched thin, but if they attack, what sort of assets can we bring to bear?"

"Airstrikes are about all we could do short term," General Appleby said, "unless you want to resort to some sort of nuclear option."

"I'm definitely not prepared to go there," President Garcia said, as he was beginning to understand the tremendous burden he'd just shouldered. "Secretary DeMarco, I want you to give them a call, and threaten the hell out of them," President Garcia said. "General Appleby, I want all of our people out of there."

They spent the next three hours working on options, and waiting on status reports from the events taking place.

"The coast guard has just intercepted the *Azrael,* and they're about to stop and board it," Paul Boothby said.

"Are they going to keep us updated?" President Garcia asked.

"We've got a P8 Poseidon on station, and we should have a video feed in just a moment."

"Put it up on the big screen."

Even though the aircraft was circling overhead at eleven thousand feet, the video was crystal clear.

"I'm going to patch in an audio feed from the coast guard ships," Major Turner said.

"*Azrael,* this is the United States Coast Guard cutter, *Jefferson County,* and I'm ordering you to heave to, and prepare to be boarded," Commander Jessup ordered.

They listened as the commander repeatedly ordered the *Azrael* to stop.

"*Azrael,* heave to immediately, or we will open fire," Commander Jessup ordered. The ship still didn't slow, so the commander ordered, "Put a couple across their bow."

The cutter's 57mm Bofors cannon belched fire, and they saw the explosions erupt about a hundred yards in front of the ship. After they'd fired two warning shots with no response, Commander Jessup was trying to decide if he should fire on the ship.

"Attention, attention, this is the captain. All crew members need to report to the ship's galley for a briefing," the *Azrael*'s captain ordered. "That goes for you two as well," the captain said to the two seamen manning the bridge.

"Who's going to steer the ship?" the helmsman asked.

"Just put it on autopilot, and get below," the captain said.

As soon as the men had left, the captain cut the power to the engines.

Commander Jessup was just about to give the order to open fire, when he saw the *Azrael* start to slow. "Prepare to be boarded," the commander called to the *Azrael.*

The *Azrael*'s captain had been ordered to scuttle the ship if they were intercepted before they reached the coast. "Lord, please take care of my family, and forgive me for what I'm about to do," the captain of the *Azrael* prayed. He opened the hidden drawer on the console and flipped the toggle switch to start the sixty-second timer on the charges. As soon as he flipped the switch, the entire vessel shook violently, as the charges detonated.

"What the hell?" Secretary DeMarco said when he

saw the explosions spray water all along the sides of the ship.

"They're scuttling the ship," General Appleby said.

The explosions had ripped a series of gaping holes in the *Azrael*'s hull, and the ship sank like a rock. No one said a word as they watched the ship disappear beneath the waves.

"Well that's that," General Appleby said as he had the major disconnect. "We may never know what their intent was, but they damn sure weren't going to be taken prisoner."

They were discussing what they'd just witnessed as the ship sank toward the bottom. It took the ship almost five minutes to reach the ocean floor, and it was still settling into the mud when the hydrogen bomb it was carrying detonated. The massive explosion instantly turned millions of gallons of seawater to steam, and when the blast reached the surface, it vaporized the coast guard cutters. The Poseidon had climbed to thirty thousand feet, and was almost fifty miles away when the blast occurred. It was moving away from the site of the explosion, but when the immensely bright light flashed around the Poseidon, it momentarily blinded them. When the pilot's vision cleared, he reversed his course so he could get a look at what happened. As the plane came back around, the mushroom cloud was already billowing far above them.

"Sir, the pilot of the reconnaissance aircraft is reporting a massive explosion," Major Turner said.

"Where, and what kind?" General Appleby asked.

"I've got the pilot, Commander Lipscomb on the line, if you'd like to talk to him directly."

"Hell yes, put him through, and see if they can send us a video feed. Commander, what have you got?" General Appleby asked.

"There has been a very large, undoubtedly nuclear explosion at the approximate coordinates where the *Azrael* went down."

"Any word from the coast guard cutters?"

"I'm going to get as close as I dare, but I don't see how any of them could have survived."

Just then, the video feed from the aircraft flickered to life on the screen.

"Oh my," Shelby Cohen said.

"Are your sensors picking up any radiation?" General Appleby asked, as he viewed the horrific scene.

"Off the scale," Commander Lipscomb said.

"Sir, unless you order me not to, I need to turn away."

"Of course, do what you need to. Nothing could have survived that. You and your crew will need to be decontaminated when you land."

"Roger that."

"Major Turner, contact the commanding officer at the naval air station, and have them standing by with a decontamination team."

"If this was the Iranians, where the hell did they get a weapon of that size?" President Garcia asked the group. "Quiet down. One at a time," he said.

But before the first one finished giving his thoughts, Major Turner returned. "The WCATWC has just issued a tsunami warning for the West Coast of the United States," Major Turner said.

"I know that was a massive explosion, but isn't that overkill?" Senator Miller asked.

"It wasn't caused by the explosion, there's been a nine-point-nine earthquake in the Cascade subduction zone," Major Turner said.

"What the hell is a Cascade subduction zone?" Paul Boothby asked.

"I was a geology major in college, so if you don't mind, I can explain," Shelby Cohen said.

"Go for it," President Garcia said.

"It's a term that denotes the area where the Juan de Fuca plate that's moving eastward has descended beneath the westbound continental crust of western Oregon. The last great Cascade subduction zone earthquake happened off the coast of Oregon and Washington in 1700. It was estimated to have been a nine-point-nine magnitude quake, and between the quake and the resulting tsunami, it caused significant damage to hundreds of miles of the coastline. It was so violent that it's believed a portion of the Washington coast sank over five feet."

"So, did the explosion cause it, or not?" President Garcia asked.

"There's really no way to tell. The quakes occur every three hundred to eight hundred years, but the timing is certainly suspect."

"Nine point nine, that's several orders of magnitude larger than the Indian Ocean earthquake, and it caused two hundred and thirty thousand casualties," General Appleby said.

"Very true. They were both subduction quakes, and some of the waves from the Indonesian tsunamis were thirty meters high," Shelby Cohen said.

"Good lord, that's what, ninety-eight feet high," Jerry Burns said. "That's insane, that would be almost a ten-story building."

"That can't be right, "Gregory Kellogg said.

"I'm afraid it is," Shelby Cohen said.

"We've got to do something," Secretary DeMarco said.

"I'm afraid there's not much we can do, other than start mobilizing the search-and-rescue crews," President Garcia said. "Major Turner, get me Timothy Gather on the phone."

"Mr. Vice President, what can I do for you today?" Timothy Gather, the head of FEMA asked.

"Timothy, I've got you on speaker with the NSC, and I take it you haven't heard yet?" President Garcia asked.

"Heard what?"

"There's been a nine-point-nine earthquake off the Washington, Oregon coast, and they've issued a tsunami warning for the entire West Coast."

"Shit. What do you need from FEMA?"

"I need you to start mobilizing every resource you can lay your hands on. If this is even half as bad as we fear, it could be truly catastrophic."

"I'm on it. I assume you'll be calling up the National Guard units?"

"Yes, and General Appleby has already issued a mandatory recall of all military personnel and placed every military installation on high alert. As soon as we understand the situation a little better, we'll coordinate with your office."

"We'll be standing by. Has something happened to President Montblanc?"

"It's a long story, and we'll explain later, but Vice President Garcia was named acting president this afternoon," Harry Miller said.

"I hope he's alright. Sorry to have gotten you off topic."

"No problem," President Garcia said. "Now let's get to work. There's going to be a whole lot of people who will desperately need our help."

"He's a good man," General Appleby said.

"That's good to know, because we are going to need everyone to step up on this," President Garcia said. "We need eyes on this," he continued.

"I've already rerouted an AWACS, and it should be over the Oregon and Washington coastline in approximately twenty minutes," General Appleby said.

"Do we know whether there's been an actual tsunami yet?" Jerry Burns asked.

"No confirmation yet, but we're expecting a call from Mallory Nimbly, the director of WCATWC, at any time," Major Turner said.

CHAPTER 21

"I've got Director Nimbly on the line," Major Turner said.

"Mallory, what have you got for us?" Gregory Kellogg asked. "Sorry, Mr. President, force of habit, I've known Mallory for years."

"Not a problem," President Garcia said. "Continue."

"The quake was felt as far east as Salt Lake City."

"Damages?"

"We've had several reports of buildings collapsing on the West Coast, but I don't have any official damage estimates yet. We've activated the tsunami warning system, and ordered coastal evacuations in Washington, Oregon, and Northern California. I've also issued a tsunami alert for the entire Pacific."

"How many people are likely to be affected?" President Garcia asked.

"Millions in the U.S. alone, but unfortunately, many of them will ignore the warnings, and they'll lose their lives."

"That's pretty pessimistic."

"Reality often is. Our current projections show the earthquake has the potential to have generated a wave that's twice the height of the 2004 Indonesian tsunami."

"I'm calling bullshit on that," Richard Wells said. "That would be over two hundred feet high."

"That's enough of that," President Garcia said. "Sorry, Mallory, continue."

"I know it's hard to believe, and it won't be that high everywhere. Most of the coastline will experience a surge of between twenty and thirty meters, however there are certain areas like bays, harbors, or lagoons that'll amplify the effect."

"Do you have an ETA?"

"The quake occurred approximately three hundred miles off the coast, and given the depth of the waters, it should be moving in the range of five to seven hundred kilometers per hour, which would put it on the coast in less than an hour from the time of the quake."

The president checked his watch and said, "That could be within the next ten minutes."

"That could be fairly close."

"Anything you'd like to share before we let you get back to work?" President Garcia asked.

"You might want to check with USGS to see if they're detecting any additional seismic activity."

"Is there something you're not telling us?"

"Nothing definitive, but given the depth and strength of the subduction quake, there's a very good chance it could cause other events."

"That's pretty circumspect, would you care to elaborate?"

"I'll try, but it may get a little involved, so bear with me. When the Cascadia subduction zone faulted, it triggered the earthquake. The issue is that fault stretches from mid Vancouver Island to Northern California. The strength of an earthquake is proportional to the size of the fault area, and several recent studies have shown that it was fully locked for at least a hundred and forty miles, thus the nine-point-nine quake."

"OK. It was a really big quake, but we already knew that."

"There's a fair amount of research that leads me to believe we could see major quakes along the San Andreas Fault, Queen Charlotte Fault, and the Mendocino Fault, just to name a few. There's also a school of thought that a megaquake like we've just seen could set off the volcanoes along the Cascade Volcanic Arc."

"Net that out for me."

"I won't bore you with the entire list, but Mount St. Helens, Mount Hood, and Mount Rainier are on the list. Seattle, Portland, and Sacramento would be especially vulnerable."

"Let's hope that doesn't happen," President Garcia said. "But I'll take your advice, and reach out to them."

"Do you believe that woman?" Walter Middleton asked. "What a load of crap. She's been watching too many disaster movies on the Syfy channel."

"She's a brilliant woman, so I wouldn't dismiss what she had to say," Gregory Kellogg said. "But I do hope she's wrong this time."

"Major Turner, see if you can get the director of the USGS for us," President Garcia said.

"This is Director Mast, who am I speaking with?"

"This is President Garcia, and I have you on the speaker with the NSC, in the White House situation center."

"No disrespect, but I thought you were the VP?" Carter Mast asked.

"Long story, but for now, I'm the acting president. If you don't mind, we'd like to ask you a couple of questions."

"Shoot."

"We just got off the phone with Mallory Nimbly. She gave us an overview of the megaquake that just occurred in the Cascadia subduction zone, and she felt that we might see some additional events as a result of the quake."

"I'm afraid she's spot-on. We've already seen hundreds of microquakes all along the West Coast, and we just had a report of steam rising from a corner of Mount St. Helens."

"Go on."

"It's too early to say whether any of this will result in a major event, but we're definitely keeping our eyes on them."

"Anything else before we let you go?" President Garcia asked.

"No, but I'll keep you informed as we get more information."

"Before you go, I'm going to put Major Turner back on, and he'll give you the direct number to reach us."

"It just keeps getting worse," President Garcia said. "Any more information on the Iranian situation?"

"Some," General Appleby said. "We lost three aircraft during the airstrikes from the Ronald Reagan task force."

"Any more details on the damage from their attack on the fleet?"

"We've reestablished contact with the fleet, and they're reporting minimal damage."

"Did we find out why we lost contact?"

"Along with the missiles, they had several submarines in the area, and they were jamming the communications with EMP pulse."

"That's new, isn't it?"

"It is. We've tested the technology, but we had no idea they had it in operation. The pulses didn't cause any real damage, but they did manage to disrupt their communication ability."

"That's good news," President Garcia said. "How are they reacting to the airstrikes?"

"Nothing so far, and they're continuing to pull back from their forward positions."

"I can't for the life of me fathom what the hell they're trying to accomplish. Tom, I want you see if the UN would be willing to broker a cease fire until we can get a handle on the rest of this."

"Right away."

The president noted a couple of frowns from the group. "Look, until we know how bad the damage from the earthquake is going to be, I don't want to chance stirring up anything else."

"Understood," General Appleby said. "I'll make sure all of our forces are on high alert, but I'll keep them on a short leash."

"Good. Have we received any updates on President Montblanc's status?"

"They've competed the on-site analysis of the aircraft, and we have an understanding of what happened to *Air Force One,* but they're still working through the other site. They haven't been able to re-create exactly what took place, but it looks like that's where the president's convoy was ambushed. They've found enough debris to identify the lead and trailing vehicles, but other than the massive crater in the middle, there's no trace of the vehicle the president's party was traveling in."

"Thanks for the update. Let's take a short break. We'll meet back here in thirty minutes."

CHAPTER 22

When Calvin Hobbs and his wife Abby retired, they'd moved into their dream home on the edge of the Columbia River Gorge. Their son Jimmy and his wife Linda had brought the grandkids for a visit, and the women were in the kitchen packing a picnic lunch for their trip to the beach.

Almost an hour before, they'd felt the whole house shake from the megaquake in the Pacific. They'd gotten used to the periodic earthquakes, but this one had knocked out the power and shattered the picture window in the living room. They were still busy cleaning up the mess when the house started shaking again.

"We need to get out of the house," Calvin said. "Jimmy, take Jeffry out the front door, and I'll get the girls out the back."

When Calvin came rushing into the kitchen, his wife asked, "What's the big deal? It was just a little earthquake." Before Calvin could respond, the house shook so violently that all of the dishes in the cabinets were flung across the room.

"Let's go," Calvin said as he helped Linda up.

The back stairs were gone, so Calvin said, "Just jump." He helped the girls up from the grass, and said, "Let's go around front."

"Damn, Dad, that was pretty intense," Jimmy said as they walked around the edge of the house.

"That was strongest I've ever felt," Calvin said.

"The house is a mess," Abby said. "I think it's leaning."

"The frame cracked during that last quake."

The third quake was the strongest of the three, and as they tumbled to the ground, the house screeched and groaned as it collapsed to one side.

"Grandpa, your house is broken," their granddaughter Melanie said.

Calvin couldn't help but chuckle and say, "Yes, it is, baby, but we'll get another one. All that's important is that we're all safe."

"Dad, isn't it too early for low tide?" Jimmy asked.

"Yes, it is."

The edge of the ridge ran about two hundred feet from the rear of the house, and as Calvin walked closer, he could see the water was receding even farther away from the beach. They hadn't been listening to the TV, so they hadn't heard any of the warnings, but Calvin knew immediately what was going on.

"Everyone get in the van, right now," Calvin said.

"What's going on, Dad?"

"There's a tsunami headed our way, and we need to get the hell out of here. Everyone buckle up," Calvin said as they were scrambling to get seated. As soon as he turned the key to start the van, he heard the strident warning being broadcast over the radio.

"What's a tsunami, Grandpa?" Melanie asked.

"It's a great big wave. Now be quiet, and let Grandpa drive." As the van accelerated away from their shattered house, Calvin was praying they'd left soon enough. He had his hands full as he drove way too fast over the rough dirt road that led to their cabin. When the van slid up onto the highway, he glanced at the rearview mirror.

"Oh dear God," he muttered.

"What's wrong, dear?" Abby asked.

He didn't bother to answer as he floored the accelerator.

"Slow down, you'll have a wreck," Abby said.

"Grandpa, there's a big wave following us," Jeffry said.

"Turn around, and put your seat belt back on," Calvin said.

"You don't have to be so mean about it," Abby said.

As Calvin stole another glance in the mirror, his blood ran cold. The onrushing wave towered far above them, and as it washed over the speeding van, it swept them up with the rest of the debris.

The Security Council was just starting to leave the room for a break when Major Turner announced, "I have Director Mast on the line."

"Put him through," President Garcia said.

"Five minutes ago, the West Coast was hit by three more quakes," Director Mast said.

"How bad?" President Garcia asked.

"The first was a five point five, the second was a six point eight, and the third was a seven point four. We're not sure if they were aftershocks or new quakes, but a seven point four is a major quake unto itself. This could be just the beginning, if Mallory's scenarios come to pass."

"Thanks for the update, and let us know if anything else happens," President Garcia said.

"The man's an idiot," Harry Miller said. "I may not be an expert on earthquakes, but everything I've ever read has said that quakes are rarely, if ever, caused by other quakes."

"You may be right, but Mallory Nimbly and Carter Mast are anything but idiots," President Garcia said. Major Turner motioned to catch his attention, "What have you got, Major?"

"This is a live feed from an AWACS, flying north over the Oregon Coast."

When the video started, Shelby Cohen said, "I know where that is. They're near the mouth of the Columbia River, and if I'm not mistaken, that's Astoria."

"You're correct," said the pilot, Colonel Walker. "The tsunami is just reaching the coast, and the wave is continuing to grow in height as it surges up the Columbia River Gorge."

They watched in horror as the wave surged over Astoria's buildings. In just seconds, the horrendous force of the water had disintegrated them into little more than kindling.

"Those poor people," Shelby sobbed.

"Colonel, can you do a slow turn so we can get a perspective of how widespread the damage is going to be?" General Appleby asked.

"Yes, sir, but it's not going to tell you much, because we can't see the end of it in either direction."

As the picture slowly rotated, they saw that the colonel was right.

"Thank you, Colonel, we've seen enough," General Appleby said. "If you see anything that we need to be aware of, please don't hesitate to contact us."

"That reminded me of the scenes from the 2011 Tohoku earthquake," Jerry Burns said.

"Let's hope it doesn't get that bad," Harry Miller said.

"That looked like it could be much worse," President Garcia said. "If even a quarter of the scenarios that Mallory Nimbly laid out happen, it will go down as the worst natural disaster of all time. Get Gather back on.

"Timothy, we just witnessed the tsunami wipe out a little town called Astoria, on the coast of Oregon. The surge impacted the coastline for as far as we could see in either direction, so you should expect casualties from Washington to Northern California."

"How bad?"

"From what we just witnessed, I'd say catastrophic, but that might even be an understatement."

"We'll do what we can, but I don't have that kind of manpower We'll need to utilize a triaged approach to where we send our resources. I'd recommend that we start with the most heavily populated areas, and work our way down the list."

"I hate it, but that sounds like a valid approach. We'll be mobilizing every resource we have, but it's going to take time."

"On my end as well, but I started everything headed west the last time we talked."

"Good man. Keep me informed."

"General Appleby, where are we at with the mobilizations?"

"We're sending everything we've got, but our biggest hang-up is going to be transportation."

"Get me the secretary of transportation," President Garcia said. Matthew Summerville had been secretary of the Unites States Department of Transportation for over twenty years, and knew every aspect transportation.

"Secretary Summerville, this is President Garcia, and I desperately need your help. We have got a major disaster on our hands, and I need to get a lot of men and material to the West Coast as quickly as possible."

"How far are you prepared to go?"

"Whatever it takes."

"That's what I needed to hear. If you'll authorize it, I'll commandeer everything that moves. Just let me know where it is and where it needs to go, and we'll get 'er done."

"Excuse me, Mr. Summerville, I need to put you on hold for a moment," President Garcia said. "Have we been able to locate the attorney general?"

"He's on a direct flight from Amsterdam," Major Turner said, "and his plane doesn't land for another twenty minutes."

"Secretary Summerville, I'm sorry, but I'm going to have to call you back," President Garcia said. "Start putting your plans together, but don't pull the trigger until we talk again."

"I'll be ready."

When William Daugherty landed, they didn't even let him get his luggage before they whisked him away. When he reached the White House, Tom DeMarco took him to one of the briefing rooms to get him up to speed.

The secretary of state had just finished laying out what they knew of the earthquakes' impact, when the attorney general interrupted.

"I'd watched some of the coverage on the plane, but this is far worse than the news organizations were reporting," Attorney General Daugherty said.

"No one's trying to hide anything, but when the earthquake hit, it knocked the electric grid offline from San Diego to Vancouver, Canada."

"Sorry, I wasn't trying to infer you were. The situation is a perfect example of why NSPD-51/HSPD-20 was instituted. Have you already involved Homeland Security?"

"Not so fast. I haven't shared everything yet. I still need to read you in on the other problems we're trying to work."

When he finished, the attorney general said, "I'm sorry, but I need a minute." After he'd taken a few seconds to process what he'd heard, he continued, "So, let me see if I understand the situation. The president's missing. The Iranians have attacked our fleet. Several large quakes and a monster tsunami have just decimated much of the West Coast. And if that weren't enough, you think it was caused by possibly the largest earthquake in recorded history, which may have been precipitated by a nuclear explosion from an attempted terrorist attack."

"I think you've got it. Are you up to meeting with the NSC?"

"I suppose."

* * *

"I've briefed the attorney general," Tom DeMarco said when they walked in.

"Good," President Garcia said. "What do you recommend?"

"Much of what you need to manage the current situation is already in effect, via the various presidential directives in force," Attorney General Daugherty said. "Anything else can be addressed by issuing additional national security, or Homeland Security presidential directives. Given the current circumstances, you should probably issue at least two. One to deal with the Iranian threats, and the other for our domestic problems."

"I'd like you all to help craft the language for the two presidential directives," President Garcia said. "Split up into groups however you'd like, and you may want to conference in Timothy Gather and Matthew Summerville. This may take a while, so this is what I'm going to do until we can put our final plans in place. I'm going to declare a national emergency, and order all National Guard units to active duty. I'm declaring martial law in all of the states west of the Mississippi, and authorizing FEMA to commandeer any transportation assets that it needs to carry out the rescue and recovery missions. Does anyone have any questions or comments?"

"I think you're alright with everything, but some are going to question the need for martial law in any state not directly affected," William Daugherty said.

"I understand, but we're not even sure that it's over, so if I'm going to err, I'm going to lean toward the more aggressive approach."

"Understood," Attorney General Daugherty said.

"We'll make sure the NSPDs cover everything you've mentioned. We can always sort it out later."

CHAPTER 23

"You look terrible," Melinda said when she walked into the situation room.

"I'm glad to see you too, but what are you doing here?" President Garcia asked.

"Special Agent Stubbs said they were relocating us."

"What about the kids?"

"We went by the college and picked them up. They sure didn't want to leave, but Special Agent Stubbs was very insistent."

"Where are they now?"

"They're upstairs. The White House staff is helping them get settled into their rooms."

"Rooms? What are they doing that for?"

"Special Agent Stubbs said that we'd be staying here for the time being."

"I guess that makes sense, considering the circumstances."

"Mr. President, excuse me for interrupting, but Mallory Nimbly needs to talk with you," Major Turner said.

"I'll go," Melinda said.

"Stay, this should just take a minute. What have you got, Mallory?" President Garcia asked.

"If you have time, I'd like to give you our initial damage estimate."

"Please do."

"I apologize if I drop off. I'm on a satellite phone, and the signal isn't very good because there's a lot of crap in the air. The tsunami has impacted the West Coast from Vancouver, British Columbia, to just south of Sacramento. The wave height has been estimated to be between eighty feet and four hundred and fifty feet. Depending on the topography, the surge carried inland from one mile to, in the case of the Columbia River Gorge, fifty miles inland."

"Oh no," Melinda gasped. "Sorry."

"That was my wife, Melinda," President Garcia said. "But that would pretty well sum up my feelings as well. Continue."

"I've touched base with all of the emergency responders that I could, but there has been very little communication from the affected areas. However, from the information I do have, I'm afraid that my initial casualty estimates may be too low."

"God, I hope not. Weren't you estimating there could be a million or more?"

"I was, but I'm relatively sure they'll far exceed that number."

"I don't know what to say," President Garcia said.

"It gets worse. I just spoke with Carter Mast with the USGS, and he believes Mount St. Helens and possibly Mount Hood could erupt at any time."

"Damn. Is there anything we can do?"

"I'm afraid it's in God's hands."

"I forgot to ask earlier, where are you located?"

"I'm in Portland."

"Shouldn't you be relocating?"

"Timothy Gather has dispatched a convoy to pick us up, but they haven't arrived yet."

"Call me back if they don't show up within the hour, and I'll send some air force choppers for you and your staff."

"Thank you, but I'm sure they'll be here anytime now."

"I was going to ask how you were holding up, but that's self-evident," Melinda said. "Do you have time to go up and talk with the kids? They're pretty scared."

"Sure. Right now it's a waiting game."

"Dad," Juanita said, as she ran over to hug him.

"I'm glad you're both here," Victor said.

"How bad is it, Dad?" Alejandro asked. "And you don't need to protect us, we're old enough for the truth."

When did they grow up? Victor wondered to himself. "It's pretty bad. Much of the West Coast has been devastated by earthquakes and a tsunami, but we'll make it through this."

"Do you think it's over?" Juanita asked.

"I hope so, honey, but we probably won't know for sure for a couple of days yet."

There was a knock on the door, and Special Agent Stubbs entered. "Mr. President, they need you in the situation center."

"I've got to go. It's going to be alright, but I'm sure glad we're all together," Victor said.

"What's up?" President Garcia asked.

"Mallory Nimbly said it couldn't wait," Major Turner said.

"Not a problem, put her on."

"We've lost touch with her, but she was concerned about something, so she had us record her message to you."

"Let's hear it."

* * *

"Mount St. Helens has erupted, and we're afraid that Mount Hood could follow shortly, and if it does, Portland could be in danger. We measured the Mount St. Helens at a magnitude three on the Volcanic Explosivity Index, but Dr. Jacobs is convinced a Mount Hood eruption could be a VEI level-seven event. Six or seven, it wouldn't really matter to us, because either way, we'd all be dead. If you—"

"That's where she got cut off," Major Turner said.

"I need a satellite view."

A minute later, Major Turner said, "It's coming up now. The plumes of smoke from the eruptions were already above thirty thousand feet and still rising when the terrifying scenes popped up."

"Shouldn't we be able to see Portland?" President Garcia asked.

Major Turner used a laser pointer to highlight its position on the screen. "It's right there, but the smoke from the pyroclastic flow has it obscured," he said.

"Get me Carter Mast, and we're going to need the team back in here ASAP," President Garcia said.

Several of them were busy with the many issues they had going, but forty-five minutes later the permanent members of the NSC were gathered again.

"What was so urgent?" General Appleby said. "I was in the middle of a strategy session with the Joint Chiefs."

"At eighteen thirty Pacific time, Mount St. Helens and Mount Hood erupted. Mallory Nimbly's team measured the Mount St. Helens' eruption at a magnitude three on the VEI scale. I've just spoken with Carter Mast of the USGS, and he's reporting the Mount Hood eruption as a level-seven event."

"I'm not familiar with the VEI scale," Walter Middleton said. "Is it similar to how they rate hurricanes?"

"It's more like how they measure earthquakes. The

scale is logarithmic from VEI two and above. In other words, from two and above, each increment is ten times more powerful."

"I've got Carter Mast, if you're ready for him," Major Turner said.

"Carter, thanks for calling back. We were just discussing the rating system for volcanoes."

"Any questions for me?"

"I assume a six or seven rating is bad, but my question is: how bad is bad?" President Garcia asked.

"A six is categorized as a colossal eruption, and a seven is a supercolossal event. We got lucky with Mount St. Helens. It was only a level three, and most of the blast hit sparsely populated areas, but Portland wasn't that lucky when Mount Hood went up."

"Hood is what, forty or fifty miles from the city? Surely it didn't affect it too badly."

"The most immediate danger from a volcanic eruption is the pyroclastic flow, and normally it wouldn't travel that far, but with a level seven event it did. The superheated flow engulfed the entire city."

"Damages?"

"I don't think we'll find any survivors, and we may not even find their bodies."

"Why would you say that?" President Garcia asked.

"The pyroclastic flow was still at fifteen-hundred degrees Fahrenheit when it reached the city."

"Oh dear God," Jerry Burns said.

"How many casualties?" President Garcia asked.

"We'll probably never know for sure, but if you said close to a million, you wouldn't be too far off."

"What can we expect next?" President Garcia asked.

"Surprisingly for eruptions of that magnitude, the seismic activity is already down to a few minor tremors."

"So there's no risk of it triggering any of the many faults that run up and down the coast?" Tom DeMarco asked.

"I definitely didn't mean to infer that. The potential for earthquakes is still there, but the explosive nature of the eruptions may have released enough pressure to lessen the chances."

"We can only hope," President Garcia said. "Thanks for the update, and I know you've got a lot on your plate, so we'll let you get back to it." The president braced himself, and stood up to address the group.

"I won't keep you any longer, but before you go, I wanted to take this opportunity to thank each of you for what you've done here today. We've got a long road ahead of us, and I'm counting on each one of you to take the lead in your areas of expertise."

"Has something else happened?" Melinda asked.

"Mount St. Helens and Mount Hood have erupted, and Portland has been wiped out," Victor said.

Melinda paused as she asked God to receive all of their souls.

"How are you holding up?" she asked when she'd finished her prayer.

"It's been a long day," Victor admitted.

"Have you eaten?"

"No, but I'm too tired to be hungry."

"You've got to eat. I'll have them bring you something."

As he sat eating, Victor was silently adding up the horrific events. When he'd finished his mental tally, he realized that no president had ever faced these levels of adversity, and he hoped he was up to the task. He closed his eyes, and took a moment to ask God for his help and guidance.

"Asking God for help?" Melinda asked.

"I was."

"Good. Go take your shower," Melinda said. "I'm going to check on the kids, and then I'll be in."

"Wait for me, I'm coming too."

Their rooms were just down the hall, and as they quietly peeked in on each of them, they were both praying for God's help to keep them safe.

"I've been expecting your call all day," Klaus said.

"This is the first chance I've had," Fredericka said. "I couldn't chance being overheard. I suppose you've seen the news?"

"Unbelievable. If we'd known it was going to cascade like that, we would have never sent the ship. It was never our intent to harm any of you. We were simply trying to force the president's hand."

"I know, but this is completely out of control. The initial casualty estimates are over a million, and that number is sure to climb. It's already so bad that the president has asked the UN to put their operation on hold until he can stabilize the situation."

"I can't tell you how badly I feel, but you've got to stay the course."

"Are you insane? There's no way my counterpart is going to follow through with his part, and without him, I've got no chance of pulling off the next phase."

"You let me worry about him, you just focus on what you have to do."

"As you wish, but if this ever comes out, nothing will protect any of us from the shit storm that will follow."

"It's far too late to worry about that."

When Klaus hung up he made the call he'd been dreading all day, but he knew he couldn't put it off any longer, and he hit the icon marked Golem.

Golem was a character from Jewish folklore, who was supposed to be the protector of the Jewish people. Protector or not, he scared the shit out of him.

"I was beginning to think you didn't want to talk with me," Golem said.

"Oh no, sir, I was waiting on Fredericka's status update

before I called you," he said as he tried to keep the quiver out of his voice.

"Do I have to guess, or are you going to update me?"

Klaus had been in and out of power several times, but he couldn't get used to Golem's complete disdain for him.

"Of course. She said they've already suffered over a million casualties, and that President Garcia has requested that the UN forces stand down until the domestic situation was stabilized."

"Son of a bitch. I knew we should have taken his sorry ass out. Have them move to stage two immediately."

"Are you sure?"

"Don't ever question my orders again. I put you in power, and I can remove you just as quickly."

"Understood. I'll contact her immediately."

CHAPTER 24

President Garcia had managed to get a few hours' sleep before the phone beside the bed rang.

"Yes?"

"I'm sorry, but we need you," Major Turner said.

"I'll be right down," President Garcia said.

"Trouble?" Melinda asked.

"I'm afraid so," he said wearily.

As he was putting on his prosthetic legs, he winced and let out a soft moan.

"Sore?" Melinda asked.

"Very. I was on my feet too long."

The lights were out when the president entered the situation room, but the glow from Major Turner's laptop provided enough light for the president to find him.

"OK, what have you got?"

"The Maine State Police stopped a semitruck at the Canadian border at three thirty this morning. The team of drivers seemed unusually anxious, so they asked to inspect their load. The truckers pulled machine guns and tried to shoot their way out, but luckily the National Guard had a squad there helping out, and they managed to neutralize them. When they opened the trailer they found what looks like a bomb."

"Where were they headed?" President Garcia asked.

"The bill of lading showed that they were supposed to drop their load off in downtown New York City."

"What have we done so far?"

"Homeland Security has dispatched a rapid response team, and the DOE's Nuclear Emergency Support Team (NEST), should be at the scene in three hours."

"So they didn't manage to detonate anything?" President Garcia asked.

"We got lucky for a change."

"They may be planning more of these. Have Secretary Greider issue an alert, and I want every plane, train, bus, and boat that enters this country searched."

"That's going to take way more manpower than they have."

"Tell them to figure it out. Hell, have General Appleby supplement their staff with his men."

As the major was furiously typing out the president's orders, President Garcia was trying to figure out what he needed to do next.

"OK, everyone has their orders," Major Turner said.

"There's no way I'll be able to go back to sleep, so let me see what else you've got." As he read through the latest status reports, he was struggling to keep his emotions in check. Page after page detailed the devastation that had struck much of the West Coast. When he finished, he said, "I need to speak with Timothy Gather."

"You're up awfully early," Timothy Gather said.

"I could say the same of you. How are we doing on getting the men and materials to the affected areas?"

"I'm using the railroads to move the stuff as far west as I can, and then we're transferring the loads to the fleet of trucks we've commandeered."

"Anybody giving you grief?"

"No. In fact all of the trucking companies have pitched

in, and we've got plenty of trucks at the rail yards. Our biggest problem is that we can only go so far before the highways become impassable."

"Speaking of that, I've just finished reviewing the aerial reconnaissance of the Portland area, and I'm declaring the entire area off-limits," President Garcia said.

Timothy didn't respond for several seconds. "I'm not sure I agree, but it'll simplify my planning. I'm going to set up my northern staging area in Spokane, but the ash on the roads has rendered them virtually impassable. The state has their snowplows out trying to clear a path, but it's going slowly because the ash keeps clogging their air filters."

"I apologize for the interruption, but there are several hundred bulldozers and road graders sitting in the Sierra Army Depot. They're outfitted for desert duty, so they'd be perfect for this job," Major Turner said.

"I didn't see that on any of the reports," President Garcia said.

"Probably because they've just arrived, but I know it's all there, because my brother-in-law is the quartermaster for the base."

"I'll contact the base commander, and instruct him to give you his full cooperation," President Garcia said.

"Great. Unless you have more questions, I'd better get back to work."

"I'm going upstairs and taking a shower, but I'll be back," President Garcia said.

"Take your time. I'll let you know if anything happens."

"I figured you'd still be sleeping," Victor said.

"I couldn't get back to sleep after they came for you," Melinda said. "Was it anything serious?"

"We're not sure yet. They stopped a truck on the Canadian border with some sort of weapon, but they killed the terrorists before they could detonate it."

"Has the whole world gone insane?" Melinda asked. "Are you going back to bed?"

"No, I thought I'd take a shower and eat a little breakfast."

"I'm kind of hungry myself. I'll have the kitchen fix us something."

They managed to eat their breakfast in relative peace, before Juanita and Alejandro came out of their rooms.

"Daddy," Juanita squealed as she ran over to give him a hug.

"Good morning, sweetie," Victor said.

"You look tired," Alejandro said.

"A little. I'm sorry we had to pull you out of school, but it was necessary."

"Mom told us some of what's going on, and there's pretty much nothing else on TV."

"Is it as bad as they're saying?" Juanita asked.

"I haven't watched any of the coverage, but I'd have to say it's probably worse than they're reporting. I've tried to keep a lid on the coverage, because we don't need any more panic than there already is."

"You're covering it up?" Alejandro asked.

"Watch your mouth, young man," Melinda said.

"It's alright, and yes, to some extent, we are." He could tell they weren't going to let it go. "You're both old enough to understand, so here it is. The Iranians have attacked our fleet, so we're technically at war with them. There was a nuclear explosion off the coast of Oregon, followed by a massive earthquake that generated one of the most destructive tsunamis ever recorded. The West Coast has also suffered a series of large earthquakes, and Mount St. Helens and Mount Hood have erupted, totally destroying Portland, Oregon. The destruction was so massive that we may never get an accurate count of the casualties, but this will go down as the most cataclysmic series of events in recorded history."

"Oh," was all Alejandro could muster.

"You didn't have to scare them," Melinda said. "Hell, you scared me."

"I'm sorry if I scared you, but our lives are going to be very different from now on."

"Thank you for being honest with us, but why did we have to come to the White House?" Juanita asked.

"Because I have to be here for the duration."

"Where's the president?"

Victor hesitated. "We don't know, and I'm the acting president until he returns."

"That's enough of that for now," Melinda said. "You kids sit down, and I'll have the kitchen bring you something to eat."

As he sat and talked with his children, Victor was reminded of why he'd stayed in the army, and why he'd been willing to take on the vice presidency. He'd heard it so many times: "I wish someone would do something," and he was determined to be that someone.

"Sir, I'm sorry, but we need you again," Major Turner said.

"Not a problem, Major," President Garcia said.

As they were making their way back down, the president asked, "Major, where are you from? Tell me a little about yourself."

"I'm originally from Northern California. I grew up in a little town called Sutter Creek, not too far from Sacramento. My dad died when I was very young, and my mom never remarried. She still lives in the same house I was born in, but she's getting up in years."

"Have you talked to her since this all started?"

"I tried last night, but they're limiting the calls into that area, so I wasn't able to get through."

* * *

The council members were already in the room when they arrived, but President Garcia took a moment to talk with General Appleby before they got started.

As the president began the meeting, the general was using one of the phones in the back of the room. He talked for a few minutes, and then he waved Major Turner over.

"Here you go, son, your mother's on the line for you."

"We're about to video conference with FEMA, Homeland Security, NSA, and the CIA, but before we do, I'd like to go around the table so each of you can ask or share anything you'd like," President Garcia said. "If you don't have anything, that's fine, but if you've got something, I want to hear it.

"William, let's start with you this time," President Garcia said.

The attorney general was a meticulous planner, so he had his thoughts already prepared on his iPad. "I'll be brief, but I'd like to bring everyone up to speed on the status of the presidential directives we worked on yesterday. I spent most of last night reviewing the existing directives, and I've taken the liberty of adding the language needed to cover virtually any contingency we may face."

"Good, so we're done with that?" the president asked.

"I believe so, but I'd like to recommend that we split each one of them into classified and unclassified sections. We'll share the unclassified sections as needed, but the rest will stay within this room."

"Is that legal?" President Garcia asked.

"There's previous precedent, and I passed it by Chief Justice Avery last night, and it's his opinion that the Supreme Court would uphold the decision."

"That's good enough for me," President Garcia said. "Next."

"Admiral Kenyan reports that they've destroyed every surface ship the Iranians had, and all but one of their submarines," General Appleby said.

"What else do they have, other than ground forces?" Mary Beth Greider asked.

"They've got some out-of-date Russian aircraft, but they're quite adept at concealing their weapons, so it's hard to be sure. However, there haven't been any more incidents since last night, and all of their ground units have returned to their original locations."

"It's over then?" Jerry Burns asked.

"At the present time I don't believe they're any credible threats to our forces," General Appleby said.

"I don't have anything to add, but Timothy Gather asked me to make his report," Jerry Burns said. "With the exception of Portland, Oregon, FEMA has established at least a token presence in every major city that was affected. Mr. Gather said that even if you hadn't declared it off-limits, it's still too hot to enter."

"How can we just ignore those poor people?" Mary Beth Greider asked.

"I understand your concerns, but they've overflown the city on several occasions, and they're convinced no one survived. The pyroclastic flow incinerated everything from where Mount Hood used to be, to about three miles past the city."

"What do they mean by 'where Mount Hood used to be'?" Harold Crowe asked.

"The eruption blew out the entire side of the mountain that was facing Portland, and the rest of it collapsed. All that's left is a pile of molten slag, that's maybe three thousand feet high. Mr. Gather sent some high-resolution photos of Portland and the area surrounding Mount Hood, if anyone would care to see them."

"We've got a few minutes," President Garcia said. "Let's take a look."

He'd sent them as a slide show, and as the pictures flowed slowly across the screen, there were several exclamations of horror.

"Good lord, that reminds me of the footage from Hiroshima and Nagasaki," William Daugherty said.

"Other than the lack of radiation, this is probably worse," General Appleby said. "At least in Japan there were survivors."

No one said a word for several seconds after the slide show ended.

"That was truly disturbing, but we need to focus our attention on the areas where we can make a difference," President Garcia said.

"Excuse me, Mr. President, I've got Charles Gibson, the lead investigator with the NEST team on the ground in Maine."

"Put him through.

"Mr. Gibson, this is President Garcia. What have you got for us?"

"We've completed our initial evaluation, and the cargo is definitely a nuclear device. We're currently estimating it at a hundred kilotons, but we'll know more when we can get it back to our lab and disassemble it."

"Origin?"

"It's very similar to the latest Pakistani devices, but we're seeing some anomalies in the fissionable material."

"Anomalies?"

"Every facility that enriches nuclear material leaves a distinct fingerprint, but this one doesn't match anything we've got on file."

"Interesting, but not much help. Were you able to disarm the device?"

"We have, and it's already loaded for transport."

"Keep us informed.

"You're up, Mr. Diaz," President Garcia said.

"The UN Security Council has agreed to postpone the attack. In the interim, they've imposed a no-fly zone over

Iran, and an embargo on all incoming shipments, except for humanitarian aid."

"That should keep them in check while we try to sort this out," General Appleby said. "What have you got for us, Gregory?"

"Not much I'm afraid," said Gregory Kellogg, the director of the DNI. "Neither NSA nor the CIA were able to determine the president's status."

"Since we haven't received any demands, wouldn't that rule out kidnapping?" President Garcia asked.

"I'm not prepared to make that call yet."

"I think that wraps it up for today," President Garcia said. "Unless there's a new crisis, the next meeting will be tomorrow at thirteen hundred. To better utilize everyone's time, anyone that has access to the secure video conference system can participate remotely, and any of you that aren't set up should get with Major Turner so he can get you scheduled for the upgrade."

CHAPTER 25

When President Garcia arrived for the meeting, he took a moment to confer with Major Turner.

"I think we've got everyone, so let's get started," President Garcia said. "I was going to start by apologizing for taking your time on the weekend, but I'm afraid it's going to be the drill for many months to come. General, why don't you lead off."

"The FEMA relief centers are fully functional in all of the affected areas, but the majority of the medical facilities are out of commission, and the temporary facilities are struggling to handle the massive influx of people needing medical care."

"What's the plan to alleviate the problem?" Tom De-Marco asked.

"The army has delivered a hundred and fifty mobile field hospitals, and there are more on the way. The air force is running hourly medevac flights to the medical centers in Salt Lake, Phoenix, and Denver, and the navy has the USNS *Comfort* and *Mercy* standing by off the coast to provide care for the most critical cases. FEMA has hundreds of trucks ferrying supplies into the relief centers, and the Corps of Engineers has set up desalinization plants to help with the freshwater shortage."

"Aren't they worried about the radiation?" Mary Beth Greider asked.

"We're monitoring it closely, but we're not seeing any significant contamination reaching the coastline," General Appleby said.

"Has anyone updated the casualty projections?" Tom DeMarco asked.

"It will be months before we know the full extent, but they'll be nothing short of catastrophic. Any more questions on the relief efforts?" the general asked.

"No? OK, I'll move on to the Iranian status. The UN has imposed the embargo and no-fly zones, but the Iranians are continuing to cause trouble. We'd thought that we'd destroyed all of their fleet, but they'd concealed a large number of their fast, missile-armed patrol boats. We're dealing with them as they show up, but they've managed to sink a couple of our supply ships."

"Good, it sounds like Admiral Kenyan has the situation in hand," President Garcia said.

"He does, however, that's not our biggest worry. They've started firing Shahab-3 missiles into Israel."

"I'd intended to cover this offline, but since you brought it up, let's go ahead and talk about it," President Garcia said. "I want to take out their missile silos, but I'd like to limit the civilian casualties. Is that feasible?"

"Yes, with some reservations," General Appleby said. "Most of their longer-range missiles are located outside of the heavily populated areas, however we believe they've hidden some of their newer generations inside the city limits of Mashhad and Isfahan."

"Those are major population centers, but we've got to get them stopped before it escalates further. What would you suggest?"

"We could use some of the naval assets in the area, but intel shows that most of them are in heavily fortified bunkers, so I'd recommend using a squadron of B2s, with the precision-guided thirty-thousand-pound MOPs (Massive Ordinance Penetrators)."

"I'd like to see the details before you pull the trigger, but I like your thoughts. Continue."

"That's all I had," General Appleby said.

"OK. Mary Beth, you're up," the president said.

"We've stopped two more incursions. The first was at a checkpoint in Laredo, Texas, and the second was in the Arizona desert, about thirty miles from Tucson."

"I hope they didn't kill them all this time," Tom De-Marco said.

"They did capture one in Texas, but before we could interrogate him, he committed suicide with a cyanide tablet hidden in a false tooth. The group in Arizona was much larger and better armed, and they had to call in helicopter gunships to subdue them. In both cases they were carrying fissionable material to be used in dirty bombs, but neither group had any functioning weapons."

"Iranians?" Tom DeMarco asked.

"For the most part, but the ones that we've identified so far don't seem to have any obvious ties to any terror-ist organizations."

"All that means is that they're getting better at hiding their movements," William Daugherty said.

"You're probably right, but we're still going to keep looking into it. Given the number of incidents we're still seeing, we're concerned that some of the groups may have slipped by us."

"Any more information on the Canadian group, or the *Azrael*?" General Appleby asked.

"We've tracked the *Azrael*'s movements back to Jakar-ta's Tanjung Priok Port. The local authorities are claim-ing that an unidentified pirate organization killed the crew and made off with the ship. However, that's pure conjec-ture, because they didn't even know it had been hijacked until the bodies started drifting ashore several days later."

"I'm still shocked that no one is taking credit for any of the attacks, and that we haven't received any ransom demands for President Montblanc," President Garcia said.

"Sorry to interrupt, but I'd like to speak to that if I may," said Margret Grissom, the director of the CIA.

"Go on," the president said.

"We've spoken with our best Middle Eastern assets, and there's absolutely no chatter anywhere. It's like he dropped off the face of the earth."

"Are we sure they weren't killed in the explosion?"

"No, and if that's what happened, we may never be able to identify their bodies. I've read the SEAL team's report several times, and it had to be a large, specialized device, because it pretty much vaporized the vehicle."

"I realize we agreed it would be better to keep the incident a secret, but it's time we go public," President Garcia said.

"It's a little late for that," Harry Miller said.

"It's never too late for the truth."

"He's right," William Daugherty said. "It may not endear us to the American public when they find out they've been deceived, but better late than never."

"Who should make the announcement?" Shelby Cohen asked.

"I think it has to be President Garcia," Attorney General William Daugherty said.

"I don't have a problem with that," President Garcia said. "I do have a question for you before we proceed."

"Shoot."

"I'm not sure it's covered under the Twenty-fifth Amendment, but I'd like to name an acting vice president."

"It's covered, but we should touch base with Chief Justice Avery just to make sure. While we're at it, I'd like to get his opinion on declaring President Montblanc and his wife dead."

"I'm not sure I'm comfortable with that," President Garcia said.

"I understand, but I don't think we have much choice."

"OK, I'll go along with it, if the chief justice agrees that it's a prudent action," the president said reluctantly.

"I'll discuss it with him and get back to you," Attorney General Daugherty said.

"It's getting late, so let's call it a day. I'll have Major Turner schedule the next meeting."

"How was your day?" Melinda asked.

"Long."

"You do look tired. How are your legs feeling today?"

"A little better. The salve the doctor gave me is helping. What did you do with the kids?"

"Juanita is on the phone with her friend Amy, and Alejandro is supposed to be working on his homework."

"I didn't think they were going to school this semester."

"The school got them enrolled in their distance learning curriculum, so they don't fall behind."

"That's great. I know this is hard on them, but I'm afraid it's also necessary."

Melinda had waited on him to eat dinner, and when they finished up she said, "It's a nice evening, let's go out to the garden to drink our coffee."

"Sounds good to me, I could use a little peace and quiet."

"This is nice," Victor said.

"You didn't say much during dinner, is something bothering you?"

He laughed and said, "Other than the obvious? Sorry. Yes, there is. In the next day or so, I'm going to have to do a State of the Union broadcast."

"You've gotten pretty good at giving speeches."

"Thanks, but it's the message that's bothering me. I'll start with an update on the events on the West Coast, and the tentative casualty counts."

"Are they worse than what they're reporting?"

"Not really, it's the next part that I'm dreading. I'm going to announce that I've been acting president since the Iranian incident in the Gulf, and that we're officially declaring President Montblanc and his wife dead."

"They've found them?"

"No, but the attorney general and the chief justice are convinced that we need to declare them dead and move on."

"That's rough alright."

"I will have a bit of good news. Charles Goodwin has accepted the vice presidency, and the chief justice is going to swear him in after my speech."

"That's good news. He's been a good partner to you."

"I don't know how I'd have gotten by without his help."

"There you go, selling yourself short again. You're a brilliant man, and pretty handsome, for a worn-out old soldier."

"Why, thank you, my dear. Let's go inside, and I'll show you how worn out I am."

"Um, that sounds good. It's been a while."

CHAPTER 26

"You've come a long way since we first met," Charles Goodwin said as he sat down in the Oval Office. "That was one of the finest speeches I've ever witnessed."

"Thanks, but a lot of the credit would have to go to you," President Garcia said.

"Bull, I might have polished the diamond, but the luster was always there."

"Excuse me, sir, I've got General Appleby on line one," Major Turner said.

"What's up, General?"

"I wanted to give you an update on Operation Thunder," General Appleby said.

"Did they take out the objectives?"

"We'll get a final assessment by morning, but first indications are a hundred percent."

"Have they retaliated?"

"They tried to launch some airstrikes, but we destroyed them before they could get airborne."

"Collateral damage?"

"I'm afraid they're going to be fairly significant. When the bunkers in Isfahan imploded, it took out most of the block."

"Damn. I hate that innocents had to suffer, but they've brought it on themselves. I've got a call tonight with Prime

Minster Weizmann, so I'll share the details then. I just hope this will convince them to back off."

"Let me know if there is anything else you need us to take care of," General Appleby said.

"That's the second time we've underestimated them," President Garcia said.

"They're desperate," Vice President Goodwin said. "That's what the Germans did in World War Two when the tide turned against them. They had weapons hidden everywhere, and it wasn't until the war ended that we understood the breadth of the underground manufacturing capabilities."

"I remember, but I'd hardly characterize their situation as dire as the Nazis'."

"Unfortunately, there are many similarities. The Germans managed to develop the V2, and launched over three thousand of them against the Allied forces. Even with their backs against the wall, they managed to field the first operational jet aircraft. And if the Allies hadn't managed to bomb and sabotage the Norwegian heavy water plant, they could have developed a nuclear weapon."

"I just hope we're as successful at stopping their nuclear ambitions."

"Speaking of nuclear, have you seen any updates from Homeland on the border incursions?" Vice President Goodwin asked.

"Nothing recent," President Garcia said.

"I'll see if Major Turner can get us an update."

"He seems like a fine young man, but I'm a little surprised to see a major in his position."

When Major Turner came in with the latest briefing folder, he said, "Here's the latest we have, but there's really nothing new. However, Margret Grissom would like a few minutes of your time."

"Did she say what she wanted?"

"No, but she was adamant that she wanted to do it in person."

"I don't have anything scheduled after two thirty, you can tell her I'll see her any time after that."

She didn't reach the White House until 9 P.M., and President Garcia met her in the Oval Office.

"Mr. President, I'm terribly sorry I'm late, but I wanted to make sure I had my ducks in a row."

"No problem, Margret, I've always got time for the CIA. So, what going on?"

"I've been struggling with the makeup of the terrorist teams that have been attacking us."

"I remember. Have you found something?"

"I've had my best people following up on a common trait we've seen in all of the attacks, and what they've found is disconcerting."

"If you're worried, I'm worried. Lay it out for me," President Garcia said.

"We've traced the backgrounds of every terrorist involved in the incursions, and none of them has ever been associated with any form of terror organization."

"They were good at covering their tracks, so what?"

"We've seen that before, but these are different, they were all dedicated family men."

"OK, but I still don't get it."

"Sorry, I left out the most important part. In all cases, their families have disappeared."

"Disappeared?"

"Without a trace. We believe someone has taken their families hostage to coerce them into carrying out these attacks. That's why they've never shown up on our watch lists."

"Why would the Iranians do that? There's no shortage of zealots."

"That's the concerning part. I'm not sure it's the Iranians."

"That's ludicrous. They just killed or abducted the president, and they've started a shooting war."

"On the first point, we're still not positive it was the Iranians. We're still trying to track down some leads, but there are several elements that don't make sense."

"What are you suggesting?" President Garcia asked.

"Just that it deserves further scrutiny."

"Leave no stone unturned, but we need to keep this quiet until you're absolutely certain."

"Of course. I haven't shared my suspicions with anyone other than you. I've got completely separate teams working on the various segments."

"I don't suppose you'd care to hazard a guess on who it is?"

"Not yet. If you have time, I do have one more thing I'd like to bring to your attention."

"I've got nothing but time."

"We're almost certain that the Iranians are preparing to move the spent fuel out of the Arak power plant."

"Isn't that the heavy water reactor they brought online a couple of years ago?"

"The same. We estimate they could extract around ten kilograms, or twenty-two pounds of high-grade Pu-239 for every year of operation, which would be enough for one to two nuclear weapons."

"Is that where the crap they're bringing across the border came from?" the president asked.

"No. We still haven't been able to determine the source."

"I thought we could ID the refining facility on almost anything."

"Normally that's true, but our databases only go back to the 1970s. Anything before that, we have to track down by hand."

"Surely it can't be that old. We took care of all that old Soviet crap years ago."

"It's not Soviet."

"Who then?"

"I can't answer that yet, but I will."

"You're just full of good news. Got anything else?"

"That's it for now."

President Garcia spent most of the night thinking about what Margret had divulged, and what he needed to do in the short term. The next morning he decided to bring in the chairman of the Joint Chiefs of Staff to lay out what he wanted done.

"Thanks for coming in on such short notice," President Garcia said.

"Never a problem," General Appleby said.

"Major, would you put the map up, please?" President Garcia asked. "This is a map of the Iranian nuclear facilities. I need you to come up with a plan to isolate the power plants, so they can't transfer their spent fuel to the enrichment sites."

"Do you want to destroy the reactors?" General Appleby asked.

"No. I simply want to cordon them off."

"We have complete air superiority, so it should be simple enough."

"Good. When can you have it done?"

"Would twenty-four hours be soon enough?"

"Absolutely, and this is not a onetime thing. I don't want anything to come in or out of those facilities."

"We'll take out every form of transportation to both Arak and Bushehr. On Bushehr, we'll have to station a guided missile cruiser nearby to ensure they don't try to move it by sea."

"Excellent. Major Turner, would you step out for a moment?"

* * *

"Turner's a good man," General Appleby said.

"I'm very impressed with his performance," President Garcia said. "Which is why I'd like you to get him a field promotion to full colonel."

"You know that's not how it works."

"I do, but I think the role he's filling necessitates a higher-ranking officer, and he's definitely the right man for the job."

"It will stir up some shit, but I'll take care of it."

When Colonel Turner brought him his briefing folder the next day, he said, "Mr. President, I can't thank you enough for the promotion."

"You're welcome, but you've earned it. What have you got for me this morning?"

"FEMA updates and some notes from the general, but nothing earth shaking."

"We sure don't need any more of that."

"Sorry, poor choice of words."

"Relax, I was just giving you a hard time. But while we're on the subject, I'd like you to set up a trip to the West Coast for me. I think it's time that I get a firsthand look at what's going on."

"I'll take care of it, but the Secret Service won't be pleased."

"That's their problem, I need to see it up close and personal. Video is fine as far as it goes, but it's just not the same as being there."

"Mr. President, I think this trip is a bad idea," Special Agent Stubbs said.

"Understood, but we're going anyway."

"Got it, and we'll be ready."

*   *   *

When *Air Force One* reached the West Coast, air traffic control routed them out over the Pacific before they'd let them turn to make a pass down the coastline. As they moved out over the Pacific, they descended to five thousand feet. The president had brought General Appleby along, and they were studying the view below.

"What's all that crap?" General Appleby asked.

"I can't tell from here," President Garcia said. "See if they've got any binoculars on board, and tell the pilot to take us down so we can get a closer look."

It took a minute or so to get clearance, but as they descended to two thousand feet, the horror became clear. The collection of debris was laced with horribly bloated bodies, and it stretched for as far as they could see. They'd both been in combat, but the scale of the carnage far exceeded anything they'd ever seen.

"Oh dear lord," Colonel Turner said.

As they continued down the coast, neither of them said a word as the ghastly scene passed beneath them. President Garcia closed his eyes and said a prayer for everyone that had lost their lives. When he finished, he said, "I've seen enough. Let's land so we can see how they're coming with the recovery efforts."

When they reached the airstrip, they had to circle for almost twenty minutes to allow several heavily loaded cargo planes to land.

"Mr. President, thanks for coming," Timothy Gather said.

"How long have you been up here?" President Garcia asked.

"I got here last Friday. I was having a hard time getting a handle on the situation, so I decided to see it firsthand."

"Understood, that's why I'm here. We just made a pass down the coastline, and I have to say that I've never seen a more disturbing sight. There are God knows how many corpses floating out there, and I need to know what you're going to do about it."

"Not much, I'm afraid. I'm aware of the issue, but I had to choose between recovering bodies and trying to keep anyone else from losing their lives," Timothy Gather said.

"I wasn't criticizing your decision. Leaders often have to make judgment calls."

"I appreciate that."

"Look, I realize we're critically short of resources, but I'm going to follow the military creed of no man left behind. As soon as we finish here, I'm going to task the navy and the coast guard with retrieving the bodies. Some of them have already drifted ashore, so I want you to redirect enough National Guard units to recover those. If you still don't have enough manpower, we'll pull in the army and marines."

"Mr. President, I don't think you understand the situation. We're barely getting by, and this is going to make it even more difficult," Timothy Gather said.

"I get it, but that's the way it's going to be. General Appleby, how many men do we have stationed overseas, and not in an active combat role?"

"I just saw that number in this morning's sit-rep. If we pulled the troop levels in South Korea, Japan, and Germany down to the absolute minimum, I'd say roughly sixty thousand."

"Do it. Would that be enough?"

"More than enough, but you know that's going to cost a fortune."

"Let me worry about that."

"That's all well and good, but given the number of bodies we're looking at, I don't know how we can possibly identify and properly process that many corpses before they rot," Timothy Gather said.

"You're right, it could take years," President Garcia said.

He thought about the problem as they continued the discussion. A couple of minutes later President Garcia said, "Since there aren't enough refrigerated facilities available to store the bodies, I'm going to have them set up a temporary storage facility outside of Fairbanks, Alaska. We can store the bodies in the permafrost until we can get them identified."

"That could work," Timothy Gather said.

"Good, I'll get the team working on the logistics. Is there anything you need in the way of equipment or supplies?"

"I wish I knew. We're just managing the chaos at the moment. The teams have been operating twenty-four hours a day since we got here, and I'm afraid they're all about to collapse."

"I was going to ask you to take us on a tour of some of the worst-hit areas, but I don't want to waste any more of your valuable time, so we'll survey it from the air."

"Thanks for that, and if we're done, I'll get back to work."

CHAPTER 27

A few days later, the president received an urgent call from Senator Miller.

"I've got several items I'd like to discuss," Senator Miller said.

"Discuss away."

"How do you intend to pay for relocating all those troops?"

"Haven't we already removed the cap on the military budget?"

"Well, yes, but that's not the reason we did it."

"Understood. What else have you got?"

"I've just learned that we're carrying out air strikes inside of Iran."

"That's true. It's code-named Lights Out, and it's intended to ensure Iran can't enrich any of the nuclear byproducts from their power plants. I'd be interested to know how you found out," President Garcia asked.

"That doesn't matter," Senator Miller said. "Besides, I'm the leader of the Senate, and I should have been informed."

"The operation was on a need-to-know basis, and you didn't need to know."

"That's bullshit, and you know it."

"I can see that we're just going to have to disagree on this subject. Have you got anything else?"

"Shelby Cohen and I have authored a resolution supporting the Israelis right to reclaim the territory that President Montblanc forced them to cede to the Palestinians. It also makes an absolute commitment to support their actions against any foreign country that they deem a threat."

"Not going to happen," President Garcia said.

"We've got the votes," Senator Miller said.

"Not to override my veto you don't."

"You wouldn't dare."

"Try me."

"I didn't know you were a Muslim sympathizer."

"I'm not going to dignify that with an answer. I think we're done," the president said as he hung up.

"He refused to even consider it," Senator Miller said.

"Why are you surprised by that? He's a frigging wetback," Shelby Cohen said.

"What now?" Senator Miller asked.

"We'll have to move to plan B."

"I know that I've been a part of this from the very beginning, but I'm not comfortable with any of that."

"That may be, but it's all we have left, and I'm going to make the call."

"I'll keep my mouth shut, but count me out," Senator Miller said.

"He's not going to like that."

Later that day, Victor was eating lunch with Melinda.

"What's wrong? You seem upset," Melinda asked.

"I had a troubling call this morning."

"You want to talk about it?"

"Senator Miller called to tell me that he and Shelby Cohen were going to pass a bill to allow Israel to reclaim the territory they returned as part of their deal with President Montblanc."

"What did you say?"

"I told him no way, and we ended up pretty crossways."

"I've always thought he was an alright guy, but Shelby strikes me as a bit of a bitch," Melinda said.

"You're sure not the first one to say that, but she's a dangerous woman to cross, because she's well connected, and absolutely ruthless."

"So how did you leave it?"

"I told him I'd veto it if they got it passed."

"Good."

"Sorry to rush off, but General Appleby and I have a call at one thirty," Victor said.

"No problem. See you tonight for dinner?"

"Yes, unless something else goes to hell."

"I know you're very busy, but I needed you on the call today," General Appleby said.

"No problem, but you don't usually ask me to sit in on your calls with the admiral," President Garcia said.

"The admiral is the one who requested it. I don't even know what he wants to cover."

When the picture appeared on the screen, they could see the admiral was in his quarters, instead of the combat operations center.

"I apologize for the secrecy, but I think you'll understand after I show you what we've discovered," Admiral Kenyan said.

"No problem," General Appleby said. "What have you got for us?"

"I'm going to show you a short video segment from a data recorder we recovered from one of our reconnaissance aircraft that the Iranians shot down. Pay close attention to the lower right quadrant of the screen."

"What are those?" President Garcia asked as they watched what looked like drones firing missiles towards the Iranian coastline. Shortly after the missiles impacted, the Iranians launched a salvo of missiles at our fleet.

"What just happened?" General Appleby asked.

"We've spent several hours analyzing the footage, and I now believe the Iranians thought they were responding to our attack," Admiral Kenyan said. "The highly sophisticated stealth technology being utilized rendered the drones and the missiles virtually undetectable. Since our equipment didn't pick them up, there's no chance the Iranians were aware of what happened."

"Why didn't the satellites pick this up?"

"Both of them were offline for maintenance."

"I thought that's why we always use two?"

"It is, but someone screwed up, and took them both down."

"We need to know who was behind this," President Garcia said.

"Agreed, but we've had no luck identifying the source," Admiral Kenyan said. "I've already sent the files on to the NSA and the CIA for analysis, but that type of drone is in service in several different countries."

"Who else is aware of this?"

"The NSA, CIA, and my six-man tech team are the only ones in the loop."

"Let's keep it that way. I assume your people know to keep their mouths shut?" President Garcia asked.

"Of course."

"I really appreciate the discretion you've shown, and we'll take it from here," President Garcia said.

"This is an almost unbelievable turn of events," General Appleby said.

"It is, but this is the second time our satellites have been offline for maintenance."

"Damn, you're right."

"There's little chance the NSA or CIA will learn anything more from the video files, but we'll give them a chance before we decide on a course of action," President Garcia said. "Coordinate with Secretary General Archambault, but I want to pull the fleet back out of harm's way until we learn more."

"A prudent move," General Appleby said. "How about the no-fly?"

"Let's leave it in place for now."

"Isn't that a bit of overkill?"

"Possibly, but if nothing else, it's helping control the arms smugglers."

"Your call. How would you feel about lowering the threat level?"

"I'm reluctant, although it might help wind down some of the tension."

When President Garcia finished with General Appleby, he placed a call to Tom DeMarco.

"What can I do for you today?" the secretary of state asked.

"I'd like to pick your brain. Do you have time to come over?"

"Sure, but what's up?"

"I'll fill you in when you get here."

"Thanks for coming over on such short notice," President Garcia said when the secretary of state arrived.

"Not a problem. What's up?"

"I need Secretary Zhang's help on some extremely sensitive matters, and I wanted your opinion on the best way to approach him."

"Sure, but it would help if I knew what we were talking about."

"Absolutely, but I need your promise that you won't discuss it with anyone before clearing it with me."

"Understood."

"We've just discovered that the Iranians were provoked into attacking the fleet," President Garcia said.

"Provoked?"

"There were three cruise missiles that struck their missile base, which they would have had every reason to believe were fired from the UN task force."

"We know we didn't do it, so who did?" Tom DeMarco asked.

"That's what I want to discuss with Zhang."

"Surely you don't think it was them?"

"Not them, or the Russians, but we've hit a dead end, and I know they have agents all over the world."

"It can't hurt to ask, but I'd be surprised if they know either."

"How should I approach him?"

"Straight up would be my recommendation. Do you want me on, or would you rather do it alone?"

"I'd like you to listen in from the other room, but I think it's better done one-on-one," President Garcia said.

"President Garcia, what can I do for you today?" Secretary Zhang asked.

"One of these days I'll call when I don't want something, but not today."

"Don't worry about it. What's going on?"

"First, I want to thank you for the supplies your country has sent, they're much appreciated."

"We were glad to help. I've been following the events on the West Coast, and I can't imagine what your people are going through. Do you have any idea how many people lost their lives?"

"Just best guesses, but we're currently estimating the death toll at one-point-seven-million people, and over a million that have lost everything."

"I saw the pictures of the bodies floating off the coast, simply horrible. What are you going to do, bury them in mass graves?"

"Unfortunately, we've been forced to do that in a few cases, but we're transporting the rest to Alaska where we'll store them in the permafrost. That way we can take the time needed to ID them and ensure that they receive proper burials."

"Admirable. I doubt many people would have gone to the trouble, faced with what you've got in front of you."

"Thanks. Before I proceed, I need to ask that you keep what I'm about to divulge a secret."

"It's difficult to give that commitment without knowing the topic, but you have my word, as long as it doesn't represent a threat to my country."

"I can assure you it presents no threat to your country. We've recently discovered the events that led up to the Iranians firing on the UN task force were precipitated by a third party."

"I'm not following you."

"Shorty before they attacked, one of their southern bases was hit by three cruise missiles."

"How did they manage to deceive you, and the Iranians?"

"The drones were utilizing some rather sophisticated stealth technology, and since the missiles came from the general direction of the fleet, they understandably thought we'd fired them. When they launched what they believed was a counterattack, we mistook it as a preemptive strike, and retaliated."

"A masterful deception, but how did you discover what really happened?"

"We had a reconnaissance aircraft in the area, and it caught the whole thing on video. Unfortunately it was shot down during the engagement, and we were only recently able to retrieve the files."

Secretary Zhang considered the issue for a moment, and said, "I'd love to accuse that bastard Baryshev, but there's nothing in it for him, so I doubt he's behind it. Do you have any idea what their endgame might be?"

"Not a clue, and that's why I need your help."

"You have my word that we'll leave no stone unturned."

"Thanks, and I'll let you know if we discover anything new on our end," President Garcia said.

"Are you going to try to clear it up with the Iranians?" Secretary Zhang asked.

"At some point yes, but that's not what precipitated the UN's ultimatum. We've got to find a way to get them to renounce their nuclear ambitions, or we're going to end up in a shooting war anyway. However, I am lowering our readiness status one level to try to diffuse the tensions."

"That should help. I think we should have weekly calls until we get this sorted out," Secretary Zhang said.

"Agreed. I'll have Colonel Turner get with your aide to set it up."

"I thought that went well," Tom DeMarco said when he returned.

"Thanks. I'm still not sure how to take him, but he seems genuine enough."

"As I told you before, if he tells you he'll do something, he will. What's next?"

"I wish I knew. I've got so many issues on my plate that I'm having a difficult time prioritizing them," President Garcia admitted.

Not used to that much honesty from a politician, it took him a few seconds to respond. "Take this for what it's worth, but if it were me, I'd get all of the NSC members in here, and put us to work."

"I'd considered that, but I hate to pull the team away from what they're doing."

"We've all got staff to handle the day-to-day issues, so you don't have to shoulder this alone."

"I'll think it over."

CHAPTER 28

He'd tossed and turned all night, but by morning, President Garcia had worked out his plan of attack.

"I need you to meet me in the situation room, at oh-nine-hundred," President Garcia said.

"Yes, sir," Colonel Turner said. "Do I need to bring anything with me?"

"No, just you."

"Sorry I'm late. The secretary of Homeland called just as I was leaving, and she wanted me to give you this."

When the president finished reading it, he said, "I need to talk with her before we get started."

"I take it you read my note?" Mary Beth Greider asked.

"I did, but I wasn't sure what you meant."

"Sorry, it was hard to describe. I've been around this town a long time, but I've never witnessed the level of rage that occurred after the joint session of Congress last night."

"This took place during the joint session?"

"No, after they'd adjourned for the evening. I was on my way to the parking garage, and as I was passing by Shelby's office, I heard her and Harry Miller having a screaming match, and I'm afraid that I couldn't resist stopping to listen in. Between taking turns calling you every name in the book and cussing each other for failing to control their people, I was starting to think it could get physical."

"So they couldn't get the votes to override my veto?"

"Not even close."

"I've been called names before, so why the urgent note?"

"I just thought you needed to know. In fact, I considered calling security; it got so bad."

"They were just pissed. I'm sure it'll be fine, but thanks for the heads-up."

"Let's get to work," President Garcia told Colonel Turner. "I want to schedule a week-long meeting to work on a go-forward plan. The meeting has to be this month, but I want you to poll the council to find the dates that work best for the majority."

"I'll get on it immediately, but they're going to want an agenda."

"They're going to help me craft a two-year strategic plan. The first part of the meeting will focus on the cleanup and rebuilding efforts for the West Coast catastrophe. The rebuilding plan will need a short term, say the next six months, and then the long-term plan. Then we'll move on to the foreign affairs portion of the meeting."

"I assume Iran will be the number one priority?"

"Yes, but not just Iran. If we can't control the Israelis' propensity to keep shit stirred up, the entire Middle East is going to go up in flames."

"Do you think a week will be enough time?" Colonel Turner asked.

"It will be if they come prepared."

* * *

Three days later, Colonel Turner came into the Oval Office with the president's briefing folder.

"What have you got for me today?" President Garcia asked.

"The daily FEMA report, an update from Homeland Security, and a rough agenda for your Monday NSC meeting."

"That was quick work. Anybody that can't make it?"

"No. Actually everyone I talked with was pumped about the meeting. They're used to being tasked instead of being made partners. Is there anyone else you'd like to include?" Colonel Turner asked.

"No, I'd like to keep this as small as possible. If we need anyone else we'll call them in."

That Sunday night, Victor and Melinda were eating a late dinner in their bedroom.

"You put in a full day," Melinda said.

"I was trying to tie up some loose ends before tomorrow's meeting," Victor said.

"It's a big deal?"

"Yes, we're going to put together a strategic two-year plan."

"With everything that's going on, that seems like forever," Melinda said.

"Tell me about it. When I agreed to take the VP slot, I'd hoped to have something meaningful to do. I guess the old saying, 'Beware what you ask for' applies."

The next morning, President Garcia stood at the door and greeted each one of the NSC members as they arrived.

"Good, we're all here, let's get started. As a courtesy to everyone, we're going to have a no cell phone, no e-mail policy while we're in session. We'll take a break every two hours to let everyone catch up, and in the case of an emergency, you need to instruct your aides to work through Colonel Turner. Everyone has the agenda, so let's start with FEMA."

"Colonel Turner is handing out an overview of our current status and a rough outline I've put together to begin our discussion," Timothy Gather said. "I've broken it into a six-month plan, and a longer-term view. I'll start with a brief overview of our current status. Your packet has a complete rundown that you can read when you have time. The thirty-thousand-foot view is that we're getting by. We're short of everything, but the Mexican and Canadian governments are operating their West Coast ports at maximum capacity to help us bring in critical supplies. The navy and coast guard have every available vessel recovering bodies. The army and National Guard units are retrieving the last of the ones that drifted onshore, and if the weather holds, they're projecting they'll be done by the end of the month. The crews at the Fairbanks storage facility have had to work around the clock to stay ahead of the flow of bodies. It's going to take years, but we're going to keep at it until everyone has been identified. Other than a few minor issues that's about it, but I'd like to take a moment to recognize President Garcia for having the fortitude to mandate this project, instead of taking the easy way out and just dumping the bodies into mass graves."

As the room stood to applaud, President Garcia was momentarily at a loss for words. Finally he managed to say, "Thank you for the kind words, but I'm sure that any of you would have done the same."

They spent the rest of the day covering the domestic issues, and at around 7 P.M., the president said, "Great job everyone. We'll have to flesh out a few of the details, but I think we've got a workable strategy."

"I just wish we could do something about southern Oregon," Timothy Gather said.

"We will, when the time's right. We'll resume at seven thirty in the morning."

* * *

"How did the first day go?" Melinda asked.

"Outstanding. We've finished the domestic portion, so we've got the rest of the week to work on the rest of it."

"Good. You seem jazzed. It must have been a great meeting."

"It was. You know I'm not into personal recognition, but I had the entire NSC stand and give me an ovation for what I did with the casualties on the West Coast."

They didn't arrive at the Liaison Capitol Hill hotel until a little after midnight.

"I like your getup, but I wouldn't have recognized you," Jonathan said.

"It's my expensive call girl look," Fredericka said. "I could say the same of you. The wig looks good on you."

"Okay, enough small talk," he said. "I got your message, but we're taking a huge risk meeting in person."

"I warned you that we'd be forced to escalate if we weren't successful," Fredericka said.

"Oh, dear God. I can't believe what we're doing. I just wish we could try to enlist the other one."

"Not going to happen. I've known him for years, and even with the leverage they've got over him there's no way he'd go for it."

CHAPTER 29

The president was up by 5 a.m., and as he did every morning, he went to the Oval Office to work until the meeting. Colonel Turner had just brought him a tray of muffins and a carafe of coffee. As the colonel was leaving the president reached for the carafe, but he knocked it over, spilling hot coffee all over the desk. When he reached across the desk to stand it back up, he slipped and knocked it off the desk.

"Damn it," President Garcia said. The president walked around to the front of the desk, and as he knelt down to pick it up, Colonel Turner saw him and came hurrying back.

"Let me get that, Mr. President, you'll mess up your clothes."

When the missile hit the wall behind the desk the explosion blew out the bulletproof glass and collapsed the wall inward. The fiery blast hurled the desk against President Garcia, but the full force of the explosion struck the colonel head-on.

The smoke from several small fires quickly filled the room as the alarms began to sound. The president was out cold, pinned beneath the overturned desk. The desk had partially shielded him from the blast, but Colonel Turner looked like he'd walked into a buzz saw. The Secret Service detail on duty reached them within seconds.

"There's been an explosion in the Oval Office, and the president is down," Agent Dibble reported over his headset.

"On my way," Special Agent Stubbs said.

When Special Agent Stubbs reached the Oval Office, Agent Dibble was checking out the president as Agent Robinson was administering CPR to Colonel Turner.

"What the hell happened?" Special Agent Stubbs asked.

"Unknown. We heard an explosion, and this is what we found when we entered."

"Perimeter security report," Special Agent Stubbs ordered.

"It was a missile, but we didn't see it until just before it hit," Lieutenant Spaulding said.

"What the hell happened to the countermeasures?"

"They must have been awfully close, because the systems didn't have time to respond before it struck the building."

"Where the hell is the medical team?" Special Agent Stubbs screamed.

"We're here," Dr. Blackshire, the resident White House physician said as he entered with his assistant Dr. Jeremy Taylor. "Jeremy, you take the colonel while I check out the president."

Dr. Taylor had Agent Robinson move aside as he placed two fingers on the colonel's carotid artery to check for a pulse. When he couldn't detect any heartbeat, he opened the portable defibrillator and said, "Move back." He had to shock the colonel several times before he finally got a pulse. "All of you get over here, I need you to help me put pressure on his wounds," Dr. Taylor said.

There was a large shard of glass stuck in his left temple, and Special Agent Robinson asked, "Should we pull that out?"

"Don't touch it," Dr. Taylor said.

"Good lord, he's cut to ribbons," Special Agent Stubbs said. "Is he going to make it?"

"If we can get the bleeding slowed down, he's got a chance," Dr. Taylor said.

"How's the president doing?" Special Agent Stubbs asked.

"I won't know if he's got brain damage until I can get an MRI and a CAT scan," Dr. Blackshire replied. "When will the medevac be here?"

"*Marine One* just landed, and they'll be transporting them," Special Agent Stubbs said.

"Let's get them to the chopper," Dr. Blackshire ordered.

"Mrs. Garcia, I'm sorry to wake you, but your husband has been injured, and they're transporting him to the Washington Hospital trauma center."

"Injured, what happened?" Melinda asked. "Is he alright?"

"He's alive, that's all I can tell you for sure," Agent Melbourne said.

"Where's Special Agent Stubbs?"

"He's onboard the helicopter with the president and Colonel Turner."

"I've got to get the kids up," Melinda said.

"One of the other agents is already working on that."

As they got into the vehicle, Juanita couldn't stop crying.

"It's going to be alright, honey," Melinda said.

"How do you know that?" Alejandro demanded. "The agent told me they were both unconscious when they airlifted them out."

"I hadn't heard that," Melinda admitted.

As she tried to console them, their armored SUV was running with lights and siren on as it weaved through the morning traffic.

When they got out of the SUV at the hospital, they were immediately surrounded by SWAT officers in full riot gear, and hustled inside.

"Mom, what's going on?" Juanita asked.

"I'm not sure, honey," Melinda said.

"Mrs. Garcia, I'm Special Agent Sereno, and if you'll come with me, I'll take you to the waiting room."

Special Agent Sereno led them through a maze of halls, until they reached the waiting room. He held the door open and said, "Make yourselves comfortable, it may be a while before the doctor comes by to brief you. Would you like something to eat or drink?"

"Some water would be good," Melinda said.

"Mom, why aren't they telling us anything?" Alejandro asked. "I'm going outside and get some answers."

"Sit down," Melinda said. "I'm sure they'll let us know something in a few minutes. See, here comes Special Agent Stubbs."

"You guys need anything?" he asked.

"We're fine, but we need to know how Victor is doing," Melinda said.

"He's stable, and they've just taken him in for an MRI and a CAT scan. The doctor I spoke with said he didn't think he'd suffered any significant brain damage from the explosion, but they wanted to make sure."

"Explosion! Brain damage! What the hell happened? He was supposed be in the Oval Office working."

"He was."

"The Oval Office blew up?"

"There was an attack, and the explosion injured the president and Colonel Turner."

"You mean someone tried to assassinate him?"

"Yes. If you don't mind, I'm going to stay with you until they let you see him," Special Agent Stubbs said.

"I appreciate that."

* * *

Vice President Goodwin was working in his office when the head of his security detail came rushing in.

"Sir, I need you to come with us," Special Agent McAllen said.

"Can't it wait? I'm in the middle of a conference call."

Special Agent McAllen hit the mute button and said, "I'm sorry, it can't. There's been an assassination attempt on the president, and they've transported him to the hospital."

"How bad?"

"Unknown at this time, but we need to get you to the White House situation room ASAP."

Vice President Goodwin un-muted the call and said, "I'm sorry, but something's come up, and I've got to cut this short."

They had an armored SUV waiting in the driveway, along with two armored SUVs with roof-mounted mini-guns for an escort.

"Don't you think this is a little much?" Vice President Goodwin said.

"Hardly, they just attacked the president in the Oval Office."

As they were pulling away Special Agent McAllen keyed his radio, and asked, "Where's my air cover?"

"It's inbound. They'll pick you up en route."

"Very well. We've just left the residence."

"Normal route?" the agent driving the lead vehicle asked.

"No, let's go the back way, just to be safe."

Special Agent McAllen was anxiously scanning the skies as they made their way toward the White House. When he spotted the helicopter gunships overhead, he let out a sigh of relief and said, "Good, they've found us."

"Who's found us?" Vice President Goodwin asked.

"Our air cover. We should be fine now."

As they made the turn underneath an overpass to get on the expressway, Special Agent McAllen spotted a semi on the side of the road. He quickly considered stopping to let the point vehicle check it out, but when he saw that it had its flashers on and traffic cones placed behind it, he decided it had just broken down. As they were passing the stalled truck, a cell phone rang in the trailer, detonating the homemade bomb.

After two hours, Melinda and the kids were beside themselves with worry.

"Shouldn't we have heard something by now?" Melinda asked.

"It takes time to do a thorough evaluation," Special Agent Stubbs said.

But after another hour had passed, he was getting concerned.

"I'm going to step out for a minute, is there anything I can get you?"

"We're fine, but would you mind seeing if they know anything yet?"

"Sure, no problem."

"What's taking so long?" Special Agent Stubbs asked the head nurse.

"Sorry for the delay, they should be almost done. Dr. Turnbow was doing the evaluation, but he's also our leading brain surgeon, and they pulled him out to try to save Colonel Turner when he coded."

"Did the colonel make it?"

"No, he didn't. I'm sorry."

"That's too bad. I'll be back in a minute, and I'll need something I can tell the First Lady."

"I'll do what I can. Wait, they must be finished, here comes the doctor."

"We've finished our evaluation of the president's injuries," Dr. Turnbow said. "He's awake, and we should have him in his room in a few minutes. I'm about to brief the family, if you'd like to accompany me."

"Yes I would, and his wife's name is Melinda."

"Melinda, I'm Dr. Turnbow, and I'm very happy to report that your husband is going to be fine. He's suffered a concussion and some cuts and bruises, but he shouldn't have any long-term issues."

"Oh, thank God. When can we see him?"

"They should have him in his room by now, so if you'll follow me, I'll take you back."

"How are you doing?" Melinda asked as she tried to hide her tears.

"Don't cry, sweetie, I'm fine," Victor said as he reached out to take her hand. "Juanita, that goes for you too. There's nothing to cry about."

"Sorry, Dad, but we were so worried," Juanita said.

"I understand. All of you come over here, I'd like to tell you something."

As they gathered around his bed, Victor said, "Look, I know this has been a terrifying experience for all of you, but if anything ever does happen to me, just know that it was God's will, and that He had another task for me."

"You don't really believe that, do you?" Alejandro asked.

"I do, but I understand your doubt. When my parents were killed, I railed against God for taking my family from me. It took me years to understand that sometimes His will isn't what we'd like it to be."

They pulled up chairs around his bed, and they talked for almost an hour before Special Agent Stubbs came in.

"I hate to intrude, but I need a moment with the president."

"That's alright. None of us have had anything to eat today, so we'll go down to the cafeteria while you two visit," Melinda said.

"What's up, Scott?" President Garcia asked.

"Vice President Goodwin has been assassinated."

"Damn. What happened?"

"His security team was moving him to the White House to stand in for you, and they detonated a semitruck loaded with explosives as they were passing by."

"Why weren't they using armored vehicles?"

"They were, but the explosion was so immense that it wouldn't have mattered if they'd been in an Abrams tank."

"I've got to get out of here," President Garcia said.

"Not until the doctor releases you," Special Agent Stubbs said.

"Then get his ass in here, because I'm leaving."

"Mr. President, I'd really like to keep you overnight," Dr. Turnbow said.

"Write up what you want done and Dr. Blackshire, the White House physician, will take care of it."

"As you will."

When Melinda and the kids got back, Special Agent Stubbs was helping Victor into a wheelchair.

"What's going on?" Melinda asked.

"We're leaving," Victor said.

"The doctor already released you?"

"Sort of."

"What does that mean?"

"He's writing up the instructions for Dr. Blackshire."

She could tell he was upset, so she moved closer, and whispered, "Has something else happened?"

"Charles has been killed," Victor said.

"Oh, dear God," Melinda said.

"We should get going," Special Agent Stubbs said.

When they reached the lobby it was filled with SWAT officers. The heavily armed men surrounded them and led them outside. They were expecting to see the armored SUV they'd arrived in, but instead there was an MRAP.

"What is that thing?" Juanita asked.

"That's a Cougar," Alejandro said. "It weighs over twelve tons, and it's built to withstand IEDs and all sorts of attacks."

"You know your vehicles," Special Agent Stubbs said.

The armored SWAT vehicles they'd pulled in for additional security were equipped with roof-mounted miniguns, and there was a virtual swarm of motorcycle and police car escorts on either end of their mini-convoy.

"This is really scary," Melinda said.

"I'm sorry, but we're not going to take any chances with your safety," Special Agent Stubbs said.

As they left the hospital grounds, they could hear the thump of the attack helicopter's rotor blades orbiting overhead. The highway patrol had cleared their route of traffic, so they made the journey in record time.

When they arrived at the White House, Alejandro said, "This looks like a war zone."

"It is," Special Agent Stubbs said.

"I think I can walk," President Garcia said.

"You're fine where you are," Special Agent Stubbs said.

"Where are you taking us?" Melinda asked.

"You're going to be staying in the basement for the time being," he said as he led them into the elevator. "We've already moved your things into your new rooms," Special Agent Stubbs said.

"I never realized all of this was down here," Melinda said.

"This is your room," Special Agent Stubbs said as he pushed Victor's wheelchair through the door.

"Dear, why don't you and the kids get settled in? I need to check on a few things."

"You need to get some rest," Melinda said.

"I will, just not right now," Victor said.

He started to get up out of the wheelchair and then he settled back and asked, "Scott, would you mind chauffeuring me around for the time being?"

As Special Agent Stubbs was pushing him down the hall, he spotted Shelby Cohen and Harry Miller getting off of the elevator, along with several members of the NSC.

"What the hell are those two morons doing here?" the president said.

"I'm not sure. Let me get you situated, and I'll find out," Special Agent Stubbs said.

When he returned he said, "When they heard about the vice president, they decided to come here. They're next in line, after the VP for the presidency, so they wanted to make sure they were available if needed."

"We won't be needing them. Thank them for me, and send them on their way," President Garcia said.

"What have you found out so far?" President Garcia asked.

"Not that much," Gregory Kellogg said. "The truck they used was hijacked three nights ago in Pennsylvania. It was carrying twenty thousand pounds of ammonium nitrate, and we believe they used the load to construct a bomb, similar to the one used in the Oklahoma City attack. The blast destroyed a nearby strip mall, and took down an adjacent overpass. All told, it killed over five hundred people."

"Are you sure you're alright, Mr. President?" Tom DeMarco asked. "You look kind of pale."

"I've been better. Any leads on the assholes that attacked the White House?"

"They're dead, but we haven't identified them yet," Margret Grissom said. "The D.C. police spotted them when they fired the missile, but when they tried to pull them over, they detonated the bomb they had onboard."

"These assholes sure don't believe in loose ends," Jerry Burns said.

"How much does the public know so far?" President Garcia asked.

"They know the vice president has been killed, and they know there was an explosion at the White House, but they don't know it was an assassination attempt," Gregory Kellogg said.

"Tom, I want you to work up a press release, and get it out to all of the news services," President Garcia said.

"OK, but how much do you want to let them know?"

"Everything, including Colonel Turner's death, but make damn sure we notify his mother before you release it. I don't want her finding out from some damn reporter, and I want a team out there to make sure she's taken care of."

"Right away," Tom DeMarco said.

"General Appleby, I think this necessitates a return to DEFCON 2, would you agree?"

"I may have jumped the gun. The vice president and I discussed it while you were on the way to the hospital, and we decided to raise it."

"No problem, you knew the situation better than anyone, and Charles was right to go along. Which brings up another topic. With all the shit we've got going down, it's imperative I name another vice president. Tom, I'd like you to take the job," President Garcia said.

"I'd be honored," Tom DeMarco said.

"Thanks. Unfortunately we know the drill, so let's get it done. If there's nothing else you need me for, I'm going to lie down for a little while. Don't hesitate to come and get me if you need to," President Garcia said.

"You blew it again, didn't you?" Klaus said when he answered his satellite phone.

"Partially," Fredericka said.

"Bullshit, you screwed the pooch. He'll just name another VP and move on."

"I'm working on an alternative," she said.

"Whatever. Do I need to look to someone else to handle this?" he asked.

"No, I just need a little more time."

"Fine, but my patience is about exhausted."

Much like the call he'd just had, he knew what to expect when his other satellite phone rang. "I know. They screwed up, but trust me, they know they have to follow through," Klaus said.

"You sorry little weasel, I'm not looking to them," Golem said. "I put you in power for a reason, and I'm about to reconsider my decision," the deep-pitched, gravelly voice said.

"I understand your concerns, but believe it or not we're making progress."

"Is there something you haven't shared with me? You know how I hate surprises."

"I had an alternate plan that I never shared with the others."

"It'd had better work out, or your ass is going to be grass, and I'll be the lawn mower."

CHAPTER 30

"It's about time you woke up, sleepy head," Melinda said.

"What time is it?" Victor asked.

"What day would be a better question."

"How long was I out?"

She glanced at the clock radio beside the bed. "Almost thirty-six hours."

"Why did you let me sleep that long? We're in the middle of a crisis."

"Tom DeMarco has been by several times to check on you, and he assured me they had the situation under control."

"I'm hungry," Victor said.

"Anything special you'd like?"

"Whatever they've got that's quick."

"This is good," Victor said as he ate his omelet.

"Are you up to a visitor?" Melinda asked.

"Sure, I feel pretty good, considering."

"You're looking a lot better," Tom DeMarco said.

"That's probably an understatement. I felt pretty rough toward the end there. How are we coming with getting you confirmed as vice president?"

"Shelby and James whined about it, but Chief Justice Avery swore me in at noon yesterday."

"Good deal, and thanks for taking it on. Who would you recommend to take your old job?"

"How would you feel about Diaz?"

"Good man. Is that your recommendation?"

"It is."

"Done deal. I'll get Colonel . . . I was going to say Turner, but he's dead. Did we get his mom taken care of?"

"General Appleby handled it."

"Good. I've lost men in combat, but I never expected to lose one in the Oval Office. It sure doesn't say much for my leadership."

"Certainly not your fault."

"Thanks for that," President Garcia said. "Who would you recommend to replace Roberto Diaz?"

"We don't have time to mess around, so why don't we bring back Larry Hatch?" Vice President DeMarco said.

"Great idea. I know he said he was tired of the grind when he stepped down, but I know he'd do it, at least short term. Give me a half an hour to get cleaned up, and we'll get to work."

"Good to see you up and around," General Appleby said when the president walked in.

"Have you and the team been here the whole time?" President Garcia asked.

"Most of us, but it's alright, we've been taking turns getting some rest. We've all decided to stay on the premises until we can get a handle on who, and why, we're being attacked."

"Any leads?"

"Thousands, but nothing that's panned out. Whoever's behind this seems to have a better than average grasp of our capabilities and procedures. If I didn't know better, I'd say we've got a mole."

"Okay. Let's follow that line of reasoning until we prove it wrong," President Garcia said. "I want to keep this to as small of a group as possible, so we'll start with you, Vice President DeMarco, and myself. Unfortunately none of us has the background to smoke them out, so who should we bring in?"

"To your point, they'll need an intelligence and/or law enforcement background, so the obvious choices would be Jerry Burns, Gregory Kellogg, Mary Beth Greider, Margret Grissom, or Roger Heinrich."

"I'm not going to be much help, because I don't know any of them well enough to make the call," President Garcia said. "Let's get Tom in here, he knows them all."

"What's up?" Vice President DeMarco asked.

"We think there's a chance that we have one or more moles in our leadership."

"The thought had crossed my mind," Vice President DeMarco said. "What do you need from me?"

General Appleby had jotted down the names as they'd been talking, so he slid the list over to Tom. "That's all the names that we could come up with."

"I would trust any of these people with my life, but if it were me, I'd go with Roger Heinrich. He was a CIA field op before he joined the NSA, and he's brilliant."

"I'm going to trust your judgment on this," President Garcia said.

"He's taking a nap down the hall, if you're ready to bring him in," General Appleby said.

"Go get him, there's no time to waste," President Garcia said.

After President Garcia had shared their theories, he asked, "Well, what do you think?"

"It would explain a lot of things," Roger Heinrich said.

"How should be proceed?" President Garcia asked.

"There are at least fifty people who are in a position to know enough to cause the problems we've been seeing. The best way to smoke out a mole—or moles—is to give each one of them a unique piece of information, and if it's used, you've got your traitor."

"That sounds pretty convoluted," General Appleby said.

"It is, but it's effective. There's one big issue you'll need to sign off on. The information has to be high-value, and require an immediate reaction."

"That sounds dangerous," Vice President DeMarco said.

"Without a doubt, and you'll need to be prepared for collateral damage."

"What sort of damage?"

"Casualties, property, who knows, but it could be significant. If we do have a traitor in our midst, they aren't going to risk exposing themselves for something trivial."

"I hate to think we could be putting more lives at risk, but we've got to have answers," President Garcia said. "What we're considering could put our lives, and certainly our reputations and careers at risk, so I'm going to work one-on-one with Roger on this."

"I'm a big boy, you don't need to protect me," General Appleby said.

"Same here," Vice President DeMarco said.

"Okay, but I made the offer. Roger, this is your top priority, and if you need anything, you let me know. If it's possible, I'd like to clear Mary Beth Greider first. I really need to know if we can trust Homeland."

"Done. Is there anyone else you'd like to see go to the head of the list?"

"They're all important, but let's do Jerry Burns next. After that use your own judgment."

When Roger Heinrich left, General Appleby said, "It makes me sick to my stomach to think we could have someone on our team that's willing to put our entire way of life at risk. What do you think: money, sex, power?"

"Could be all of that, or it could be that they think they are standing up for what they believe. Zealots often change history. Sometimes it's for the common good, sometimes not, but never forget, history is written by the winners," President Garcia said.

"Like Thomas Jefferson and the boys," Vice President DeMarco said.

"I hate to think that we could be on the wrong side, but yes, very much like that," President Garcia said.

"That's enough of the philosophical bullshit," General Appleby said. "Let's play the hand we've been dealt."

"You're right," President Garcia said. "Let's take a ten-minute break before we start the status meeting."

When they resumed, the president said, "Let's start with FEMA."

"The situation on the West Coast is starting to stabilize, but they still need manpower and supplies," General Appleby said.

"Do we have anything left in reserve?" President Garcia asked.

"Colonel Wilhelm, would you put the latest report up on the screen for us?" General Appleby asked. "Sorry, I just remembered you haven't met Colonel Turner's replacement. Colonel, would you come over here so I can introduce you to the boss? Mr. President, this is Colonel Jerry Wilhelm."

"Nice to meet you, Colonel," President Garcia said. "Tell me a little about yourself."

"I'm an army brat. I was born in Germany, and Dad's assignments took us all over the world. When he retired, we moved back to West Virginia where I finished high school. I attended West Point, and after I graduated, I've spent most of my career with the army's Special Forces, working mostly counterterrorism missions."

"What he didn't say is that, like you, he holds a Silver Star and several Purple Hearts, and that he graduated top of his class at West Point," General Appleby said. "I hand-picked him for this assignment because I want him on the fast path to flag officer."

"I look forward to working with you, Colonel," President Garcia said.

"OK, back to work," General Appleby said.

As they studied the latest logistics reports, they quickly identified several critical needs.

"What are we doing about the food and fuel issues?" President Garcia asked.

"When we lost the West Coast terminals and the refineries, it put a real crimp in our domestic production. Luckily, the lion's share of our refinery capacity is in Texas and Louisiana, so we've had them ramp up to full capacity. The port capacity is a bigger problem, but we're trying to turn them around as fast as we can. The Chinese and the Russians are sending what they can, but we really need the Venezuelans to step up."

"What sort of reserve supplies do we have at the stateside bases?" President Garcia asked.

"Mostly canned goods, MREs, et cetera."

"Send everything we have. It may not be the best, but at least they'll eat. How about the cleanup?"

"Timothy Gather just reported that they've wrapped up the body retrieval."

"That's great. What's next?"

"They've just begun moving the heavy equipment into Seattle and Sacramento. Once they have everything in place, both groups will begin working their way toward the Portland area."

"He'd better not enter the quarantine area."

"The plan calls for the California team to stop thirty-five miles south of Portland, and the Washington task force will stop twenty miles north of Mount Hood."

"Good. I was afraid he was still trying to buck me on that."

"No, he understands, but even if he wanted to, they simply don't have the resources to do it."

"I think I'll call the Chinese and the Russians and see if there is anything else they can do," President Garcia said. "Tom, you know President Conteras, don't you?"

"Well. He and I were roommates at Yale, and we've stayed in touch since he returned to Venezuela."

"Good. I want you to see what it would take for them to ship us some gasoline and fuel oil."

"He's going to want something in return."

"What will it take?"

"He needs money, and a few old F-16s would probably seal the deal."

"Go for it."

They'd been at it for hours when President Garcia said, "Sorry, boys, I think I'm done for the day."

"Damn, it's later than I thought," Vice President DeMarco said. "You lose track of time cooped up down here."

"OK, we'll hit it again tomorrow," General Appleby said. "Maybe we can get a decent night's sleep for a change."

"Mr. President, I need a moment of your time," Special Agent Stubbs said.

"Sure Scott, what have you got?" President Garcia said.

"We need to move the vice president to the Cheyenne Mountain facility."

"Why? Isn't he safe enough here?"

"Possibly, but the protocol for this type of situation requires that you and the vice president be housed in separate locations, so we can maintain the continuity of government in case of another catastrophe."

"Damned unhandy, but I suppose it makes sense."

"Good, I'll have him transferred by morning."

"What can I do for you, Agent Stubbs?" Vice President DeMarco asked.

"I need you to pack your things and meet me in the hall."

"I haven't had a chance to unpack yet, but what's going on?"

"We're going to transfer you to the NORAD Cheyenne complex."

"Tonight?"

"Yes, sir, I've got a helicopter standing by to transport you to the airport."

Vice President DeMarco slept on the flight to Colorado Springs, but he woke up when the 747 touched down.

"Good, you're awake," Colonel Littleton said.

"Where are we?" Vice President DeMarco asked.

"Colorado Springs. There's a helicopter waiting to take you the rest of the way."

It was a short flight to the facility, and when the chopper touched down, the base commander greeted the vice president. "Welcome to Cheyenne Mountain," General Robertson said.

"Thank you, General," Vice President DeMarco said.

"Have you been here before?"

"No, I haven't, but I've read a lot about it."

As they walked through the tunnel into the mountain,

Vice President DeMarco said, "This must've have taken a hell of a lot of digging."

"More blasting than digging, but it's been a work in progress since the sixties."

As they rounded the corner to enter the main facility, Vice President DeMarco said, "That's a hell of a door."

"It's designed to withstand a nuclear explosion."

Once inside the main complex, they took another elevator down three more levels.

"This floor will be your new home until the all-clear is given," General Robertson said as he opened the door to his quarters.

"Thanks, this should do fine."

"There's a mini communications center in the den, and it's robust enough for you to take all of your meetings from here if you'd like."

"Good deal. I'm supposed to be in a session of the NSC at oh-six-hundred."

"No problem. Sergeant Adams will show you how to operate the system."

"You made it," President Garcia said when they'd established the video link.

"I just got here a few minutes ago," Vice President De-Marco said.

"We don't have much to talk about today, but it's good to know you aren't going to have any problems participating, because I'm going to need a lot of input from you."

After a short meeting, President Garcia said, "That's it for today. Finish getting settled in, and we'll touch base again before the end of the day."

CHAPTER 31

"How long are you bastards going to hold us prisoner?" President Montblanc demanded when the guards delivered their dinner.

The burly guard didn't say a word as he set down their trays. He took a moment to check their supply of drinks before he left, locking the heavy metal door behind him.

"I don't know how much longer I can stand this," Deborah Montblanc said.

"I'm so sorry that I got you into this," Peter said.

"I'm not blaming you, but what the hell do they want from us?"

"I don't have a clue. They haven't even tried to interrogate me," Peter said. "Hell, I don't even know what country we're in, let alone who's holding us."

When the guards got back to the control room, Chris Collins said, "Damn, that sure is a fine-looking woman."

"Have you been watching her shower again?" Richard Ellis asked. "I told you to stop that shit, and I'm not going to warn you again."

"No, it's just that there's something about her that turns me on."

"Whatever, but I need you to focus on the mission. This

means a lot of money to us, and I don't want you screwing it up. Am I clear?"

"Yes, boss, I got it."

They'd gone almost three weeks without any new incidents when the alert message came in during their morning status meeting.

"There's been an incident in the Gaza Strip," Colonel Wilhelm said.

"What this time?" President Garcia asked.

"The Israelis have started a sweep through the area, and if the first reports are correct, they are slaughtering innocent civilians."

"That seems out of character for them. Did someone attack them first?"

"Not that we're aware of," Colonel Wilhelm said.

"See if you can get Prime Minister Weizmann for me," President Garcia said. "I may need the vice president's help on this, so make sure he gets a feed of the call."

"You want him on the call?"

"No, just a one-way feed, but I do want him on the phone so I can get his input."

"I was expecting your call," Prime Minister Weizmann said.

"What the hell are you up to now?" President Garcia asked.

"Right to the point, as always. We're reclaiming our territory, and while we're at it, we're going to add a buffer zone to stop these animals from firing missiles into our territory."

"Have there been attacks?" President Garcia asked.

"Not lately, this is simply a preventative measure."

"We've received reports of heavy casualties, and that your forces are indiscriminately killing innocents."

"Hyperbole. There have been a few unfortunate incidents, but we don't have time to mollycoddle them."

"You need to stand down, immediately."

"When we reach our objectives."

"Which are?"

The prime minister sighed, and said, "We'll stop when we've driven them back far enough to ensure my people's safety."

President Garcia muted the call and asked, "What's the range of the Hamas/Hezbollah missiles?"

"They don't have a lot of them, but the Fajr-5 is approximately fifty miles," General Appleby said.

"If I remember correctly, at its widest point, Palestine is only a hundred and seventeen kilometers wide," President Garcia said.

"That would be close."

"That means they intend to push them into the sea, or at least out of the country. Mr. Weizmann, I must demand an immediate halt to your advances," President Garcia said when he un-muted the connection.

"Sorry, no."

"You're going to force me to take action if you don't."

"Do what you must," Prime Minister Weizmann said as he hung up.

"He's certainly an intractable bastard," President Garcia said.

"So, what are you going to do?" Vice President DeMarco asked.

"One part of me understands what he's trying to do, but I can't let them turn every Arab country in the world against them, and us."

"I agree, but we don't have much leverage," General Appleby said.

President Garcia had studied Israeli tactics while he was at the Marine Corps War College, and he knew they rarely varied their approach. "I assume they're leading with their armor," President Garcia said.

"That and airstrikes. The Palestinians don't have a snowball's chance in hell against them."

"Even that is a bit of an understatement," President Garcia said. "OK, this is what we're going to do. I'm going to declare a no-fly zone over the entire area. We'll need to have the air force coordinate with Admiral Kenyan's forces to pull it off, but without air support, the Hamas and Hezbollah forces should be able to stop their advances."

"You're willing to fire on the Israelis?" Vice President DeMarco asked.

"I don't want to, but I don't see any other course of action. However, if one of you has a better plan, I'd love to hear it."

They had to admit the president had balls, but they knew it was a desperate gambit.

"I don't, but you do realize that you'll be finished in Washington," Vice President DeMarco said.

"Probably true, but if I can keep this from escalating, it'll have been worth it. Tom, while the general is pulling his part together, we need to get Roberto Diaz up to speed. Then we'll brief Paul-Henri Archambault, because we're going to need his help with the UN Security Council."

"I don't think you'll catch much flack from the council," Vice President DeMarco said.

"We'll get back together at fourteen thirty, and if we're ready, I'll call Prime Minister Weizmann."

They had to postpone the meeting until 1530, because the general needed a little more time.

"The vice president is coming online," Colonel Wilhelm said.

"Sorry for the delay, but we had a couple of issues we had to deal with," General Appleby said.

"No problem," President Garcia said. "Are you ready?"

"Everything is in place, but we're going to be stretched pretty thin."

"Tom, have we heard back from the UN?"

"I just got off the phone with Paul-Henri, and as I thought, the council gave us a unanimous vote on your plans."

"Alright, let's give Prime Minister Weizmann a call."

"Good evening, Mr. President," Prime Minister Weizmann said. "I didn't expect to hear from you so soon."

"As I told you when we last spoke, I can't allow you to proceed with your plans. I'm calling to inform you that we're instituting a no-fly zone over the entire region. If we see any military aircraft take off, we will shoot it down, and that includes helicopters. You have one hour to land your aircraft, before we begin shooting them down."

"You arrogant fool," Prime Minister Weizmann said. "We're your ally, and your government is sworn to defend us."

"And we will, but we won't allow your naked aggression. If the no-fly zone doesn't convince you to stop, I'll be forced to take further action."

"You can't threaten us."

"It's not a threat. Now do the right thing, and stop this madness."

The prime minister muttered a curse, and dropped off of the call.

"What happens next?" Vice President DeMarco asked.

"Now we wait," President Garcia said. "We might as well go through the status reports while we wait."

They'd been working for almost two hours when Colonel Wilhelm said, "The prime minister is demanding to speak with you."

"Put him on," President Garcia said.

"You murderous bastard, you've shot down six of our

aircraft, and damaged another ten," Prime Minister Weizmann said.

"A regrettable loss of life, but I warned you," President
Garcia said. "Have you halted your advances?"

"Hell, no. I'm not going to let a Chicano bastard like
you meddle in our affairs."

"I'm not going to dignify that by asking for an apology, but if you don't halt the attacks, I'm going to order
our aircraft to start destroying your armored forces, and
if that doesn't convince you to stop, I'll have them start
strafing your ground forces."

They could see that Prime Minister Weizmann was so
mad that he was about to have a stroke. The prime minister muted the call to confer with his staff. They couldn't
hear, but it was evident that they were engaged in a heated
discussion.

When he finished, he returned to the call, and said, "It's
done, but don't think that you've heard the last of this."

"You've done the right thing," President Garcia said.

"You can go to hell."

"Boy, is he pissed," Vice President DeMarco said.

"Oh, well," President Garcia said. "At least I got his
attention."

As they often did, they met late that night to discuss the
day's events.

"I can't believe the stupid wetback had the balls to make
that sort of move," Fredericka said.

"I warned you," Jonathan said. "He may be politically naive, but he's a tough bastard. What now?"

"We've got to take it to the next level," Fredericka said.

"Next level! We've already committed high treason."

"So what's your point?" she asked. "Like our forefathers,
we've got to go all-in. Our only other option is to give up the
very beliefs that make us who we are. This nation needs to
return to the beliefs that made us great."

He knew where she was going, and while he agreed with most of it, he didn't feel like listening to her preach at him. "Don't start with your bullshit rants against abortion, gay marriage, and that the immigrants and non-whites are ruining the country. This has gotten completely out of hand."

"I'll admit I never intended to kill millions of our countrymen, but who could have known?"

"I'm not blaming anyone, but maybe God is trying to send us a message."

"I refuse to believe that. God is on our side, not the mongrels that have taken over our country," she said. "It's time to use our bargaining chip."

"You're probably right, but I've got to work on another cover story. Paul-Henri and President Garcia aren't going to believe that Ayatollah Rostami is behind it."

"I thought we'd agreed on a splinter group working behind the scenes on Iran's behalf," she said.

"We did, but I need to tighten up a few details before we pull the trigger."

"How long?"

"I should be able to finish up by next week."

"Fine, just let me know what you need me to do," she said.

A few days later, Richard Ellis said, "Larry and I are going to make a supply run. We should be back by six, so just hold off on feeding them dinner until we get back."

"Why can't I go instead of Roberts? I could use a piece of ass," Chris Collins whined.

"You horny bastard. Have you forgotten what happened last time you went to town?" Richard Ellis asked.

"It wasn't my fault. I didn't know she was married, and I didn't mean to kill her husband."

"You never do, but the authorities have an all-points bulletin and a reward out for your sorry ass."

"OK, but can you bring back some more Jack?"

CHAPTER 32

He'd been expecting the call for days, but when he saw the caller ID, his heart almost stopped. "Ayatollah Rostami, how may I be of assistance?" asked Mostafa Ramadani, the head of the Ministry of Intelligence and National Security of the Islamic Republic of Iran (MISIRI).

"The guardian council tasked you with finding out who orchestrated the attack on President Montblanc and his wife, and I'm calling to get your report," the supreme leader, Ayatollah Rostami said.

"I'd rather not discuss this on the phone," Minister Ramadani said.

"Fine, I'll expect you in my office by fourteen thirty."

When Minister Ramadani entered the ayatollah's office, he was struck by its extreme austerity.

"Take a seat here beside me," the ayatollah said. "I'm quite disappointed in you performance so far. I thought I'd been clear that we needed your final assessment of the events surrounding the attack on President Montblanc."

This isn't starting well, he thought to himself. "As I indicated in my initial report, the attack was carried out by a renegade group, Takavar commandos, from the Lashgare division. They'd deserted the previous year, along with Colonel Tavaazo and Major Hamdi."

"That doesn't look very good for us," Ayatollah Rostami said.

"It gets worse. They used a Russian Antonov AN-225 that was on lease to the National Iranian Oil Company to make their escape."

"Someone has gone to a great deal of trouble to make it look like we're behind this, but how do you abduct the president of the United States, and just disappear?"

"Whoever orchestrated this has covered their tracks well. However, we've just had a breakthrough on their whereabouts."

"How did you come by this information?"

"The Americans put up a fifty million dollar reward for information leading to their recovery. However, we'd quietly offered a hundred million, and it paid off last week. A group of Colombian drug smugglers stumbled on the crash site in a remote section of jungle, and they came to us with their discovery instead of to the Americans."

"Why wasn't I informed?"

"I didn't want to come to you until we'd researched what they had."

"So, what did you find out?" Ayatollah Rostami asked.

"It was definitely the Antonov they used in the operation, but it exploded at low altitude, and the debris field was spread over an extensive area."

"They were taken in Egypt, how the hell did they end up in Colombia?"

"The aircraft did, but our team was certain that the president and his wife weren't on board when it went down."

"I want to speak with the leader of the recovery mission."

"Me too, but we lost touch with them shortly after they made their report."

"This doesn't make sense. Normally you don't take hostages unless you intend to make some sort of demand," Ayatollah Rostami said.

"I agree, and why did they make it look like we were behind it?"

"You're the head of intelligence, isn't that your job to figure it out?"

"Sorry, of course it is, but much like the attack on our missile base that precipitated our firing on the American fleet, someone is trying to paint us into a corner."

"I authorized the counterattack. Are you saying it wasn't the Americans?" the ayatollah asked.

"I am. One of our double agents in the Chinese security force tipped us off to it not long ago."

"Again, why wasn't I informed?" the ayatollah growled.

"He wasn't willing to divulge the details, or how he found out, so I've been holding back from telling you while I tried to confirm his story."

"Jews?"

"Possibly, but that would be a dangerous game to play. They'd be risking their very existence if the Americans ever found out. Besides, why would they take that sort of risk, when the UN was about to do their dirty work for them?"

"Who knows, but I need you to get to the bottom of this."

"Believe me, I wish I had more, but the trail has gone cold, and unless we can turn up a new lead, we're not going to figure it out before the UN storms in here and takes us out."

"I'm working on that," Ayatollah Rostami said. "If you uncover anything new, it's to be my eyes only. Are you clear on that point?"

"Yes, sir."

CHAPTER 33

Christmas was in two weeks, but the overnight snow-storm had caught everyone by surprise.

"I thought we were only supposed to get a few flurries," Melinda said as she looked out at the two-foot drifts in the garden.

"Surprise there. I wish I could screw up more than half the time and still have a job," Victor said. "What are you guys up to today?"

"You forgot, didn't you?" Melinda asked. "We're all going to the mall to do our Christmas shopping."

"Oh, crap. I'm sorry, but there's no way I can get away today, and I'd rather you didn't go without me."

"But Special Agent Collie has gone to a lot of trouble to set this up," Melinda said.

"I'd still rather you didn't go."

"We've talked about this. We can't continue to be prisoners in our own home."

"I know it's been hard on all of you, but we still don't know who's behind all of this."

"Special Agent Collie felt like they could handle one trip to the mall."

"What changed? When I talked with Special Agent Stubbs, he told me there was no way they could guarantee our safety in a crowed area like the mall."

"I don't know, but Agent Collie has assured me they have a plan."

"OK, but I still don't like it. What time are you taking off?"

"They're picking us up at seven thirty."

"Be careful, and do what the agents tell you," Victor said.

"Quit worrying, we'll be fine."

When their armored SUV pulled up in front of the Mazza Gallerie, Juanita asked, "Where are all the people?"

"They don't open until ten," Special Agent Collie said, "but we got them to open this section of the pavilion early."

When they went inside, all of the eighteen fashionable shops were deserted, except for the sales clerks.

"This is really weird," Alejandro said.

"It is a little disconcerting," Melinda said. "At least we don't have to wait in line. Let's split up, and we'll meet back here at nine fifty-five."

Each of them had a team of agents accompanying them, so they didn't have to worry about carrying their packages.

"It looks like you guys made a real haul," Special Agent Collie said as they loaded their packages into the SUVs.

"I can't thank you enough for letting us get out," Melinda said.

President Garcia felt bad about not going, so he'd asked Special Agent Collie to give him a call when they left the mall. When they pulled up at the White House, Victor came out to help them carry in their packages.

When the device hidden in the headliner received the high frequency signal, it started a ten-second countdown.

The kids were still gathering up their stuff, so Victor took Melinda's packages as she exited. As they were walking away from the SUV, Melinda was scolding him, "You shouldn't be out in this weather without a coat."

When the C4 detonated, the SUV's armor plating contained most of the blast inside the vehicle. Victor and Melinda were several yards away, but the open door focused the force of the blast toward them, hurling them face-first across the driveway into a pile of snow. The blast had knocked them both out, so they didn't see the secondary phosphorus charges ignite, setting off an inferno inside the shredded interior.

When Victor came to, they were lying side by side in the hospital beds they'd set up. Victor was still trying to clear his head when Dr. Blackshire bent over his bed to check his vitals.

"What happened?" Victor asked.

"There was an explosion," Dr. Blackshire said.

"Are Alejandro and Juanita alright?"

"I'm so sorry, they're both dead."

"Dear Father in heaven, please receive their souls into your kingdom, and please help Melinda through this," Victor prayed. "I need you to take me to them, right now."

"Mr. President, that's not a good idea."

"And why the hell not?"

"In addition to the explosives, the terrorists used a secondary phosphorous charge."

He'd seen what phosphorous could do, so he knew the doctor was giving him good advice. "How's my wife doing?"

"She'll be fine. I've got her sedated, because I wanted to speak with you first."

"I appreciate that."

"She should come around in a few minutes, but is there anything I can do for you, other than leave you to your thoughts?" Dr. Blackshire asked.

"I'm good, and Doc, thanks for allowing me to handle this with my wife."

He'd been lying there trying to think of a way to break the news, when he realized Melinda was awake.

"How are you feeling?" Victor asked.

"What happened?" Melinda asked, still not quite coherent.

"There was an explosion."

"Explosion! Are the kids alright?"

As Victor struggled to get the words out, she started wailing. Her anguished screams broke his heart, but he knew that nothing he could say or do could ever console her. They had him hooked up to a monitor and an IV, but he managed to reach her side.

Hearing her cries, the doctor and nurses stayed away until Melinda's screaming had subsided to whimpering sobs of sorrow.

"You should get back in bed," Dr. Blackshire said.

"Can you give her something?" Victor asked.

"Don't you dare," Melinda screamed. "I don't need sleep, I need to see my babies."

"I'm afraid that's not possible," Dr. Blackshire said. "We've already transferred them to Andrews."

"Why?"

"We didn't want them in the city morgue."

Hearing the words set her off again, but after a minute or so she managed to compose herself. "I still want to see them," she said.

"That's not a good idea," Dr. Blackshire said.

"That's bullshit, I don't care if it's dangerous," Melinda said.

"It's not that, there's just not much left."

This time she passed out.

"You've got to give her something," Victor pleaded.

"Certainly, but give me a moment to make sure she's alright." When Dr. Blackshire finished, he said, "I've given her a shot, and it should keep her asleep until morning, but she's going to need counseling."

"Would you ask Special Agent Stubbs to step in here for a moment?" President Garcia asked.

"Agent Stubbs isn't here."

"Fine, I'll deal with Special Agent Collie."

"He's not available either."

"What the hell? Find one of the other agents and send him in."

"Mr. President, I'm Special Agent Guthrie, and I can't tell you how sorry I am."

"I don't want to hear your excuses," President Garcia said. "I want you to fly Father Mendoza in here by morning."

"Father Mendoza?" Special Agent Guthrie asked.

"He's the priest from our church in Albuquerque. My secretary can give you the address, and I want him here when Melinda wakes up, and while you're at it, have them pick up Melinda's mother, Mrs. Esmeralda Santiago, as well."

"Yes, sir, I'm on it."

After Agent Guthrie was gone, the president sat on the side of his bed. The powerful sedative had knocked Melinda out, but as he sat watching her sleep, he could hear her anguished whimpers.

"Dear Lord, why are you doing this to us?" he lamented. As he choked back his tears, he prayed, "Forgive me, Lord, I know we don't always understand your plans for us, but this is so hard. Please take our children to your side and keep them safe with you until Melinda and I can join you, and them, for all eternity.

"And Lord, please give me the strength to help Melinda through this, and give me the strength to lead our country out of the darkness that has befallen it, and Father, I beg your forgiveness for what I may have to do."

When he'd finished praying, he took a moment to compose himself before he pushed the call button and barked, "Nurse, I need a phone in here, and I need to talk with the vice president ASAP."

"The doctor said that you need to get some rest," the nurse said when she came in.

"Please do as I ask."

She could tell he wasn't in any mood to wait, so she said, "Yes, sir, I'll see to it immediately."

"Victor, I don't have the words to express my sorrow for your loss," Vice President DeMarco said.

"I appreciate that, but I'm not looking for sympathy," President Garcia said. "I know it's not the Christian way, but I want retribution on the sorry bastards that killed my kids."

"As any man would. What do you want us to do?"

"I wish I knew. I've got the Secret Service flying in Melinda's mother and our old parish priest, but where the hell is Special Agent Stubbs?"

"I have no idea, but I'll find out."

"What have we found out about the attack?"

"The team protecting your family didn't follow protocol, but that's not what got them killed. The phosphorus charges destroyed most of the evidence, but we did find a fragment of the detonators they used. It was a highly sophisticated, ultra-high-frequency trigger, and even if they had activated the cell phone jammer like they were supposed to, it wouldn't have prevented this particular device from working."

"They had to be really close for that to work," President Garcia said.

"Exactly. The tech I talked with said that it has a range of less than a hundred feet."

"Oh, dear God, it was one of our own people?"

"Without a doubt."

"Round up everyone that was out there."

"We've isolated everyone that was even remotely involved, but Special Agent Collie has disappeared."

"Disappeared?"

"No one has seen or heard from him since the attack."

"That sure as hell seems suspicious. It's one thing to try to kill me, but they've destroyed my family, and I'm going to kill every one of the sorry sons of bitches," President Garcia growled. "I trusted him to protect my family, and if he's involved, he'll go to the head of the line."

"Understandable."

"Has Roger had any success yet?"

"Still working on it, but nothing yet."

They'd been talking for several minutes when President Garcia said, "Tom, I'm sorry, but I'm not feeling very well. Could you hold down the fort for a little while?"

"That's why you've got me. I'll call back and have the doctor come in when we're done. Now get some rest, and we'll talk in the morning."

The doctor gave him a light sedative so he could rest, but the nightmares started as soon as he was asleep.

When her satellite phone rang, she knew it wasn't going to be good news. "I've told you never to call me during the day," Fredericka said.

"I thought you'd want to know that our plan went astray," the muffled voice said.

"Speak up, you imbecile."

"I'm sorry, but I've got to be quiet so that I'm not overheard. I said the plan has failed. His children were killed, but the president and his wife survived."

"Shit, it just keeps getting worse. This is what I—"

"Somebody's coming, I've got to go," he said, cutting her off.

Damn it to hell, I'm surrounded by gutless assholes, she thought to herself. She put her head down on the desk. After several minutes of contemplation, she still couldn't see a way out, but she decided to call one of her coconspirators. *I should have never let that sorry little bastard pressure me into this shit,* she thought to herself as she dialed his number.

"Don't tell me, we failed," Jonathan said when he picked up.

"How'd you know?"

"It's all over the TV. How did the dumb-ass manage to kill his kids, and not get him?"

"Who knows, he wasn't where he could talk."

"I told you I didn't want to go through with it, and now this happens. Dear God in heaven, what have we done?"

"Buck up. We need to meet."

He didn't answer her.

"I said we need to meet."

She was about to go off on him, when she heard the gunshot.

She knew what he'd done, but she didn't hang up.

"Oh my God, he's killed himself," a female voice screamed.

"Damned coward," she muttered as she hung up.

"I warned you about him," Klaus said when he answered.

"How did you know?" Fredericka asked.

"I've got my ways. They called me before they called nine-one-one. You sure aren't on a roll."

"Not my fault," she said. "We had a flawless plan."

"You're truly a clueless bitch. How are you going to clean this mess up?"

"I sent a cleanup team, but he'd already made a run for it."

"Damn, we don't need him rolling over on us."

"Don't worry, we'll get him."

"You'd damn well better."

"I understand."

"Once you've taken care of that, you need to finish the task."

"How the hell do you think I can accomplish that?"

"Your problem."

CHAPTER 34

When President Garcia woke the next morning, he immediately turned over to check on Melinda. She was still asleep but he could tell it wasn't a peaceful sleep as she vacillated between whimpering and cursing. He knew how she felt. Even with the sedative they'd given him, the nightmares had raced through his mind all night. He threw back the blankets and swung his legs over the side of the bed. They'd removed his prosthetics after he'd fallen asleep, so he pushed the call button.

"Yes, sir, do you need something?" the nurse asked.

"I need someone to bring me my legs."

"I'll be right in."

The nurse pushed the tray with his legs over to his bedside. As Victor reached for one of them, the nurse said, "You've bled through your stockings. Let me take a look before you put them back on." She had to use a washrag to moisten the stockings before she could peel them off. "Let's get you cleaned up, and then I'll put some of this salve on those sores." When she was finished dressing the wounds, she told him, "You need to leave the left one off for a day or two."

"It'll be fine."

"As you wish, but it's going to hurt like hell."

"Nothing new there. Have Mrs. Santiago and Father Mendoza arrived yet?" President Garcia asked.

"I haven't seen Mrs. Santiago, but Father Mendoza arrived a little after midnight. He spent most of the night by your bedsides."

"I'd like to talk with him."

"He just stepped out to get a bite to eat, but he should be back anytime now. I can go and get him if you'd like."

"Let him be until we're done." When she'd helped him reattach his prosthetics, he slid off the bed and moved to Melinda's bedside. "Wake up, dear," Victor said.

She awoke with a start. "Please tell me it was just a bad dream," she pleaded.

He bent over and whispered, "I'm so sorry, but they're gone."

When she broke down again, he struggled to hold his emotions in check. "I know it hurts, but they're with God, and we'll see them again one day," Victor said.

"I know, but it's just not fair, they were just kids."

"I don't pretend to understand why God lets bad things happen, but their deaths have to be part of His plan."

"I've heard you say that many times, but you don't really believe it, do you?" Melinda asked.

"It's hard, but as I told you all the other day, I do truly believe it."

"I don't think I can go on," Melinda said.

"Yes, you can, and you know that they'd want you to remember them as they lived, not as they died."

"But they were my babies," Melinda sobbed.

"As they were mine, but nothing we can do will bring them back. All we can do now is live our lives as God wills, and hope that He sees fit to reunite us with them on our judgment day."

"I wish Father Mendoza was here," Melinda said.

"He's waiting outside," Victor said.

"How?"

"I had them fly him in last night. The nurse said he spent most of the night at our bedsides."

* * *

Father Mendoza spent the next hour praying with them, and when he finished, Melinda said, "Father, I've got to be honest with you. I'm not sure I'll ever believe that this was God's will, but I'll keep trying."

"That's all anyone can do," Father Mendoza said. "Faith is often difficult. Even as a priest, I sometimes find myself questioning the very existence of God, but in the end, my faith in Him wins out."

"I hope I can get there again," Melinda said. "I just wish you could stay with us."

"The cardinal has arranged for me to stay with you for as long as I'm needed," Father Mendoza said.

"But what about your church?" Melinda asked.

"Father Genovese has taken over for me."

"Thanks be to God for your coming, but I've got things that I must attend to," President Garcia said.

"I understand, but before you go, I've seen the rage in your eyes. Be careful you don't lose yourself in your quest for revenge," Father Mendoza said.

"It's a chance I'll have to take, because I'm going with the Old Testament on this one: an eye for an eye, and a tooth for a tooth."

"And I would tell you to remember Christ's words on mercy and forgiveness."

"I get it, but I've got a job to do, and if I lose my soul doing it, so be it."

After Victor was gone, Melinda asked, "Father, would you pray with me?"

"Certainly, child, but don't doubt that Juanita and Alejandro are with God."

"No, I want you to help me pray for Victor's soul, for I fear he's about to do some truly awful things."

"We'll pray for his soul, but while God does say that

we should turn the other cheek, there's still a place for an eye for eye in some situations."

"Why didn't they bring Melinda's mother with them?" President Garcia demanded.

"Special Agent Guthrie didn't tell you?" Colonel Wilhelm asked.

"Tell me what?"

"She had a stroke when they told her the news, and she died before they could get her to the hospital."

President Garcia grabbed the wall for support. "God, why us?" he asked. "Sorry. Tell the council that I'll need a few minutes."

"Right away," the colonel said as he marveled at the president's ability to cope.

Victor had Father Mendoza step out into the hall to share the news.

"I have no words," Father Mendoza said.

"Me neither, but I've got to tell her. Would you mind coming back in with me?"

"That's why I'm here."

When Victor told Melinda of her mother's untimely death, Melinda's response took them by surprise.

"I dreamed she died last night. She told me not to worry about her, because she was going home, and that she and my father would look after the children until we got there. I hate that I didn't get to say good-bye, but I take solace in knowing she's with God, and that she's looking after Juanita and Alejandro. I know you need to get to work, but would you mind asking the nurse to bring my clothes in? I'd like to go back to our rooms."

"Sure, and I'll come back and check on you as soon as I can," Victor said.

"Thanks, but Father Mendoza and I will be fine."

CHAPTER 35

When President Garcia walked into the situation room, the NSC was preparing to work through the intelligence they'd gathered on the attack. Vice President DeMarco was chairing the meeting via videoconference, but when he saw the president enter, he stopped in midsentence and stood up. When the rest of the council members realized what was happening, they rose to their feet.

"Thank you, but please take your seats," President Garcia said. "Before we resume, I'd like to take a moment. I realize that all of you will want to express your sympathy for the loss that my wife and I have suffered, but it's not necessary. I'd rather that we focus on finding the low-life scum who are trying to destroy our way of life. Now, please resume what you were doing, and I'll have Tom catch me up on what I've missed."

"We were late getting started, so you haven't missed anything," Vice President DeMarco said. "We took a break while I took a call from the D.C. chief of police."

"What did he want?" President Garcia asked.

"He was giving us a heads-up that they'd received a nine-one-one call from Senator Miller's office."

"Has there been another attack?"

"No. The caller said that he'd committed suicide."

"When?"

"They received the call at nine thirty. Their officers had just arrived on scene, and the initial report was that he'd shot himself."

"Horrible, simply horrible," Jerry Burns said. "The whole damn world has gone crazy."

"I know you were just getting started, but I'd like to call a short recess," President Garcia said. "Tom, I'd like for you to stay on, and General Appleby, I'll need you as well."

When the rest of the council had left, President Garcia asked Colonel Wilhelm, "Is Roger Heinrich in the building?"

"No, but I can get him over here if you need him."

"We've got a secure line to the NSA, don't we?"

"Of course. Would you like me to see if he's available?"

"Yes, but make sure he knows that I need him right now."

"OK, he should be coming up on the main screen in just a moment," Colonel Wilhelm said. "Would you like me to step out?"

"Yes, please. We'll call you if we need anything," President Garcia said.

"I assume you're calling about Senator Miller?" Director Heinrich asked.

"You NSA guys don't miss much, do you?" General Appleby said.

"Actually, it's already on the channel seven ABC news alert," Director Heinrich said.

"Does this tell us anything?" President Garcia asked.

"Possibly. He wasn't on my list, but I'm going back though everything we have on him to see if there's something else going on in his life that could have led to this."

"How's the varmint hunting going?"

"I planted the first batch last week, and if I don't see any results in a day or two, I'll move on to the next group."

"I wish we could go faster, but I understand why we can't."

As they prepared to wrap up the call, Director Heinrich said, "Mr. President, on behalf of everyone at NSA, I'd like to convey our heartfelt sympathy at your family's horrific loss."

"We appreciate that. It's the hardest thing I've ever had to face."

"I feel like we've failed you at every turn, and if you'd like, I'll tender my immediate resignation."

"Hell, no, I need you to help us smoke out the sorry pieces of shit."

"Thanks for that, and I'll call as soon as I know something."

"OK, let's get the team gathered back up. We've got work to do," President Garcia said.

"Sorry for the delay," President Garcia said when they'd returned. "General Appleby, let's start with you."

"The Israelis are holding their positions as they agreed, but if the Palestinian factions keep screwing with them, they're not going to stay put for very much longer."

"What sort of incidents?" Mary Beth Greider asked.

"Mostly suicide bombers, but there's been at least one incident involving a sarin gas attack."

"Still that crap that got loose out of Syria?" Walter Middleton asked.

"Afraid so. We know that they lost control of several tons of the stuff, and we've only been able to recover a fraction of it."

"Anything else?"

"On the domestic front, the navy and coast guard have delivered one million, seventy thousand bodies to the Alaskan facility."

"Don't take this wrong, but weren't we expecting a much larger number?" Timothy Gather asked.

"Thank God for that," President Garcia said. "But Timothy's right, I believe the initial estimates were in excess of two million. Why were we off that badly?"

"I'm not sure we were," General Appleby said. "You're forgetting that we haven't entered the Mount Hood/Portland quarantine area. Portland alone could account for another five- to six hundred thousand people, not to mention the population in the areas between the volcano and the city."

They were all aware of the projections, but no one said a word as the enormity of the disaster hit home.

"I hope none of you mind, but I'd like to lead us in a short prayer for everyone we've lost," President Garcia said.

"General, please continue," President Garcia said when he'd finished.

"That's it for me."

"OK, we're running a little behind, so we'll let FEMA go next, so he can catch his flight."

"Now that the recovery phase is complete, we're moving into the reconstruction phase. We'd been seeing an escalation of looting, but with the recent addition of the NATO troops, we should have the situation back under control by the end of the month. We've finalized all the contracts for the roadway and bridge reconstruction projects, however we're projecting that it's going to take at least ten years to complete the efforts."

"I guess we won't have to worry about there being enough construction jobs for a few years," Vice President DeMarco said.

"We'll finalize the contracts for airport and air traffic control upgrades by the end of the month. The air traffic control portion will be complete by the end of next year. We'll have some of the less damaged airports back online by next year, but the ones near the coast could take another three years."

"How about health care?" General Appleby asked.

"It's not a pretty story. We're still experiencing a severe shortage of trained medical staff, but the French, Canadian, and British governments have sent us every military doctor and corpsman they could spare. The hospital reconstruction projects are projected to run for up to five years."

"That's a long time," Vice President DeMarco said.

"It is, but the housing situation is even more problematic. The scale of the disaster has overwhelmed the resources of the insurance companies, and it could take decades to rebuild."

"Screw that," President Garcia said. "We're not going to let money get in the way. We've been helping out the rest of the world for years, it's about time for some payback. Colonel, I need you to get Ambassador Hatch on the teleconference."

"Mr. President, what can I do for you today?" Larry Hatch asked.

"We need a shitload of money to rebuild the country, and I want you to work with Paul-Henri Archambault to get the UN member nations to step up and help us out. Do you think you can pull that off?"

"Who knows with the UN, but I do know that for a change, there's a lot of sympathy for what we're going through."

"Good to hear. Before we let you go, what's the Security Council's temperature on the Iranian situation?"

"Paul-Henri and I discussed that yesterday. He'd like to bring it to a conclusion, but he understands our need to hold off. He's asked that we maintain the no-fly zone until we're ready to reengage."

"I'll agree to do that if he can help us bring in some cash."

"That's a great ploy, I'll use it."

"Great, let me know if I can help."

* * *

"What can Treasury do for us, Mr. Middleton?"

"That's a question better posed to our congressional partners."

"Partners? If only that were true," President Garcia said. "Tom, I want you to take the lead on this. See what you can get out of Shelby Cohen—and I forget, who's in line to take Miller's position?"

"That would be Senator Harry Bullard. He's a dear friend, and if anyone can do it, it will be him."

"Great, get to it," President Garcia said. "Mary Beth, you're up."

"As director of Homeland Security, I feel like we should rename it to insecurity. The incident with your family was just one of ten different attacks we've suffered in the last week. Every time we think we've got a solid lead they adapt and disappear."

"Is there anything else we should be doing?" President Garcia asked.

"The FBI director and I are convinced that you need to impose the martial law decree nationwide."

"Whoa, that's a bit extreme," Paul Boothby said.

"I'll take it under consideration," President Garcia said. "Let's move on."

"Please give it some thought before you turn me down," Mary Beth Greider said.

"I will, now please continue."

"We've also seen a huge surge in illegal border crossings."

"Why now?" William Daugherty asked.

"It's become obvious that we're out of resources, and they see it as an opportunity to enter the country. Personally, I think most of it is being driven by the new immigration policies, and the damned wetbacks are taking advantage of the situation," Harold Crowe said.

Everyone in the room expected the president to take

the secretary of Energy to task for his comment, but he ignored him. "It will be several months before we can free up the National Guard units to beef up the patrols, so I'll have the air force station another hundred drones along the borders. I don't want them firing on anyone, but it will let us be more effective with the interdiction efforts," President Garcia said. "Continue, Mary Beth."

"We've finally identified the source of the nuclear material in the Maine incident."

"Finally. Where did it come from?" President Garcia asked.

"Pantex."

"The storage facility in Texas?" Roger Heinrich asked.

"The same. We're now certain the material came from a shipment of Soviet-era weapons they decommissioned in the early nineties."

"I thought that facility had an impeccable security reputation," Harold Crowe said.

"It did, but when we audited the facility, we found over fifty discrepancies that amounted to almost a ton of missing plutonium."

"Any leads on who, or how it's being done?" President Garcia asked.

"The chief of security has disappeared, along with most of his staff. We've interrogated every employee and contractor that's worked there in the last two years, but so far we've got nothing."

The room fell silent for a few seconds, before multiple people started firing questions at Mary Beth.

"Hold on, one at a time," President Garcia said. "She's already told us that she has no idea how it happened, so unless you've got something else you need to ask, just let it go. Mary Beth, is there anything you need to continue your investigation?"

"Any help would be appreciated, but if we're ever going to get to the bottom of it, the intelligence community will have to do it, because I've exhausted my resources."

"You heard the lady. Mr. Heinrich, Mrs. Grissom, and Mr. Burns, the balls are in your court, and I expect each one of you to do whatever it takes to ferret out the perpetrators. Anything else?"

"No, I think that's plenty for today."

They spent the rest of the afternoon on lesser issues, but the president couldn't get Mary Beth's report off of his mind. When they were wrapping up, he said, "I need General Appleby, Vice President DeMarco, and Attorney General Daugherty for a few more minutes, but the rest of you can get back to work. Colonel Wilhelm, you can stay as well," President Garcia said.

"Tom, what are your thoughts on Mary Beth's recommendation to expand martial law?" President Garcia asked.

"I'm for it, if Chief Justice Avery and William give it their blessings," Vice President DeMarco said.

"Given the circumstances, I don't see any issues with it," Attorney General William Daugherty said.

"General?"

"I'm fine with it in concept, but we're already dangerously overextended. What kind of effort are you going to want?"

"Curfew enforcement, more checkpoints, and we still haven't locked down the borders," President Garcia said.

"Don't I know it," General Appleby said. "I can already tell you that I don't have enough manpower to seal off that many miles of border."

"What about drones?" Vice President DeMarco asked.

"If I used all of our reserves I could probably monitor them, but I still wouldn't have the manpower to respond."

"I realize I just said it was off the table, but what if I authorized you to use them for lethal force?" President Garcia asked.

"Maybe, but is that even legal?"

"William?"

"A qualified yes, but we'll need to give the proper warnings and notifications. It would undoubtedly stir up a buttload of criticism, but there are many countries that already take that sort of action."

"Good enough for me," President Garcia said. "William, coordinate with the chief justice and General Appleby on the timing, but I'd like to put this in place as quickly as possible. Colonel, have we located Special Agent Collie yet?"

"No, sir, but they did find Special Agent Stubbs."

"Is he alright?"

"He's alive, but he's in rough shape."

"Where is he now?"

"They've taken him to Walter Reed."

"When he's up to it I need to talk with him," President Garcia said. "I'm sorry, gentlemen, I feel like shit again, and unless one of you has something else, I'd like to call it a day."

CHAPTER 36

As the days passed, Victor was pleased with Melinda's progress.

"This is a grand breakfast," Father Mendoza said. "I'm used to eating a cup of microwave oatmeal."

"There are some perks that come with the job," Victor said.

"And burdens," Melinda said.

"I'm so sorry, dear, I didn't mean to sound so cavalier."

"Oh, you're fine. I'm never going to stop missing them, but I know they're in good hands. It's just that I can see the toll this is taking on you, and I've got to wonder if it's worth the price."

"Unfortunately, the price of freedom is often paid in blood. I've spent most of my life trying to defend this country, and even if it results in my death, I'll never stop believing it's worth the sacrifices. Sorry if I got a little preachy."

"I can relate," Father Mendoza said.

"Sorry to abandon great company, but I've got work to do," Victor said. "Anything you need before I take off?"

"We'll be fine, dear. We're going to work on the plans for the kids' headstones. I meant to ask last night: is tomorrow going to be alright for their memorial service?"

"Yes, unless something catastrophic happens."

"Good. I don't suppose you have any idea when we'll be able to bury their ashes?" Melinda asked.

"Son of a bitch," Chris screamed. Insane with pain and anger, he pulled the president to his feet and snapped his neck.

"Oh shit, what have I done?" Chris said as he dropped President Montblanc's lifeless body.

I'm in deep shit now, he thought to himself. *I've got to get the hell out of here before they get back.* As he turned to leave, he heard Deborah whimpering on the floor.

Hell, they're going to track me down and kill me anyway, I might as well get one last piece of ass.

"I'm going to show you how a real man does it," he said as he picked Deborah up and threw her on the couch. He ripped her dress off, and said, "Damn, girl, you look even better in person."

He tore her bra and panties off, and pulled his pants down.

"Please don't," she said.

He raped her for almost thirty minutes, and when he was done he said, "Sorry about this, you really were a good piece of ass."

After he'd choked her to death, he pulled his pants up and hurried away.

When Richard Ellis and Larry Roberts finally got back from town, Richard asked, "What the hell is that door doing open?"

When he saw the carnage in the Montblancs' room, all he could say was, "Oh my God, no."

Larry heard his cry and came running in. "Shit, the crazy bastard has killed them both."

"I've told you never to call me on an open line," Jonathan said.

"They're dead," Richard Ellis said.

"Who's dead, you halfwit?"

"President Montblanc and his wife."

"You incompetent bastard. What the hell happened?"

"We'd gone to town for supplies, and when we returned they were dead and Collins was missing."

"I warned you about him, but none of that matters now. Make sure the bodies aren't found, and then you and your team need to get back here ASAP."

"I'll take care of it."

"What did he have to say?" Larry Roberts asked.

"We need to dispose of the bodies, and then we'll burn this place to the ground."

"What then?"

"I know how they handle loose ends, so we're going to disappear, and hope they never find us."

It was four in the morning when her satellite phone rang. *Shit, this can't be good,* Fredericka thought to herself. "What now?" she asked.

"The president and his wife are dead," Jonathan said.

"How?"

"One of the sociopaths on Ellis's team went rogue. I've had them dispose of the bodies, and I'll have someone take care of Ellis and his men, but this screws up everything. I'm going to have to think about our next moves, so I'll give you a call in a few days."

"I can do that, but stay out of the booze, and don't go in their rooms while we're gone."

"Sure, boss, whatever you say."

As soon as they'd left, Chris went to his footlocker and got his crack pipe and a bottle of Jack Daniel's he'd hidden there. "Ah, that's better," he said as he took a long drag off the pipe. He'd been saving all the latest video of Deborah's activities, particularly the ones where she was naked. So once he was good and wasted, he spent several hours watching her. They usually turned the lights off before they made love, but he'd managed to get a couple scenes of Peter doing her.

By then he was getting really horny, but after way too much booze and crack, he passed out for a couple of hours.

Their trip to town had taken longer than they'd planned, and Richard was getting worried about what Chris could be up to. Trying to make up time, he was driving too fast, and when he swerved to miss a deer, the truck slid off the road into the ditch.

"Damn it, the tire's flat," he said when he got out to survey the damage. As they began changing the flat, Richard said, "I sure hope Chris did as I asked. That crazy bastard gets even more unstable when he gets drunk or high."

"I'm sure he's alright," Larry Roberts said.

When Chris came to, he looked at his watch, and thought to himself, *Damn, it's getting late, they should've been back by now.* He hadn't eaten all day, and he was starting to get a migraine, so he went to the kitchen to fix something to eat. *Hell, I don't want to have to screw with this later, I'll just feed them while I'm here,* he thought to himself. After he'd warmed up their meals, Chris opened the door, and pushed the meal cart inside.

"Are you people ever going to tell us what you want?" President Montblanc asked.

By then Chris's head hurt so badly he thought it might explode, and he didn't feel like listening to the president's crap.

"You low-life piece of shit, I'm talking to you," President Montblanc said.

You'd better watch your mouth, little man, Chris thought to himself. He put their trays on the table and turned to leave. Deborah was sitting on the couch, and despite his pounding head, he was still horny from watching the video. *Damn, I sure would like to have some of that,* Chris thought to himself.

"Hey, darlin', how about I take you out of here, and show you how a real man bangs that pretty little ass of yours," he said.

Shocked to hear him speaking English, and with a Southern drawl, President Montblanc said, "Watch your foul mouth, you sick bastard, and since when do you speak English?"

"Piss off, old man. Come here, you little bitch," Chris said as he grabbed Deborah by the hair and pulled her off the couch.

"Take your hands off of her," President Montblanc said as he slammed his fist into Chris's jaw.

"You little shit," Chris said as he tossed Deborah to one side. "I'm going to teach you some manners. Then I'm going to make you watch while I bang your old lady like a drum."

The president wouldn't have stood a chance against Chris sober, but he was still half stoned, so the fight went on for several seconds. President Montblanc knew he was overmatched, but he managed to hold his own until Chris pinned him down. Desperate, the president tried to gouge out Chris's right eye.

"I'm so sorry, but it's going to be a while yet."

"I understand, and that part's not that important. Once we get them back, we can keep their urns with us until we can put them beside Mom and Dad."

When the president reached the situation room he was surprised to see that Special Agent Stubbs was waiting to talk with him.

"It's good to see you up and about," President Garcia said.

"Thank you, sir. The doctors wanted to keep me another day, but I just had to tell you this news in person. Homeland captured Special Agent Collie last night in Miami as he was trying to board a fishing boat headed to Cuba."

"Cuba. How are they involved in all of this?"

"We don't think they are. It was just the closest country he could reach that wouldn't extradite him."

"It makes me sick to my stomach that we've got traitors like him in our midst," President Garcia said.

"No doubt about that, but he's going to wish he was never born by the time we're finished with him."

"As much as I want to choke the life out of him with my bare hands, I don't want us bending any laws for the sake of revenge," President Garcia said.

"No worry there. We've already cleared our interrogation protocols with Chief Justice Avery."

"I realize it's an irregular request, but I'd like to spend a few moments with him before they transport him," President Garcia said.

"Shouldn't be a problem. We've already transferred him to a holding cell at Andrews, and he's not due to leave for Guantanamo until twenty-one hundred hours."

"Avery okayed that?"

"In a heartbeat. His exact words were, 'There's never been a clearer case for treating a U.S. citizen as an enemy combatant.' Excuse me for a moment, and I'll make the arrangements.

"Done. He'll be here at eleven thirty," Special Agent Stubbs said.

"Thanks," President Garcia said. "How did they manage to take you prisoner?"

"Unfortunately I don't remember a great deal. I was getting out of my car in the parking garage at my apartment building. I'd just locked the car door, and as I turned to leave, I felt a sharp sting in my neck. I remember pulling the dart out of my neck, but it paralyzed me within seconds, and I passed out shortly after I hit the floor."

"So they tortured you for information?"

"I have no idea how I got so beat up. They must have kicked the shit out of me for the pure hell of it, because I don't remember anyone asking me anything."

"I wonder why they didn't just kill you," President Garcia said.

"Not a clue, but if Collie knows anything, I promise you we'll get it out of him."

They continued talking for a few more minutes before the president said, "I need to make a few calls. There's an empty room down the hall. Why don't you get some rest until Collie gets here?"

"General Appleby needs a moment of your time," Colonel Wilhelm said.

"Sure, send him in," President Garcia said.

"If it's alright I'd like to conference in the vice president," General Appleby said.

"You feeling any better?" Vice President DeMarco asked.

"In body, but I've got to admit that I may never get over them murdering my children," President Garcia said.

"Nor should you," General Appleby said.

"Enough of that," President Garcia said. "What are you two plotting?"

"We'd like to give you an update on the border security issue," Vice President DeMarco said. "We had to use every available drone, but we've managed to cover the zones that have the highest level of activity."

"That's good, but how about the rest of it?"

"Once we've retrieved the surplus drones from our overseas commands, we'll be able to cover approximately ninety-five percent of the border. In the interim, we're going to reposition surveillance satellites to cover the open areas, and we'll use the state police units to respond to any threat we detect."

"That sounds pretty convoluted," President Garcia said.

"It's not a perfect solution, but it's a hell of a lot better than it was," Vice President DeMarco said.

"Absolutely, and General Atomics, Boeing, and Northrop Grumman have already agreed to ramp up their production to deliver the rest of the drones we need," General Appleby said.

"Any pushback yet?" President Garcia asked.

"A ton. There are three bills in Congress right now to shut the programs down, but none of them have enough votes to survive a veto from you," Vice President DeMarco said.

"Anything more on the Pantex situation?" President Garcia asked.

"We've identified the lots, and the approximate dates the materials were removed from the facility, but not who did it," General Appleby said.

"Damn. What have we done to prevent another occurrence?"

"Since they're not actively decommissioning anything, I've had them seal the facility and furlough the workers," Vice President DeMarco said.

"Extreme, but it should give us some time to complete the investigation," President Garcia said. "I need to give you a heads-up on something. Later today, I'm going to be meeting with Special Agent Collie."

"They caught the bastard?" General Appleby asked.

"Last night in Miami."

"Too bad they didn't just kill the sorry piece of shit," Vice President DeMarco said.

"Trust me, I'd gladly do it myself," President Garcia said. "But I'm glad they didn't. They'll be transferring him to Guantanamo for interrogation after I meet with him, and we need information worse than we need another dead body. Collie will be here at eleven thirty, and you're welcome to sit in."

"I'll pass," General Appleby said. "I'm not sure I could control myself. I've got to ask, why would you put yourself through seeing him?"

"I want to look him in the eye and ask him why he did it," President Garcia said.

"You can't believe he'll answer you?" Vice President DeMarco asked.

"Not really, but I've got to ask."

"If you really don't mind, I would like to be there when you ask him," General Appleby said.

"I wouldn't have offered if I minded."

After Vice President DeMarco dropped off, they spent some time discussing what they wanted to accomplish in the coming months.

"Mr. President, sorry to interrupt, but they're about to bring Collie down," Colonel Wilhelm said. "Where would you like to hold your meeting?"

"Here's fine."

They were used to seeing him in a suit, and they almost didn't recognize him when they brought him in and handcuffed him to one of the chairs. He was dressed in a T-shirt, and cutoffs, and he looked and smelled like he hadn't bathed since he'd gone on the run. He was seated at the far end of the massive conference table, so they got up and walked down to him.

President Garcia was studying his face for a clue of what he was thinking, but General Appleby jumped right in. "You're a sorry piece of shit," General Appleby said.

"Sticks and stones," Mr. Collie said.

"We'll see how glib you are after a few days at Gitmo," President Garcia said.

"You can't do that. I'm an American citizen, and I have rights."

"You forfeited those when you turned terrorist," President Garcia said. "Not that I really care, but why in God's name would you betray our country?"

"Our country? You and your people have taken over my country, and we're going to take it back."

"So, you're nothing more than a petty bigot, trying to justify your actions through some misguided sense of patriotism," General Appleby said.

"Bigot? Maybe, but don't accuse me of not being a patriot."

"Patriots don't murder children," President Garcia said.

"It wasn't our intent to harm your family, but collateral damage happens."

"You sick bastard," President Garcia said. "You keep saying 'we,' who else is in this with you?"

"Like I'd tell you. But I will tell you this. This country has lost its way, and once we've gotten all of you and your kind cleared out, we can get back to standing with our friends and allies to stamp out the Arabs that are trying to impose their way of life on the rest of the world."

"I've heard enough of this bullshit," President Garcia said. "Get this sorry piece of shit out of here."

Special Agent Stubbs was waiting in the hall when they brought Mr. Collie out.

"So you survived," Mr. Collie said.

"No thanks to you," Special Agent Stubbs said. "We've

got a really nice room all prepared for you, and Mr. Strauss is going to show you a really good time."

In spite of himself, Mr. Collie felt a cold chill come over him. Leonard Strauss had been practicing his craft for decades, and was legendary for his ability to inflict horrific pain without actually killing the subject. He'd been the one that had broken Osama bin Laden's replacement when they'd captured him in Saudi Arabia the previous year.

"I'll never talk," Mr. Collie said.

"More power to you, but at the very least you'll suffer before you die, and I hope you burn in hell for all eternity for what you've done."

"What a piece of shit," General Appleby said.

"I don't disagree, but I sensed he was being honest with us," President Garcia said. "He really believes in what he's doing."

"Unfortunately, I think you're right. What do you think he meant by working with their allies to rid the world of the Arab threat?"

"No way to know, but the sad thing is that we're not that far apart in that belief," President Garcia said. "We're about to launch an all-out attack on the Iranians if they didn't bend to our will. Speaking of attacks, have we heard anything out of the UN Security Council, or Secretary General Archambault?"

"No, but I was going to call Paul-Henri this afternoon," Vice President DeMarco said. "I don't suppose you've heard anything else out of Prime Minister Weizmann?"

"No I haven't, and that can't be good. Colonel, would you get Roger Heinrich for us?"

"What can the NSA do for you today?"

"What have the Israelis been up to lately?" President Garcia asked.

"No good, as usual. They've made six incursions in the last twenty-four hours alone, two in the Gaza Strip and four into Jordan. They must think something is going on in Petra, because they keep sending sapper teams in to blow up shit."

"I don't remember anything of significance in Petra," General Appleby said.

"There's not, as far as we know, but they seem to have a hard-on for something there. So why all the interest in them?"

"I'm going to give the prime minister a call, and I wanted to see if there was anything specific I needed to get on his ass for," President Garcia said.

"Not that they don't deserve the ass eating, but they've been relatively good, for them."

"Before we let you go, have you made any progress on our other little project?"

"Yes and no. Senator Miller was definitely dirty, but I haven't tracked his actions back to anyone else yet. I've put out ten more pieces of bait; maybe we'll get someone to take the hook."

"Keep us posted."

"This is taking too long," General Appleby said.

"I agree, but what else can we do?" President Garcia asked.

"If it's alright with you, I've got a couple of things I'd like to try."

"What did you have in mind?"

"I'd rather not tell you. That way you can have plausible deniability if it goes to hell."

"Have it your way."

CHAPTER 37

When the alarm went off at four thirty, President Garcia muttered groggily, "Damn, that was quick." He gently slid the covers back so he could sit up, and swung his legs over the side of the bed. He used the cane he kept beside the bed to pull the cart closer so he could retrieve his prosthetics. The nurse had left a tube of the salve on the cart, so he doctored his sores before he slid the stockings over his stumps. His left leg was getting better, but it still ached when he first put on the artificial limb. He gave it one final adjustment before he steeled himself against the pain and slid off the bed. He saw that Melinda was curled up in a ball from the chill of the air conditioner. He pulled the blanket up to cover her and gave her a gentle kiss before he went to get dressed.

"You're up and about pretty early," President Garcia said when he walked into the room where they ate.

"You're one to talk," Margaret Webster said.

"Have you and Larry gotten settled in alright?"

"It's quite a change from the observatory, but we're doing fine. What would you like for breakfast?"

"Have you got any more of those sweet rolls?"

"I made a fresh batch last night. Would you like some coffee while I warm them up?"

"Yes, please."

"Here you go. Anything else you'd like?"

"A little conversation, if you have the time," President Garcia said.

"Like I wouldn't have time for the president of the United States," she said with a chuckle.

"You spend a lot more time with Melinda than I get to. How's she doing?"

"It's funny, I'd expected her to mope around, but she's managed to put the kids' deaths in perspective. Thank the lord I've never had to go through it, because I don't know if I could get over it."

"I hope it's not just an act to help me cope, but I know that she's convinced, as I am, that they are in a better place, and that her mom is there with them."

"She's told me that very thing, and you're right, there's no doubt in her mind."

"Thanks, Margaret, that helps."

"Good morning, Colonel," President Garcia said when he entered the briefing center. Special Agent Stubbs had convinced him to not work upstairs until they'd come up with a plan to secure the grounds, so he was using the briefing center as his office.

"Good morning, Mr. President," Colonel Wilhelm said. "How about a cup of coffee? I just made a fresh pot."

"Sure. What have we got this morning?"

"We have just received word that the aircraft ferrying Special Agent Collie to Guantanamo has gone down in the Gulf."

"What the hell happened?" President Garcia asked. "And why am I just now hearing about it?"

"Guantanamo dropped the ball and didn't report them missing until early this morning."

"Collie?"

"They're sweeping the route they should have been on, but so far no trace of the aircraft."

"That's the shits. We just got our hands on the sorry bastard. You make damn sure everyone knows to let us know if they find something."

"Yes, sir."

"Other than that little piece of good news, what else have we got?"

"I think you've got sit-reps from everyone in the world. They must've all been worried that you'd forgotten them, because your in-box was full this morning."

"Let's get to it."

Most of the reports contained the normal updates, but when he got to Margret Grissom's report, he couldn't open the attachment. "Colonel, would you mind helping me with this report from the CIA? I can't get it to open," President Garcia said.

"Sure, let me take a look. This is odd. They've never used this encryption algorithm on a status report. Give me just a minute to pull the key down off the server.

"There you go, it should open up now," Colonel Wilhelm said.

When the president opened the attachment, it contained a folder of pictures and a short note.

"*Until you give me instructions on how you want to handle the situation, I'm treating this as for your eyes only,*" Margret's note read.

He opened the folder marked crash scene photos, and a slide show popped up. The photos were from a crash site in Colombia, and as they slowly scrolled across the screen, they were accompanied by a verbal explanation of what he was viewing.

"This is a photo of what's left of the main fuselage to the Antonov they used to transport President Montblanc and his wife out of Egypt. It was flying down a valley, on its way to a runway that's normally used by one of the local drug lords, when it exploded in midair."

He stared at the photos of the crash for several minutes until he moved on to the next set.

"This is what's left of the crew and passengers. As you can see, the bodies are for the most part unrecognizable without using forensics, but according to the data we captured, the team that worked the site had verified that the president and his wife weren't among the victims."

He let the slide show run to the end and said, "Colonel, I need to see Director Grissom as soon as she's available."

"I wondered what was up. They've just cleared her, and she's on her way down."

"Margret, it's good to see you, but where the hell did you get these?"

"That's why I've come. We got a tip that a Colombian drug lord had just come into an extraordinary sum of money, so I sent a team down to check into what was going on."

"The CIA generally doesn't concern themselves with drug lords."

"This was a little different. The tip came from a Colombian intelligence officer we turned a few years ago, and he was adamant that we needed to look into it. He wouldn't give us anything specific, because he was scared to death it would be traced back to him.

"When our team got there, they got into a firefight with a group of unidentified foreign operatives. Unfortunately they were all killed, but we did manage to retrieve a jump drive that contained the photos you just viewed, along with the results of their forensic testing. They'd destroyed all of the physical evidence, so all we have are the photos and the DNA analysis they carried out on the body parts they'd recovered."

"Colombia? Why would they take them to Colombia?" President Garcia asked.

"That's just it, we're not sure they were ever there. They

must have dropped them off somewhere else. Other than verifying the attack was carried out by a Colonel Tavaazo and a group of Takavar deserters, we're not one damn bit closer to finding President Montblanc."

"You were right to keep this quiet. If we actually knew anything, we'd go public with it, but this is going to raise more questions than it answers. Did I understand you correctly? This Colonel Tavaazo and his men were deserters?"

"Correct. They bugged out last year, and had put out feelers that they were for hire."

"This just gets more bizarre. Let me know if you find anything else."

When she was gone, President Garcia said, "Colonel, I need to talk with General Appleby and Vice President DeMarco."

"Sorry, I'm late, traffic was awful this morning," General Appleby said. "Ever since they closed off all of the streets around the White House, it's been almost complete gridlock."

"Sorry about that, but the Secret Service was adamant," President Garcia said.

"Understandable, but it's still a pain in the ass. Are we getting Tom on?"

"He's on a conference call, but he should be joining us in a few minutes. You want coffee and some breakfast?"

"Coffee would be good."

"Sorry, I needed to take that," Vice President DeMarco said when he popped up on the big screen.

"Anything important?" President Garcia asked.

"Yes. When we're done with whatever you've got for us, we need to touch base with Roger."

"It wouldn't hurt for him to hear what I've got as well, so let's go ahead and conference him in."

* * *

"Good morning, gentlemen," said Roger Heinrich, the director of the NSA.

"I've just finished a briefing with Director Grissom," President Garcia said.

"What's the CIA been up to?" Director Heinrich asked.

"I'll send you all the data I've got on this when were done, but they've come up with some interesting information regarding President Montblanc."

"They've found Montblanc?" General Appleby asked.

"No, but they've found the team that grabbed him and the aircraft they used at a crash site in Colombia. The Iranian commandos that carried out the attack were deserters, turned mercenaries, and they were all killed when their aircraft exploded in midair."

"Deserters? Interesting. How did they come by this information, and what about the president and his wife?" Vice President DeMarco asked.

"They retrieved the information from the team that was sanitizing the site, and if their analysis was correct, the president wasn't on board when the aircraft went down. Unfortunately none of them survived, so we couldn't interrogate them."

"So it was the Iranians?" Vice President DeMarco asked.

"I wouldn't jump to that conclusion," Director Heinrich said. "We've had reports of their desertion, and their attempts to turn mercenary."

"This doesn't make sense," General Appleby said. "They took a huge risk to abduct him, and then we don't hear a word about it."

"I'll have my analysts go back through anything that even vaguely refers to them," Director Heinrich said.

"Good. Tom, I believe you had something that the group needed to hear," President Garcia said.

"In the last forty-eight hours we've seen several large

money transfers, and there's been a sharp spike in encrypted traffic on an anonymous proxy server that we monitor."

"OK, you're going to have to dumb that down for me," President Garcia said.

"The proxy server is used to mask the identity of the sender, and the message traffic is using an encryption algorithm that we haven't seen in years, one that we've never been able to decrypt. The money was wired to a series of front companies and was withdrawn in cash within minutes. We've pulled all of the video from the banks, but they used homeless people they'd dressed up to look like executives to withdraw the funds, and none of them had a clue about who had hired them," explained Director Heinrich.

"Some sort of money laundering scheme?" Vice President DeMarco asked.

"If that's all it was, there are much simpler techniques they could have used."

"Didn't we institute a mandatory protocol to the banks last year to address this sort of thing?" Vice President DeMarco asked.

"Good memory," Director Heinrich said. "Every financial institution is required to record the serial numbers of every bill in a cash withdrawal of over a hundred thousand dollars."

"What good does that do?" General Appleby asked.

"Every bank is scanning large cash deposits to record the serial numbers. It won't do much good if they just spend the money, but if they deposit it, we'll be able to trace it."

"I don't see why any of this is relevant," President Garcia said.

"It may be nothing, but I don't believe in coincidences."

"You're the spook, but I'm not going to worry about this until you can tie it back to something," President Garcia said. "Speaking of that, have you had any bites yet?"

"Possibly. We've intercepted a series of transmissions that contained several pieces of the information I'd put out there."

"You mean you got multiple hits?" President Garcia asked.

"Four, to be exact, but we weren't able to pinpoint the final destination, because they were using malware to IP skip the transmission all over the Middle East."

"Damned Iranians," General Appleby said. "We should put the hammer down on them."

"Again, I wouldn't jump to that conclusion," Director Heinrich said. "Someone has gone to extraordinary lengths to make it look like them, but I'm beginning to doubt they've been behind any of it."

"OK, I get it. You have doubts, but how about the assholes that passed the information along?" Vice President DeMarco said.

"I'm not ready to declare them traitors, but all of this tracks back to highly placed, well-thought-of members of the House of Representatives."

"Names?" President Garcia asked.

"Terry Griffin, John Chandler, Barry Lauder, and Elisabeth James."

"They're all members of the House Committee on Foreign Affairs, and Lauder is the chair," Vice President DeMarco said. "I've worked with every one of them, at one time or another, when I was secretary of state, and I can't believe any of them would betray this country."

"I understand, but there's a clear trail back to each one of them," Director Heinrich said. "Who knows why people do things, but let me dig a little deeper before we accuse them of anything."

"Gentlemen, we knew we might not like what we found when we started this, but we've got to let the evidence guide our decisions, not emotions. I'll give you another few days, but then we need to address the issue," President Garcia said. "I've got another appointment with the doctor in ten minutes, so if you don't have anything else, we'll conclude for the day."

CHAPTER 38

Three days after Director Heinrich had made his initial accusations, he called the president with an update.

"Good afternoon, Director Heinrich," President Garcia said.

"I'm afraid this call may ruin your day," Director Heinrich said.

"How so?"

"I've got final verification of the traitor's actions."

"Damn, I was hoping you'd made a mistake. Oh, well, they made their decisions, and now I've got to make mine."

"If you don't mind me asking, what are you going to do?"

"I'm going to have Homeland pick them up, but I think I'll give Shelby a heads-up before I do," President Garcia said.

"I wouldn't if it were me. Before you drop off, I've got one other piece of news for you."

"Good, I hope."

"Not so much. I'm reasonably sure Steven Bergmann, Timothy Gather's right-hand man, is in on it."

"Oh, hell. Timothy thinks of him almost like a son. I'm going to have to think about this a little more before I pull the trigger."

"Your call, but I wouldn't wait very long, because I'm afraid I may have a leak inside my organization as well."

"I never asked, but how many people know about this little task we have you working on?" President Garcia asked.

"Just two, besides me. Jamie Johnson and Robert Taylor. They've worked for me for years, and I'd trust them with my life."

"You've trusted them with all of our lives, but if you trust them, that's good enough for me."

President Garcia took a few seconds to get his thoughts organized before he called Colonel Wilhelm back in.

"Colonel, have we gotten any updates on the search for Agent Collie?"

"Yes, sir. They've called off the search."

"How the hell does an aircraft just disappear with all the technology we have today?"

"I have no idea, but they didn't even find any debris."

"Sorry, I didn't mean to snap at you, but it's frustrating as hell. Would you mind checking to see when I can have a few moments of General Appleby's and Vice President DeMarco's time?"

"They're on a video conference, but it's scheduled to end in about ten minutes."

"Good afternoon, gentlemen. I'd like to discuss a call I just had with Mr. Heinrich."

"That usually doesn't mean good news," General Appleby said.

"And I'm afraid it doesn't this time either," President Garcia said. "He called to let me know he was highly confident that the representatives are indeed working against us."

"I'm not surprised, after what he'd shared last time," Vice President DeMarco said.

"No, me neither," President Garcia said. "However, he'd come up with another name since our last conversation. He now believes Steven Bergmann may be involved as well."

"Gather's son?" General Appleby asked.

"Actually he's not his son, but he does treat him like a member of the family."

"You can't think Timothy's involved," Vice President DeMarco said.

"No, of course not, and Director Heinrich's not a hundred percent on Steven yet."

"Shit, it just keeps getting worse," Vice President DeMarco said. "You don't know who you can trust anymore."

"In this town, I'm pretty sure that's always been true," President Garcia said. "I was considering giving Shelby a heads-up before I move against them. What do you two think?"

"I wouldn't do it," General Appleby said. "The bitch sure hasn't cut you any slack."

"True, but I still need her support."

"I don't see any reason not to, unless you doubt her as well," Vice President DeMarco said.

"I've definitely got my issues with her, but I doubt she'd risk her career over this," President Garcia said. "This does verify my worst fear, that we, or at least I, have enemies within the organization."

"I'm not naive enough to think that many of them aren't true bigots, but I doubt this is personal," General Appleby said.

"Actually I'd be happy if it were personal, otherwise it means they're trying to destroy our nation from within, and I simply won't tolerate that," President Garcia said. "Gentlemen, thank you for your time. I'm going to give Homeland a heads-up, before I call Shelby."

* * *

General Appleby returned to the other conference room to get on his next call with Vice President DeMarco. "Damn, I'd sure as hell hate to have to make that call," General Appleby said.

"For sure. Shelby's a bitch on her good days," Vice President DeMarco said. "I had a lot of doubts about the president when he took over, but he's a stand-up kind of a guy."

"I never doubted that. He's a marine, and a damned good one by the looks of his service jacket."

After President Garcia had made his call to Secretary Greider to arrange for conspirators' arrests, he took a moment to reflect on what he wanted to say before he dialed the Speaker's number.

"President Garcia, what can I do for you this fine afternoon?" Shelby Cohen asked.

"I'm afraid I've got some disturbing news that I need to brief you on. At approximately sixteen thirty today, agents from Homeland Security will be arresting Terry Griffin, John Chandler, Barry Lauder, and Elisabeth James," President Garcia said.

"You spic bastard, I'll have your ass if they do."

He hadn't been expecting a diatribe, but he managed to say, "I'm sorry, but we are, and you need to calm down."

"What kind of trumped-up bullshit are you trying to pull now?"

"I've received verification that they've been passing classified information to our enemies, so this isn't negotiable. I simply wanted to give you a heads-up before we arrested them."

As much as she hated his kind, she couldn't believe she'd spouted off like that. "Mr. President, I'm terribly sorry for running off at the mouth like that. It's just that I've known, and worked with them for years, and I can't believe any of them would do anything to harm this country. However, you'd better have your ducks in a row, or I'm going to come after you with the full weight of the House."

Some apology, he thought to himself. "I assure you I wouldn't have taken this extreme action if I weren't completely sure of the facts. I'll give you a call in the next day or two to discuss this further." he said.

Colonel Wilhelm had been sitting halfway across the briefing center, but he'd heard Shelby Cohen's rant. When the president got off the call, he got up, and walked over to him. "Is there anything I can do for you, sir?"

"No, thanks, but it seems I don't have many fans in this town," President Garcia said. "On second thought, would you mind getting Director Heinrich for me?"

"Who crapped in your Post Toasties?" Director Heinrich said when he saw the president's expression.

"That obvious? I just got off a call with Shelby Cohen."

"Didn't take the news very well?"

"Hardly, she called me a spic bastard."

"Sorry, I shouldn't have giggled, but you've got to admit, for a broad, she has balls."

"Brass ones for sure, but that's not why I called. Homeland will be picking them up in a little over an hour. They're going to take them to the detention center at Edwards for processing, and I'd like to get your recommendation on who should do the initial interrogations."

"I'd like to say Leonard Strauss, but his methods might be a little extreme to use on elected officials, at least for now. I've got a guy I'll send over. His name is William Steward, and he spent the last three years interrogating Taliban prisoners."

"We can't have him torturing anyone," President Garcia said.

"Understood. That's not his style; this guy is the best I've ever seen at getting inside someone's head. He speaks like a bazillion languages, and he's the smartest son of a bitch I've ever been around. If he can't get them to open up, no one can."

"Sounds good. They may not have them in place until sometime tonight, so why don't you have him show up first thing in the morning."

"Will do."

President Garcia spent the rest of the afternoon working through the never-ending list of issues that came in every day. Mary Beth had promised to call him as soon as they were done, but when he hadn't heard anything by 1800, he decided to see what was going on.

"Sorry I haven't called you," Mary Beth Greider said. "When my agents got there, they'd all left for the day, and we haven't been able to locate any of them yet."

"Where the hell did they go?"

"We've already been to their residences, but no one seems to know where they are. I've flagged them in the no-fly lists, and put out all points bulletins to the locals, but nothing yet. Someone had to have tipped them off."

"Bitch," the president muttered.

"Were you talking to me?" she asked.

"No, sorry about that. I'd given Shelby Cohen a heads-up, and she must have warned them."

"Loose lips, as the old saying goes."

"It seems that I should have listened to General Appleby. Sorry I screwed us up, but stay after them."

"If they're still in the country, we'll find their sorry asses."

When they finished, he called Roger Heinrich. "You can cancel your man," President Garcia said.

"What happened?"

"Homeland can't find them. Shelby must have tipped them off, and they made a run for it before the agents got there."

"You going after her?"

"Probably should, but it'd be my word against hers. But don't think I'll forget it."

"Don't let it get you down, because I think we're real close on the rest of the list. In fact I may have something for you in the next day or two."

"I sure hope so. I could use some positive news for a change."

"You look like you've lost your last friend in the world," Melinda said when he walked in.

"I'm not sure I ever had one, other than you," Victor said as he plopped down on the couch.

"You look exhausted," Melinda said. "I'll have them bring a couple trays, and we'll eat in here tonight."

"Good idea. How was your day?"

"As opposed to what? They won't let me out of the basement. All I can do is watch movies, TV, or read. I think I'd have gone mad by now if Father Mendoza wasn't here to talk with, although I think he's starting to get cabin fever as well."

He pulled her down into his lap and said, "I'm so sorry. I've made your life hell."

She tenderly touched his face and said, "Au contraire, my dear. My life wouldn't be worth living without you, and don't you ever dare forget it."

"But the kids, and your mom."

"Don't you dishonor them by thinking it was anything you did. As you often told us, there are bad people in the world, and someone has to stand up against them, and in this case, my dear, it's you that's drawn the short straw. God has a plan for you and me, and we're just going to have to buck up, and get 'er done. As Larry the Cable guy would say."

The president laughed and gave her a kiss. "I love you so much, and thank you for helping me get through this."

"That's the least I can do. Let's go to bed, and you can thank me properly, if you're up to it."

"If I'm ever not up to that, just shoot me."

Late that night Fredericka's satellite phone rang. She'd been anticipating the call, although she wasn't looking forward to the conversation.

"What the hell were you thinking?" Klaus asked.

"I couldn't bring myself to give the order."

"What have you done with them?"

"They're on a remote ranch in Wyoming, and no one will find them up there."

"They'd better not. How are you coming with your other assignment?"

"If we go that route, it's going to take time."

"More money?"

"Money isn't the issue. Many of them are scared to death by the lengths you've already gone to, and several of them won't back any more of your little schemes."

"Watch your mouth, bitch. You forget who you're talking to. There's nothing I won't do to ensure our survival; I thought you'd realized that by now."

Oh, I know how you are, you little shit, she thought to herself. "I do, but this has gotten out of hand, and I'd be lying if I told you that I haven't had second thoughts myself. If we don't pull this latest gambit off, I'm out as well."

"Don't make that mistake. Just get on with it. Before I forget, did you take care of that Collie issue?"

"I have."

"Excellent work for a change."

* * *

"What have you found?" Ayatollah Rostami asked.

"Nothing, absolutely nothing. In fact, the Chinese agent who tipped us off that it wasn't the Americans who fired first has gone missing," Minister Ramadani said.

"It's got to be Israel."

"I can't say you're wrong, but we have no proof. What good would it do to accuse them? The whole world knows we hate each other."

"Very true, but we've got to get them to show their hand, or the UN is going to come in here and take us out."

CHAPTER 39

The president's alarm went off at 0400. Not wanting to disturb Melinda, he gathered up his shaving kit and clothes, and walked across the hall to one of the unoccupied rooms to take his shower. When he'd finished, he considered calling the kitchen to get some breakfast, but he decided he'd get some work done before everyone got in for the day.

The night-lights in the briefing center let him make his way to his makeshift office in the rear of the room. When he opened his e-mail, he saw that Roger Heinrich had sent him a cryptic note at 0130. All the note said was that he and his two helpers had uncovered some startling new information, and he wanted to discuss it with him as soon as possible.

Colonel Wilhelm wasn't shocked when he came in and saw the president hard at work.

"Colonel, would you get with Roger Heinrich's assistant, and set up a call?" President Garcia said.

"Right away. Would you like me to have them bring your breakfast down here?" Colonel Wilhelm asked.

"Sure, and if you haven't eaten, have them bring some for you as well."

* * *

Roger's assistant wasn't in yet, so the colonel sent a meeting request. When he finished, he sat down beside the president to have breakfast. They'd almost finished, when the phone rang.

"How?" Colonel Wilhelm asked. "I'll let him know right away."

When he hung up, President Garcia asked, "What's wrong?"

"When Mr. Heinrich's assistant got in a few minutes ago, he saw that their tracking system was showing that Roger was still in an impromptu late-night meeting. When he went to check on him, he found the director and two of his men dead in the conference room."

"Does he know what happened?"

"He said there was no sign of a struggle, and no obvious cause of death."

"Jamie Johnson and Robert Taylor?" President Garcia asked.

"Why, yes. How'd you know?"

"Dear God, they're everywhere. I need to talk with General Appleby and Vice President DeMarco ASAP. Call NSA and tell them to lock down everything until I can get the FBI and Homeland over there to take over."

Vice President DeMarco had just called in, when the general arrived.

"What's up?" General Appleby asked.

"They've killed Roger Heinrich and the two men he was working with," President Garcia said.

"How, when?" Vice President DeMarco asked.

"Sometime during the night. As to how, we won't know that until they do the autopsies. If they can get to the director of the NSA in his own building, this has to go far deeper than we'd feared. General Appleby, I want you and your family down here immediately. We're on complete lockdown until we can get a handle on this."

"I don't understand how they can always be one step ahead of us," General Appleby said.

"Me neither, but I'll be dammed if they're going to beat us," President Garcia said.

"Had he shared the list of people he was vetting with you?" Vice President DeMarco asked.

"No, he didn't want to bias us against anyone unnecessarily."

"Shit. That puts us back at square one," General Appleby said.

"For the time being," President Garcia said. When he saw the general pour himself another cup of coffee, he said, "I was serious. I want your family down here before noon."

"My wife is going to pitch a bitch," General Appleby said.

"Blame it on me, but this isn't negotiable. Colonel, I'm calling a full NSC meeting for ten o'clock tomorrow morning."

"Several of them are spread out around the country," Colonel Wilhelm said.

"Do whatever is necessary, but I need each and every one of them on the premises. Except for the vice president, there can be no exceptions unless you clear it with me. Understood?"

"Crystal."

After the colonel scurried off to start making the necessary arrangements, General Appleby asked, "Do you really think that's necessary?"

"Yes. That's it for now. You need to see to your family."

Once General Appleby had left, the president placed a quick call.

"Mr. President, what can I do for you?" William Steward asked.

"First, I was terribly sorry to learn of Roger's death. I know you two were close."

"We were. I can't believe someone managed to murder them, particularly here. That means we have traitors inside our organization as well."

"Which brings me to the purpose of my call. We're holding a NSC meeting at ten A.M. tomorrow, and I need you to be here by eight."

"Whatever you need, but may I ask the purpose?"

"No, I'll fill you in when you get here. It would be better if you don't tell anyone where you're going. Why don't you just call in sick, and then come on over."

Next he called Director Greider.

"Good afternoon, Mr. President," Mary Beth Greider said.

"Damn, it is afternoon," he said as he glanced at his watch. "I know you have your best people on Mr. Heinrich's case, but I don't want anyone briefed on your findings until you clear it with me. Also, I need you to compartmentalize the investigation to as small a team as feasible. Use only people you would trust your life to."

"OK. Can I ask what you're up to?"

"I'm shocked you had to ask. It's obvious that someone has infiltrated every aspect of our society, and will use any means necessary to achieve their goals."

"Actually, I've been thinking along those same lines for some time. I just thought it was my innate paranoia coming out. The three-man team that's assigned to Roger's case are people I'd trust with anything, including my life."

"Good. I'd like you to get here by nine tomorrow. Is that going to be a problem?" President Garcia asked.

"Not at all."

When he finished his call, President Garcia called Special Agent Stubbs in.

"Please sit here beside me," President Garcia said when he arrived. "How's your health?"

"I'm getting stronger every day. The doc says I should

be back to normal in a few more weeks," Special Agent Stubbs said.

"Good to hear. Did the colonel give you a heads-up that we're going to have some more guests?"

"Yes, sir. We dispatched a team to help them get relocated as soon as we got the news. The general's family arrived just before you called. We've opened up another section to ensure they are as comfortable as we can make them."

"Good work, as always. Are you aware of the NSC meeting in the morning?"

"I am, and we're bringing in extra agents, and SEAL team eight will be onsite as well."

"Bit of overkill, isn't it?"

"Not after what happened to your family. Sorry. I shouldn't have said that."

"No, you're right."

"You have NSC meetings all the time. What's special about this one?"

"Do you happen to know William Steward?" President Garcia asked.

"I do. He and I pulled an operation with the previous administration. Why do you ask?"

"He's going to be joining my staff, and I'm going to need the three of us to work very closely for a while."

"Whatever you need."

"I'm going to be briefing him on his assignment around eight in the morning. Why don't you drop by about eight fifteen, and I'll fill you in as well."

"How was your day?" Melinda asked when he came in.

As he slowly lowered his aching body onto the couch, he said, "It was unusually tiring. I must be getting old."

"You started at four this morning. What did you expect?"

"Sorry, I tried not to wake you."

"You're fine. I've gotten to where I only sleep about a half an hour at a time. The doctor gave me some sleeping pills, but they don't seem to help."

"You should tell him."

"I will. Given what you go through every day, what was so bad today?" she asked as she curled up beside him.

After he'd shared the events of the day, she said, "Damn, that's tough. I don't think I met Roger more than a couple of times, but he seemed nice. Wasn't he the one that was helping you determine if there are any fifth columnists working against you?"

"Yes, he was. He was a stand-up guy and a true patriot. He'd already identified several highly regarded members of the House that were involved."

"Congressmen. Good lord, how much trouble is the country in?"

"It could end up being worse than the Civil War. I'm convinced Roger had ferreted out some more of them, and that's probably what got him killed. Whoever took out Roger and his men have to be NSA insiders, who are among the most scrutinized members of our intelligence community."

"That's horrific. I can't even imagine a way through what you've already found out, but I know you'll find a solution."

"Thanks, sweetie, I just wish I'd had a chance to learn my way around this wretched town before this happened."

"Listen to yourself. You've just been taking their shit. If I didn't know better, I'd say you were wanting to tuck tail and run," she scolded.

"Hell, no. We'll improvise, adapt, and overcome. A marine never quits. *Semper fi, do or die*," he said proudly.

"Now that's the man I know and love."

Completely spent, he slept through the night, but his mind never stopped racing through the various scenarios he might be facing. When he woke the next morning, he found himself strangely excited at the prospects that lay ahead. He was back in the situation room by 0430, and he and the colonel once again shared breakfast and talked.

"You're making a habit of this," Colonel Wilhelm said.

"I know, but I seem to get more done like this," President Garcia said. "I'm going to need a room with absolute privacy for a couple of my meetings today."

"No problem. I'm not sure why they built it that way, but there's a room on the level below this one, and it's electromagnetically shielded and soundproofed."

"That should do, but I thought this was the lowest level."

"No, there's a rather expansive floor below this one, and there may even be a level below that one."

"Do you have any family in the city?" President Garcia asked.

"Just my wife. We've only been married a short time, so we don't have any children yet."

The president picked up his tablet and texted Special Agent Stubbs.

"Yes, sir," Special Agent Stubbs said when he walked in.

"I want you to send a detail out to pick up Colonel Wilhelm's wife. Make sure to bring everything she needs for a protracted stay, because they're going to be staying with us for the duration."

"Am I in trouble?" Colonel Wilhelm asked.

"Not with me, but there are people working against me that might try to use your family against me, and if I can help it, no one else's family is going to suffer over this. When you've taken care of that, come back, because I need to talk with you," President Garcia said.

Twenty minutes later, Special Agent Stubbs returned.

"The colonel's wife will be here within the hour," Special Agent Stubbs said.

"Good. Have a seat. William Steward should be here in a few minutes, and I'm going to go ahead and brief you on the purpose of his visit, and what I'll be needing from you and your team."

"Yes, sir."

"Mr. Steward is an NSA operative, but his specialty is interrogation. I've arranged for a room on the level below this one for him to set up shop. While the NSC meeting is in progress, I'll from time to time send a member of the council down to visit with him."

"You're going to interrogate the members of the National Security Council?"

"Yes, I am, and if any of them don't pass muster, I'm going to put them on a plane to Guantanamo Bay, where they'll be held until I can decide what to do with them."

"Is that even legal?"

"I really don't know, and I'm sure as hell not going to get anyone's opinion on it until I know who I can trust. I know I'm placing you in a terrible situation, but as the leader of this nation, I'm faced with a no-win situation if I can't ferret out the traitors embedded throughout our government."

"What if I say no?" Special Agent Stubbs asked.

"Then I've misjudged you. I pride myself on being a good judge of men, so if I've got to stake my career, and probably my life on someone, I'm going with you."

"I'm in."

"Excellent. Don't take this wrong, but I have to ask. Is there anyone on your team you wouldn't trust your life to?"

"Actually there are two, but I'll take care of that as soon as we're done, and I know just the men to replace them with."

"Good," President Garcia said as he stood to shake Special Agent Stubbs's hand.

CHAPTER 40

After the attack on the White House, they'd cordoned off all of the streets around the compound to give them a buffer zone. Only official vehicles were allowed inside the perimeter, so everyone had to leave their vehicles at the checkpoints. Then they had to go through an inspection that made airport security look trivial. Once they passed inspection, the security team would bus them the rest of the way.

Anyone who was going to enter the lower levels was patted down, walked through a metal detector, and an explosive sniffer, before they were issued the RFID badge that would allow them to enter the elevator.

As the Security Council members were arriving for the meeting, President Garcia was sitting in a small observation room watching them file in, trying to imagine which of them wouldn't survive what was about to go down. When they were all present, he walked over across the hall to begin the meeting. They all stood as he entered.

"Please take your seats."

"I thought they were going to strip search me when I came in," Jerry Burns said.

"Don't laugh, they did strip search me," Major General Wells, head of NORAD, complained.

"Sorry about that," President Garcia said. "But they have a different protocol they follow for anyone that's not a regular member of the council. This may be a long day, so please make yourselves comfortable. When you need a break, or something to eat or drink, please go ahead and take care of it, because we're going to work straight through. At some point during the day, each one of you will be asked to spend a little time with a project manager that I've brought in to help me get organized. He'll be asking you a battery of questions so I can gain your perspectives on several different topics, and I would ask you to treat the interview like you're speaking directly to me."

"I've never heard of such a thing," said Gregory Kellogg, the director of National Intelligence. "I'm not sure I'm comfortable with the process."

"I understand it's a different approach, but please give it a chance," President Garcia said.

They spent the morning working through a laundry list of issues. Around noon the president excused himself to take a quick break.

As he walked into the bathroom, Walter Middleton, the secretary of the Treasury followed him in. "Sorry to stalk you, but I'm not going to do your little exercise," Secretary Middleton said.

"I'm not going to ask why, because it's not optional," President Garcia said.

"Bullshit. I'm not some schoolboy you can order around. I've been at this game for a long time, and you're . . . you're . . ."

"Just a Mexican," President Garcia interjected.

"I probably wouldn't have put it quite that crudely, but something like that."

"I'm only going to say this once," President Garcia said quietly. "Either do the interview, or you're out."

"You can't threaten me."

"Just stating facts. What's your answer going to be?"

"As I said, no."

President Garcia opened the bathroom door and motioned to the Secret Service agents waiting in the hall. "Agent Williams, would you and your team please escort Mr. Middleton to section eleven."

"What the hell is this?" Secretary Middleton asked.

"Please come with me, sir," Agent Williams said as he took him by the arm.

"Take your meat hooks off of me."

"Sir, you need to calm down, and follow me, or I'll be forced to restrain you."

Secretary Middleton jerked his arm away, but when he did, one of the other agents stuck a Taser in the middle of his back. Incapacitated, they gabbed both of his arms to keep him from falling, and carried him away.

When President Garcia rejoined the meeting, he said, "Secretary Middleton has been taken ill, and has gone home to rest."

The meeting wasn't a total sham, and they managed to work through several important issues. At 1800, President Garcia said, "It's getting late, so why don't we call it a day. I'd like to resume at oh-seven-hundred. Thanks for all of your hard work, and I'll see you in the morning."

Once they were gone, William Steward came in to brief him on his findings.

"How did we do?" President Garcia asked.

"Not counting Secretary Middleton, I've talked with all but one of the council members."

"Findings?" President Garcia asked.

"Understanding that this is not an exact science, I'd dig into Secretary Summerville's and Mr. Daugherty's recent activities. Other than that, I think the rest of them should be fine."

"Thanks, We've still got Secretary Middleton in custody. Would you mind spending some time with him before you go?"

"No problem."

* * *

"Is this guy for real?" General Appleby asked.

"I really don't know much about him, except that Roger Heinrich swore by him," President Garcia said.

"I still can't believe they were murdered in a secure facility like NSA," Vice President DeMarco said.

"That's why I've resorted to these extreme methods," President Garcia said. "There can be no security if you can't trust the people on your team."

"What are you going to do with Secretary Middleton?" Vice President DeMarco asked.

"That depends on Mr. Steward's assessment. If he doesn't view him as a risk, I'll simply replace him. If he's an active partner in any of this, he's on his way to Gitmo."

"If he's really a part of it, he should die," General Appleby said.

"One side of me agrees with you, but I'm not going there unless there are no other options," President Garcia said. "I'm totally spent, so let's call it a day. Since Mr. Steward will be staying over, we'll meet with him at oh-six-hundred."

Mr. Steward arrived early for the meeting, but President Garcia had been working for over an hour. "You must be an early riser," William Steward said.

"All my life, but it's gotten worse since I've taken on this job," President Garcia said.

"I've read that the stress of the office will make you age twice as fast," William Steward said.

"I can believe that, and with all the shit that's happened since I was thrust into the job, I could believe three or four times. So, what about our esteemed secretary of the Treasury?"

"Not as tricky as he thinks he is. I can't give you specifics, but he's definitely up to his ears in it."

"Thanks, we'll take it from here. We may be calling on you from time to time, so don't go far."

"Honestly, I don't have any place else to be. My wife left me years ago, and NSA is all I have left."

General Appleby arrived at 5:55 for the scheduled meeting. "Where's Mr. Steward?" he asked.

"Come and gone, but we had a nice chat," President Garcia said. "Let's get Vice President DeMarco on, so I can fill you both in on what Steward had to say."

"Good morning, Tom," President Garcia said. "I have to apologize, Mr. Steward has already come and gone, but I'd like to take a few moments to fill you both in on what he had to say."

"So what's the verdict on Middleton?" Vice President DeMarco asked.

"Dirty."

"Now what?" General Appleby asked.

"I hate to do it to an American, but I think Cuba is the only safe solution," President Garcia said.

"I wouldn't lose any sleep over it," General Appleby said.

"I'd second the thought," Vice President DeMarco said. "What are we using for a cover story?"

"Heart attack?"

"Why not? He's an old fat guy," Vice President De-Marco said.

"It's settled then. He'll be in Gitmo by nightfall. Since he's never coming back, I'm going to have Leonard Strauss see if he can't get some specifics out of him."

"Damn, all you'd have to tell me is that he was going to work me over, and I'd sing like a bird," General Appleby said.

"Strauss is on another assignment for the next three

weeks, but I'll have them drop him off in Guantanamo when he finishes."

"What do you want to do about the other two?"

"I'd like to send them with Middleton, but I'm afraid it might look suspicious if all three of them suddenly dropped dead. The attorney general is easy enough, I'll just fire him, but I'll need to convince Summerville to resign."

"Why don't you let me handle Summerville?" Vice President DeMarco said. "Our families have known each other for generations, and I think I can put it to him where he'll go quietly."

"Thanks, and I'm going to break the news to Daugherty before we resume," President Garcia said.

"Then I'll visit with Matthew while you're speaking with him," Vice President DeMarco said.

The council members had all shown up at least thirty minutes early, so they pulled the two traitors aside to break the news.

"What do you have on tap for us today?" Attorney General Daugherty asked.

"William, you've done a fine job for this country, but it's time that you step aside," President Garcia said.

"Who are you to tell me I'm out? I've spent my entire life serving this country, and there's no way in hell that I'm going to let an ignorant wetback take my life's work away from me."

"I'm not going to dignify your narrow mindedness by responding. I believe the statute reads that the attorney general serves at the pleasure of the president, and it no longer pleases me to have you represent this country."

He'd already briefed Special Agent Stubbs on what was going down, so he was waiting outside when the president opened the door and said, "Special Agent Stubbs, would you escort Mr. Daugherty out?"

The president could hear him muttering curses under his breath. "If you have something you'd like to say, look me in the eye and say it," President Garcia said.

He started to respond, but when he saw the president's steely glare, he thought better of it. "No, I guess not, but you haven't heard the last of this."

When he saw them lead the ex–attorney general out, General Appleby joined the president. They had a few minutes before the meeting was scheduled to resume, so they called the vice president.

"How'd yours go?" President Garcia asked.

"He's agreed to step down, and he's going to say that it's so he can spend more time with his family," Vice President DeMarco said.

"Good deal, but we're going to need to keep an eye on them, particularly that asshole Daugherty. I'm usually a decent judge of character, but he sure had me fooled," President Garcia said. "Would either of you like to recommend their replacements?"

"What would you think of Walter Hagan as attorney general?" General Appleby asked.

"Wasn't he the army's judge advocate general a few years back?" President Garcia asked.

"That's him. He's getting up there in years, but he'd do a good job."

"He's a great choice, and he's well thought of in Congress," Vice President DeMarco said. "And Wally Windom would be a perfect fit for Transportation."

"Never heard of him," President Garcia said.

"He's run the Texas DOT for years, but I know he's close to retirement. He'd do it if I asked him to."

"If you like him, I like him," President Garcia said. "How about the Treasury position?"

"I'd go with Jeremy Scalph," Vice President DeMarco said. "He's a past member of the Board of Governors of the Federal Reserve. He's between gigs, so I'm sure he'll jump at the chance."

"Great, that takes care of the openings," President Garcia said. "Tom, would you mind handling the paperwork?"

"No problem."

"I hope they don't take forever to confirm them," President Garcia said.

"Given the circumstances, and the candidates' reputations, it shouldn't be an issue," Vice President DeMarco said.

"Good. When we get in there, I want us to focus on our domestic issues," President Garcia said.

"What about the UN and that whole Middle East mess?" General Appleby asked.

"If you two are in agreement, I'm going to ask the secretary general to stand down until we can stabilize our domestic issues."

When the news hit the press the next day, Fredericka locked her office door and hit autodial on her satellite phone.

"I thought you didn't want to talk during the day," Klaus said.

"I don't, but this couldn't wait. They could be on to us. Secretary Middleton has died of a massive heart attack, President Garcia has removed the attorney general, and I believe they pressured the secretary of Transportation to resign."

"I can understand the secretary of Transportation, he's a pompous asshole, but I thought he valued Daugherty?"

"As far as we knew, he did. I've reached out to both of them, but they haven't returned my calls."

"That's not good. Do you think they'll keep their damned mouths shut?"

"I don't think Summerville would ever talk, but I have doubts about Daugherty."

"Then take care of it, and be quick about it. We've got far too much at risk to let him screw it up."

CHAPTER 41

The knock on their bedroom door woke President Garcia from his first sound sleep in days. He sat up in bed and said, "Come in."

Special Agent Williams walked quickly to the side of the bed and handed him the message. After he'd read it, he didn't know whether to cheer or cry.

"Thanks. Tell them I'll be there in a few minutes," President Garcia said.

"What's wrong?" Melinda asked.

"William Daugherty and Matthew Summerville were just killed in a car wreck."

"How awful, but why wake you?"

"They were the two men I just replaced."

"I still don't get it."

"Just go back to sleep, this shouldn't take very long."

When he walked into the briefing center, General Appleby already had Vice President DeMarco up on the videoconference.

"Sorry, it takes me a little longer to get dressed," President Garcia said.

"I wouldn't have even disturbed you if it weren't for the status update we just received from Mr. Steward," General Appleby said.

"Steward. Is he still on that special assignment in Rota?" President Garcia asked.

"Yes, and the Tunisian he's interrogating just gave up something I felt you should hear right away."

"Let's hear it."

"We grabbed him because we'd received a tip that he was involved in President Montblanc's disappearance, and he just divulged that the president and his wife have been murdered."

"Oh, dear God. Have we been able to verify his story?" President Garcia asked.

"Nothing definitive yet. He swore they'd destroyed their bodies, so we may never be able to verify his story," Vice President DeMarco said.

"Now that we have dates, times, and locations, we'll try to corroborate his story from NSA satellite surveillance," General Appleby said.

"Even if we do, I think we should keep a lid on it until we can prove who's behind it," Vice President DeMarco said.

"Probably true," President Garcia said. "Was Steward able to get him to divulge who he was working for?"

"Steward's convinced he doesn't know," General Appleby said. "He was receiving all of his instructions via an unregistered satellite phone they provided, and a front company in the Cayman Islands was paying him by wire transfer. He admitted that he provided the aircraft they used, and paid off the Iranian mercenaries that carried out the attack. However, Steward is convinced he was just brokering the deal, and didn't have any real skin in the game, other than money."

"Damn, for a minute there I thought we might be getting close," President Garcia said. "Tell me about the car wreck."

"Their limo was run over by a semi at two A.M. on the Beltway, about three miles from the Woodrow Wilson Bridge. It had pulled over for some sort of mechanical issue when a truck driver evidently fell asleep and drifted off the road. The limo driver was outside working on the car, and was able to get out of the way, so we have a fairly clear picture of what occurred. The highway patrol supervisor I spoke with said there wasn't much left, because the limo had caught fire after the truck ran over it."

"I wonder what they were doing out at that time of night," President Garcia said.

"They were returning from the big GOP fund-raiser that Stevan Baldridge and John Steadman were hosting at the Verizon Center," General Appleby said.

"That's right," President Garcia said. "Tom and I were supposed to attend, but the Secret Service nixed it at the last minute. They had their wives with them, didn't they?"

"Given the catastrophic nature of the crash, I doubt they know who was in the car," General Appleby said.

"Colonel Wilhelm, would you have the police do a welfare check on their wives?" President Garcia asked.

"Any chance it wasn't an accident?" Vice President De-Marco asked.

"Considering what's occurred lately, I'd have to say it's certainly a possibility," General Appleby said.

They'd been discussing the evening's events for almost half an hour, when Colonel Wilhelm returned. "The local police did a welfare check on both residences, and it looks like their wives were with them," Colonel Wilhelm said.

"I hate to admit it, but I don't really care that those assholes are dead. But their wives didn't deserve to die," President Garcia said. "Thank you, Colonel. You can go back to bed if you'd like," President Garcia said.

"Thanks, I think I will."

"We'll be right behind you. Before you turn in, would you reschedule the morning meeting for thirteen hundred?"

* * *

They were about to call it a night, when the colonel returned.

"I thought you were going to turn in," President Garcia said.

"I was, but we just received a flash message from the NSA, and there's been a major nuclear event in Tehran," Colonel Wilhelm said.

"When?" General Appleby asked.

"Six minutes ago. First indications are that it was a MIRV, carrying eight warheads."

"Won't be much left," General Appleby said.

"Please tell me we didn't fire the missile," President Garcia said.

"I wish I could, but NSA tracked the trajectory back to the approximate position of the UN task force in the Gulf of Oman," Colonel Wilhelm said.

"I thought they were supposed to be gone by now."

"The UN Security Council requested that they hold off until Friday."

"Damn it to hell. I need to talk to Admiral Kenyan, right now," General Appleby said.

It only took the colonel a couple of minutes to establish a connection to the bridge of the admiral's flagship.

"I assume you're calling about the submarine we just sunk," Admiral Kenyan said.

"Submarine? That may be part of this, but we're calling about the missile that just wiped out Tehran," General Appleby said. "Please tell me it wasn't one of ours."

"I wasn't aware it was a nuclear attack, and I can assure you we didn't fire the missile. It was fired from an unidentified submarine. One of the frigates patrolling our perimeter actually observed the missile launch. I believed they were attacking us, so I immediately ordered a counterattack. We've seen a significant amount of debris come to the surface, so we're assuming it was destroyed. We're sweeping the area to retrieve what we can, to try to identify it."

"I was almost certain we weren't behind it, but we had to check," General Appleby said. "Have you observed any other attacks?"

"No, but I can assure you we're on high alert," Admiral Kenyan said. "You said it was a nuclear explosion. How big?"

"It was an MIRV, and first estimates are eight approximately five-hundred-kiloton warheads."

"Those specs are damn close to our Trident II, W88 warheads. Poor bastards, there won't be much left if it was anything close to that."

"What's your status?" General Appleby asked.

"We haven't suffered any damage, and our British contingent is sweeping the area to make sure there aren't any more of them. Do we need to alter our plans to return to base?"

"Not at this time. Let us know if anything changes, and I'll keep you updated as the situation becomes clearer," General Appleby said.

"Do any of you happen to know the current population of Tehran?" President Garcia asked.

"It's about eight-point-three million in the city itself, but the surrounding area has another five million or so," Colonel Wilhelm said.

"I know there were eight warheads, but do we know whether it was an air burst weapon?" President Garcia asked.

Colonel Wilhelm scanned the latest data from NSA and said, "They were all air bursts, and as you would expect from that type of weapon, the eight concentric circles of almost total destruction were overlapped."

"That means there will be millions of casualties," President Garcia said.

"Guaranteed, and the lucky ones died immediately," General Appleby said. "Given the radiation levels we've measured so far, we can expect the casualties to climb dramatically as time passes."

President Garcia closed his eyes as he said a quick prayer. "Colonel, see if you can get me a link to Ayatollah Rostami," President Garcia said when he finished.

Surprisingly the call went through immediately.

"You evil infidel scum, have you called to gloat?" Ayatollah Rostami said.

"No. I've called to offer any assistance we can," President Garcia said.

"So you exterminate millions of my people, and then you act like you care?"

"It wasn't us. I just—" President Garcia started.

"Liar," the ayatollah screamed as he cut the president off. "The missile came from your fleet in the Gulf of Oman. We saw it immediately, or I'd be dead, along with the rest of the city. I don't have the wherewithal to strike your country directly, but let's see how you like seeing your people slaughtered without mercy," the ayatollah said as he hung up.

"Get him back," President Garcia said.

After several tries to reestablish the link, the colonel said, "I'm sorry, sir, they're rejecting the call."

"Colonel, I need Admiral Kenyan back ASAP," General Appleby said. After a couple of minutes, General Appleby asked, "What the hell is the holdup?"

"We've tried video and voice, but we can't make a connection. I've got NSA checking to see if there's some sort of satellite glitch."

Just then, Randy Gosford, the new director of NSA, came on the video. "Sorry it took so long. The Iranians have launched a missile attack against Admiral Kenyan's command. The attack consisted of sixty-five missiles, but their antimissile defenses knocked down all but thirteen. Unfortunately, seven of those were nukes, and initial indications are that none of the surface ships survived."

"Are you sure?" President Garcia asked.

"I've already received verification from two of the six submarines that were guarding the fleet," Director Gosford said.

"Thank you, Director, I'll get back to you," President Garcia said. "See if you can get Rostami."

"So, how does it feel?" Ayatollah Rostami asked.

"As I said, we didn't do it. The missile was fired from an unidentified submarine, in the same general location as our fleet."

"What proof do you have?"

"I'd spoken with the Admiral Kenyan shortly before I called you the first time. We recorded the call if you'd like to see it for yourself."

The video stream was ultra-high-definition, and as the ayatollah studied their faces, he realized they were telling the truth.

"This is the second time I've been duped into thinking you'd fired on us," Ayatollah Rostami said. "Someone is trying to get you to wipe us off of the face of the earth."

"So it seems," President Garcia said. "It isn't the first time it's happened to us either. We'd been assuming you were behind the abduction of President Montblanc, but we've recently uncovered evidence that proves it wasn't your government."

"I'd never bothered to deny it, because I knew you wouldn't believe me," Ayatollah Rostami said. "So where do we go from here?"

"The path forward is likely to be convoluted, but you and I have to work through it, before this escalates any further," President Garcia said.

"Agreed, but I hope you have some idea how, because I don't see much hope on my end," Ayatollah Rostami said.

"If it were just our two nations it would be hard, but

the fleet contained a cross section of UN peacekeeping forces, and they're not going to be pleased to see me working with you."

"That's a certainty, and I don't have any credible way of starting a discourse with them," Ayatollah Rostami said.

"No, you don't, but I'm hoping they'll listen to me. As soon as we're finished, I'm going to sit down with the Paul-Henri, and to try sketch out our first steps."

"I'll be waiting. Before you go, were you serious about wanting to help?"

"Certainly, although we're not in a hell of a lot better shape than you. What can I do?"

"Most of our medical infrastructure is gone, and we have little in the way of supplies, or food."

"We're stretched pretty thin, but I'll see what I can get out of the UN. Either way, I'll get you everything I can. By the way, what's your situation?" President Garcia asked.

"I'm currently in an underground, blast-proof bunker, near the center of the city. It's self-contained, and we have enough resources to last about six weeks. After that, who knows?"

"Understood. I'll get to work on that as well."

"Many thanks."

"How in the hell are you going to talk the UN Security Council into helping them, instead of finishing them off?" General Appleby asked.

"I'm going to share everything we've learned so far. It should be more than enough to convince them this is being orchestrated by a third party," President Garcia said.

"There's some pretty sensitive stuff in there," Vice President DeMarco said. "Are you going to sanitize it first?"

"Nope. I'm going to show them the raw Intel."

"It's done," Fredericka said.

"I saw the news," Klaus said. "Your man did an excellent job of making it look like they did it."

"He'd better have for what he charged."

"He wasn't part of your normal team?"

"Unfortunately I was forced to use an independent contractor. My internal resources have been pushing back."

"Should we be worried?"

"Probably, but what choice do we have? If we're ever found out, we'll either be sent to Cuba, or executed as traitors."

"Are you going to be able to pull off the next two initiatives?" he asked.

"I won't have too much trouble with the first one, but the second is going to be problematic. Even some of my closest supporters have started to question what I'm asking them to do."

"Get them in line."

I dare him to talk to me like that, I've risked everything for this, she thought to herself. "Yes, sir. I'm sorry, but I need to go."

CHAPTER 42

Even though their relationship had been badly strained by recent events, Shelby Cohen decided to give Vice President DeMarco a heads-up.

"Shelby, it's good to hear from you," Vice President De-Marco said.

"It has been too long. We'll have to do lunch once this all calms down. How much longer is the Secret Service going to have you and the president locked down?"

"No way to tell. I don't mean to rush you, but I've got a Security Council meeting in ten minutes."

"No problem. I just wanted to let you know that I'm going to be submitting two pieces of legislation sometime this week. The first is a bill to provide Israel with a hundred M1A2 Abramses, forty of the new generation of Raytheon's ABM systems, and seventy-five F35As."

"There's no way in hell the president will let that go through after all the shit Ben Weizmann has pulled."

"There's more. The second is a resolution to begin the UN-mandated air-and-ground assault on Iran by the end of next month."

"Have you lost your mind? Tehran was just nuked, and you want to begin an all-out assault against them? I know for a fact that the president is committed to providing them aid, not attacking them."

"Unacceptable. Now is the time to remove them as a threat to world peace, once and for all."

"At one time they may have been a threat, but they're in no position to threaten anyone. Even if you do manage to ram this through Congress, the president will veto it, and besides, the UN would never go for it either."

"I don't understand. I know there was some unfounded animosity from President Montblanc, but I always believed you and President Garcia were advocates for Israel."

"To a point we are, however the Israelis' actions of late have given us both pause. I'll make a deal with you. I'll see if I can get the president to go along with the arms transfer, if you'll back off the attack bullshit."

After a long pause, she said, "Deal, but I'm not going to hold off forever."

"Sorry I'm late. I was on a call with the Speaker of the House," Vice President DeMarco said when he joined the call.

"What's Shelby scamming now?" President Garcia asked.

After the vice president had laid out her plans, the president said, "Wow, she sure has a set. I hope you told her there wasn't a snowball's chance in hell."

"I did, but I think it would be prudent to let the request for arms go through. If you do, I've got her to agree to back off on pushing forward with the UN plan."

"I'm having to fight Congress for every penny to rebuild this country, and she wants to give away a trillion dollars to a country that is, at best, a marginal ally."

"She does, and what's more she thinks she has the votes to get it done."

"I know you're right, but it sure seems to me that they have their priorities all screwed up."

"Agreed, but I think you should pick your battles with her."

"OK, but if I agree to it, I want you to get her to appropriate a like amount for domestic rebuilding, and humanitarian aid to Iran."

"She won't like the Iranian part, but I think I can convince her."

"I know I'm naive about Washington politics, but how can she wield that much power?" President Garcia asked.

"She doesn't, the lobbyists are the power behind the throne in this city. They exercise a tremendous amount of leverage in both Houses, and even the courts."

"This shit gives me a headache. Let's move on. What's on the agenda for today?" President Garcia asked.

"First up is Timothy Gather. He's going to give us an overview of the West Coast situation. After that, NSA has an update on Roger Heinrich's murder. And last but not least, Homeland has a status report on border security."

When they made the connection to the FEMA field office, they were expecting to see Timothy Gather. Instead, the assistant director, Moll Bannister, was sitting at his desk.

"Good afternoon, Miss Bannister, we're supposed to be having a call with Mr. Gather," General Appleby said. "Is he available?"

"I need to apologize. We should have called you, but it's been a madhouse around here all day. Mr. Gather had a heart attack this morning, and has since died."

"My God, he was only forty-five and in great shape," Vice President DeMarco said.

"It came as a complete shock to all of us. He'd just returned from a field trip to the Portland area, and was complaining that he didn't feel well. He was on his way to our field hospital when he had the attack. They tried to revive him, but he never came around."

"We can do this another time," President Garcia said.

"Thank you for your concern, but he'd have wanted us to carry on," Miss Bannister said.

"Fine, if you're up to it," General Appleby said.

"I am. I'm happy to report that the first phase of our rebuilding effort is on time and on budget. Starting next week, we'll begin moving half of our staff to the West Coast office in southern Washington to begin the assessment of the Mount Hood disaster."

"Why? I didn't think there was anything left," President Garcia said.

"There's not. Most of us were trying to talk Timothy out of it, but he was adamant that we sweep the area for casualties before we made a final determination on what our next steps should be."

"Hold right there," President Garcia said. "You could probably talk me into sweeping the area for bodies, but I don't want to waste any resources on a fool's errand. I've flown over the area, and for the foreseeable future we just need to cordon it off and leave it for later."

"Mr. Gather believed that given time, we could rebuild."

"I know, but that's not going to happen. We simply don't have the resources."

"Understood. How would you like to proceed?"

"Do your sweep, although I wouldn't waste a lot of time on it. When you finish, I want you to have the Corps of Engineers begin erecting a security fence around the entire area."

"That's a lot of land."

"It'll be quicker than trying to salvage and rebuild. When they're finished, I'll have Homeland Security institute an armed drone patrol around the entire area to ensure that the looters stay out of there. At some point we may turn it into a national monument, or some future generation might be willing to spend the resources to rebuild, but not now."

"I'll get on it immediately," Miss Bannister said.

"Good. Would you mind staying on for a few more minutes?" President Garcia asked.

"No problem."

He muted the call and asked, "Do any of you have any objections to me promoting Miss Bannister to Mr. Gather's job?" No one objected, so the president un-muted the call and said, "Congratulations, Miss Bannister, you're the new director of FEMA."

"Thanks. Filling Timothy's shoes will be a challenge, but I promise to do my best," Director Moll Bannister said.

"That's all any of us can do, but Timothy spoke highly of you, and I'm sure you'll do fine. If you need anything, please feel free to give me or Vice President DeMarco a call."

When they'd hung up, President Garcia said, "Mary Beth, I want his body back here ASAP, and I want your best forensic team to go over it to make sure it really was a heart attack."

"A little paranoid?" General Appleby asked.

"After all the shit that's happened? Let's hope the next one goes better. Colonel, we're ready for Mr. Gosford."

"Good afternoon," President Garcia said. "First let me congratulate you on a job well done. NSA hasn't missed a beat since you took over."

"Thank you, Mr. President. I just wish it had been under better circumstances. Roger was one of my closest friends," Randy Gosford said.

"A great loss for sure. What have you got for us today?"

"We've determined how Roger and his team died," Director Gosford said. "There was a canister of sarin gas hidden under the table, and it was set to go off a minute after Roger sat down at the table."

"How would they know that? From what I've read, the meeting was impromptu, and wasn't on his schedule."

"The device was fitted with a portable RFID scanner, and whoever placed the device had access to Roger's code."

"Who would have that kind of access?"

"That would be almost anyone in the building. Besides, it's not the kind of information they'd compartmentalize."

"So there's not much chance of catching whoever did this?" President Garcia asked.

"That wasn't the issue. We identified the perpetrator almost immediately."

"So you have them?"

"We have her body. It was Roger's longtime personal assistant, Ann Breuer, but when we went to arrest her, someone had broken into her flat and strangled her."

"Ruthless bastards. Do you have any idea who she was working with, or for?"

"Not a clue. She went to work for Roger right out of college, and there's nothing in her background that would indicate she was part of a terror organization."

"Great, another dead end. Did you find out anything on the other assignment I gave you?"

"We've hit a dead end there as well. I'd been hoping to read Roger's notes, but someone had reformatted his computer's hard drive."

"I thought everyone's data was automatically backed up to the central server," General Appleby said.

"It is, but that had been erased as well, along with all of the tape backups for his department."

"All I know to tell you is keep at it. Homeland, you're up."

"Since my last report, we've successfully interdicted eleven attempts to smuggle WMDs into the country," Mary Beth Greider said. "Six of them involved nuclear materials, and the rest were sarin gas shipments."

"Good job, but it doesn't seem to be slowing down," General Appleby said.

"No it hasn't, but there's something odd going on."

"How so?"

"In every instance they could have detonated their loads, but none of them did."

"Thanks to you, and your team's quick response," Vice President DeMarco said.

"I wish I believed that. It's almost like they never intended to use them."

"You're not making any sense," President Garcia said.

"I know, and I apologize for that, but something is just not right."

"Follow your instincts, but I think it's just great work," General Appleby said.

"I intend to. The only other thing I've got to report is that per your orders, I've instituted drone surveillance around the perimeter of the Portland quarantine area."

"That was quick work," President Garcia said. "I didn't think they'd even completed the enclosure."

"They're not even close, but since I had plenty of drones, I went live ahead of schedule."

"Where did you get the drones?" General Appleby asked. "I thought we'd used them all."

"Aeronautics Defense Systems just shipped us fifteen hundred of their new stealth drones. They're fully weaponized and virtually undetectable."

"Isn't that an Israeli company?" Vice President DeMarco asked.

"It is. Between them, Elbit Systems, and the Israel Aerospace Industries, they accounted for over four-point-six-billion dollars of drone shipments last year."

"I thought we owned the drone market?" General Appleby asked.

"We could have if we hadn't put so many export limitations on the U.S. companies. Besides that, we're no longer competitive. Elbit makes a drone that can carry twice the payload of any of our models, and it can stay aloft for over thirty-six hours."

"Damned impressive," General Appleby said.

"Mary Beth, thank you for the update, and we'll be in touch," the president said.

"That was a little strange. I guess the pressure's getting to her," General Appleby said.

"I wonder," Vice President DeMarco said. "I've seen her intuition in action, and she's rarely wrong when she senses something's amiss. We'd be well served to poke around a little."

"What did you have in mind?" President Garcia asked.

"I've been following up on a couple of leads of my own, and I think at least one of them might tell us whether she's right."

"Out with it," President Garcia said. "The time is past for you to try to go it alone."

"I suppose you're right. You know the old saying, follow the money?"

"Of course."

"Well, that's the tack I took. I had Phillip Aberle pull the financial records on Congress, and everyone that holds a top secret and above clearance."

"I know he's the director of the IRS, but there's no way he could do that and keep it a secret," President Garcia said.

"You can if the NSA is feeding you the requests under a presidential order," Vice President DeMarco said.

"I never signed anything like that."

"I warned you it was better if you didn't know."

"What did you find?"

"That's the thing. Roger never gave me specifics. All he'd shared was that there could be close to a hundred in Congress alone."

"Lord save us," President Garcia said.

"When you say involved, what does that mean?" General Appleby asked.

"I wish I had the answer to that. He was using a combination of his research and the IRS data to pare the list down to a manageable size."

"So we're stuck knowing that Congress could be full of traitors, and we have no idea which ones?" General Appleby said.

"That's it in a nutshell."

"Wonderful. I want you to connect with the new director, and restart the program. Only this time, make damn sure he keeps it to himself."

"I wasn't expecting your call until next week," Klaus said.

"I need more money," Fredericka said.

"I just sent you ten million last week. I thought you were afraid they'd track it back to you?"

"I am, but I don't have any choice if you want this to happen."

"I thought we had friends in high places?"

She laughed and said, "We do, if the price is right. Some of them are truer to the cause than others."

"Very well, it will be in the account by morning."

CHAPTER 43

When President Garcia heard the knock on their bedroom door, he couldn't help but groan. "Just a minute, I'll be right there."

"I'm very sorry, but they need you in the briefing center," Special Agent Valdez said.

"President Garcia, thank you for taking my call. I'd feared our two countries weren't going to be able to remain allies, but the arms shipments will go a long ways toward repairing the past misunderstandings," Prime Minister Weizmann said.

"I wish I shared your feelings," President Garcia said. "I view it as more akin to a deal with the devil. However, you and I can fix at least some of this, if you'll listen to reason."

"You never let up, do you?"

"Not when it's this critical. You've made your point, and regardless of how it happened, Iran is no longer a threat to anyone," President Garcia said.

"History will be the judge of that, but after the losses you've suffered at their hands, I'm surprised your country hasn't wiped them off of the face of the earth."

"I'd be lying if I said it hadn't crossed my mind, but I'm committed to finding a peaceful solution to this mess."

"Why would you waste your time? Those animals are incapable of live and let live."

"Because it's the Christian thing to do."

"Don't get me wrong, I'm as religious as the next man, but this goes way beyond that. I know you think you are doing what's right, so I'm going to give you a few weeks to convince me. After that we'll be forced to take independent action."

"Would you like some breakfast?" Colonel Wilhelm asked when the president finished the call.

"Might as well," President Garcia said. "Get some for yourself while you're at it."

"I hated to disturb you, but I thought you would want to take his call," Colonel Wilhelm said when he returned with their trays.

"Of course I did, and don't ever worry about doing your job. What do we have scheduled for today?"

"The only thing you have so far is your standing meeting with Vice President DeMarco and General Appleby."

"Good. Unless it's an emergency, don't schedule anything else for today."

"I expected a bigger crowd," General Appleby said when he walked in.

"The president said he wanted to work on a few things, and asked that I not schedule anything else," Colonel Wilhelm said.

"I wonder what's up," Vice President DeMarco asked.

"He didn't say," Colonel Wilhelm said. "But he should be back in a couple of minutes."

"Sorry about that," President Garcia said when he returned. "I was supposed to wake Melinda up this morning, and I almost forgot."

"So what have you got planned for today?" Vice President DeMarco asked.

"We need to put a team together to extract Ayatollah Rostami and his entourage from their bunker," President Garcia said.

"Do we have the current radiation levels?" General Appleby asked.

"In the folder in front of you," Colonel Wilhelm said.

"Damn, that's really hot."

"Do you think we can get a team in and out safely?" President Garcia asked.

"If we use some of the Ospreys we've retrofitted with shielding and add a positive air system, it might be feasible," General Appleby said.

"Would you work on that for me? The ayatollah's bunker only has another twelve days of resources left."

"We've never tried an operation like this, so I'd like to involve the CIA's Special Operations group," General Appleby said.

"Use any resource you need, but I need this to happen."

"Gotcha. I'd like to do this in person. Would it be alright if I spend a few days at Langley?"

"That's your call," President Garcia said.

"I'd like to get started, unless you need me to stay for the rest of the meeting."

"You can take off. We're going to have a quick call with Randy Gosford, but I don't imagine we'll get much done today."

"General, I'd rather you didn't leave the premises," Special Agent Stubbs said.

"I understand, but I need to handle this in person, so I'm going to overrule you on this one," General Appleby said.

"Give me a few minutes, and I'll arrange for transportation."

"No need. I've already called for a chopper, and it should be landing in a few minutes."

"How about a protection detail?"

"Got it covered. The CIA has a team on board."

"I'll walk up with you," Special Agent Stubbs said. The chopper was just landing on the lawn as they walked out. "I've never seen a bird like that," Special Agent Stubbs said.

"It's a Sikorsky S-97. It's a prototype, and I think they've only built six so far. Its hull is made of composite materials, and its hybrid propulsion system gives it a top speed of over two hundred knots."

"It's good to see you again," Margret Grissom, the director of the CIA said when he arrived at the Langley, Virginia, facility.

"It has been awhile since we've talked in person," General Appleby said.

"Thanks for helping out on this. President Garcia has put the highest priority on the mission, but as you know, no one has ever gone into an area that was this hot. You know I always love a challenge, but damn. That's enough bitching, let's get to it. Have you ever met John Chambers?"

"I can't say that I have. What's his background?"

"He's a career CIA operative, but he's planned and executed some of the most complex missions imaginable. He's the one who developed the plan that enabled the Japanese to finally get a handle on the Fukushima meltdown."

"Impressive, but I'm afraid this is way beyond even that," General Appleby said.

"Agreed, but if John can't figure it out, no one can."

"OK, when can we meet with him?"

"He's waiting on us."

* * *

"General, I'd like you to meet John Chambers," Margret Grissom said.

"Good to meet, you, but I've got to warn you that Margret has made some pretty big promises on your behalf."

"Good to finally meet you in person, General. You probably never knew it, but we've worked together before. Do you remember the OP you led into North Korea?"

"Do I. If those rangers hadn't gotten there when they did, I wouldn't be standing here. How were you involved?"

"I was the one that made the call to send them, and I actually led the mission."

"I thought you said he was career CIA?"

"I am, but I was undercover as a colonel in the ranger battalion at the time."

"I've waited almost fifteen years to thank you," the general said as he took his hand. "So, do you have any thoughts on this mess?" General Appleby asked.

"I do, but I don't have a lot of time to explain, because I've got a chopper standing by to take me to Edwards."

"How long until you can give it a go?"

"The positive air kits for the Ospreys are being installed as we speak, and we'll leave as soon as I arrive," John Chambers said.

"Aren't you a little old for active OPs?"

"Probably, but I need to be there for this one."

"I've tried to convince him not to go, but I think we're going to have to go with his instincts," Margret Grissom said.

"Then Godspeed, and let us know if there's anything else we can provide," General Appleby said.

"What have you screwed up now?" Klaus asked.

Sorry bastard, Fredericka thought to herself. "It has nothing to do with me. They're sending a CIA operative by the name of John Chambers to lead a mission to rescue Rostami, and bring him to Washington."

"Damn. I can't let that happen. Thanks for the heads-up, and I'll take it from here."

CHAPTER 44

When John Chambers's helicopter landed at Edwards Air Force Base, his next ride already had its starboard engines fired up. As he hurried up the portable ramp into the aircraft, he found himself wishing he was twenty years younger.

"Welcome aboard, sir. We've already been cleared for takeoff," the air force lieutenant said. "Take any seat you'd like, but make sure you buckle up because we're leaving hot."

"Thanks. What's our flight time going to be?"

"Approximately eleven and a half hours, depending on the weather."

John had been on the presidential aircraft before, so he knew where he wanted to sit. As the 747 roared down the runway, he thought back to the last mission he'd gone on. It was supposed to be a simple operation to rescue some American tourists that had been taken by a group of Somalian pirates. The first part of the mission had gone as planned, but after they'd freed the hostages, an RPG had hit their helicopter as they were leaving. He could still remember the horror in the woman's eyes as their helicopter had spun toward the ground. He'd survived the crash, but he'd suffered burns on over 40 percent of his body, and they'd kept him in a medically induced coma for weeks to let them heal.

He hadn't done any fieldwork since, but he found himself enjoying the rush of adrenaline that came with a mission. They picked up a tailwind along the way, and eleven hours later, they began their descent into the Incirlik Air Base in Turkey.

As John Chambers was exiting the aircraft he said, "Thanks, good flight. Are you going straight back?"

"No, we've been ordered to wait on you," Colonel Etheridge said. "Do you have any idea when you'll be finished?"

"One way or the other, I'll be done in four days tops," John Chambers said.

"We'll be standing by. The tower said they were sending a car for you."

After John had gone, the copilot asked, "I wonder what he meant?"

"Hard to say. They didn't brief me."

When the staff car stopped beside the aircraft, two heavily armed airmen got out. "Mr. Chambers?" the sergeant asked.

"That's me. You boys my ride?"

"Yes, sir. Do you have any luggage?"

"No, just my briefcase."

"Please get in, and we'll take you to the command post."

"Welcome to Turkey," Colonel Smotherman said. "I believe we've got everything on your list, but what the hell are you going to do with that many Class A radiation suits?"

"We're going into Tehran, and I'm hoping they'll keep us alive long enough to complete the mission."

"Tehran? Have you lost your mind? It's so hot it glows in the dark."

"Regardless, we're going in. I've been ordered to retrieve the ayatollah, and that's what I intend to do."

"I've got a room for you in the officers' billet," Colonel Smotherman said.

"No need. I slept on the flight, and I'd like to get going. We've only got a few days before they run out of air."

"Your call. I've assembled the team you requested, and they're standing by."

"Thanks, and if you don't mind, I'd like to meet them before we take off."

The team was being housed in one of the large hangars that lined the airstrip, and when they walked in, the team jumped to attention.

"Stand at ease," John Chambers said. "I'm not military, and even if I was, we're not going to have time for that. I know you've been briefed, but I'd like to take a moment to let you know what we're facing. We're going to rescue the supreme leader of Iran, Ayatollah Rostami and his staff. Shortly before Tehran was hit, they took shelter in an underground bunker near the center of Tehran. The bunker is intact, but the entrance is buried under several feet of rubble. Normally it wouldn't take more than a few hours to clear a path, but due to the residual radiation we'll have to wear the HAZMAT suits at all times. Unfortunately, they don't provide complete protection from the radiation, but we're going to get in and out as quickly as possible. Does anyone have any questions?

"Go ahead, ask your question," John Chambers said, when he saw a hand go up.

"Why are we risking our lives to save that murderous bastard?" Captain Bingham asked.

"Orders, but I can tell you the president declared this mission his highest priority."

"Damned politicians," one of the men muttered.

"I don't care who said that, but let me set you straight. The president is a highly decorated veteran, and he's been there and done that, so I'm not going to tolerate that sort of bullshit. Our time is short, so gather your shit and let's mount up."

When their aircraft broke through the clouds covering the city, John Chambers was taken aback by the destruction that unfolded below them. "Good lord. I've studied the satellite images, but this is unbelievable."

"The beauty of modern technology," Major Cruz said. "The destruction from a nuclear blast falls off quickly as you move away from the center of the blast. However, the MIRV technology maximizes the destruction by overlapping the multiple warheads' circles of complete destruction."

"We'll be on the ground in three minutes," the pilot announced. A few seconds later John Chambers could see the V22's massive propellers begin changing attitude to allow them to land like a helicopter. They'd hoped to land near each other, but the debris fields forced them to spread out.

"Have your men get the bobcats unloaded while I verify where we're going to be working," John Chambers said.

"We're on it," Major Cruz replied.

"Make sure everyone has their dosimeters on," John Chambers said. As he picked his way through the debris field, he noticed the graphite-colored dust swirling around his feet. He unclipped the Geiger counter on his belt and took a reading. As soon as he heard the fast-paced chatter, he knew it was bad before he even checked the digital readout. *Damn, we'd better work fast,* he thought to himself.

There wasn't much left of the palace, but he'd studied the floor plan for hours. When he reached the section where the stairs to the bunker were supposed to be, a mountain of debris covered it. "I've located the entrance to the bunker," John Chambers called over his headset. "Follow my homing beacon, and get your asses moving."

When they reached his position, John Chambers said, "Back the trailers up on either end. We'll use both excavators until we start down the stairs." As he watched the bobcats feverishly scooping up the debris covering the stairway, John noticed the major checking his dosimeter. "How we doing?" John Chambers asked.

"It's slow going. Some of the debris is so heavy that were having to use both of the bobcats to drag it out of the way."

"It should get better as we reach the bottom of the pile."

"You're probably right, but it's way too hot," Major Cruz said.

"I know, the levels are much higher than expected. Make sure the men are rotating back to the aircraft every four hours, and I want you to go back to the aircraft and wait there until we're finished."

"I'd rather stay with you," Major Cruz said. "One of us needs to be able to function when we pull them out of there."

"Do as I ask. Now get going, I need to call in with a status update."

"We should reach the bunker in about twenty hours," John Chambers said.

"Good work. I'll let them know to be ready. How's your team holding up?" General Appleby asked.

"The radiation levels are almost twice what we were expecting. I'm going to have all the men doing the excavation return to base as soon as we reach the blast doors. They've already exceeded the exposure limits we agreed on, but they've all volunteered to see it through."

"We've got a full decontamination team standing by, and you can be sure we'll do everything we can for them. How about you?"

"It'll be alright."

"Very well. Contact me again when you reach the bunker."

Once they reached the lower level they had to clear the last few feet by hand, and when they finished, John Chambers told them, "I want all of you back on the aircraft immediately."

"Don't you want us to help you evacuate the bunker?" Sergeant Mitchell asked.

"Not necessary. They've got rebreathers, and they won't be out in it long enough to cause any real damage. Now get your assess moving, and thanks for hanging in."

John had been fighting the feeling for several minutes, but he finally had to crack open his suit enough to puke. He stayed bent over until all he could manage was a dry heave. "I'm outside the blast door, have them open up," John Chambers said.

The general motioned to Director Gosford to place the call. "We're calling now."

"Good. You might ask them to hurry, it's getting pretty bad out here." As the seal on the door broke, there was a huge rush of air. "It's opening now. I've got to go. I'll call you when we're airborne." When the door was open far enough John squeezed through.

They were all gathered by the door, and the ayatollah was standing at the front of the group.

"Sir, we need to get going," John Chambers said.

"We're ready," Ayatollah Rostami said.

"Make sure you seal your masks before you exit the bunker."

Director Gosford had briefed them on how many people the aircraft could accommodate, so they'd already split up into groups.

"Mr. Rostami, you'll be flying with me. Now if you're ready, let's move out."

As the remaining Ospreys were climbing away from

the city, Ayatollah Rostami removed his mask and said, "Mr. Chambers, I can't tell you how much we appreciate your team's efforts, and if there's ever anything I can do for you, all you have to do is ask."

"No thanks needed. It comes with the territory, but there's one thing you can do."

"Name it. If it's within my power, I'll do it."

"Work out something with President Garcia to end all of this needless slaughter."

"You have my word that I'll try."

"Everyone listen up," John Chambers said. "You all need to disrobe, and put on one of the jumpsuits that are hanging on the bulkheads."

"Is that really necessary?" Ayatollah Rostami asked.

"Yes, sir, it is."

As John was stripping off his suit and undergarments, he took a quick glance at the others and said, "That means everything." He felt like he needed to puke again, so he held an airsick bag to his face, but all he could do was dry heave.

Once everyone had changed, the crew gathered the clothing and jettisoned it.

"When we land you'll be put through a complete decontamination process," John Chambers said. "After that you'll be evaluated for further treatment."

"We weren't exposed for that long," Ayatollah Rostami said.

"For your group it's more of an insurance policy," John Chambers said.

"Your teams were wearing HAZMAT suits, surely that would have provided enough protection."

"To a point, yes, but we understood the risks."

As the Ospreys were landing, they could see the ambulances racing across the runway toward them. A large team of medics met them as they were walking down the ramp.

"Ayatollah Rostami, I'm Dr. Jamison, and I'll be

conducting your evaluation. As soon as we get you checked out, the president has a plane on standby to transport you to Washington."

"What about my staff?"

"Once your team has been cleared, we'll be hosting them until your return."

"Very well. Let's get to it."

Since the ayatollah hadn't been exposed for any length of time, it only took a few hours to clear him.

"You're all set. The sergeant will take you to your aircraft," Dr. Jamison said.

"Before I go, I'd like to check the status of John Chambers and his men," Ayatollah Rostami said.

"They're still working on them, but other than John, we don't believe any of them are going to suffer any long-term health issues."

"That's great news. How about Mr. Chambers?"

"He was exposed for far too long, and he's a lot older than the rest."

"What does that mean?"

"It means he probably won't survive."

"I'd like to see him before I go."

"I'm afraid he's in quarantine."

"Oh. Isn't there some way I can talk with him?"

"Give me a moment," Dr. Jamison said as he picked up the phone.

"Okay, here's the best I can do. They've moved him to one of the rooms with a viewing window and an intercom. The doctor who's treating him thinks he can wake him up long enough for you to have a short conversation."

The ayatollah watched as they wheeled John's bed up to the window. They had all sorts of IVs attached to him, and his eyes were closed. The doctor injected a shot into one of his IV tubes to wake him up.

"He's in a lot of pain, so I don't want to keep him awake any longer than necessary," the doctor told them.

When the ayatollah saw his eyes open he asked, "John, can you hear me?"

"Yes, but you needn't have come," John Chambers said.

"Yes, I did. I wanted to tell you again how much I appreciate your valiant efforts, and I'll do everything possible to fulfill your request."

"Many thanks, and there's worse things to die for," he said. He started to say something else, but he let out a low moan, and passed out.

"I'm sorry, but that's all I can allow," the doctor said.

"Do everything you can for him," Ayatollah Rostami said.

"You can count on that, but I'd be shocked if he lasts through the night."

"I wish I could stay, but I've got critical matters to attend to."

As the ayatollah's plane raced through the night sky, he was gazing out at the full moon. He was the religious leader of his nation and much of the Arab world looked to him for guidance, but he wished he had a better vision of how to reach a peaceful resolution to their problems.

It had been a long day, but he opened his bag and removed his prayer rug so he could say his final prayer of the day. When he finished he felt better about what lay ahead. He still didn't know the specifics, but he knew in his heart it was going to work out.

"I've just learned they've rescued Ayatollah Rostami, and that he'll be landing at Edwards in seven hours," Fredericka said.

"Shit, I thought I had that handled," Klaus said.

"Listen, you haven't been doing that well yourself," she said.

"You'd do well to watch your mouth. What are you going to do about this?"

"There's nothing I can do. It's a CIA mission, and they've got it locked down."

"Very well. I'll see what I can do from my end."

CHAPTER 45

"Ayatollah Rostami's plane is two hours out," Colonel Wilhelm said.

"They're running a little late, aren't they?" President Garcia asked.

"They had to alter their altitude to get over some weather, and ran into headwinds."

"I'm just glad we were able to extract him successfully," General Appleby said.

"Any more updates on John Chambers and the rest of his team?" President Garcia asked.

"Six of the men are in critical but stable condition, and the rest should be released by the end of the week," Colonel Wilhelm said.

"How about Chambers?" General Appleby asked.

"He died at oh-four-hundred."

"That's too bad," President Garcia said. "Did he have any family?"

"No, he never married, and his parents passed away several years ago," Colonel Wilhelm said.

"I want him buried at Arlington, with full honors," President Garcia said.

"A little unusual since he wasn't military," Colonel Wilhelm said.

"He deserves to be buried there, and I won't take no for an answer," President Garcia said.

"I agree, and there's certainly more than enough precedents," General Appleby said. "I'll make a couple of calls."

As they started working the issues of the day, General Appleby asked, "Is there something bothering you?"

"I can't put my finger on it, but I'm worried about the ayatollah."

"They're running a little late, but they haven't reported in problems."

"I know, but I've got a bad feeling."

"If you're that concerned I can scramble some F-35s to lead them in," General Appleby said.

"Good thought, do it," President Garcia said.

When the general got off the phone, he said, "They're on their way. They should reach them in a little over forty minutes."

They'd been working for just over an hour, when Colonel Wilhelm came back in.

"There's been an attack on the ayatollah's aircraft," Colonel Wilhelm said.

"Is he alright?" President Garcia asked.

"Yes, the F-35s took care of the threat."

"What happened?" General Appleby asked.

"The squadron commander said they were attacked by four F-16s from the North Carolina Air National Guard," Colonel Wilhelm said. "The F-35s flamed three of them before the fourth pilot realized who was shooting at them, and broke the attack off. He said their commanding officer, a reserve commander by the name of Franklin Brown, ordered the attack. He told them terrorists had seized the aircraft, and were intending to crash it into the Pentagon."

"I'd like for Strauss or Steward to spend a little time with this Commander Brown," President Garcia said.

"First, we'll have to find him."

"There's no way a reserve colonel could have known about the flight, so someone had to have tipped him off. Use whatever resources you need, but we need to find him."

"I've already spoken with Gosford, and he's all over it," General Appleby said.

"Sorry to interrupt," Colonel Wilhelm said. "But Ayatollah Rostami's plane just landed."

"Good. Are the Sikorskys standing by?"

"They landed just ahead of him. He should be here in about twenty minutes."

When the ayatollah stepped off the elevator, the president was waiting to greet him. "Mr. Rostami, it's good to finally meet you in person," President Garcia said.

"Thank you. I wasn't sure I'd live long enough for this day to happen."

"Are you up to getting started?" President Garcia asked.

"Absolutely."

When they entered the situation room, General Appleby got up to greet the ayatollah.

"Would you like something to eat or drink?" Colonel Wilhelm asked.

"I'd take some hot tea, and some fruit, if you have it," the ayatollah said. "I'd never seen an aircraft like the one that brought me here. It was very impressive."

"It's a Sikorsky S-97, and we've only built a few of them so far. It will be our next-generation attack helicopter once we get it out of the prototype phase," General Appleby said.

"Before we get started, do you have any updates on John Chambers?" Ayatollah Rostami asked.

"He died during the night," President Garcia said.

"I was afraid he might. I made a promise to him that I'd like you to be aware of. I promised that I would do everything in my power to bring an end to all of this needless bloodshed, and I intend to fulfill that promise."

"Good, we're on the same page with that," President Garcia said.

"I just hope it's still possible," Ayatollah Rostami said.

"I've always believed that anything is possible if you have faith and are willing to put the effort into it," President Garcia said. "I didn't want to do this in a vacuum, so I've invited Paul-Henri Archambault to sit in with us. I hope you don't mind?"

"I'll reserve judgment on that, but I'll go along for now."

When the secretary general arrived, they sat down to try to work out a path forward. The ayatollah didn't hold the secretary general in high regard, but after a seven-hour round of discussions, he had to admit he was a much different man than he'd imagined.

"This has been a good start," Ayatollah Rostami said as they called it a day. "Paul-Henri, I've misjudged you all these years. I've always considered you a rabid anti-Muslim, but I don't believe that now."

"I'm glad. I'd always hoped we could sit down and work through our miscommunications, but the process always got in the way. It's quite sad that the world had to come to the precipice before it happened."

"Mr. Secretary, I'd like you to spend the night with us," President Garcia said.

"OK, but why?"

"I'm afraid for your safety."

"I don't have a lot of enemies. Is there a reason for your fear?"

"Before I go there, I need your word that you won't share what I'm about to tell you with anyone, unless you clear it with me."

"It's hard to promise that before I know what you're going to say, but you have my word."

The president spent almost an hour laying out what they knew, and what they suspected. When he finished, Paul-Henri was speechless.

After several minutes, Ayatollah Rostami asked, "Mr. Secretary, are you alright?"

"Not really. Did you know all of this?"

"No. The president had shared a little of it before they rescued me, but this is the first time I've heard the whole story."

"I wish I could say that we knew the whole story," President Garcia said.

"So you really believe there are people within the highest levels of your government that are trying to destroy the United States?" Secretary General Archambault asked.

"We're not confident that we understand their endgame, but they have been willing to resort to extreme measures to attain their goals."

"I'll take you up on your offer. It will give me some time to think through what you've laid out," Paul-Henri said.

"Great, if it's alright with everyone, we'll resume at seven in the morning."

"You look like you're in a better mood," Melinda said.

"A little. I spent the day working with the secretary general of the UN and Ayatollah Rostami," President Garcia said.

"Rostami! What's that murdering bastard doing here?" Melinda demanded.

"Slow down. He's as much of an innocent dupe as the rest of us. I haven't wanted to burden you with any of it, but we've discovered a number of traitors spread throughout all levels of our organizations."

"Traitors. You mean it could have been Americans that murdered our children?"

"It's very possible that some of them had a hand in it."

"Lord save us."

"I'll second that thought. I can use all the help I can get."

"I thought you might call to gloat," Klaus said.

"Maybe a little, but what the hell do we do now?" Fredericka asked. "They're starting to figure this out, and I'm afraid it could all come out if we don't finish what we've started."

"At this point, I'm open to anything," he said. He listened for several minutes before he said, "Good God, woman, do you have any idea what you're asking of me?"

"No more than you've asked of us. It's time to shit or get off the pot, as they say."

"The president was quite clear the last time we talked, and if I'm to do this you're going to have to hold him in check," Klaus said.

"If no one backs out on me I may be able to block him, at least temporarily, but it's going to be close."

"OK, I'll do it," he said. "But if this doesn't work we're all finished."

CHAPTER 46

When they reconvened the next morning, they were all anxious to finalize a plan.

"How did you sleep?" President Garcia asked.

"Surprisingly well," Ayatollah Rostami said.

"How about you, Paul-Henri?"

"Not very well. I just couldn't stop thinking about what you shared yesterday. I've always been a little naive when it comes to the depths that some people will sink to, but I'll never understand how anyone could turn against their own people."

"That's the point," President Garcia said. "Zealots are always sure they're in the right."

"I've taken the liberty of putting some talking points together from yesterday's discussions," Vice President DeMarco said. "I'll give you a moment to look them over, and then I'll make whatever changes we come up with."

When it looked like they'd all finished, President Garcia said, "Let's just start at the top of the list, and work our way through the recommendations."

"I think Mr. DeMarco did a great job, but I'd like to clarify the first point," Ayatollah Rostami said. "In principle I'm fine with the peacekeeping troops, but I'd want a concise definition of their mission and the length of stay."

"Understandable," Secretary General Archambault said. "The mission would be to maintain order, and ensure that terrorists don't try to make off with any of your advanced weaponry. As to the duration, I'd like to leave that up to you."

"I'm not as concerned with terrorists as I am the Jews," Ayatollah Rostami said. "They've got to realize we're almost defenseless, and I'm afraid they'll take the opportunity to finish us off."

"I wish I could say you're wrong," President Garcia said.

"Alright, I'll amend the mission statement to include protection from any foreign invader," Vice President De-Marco said. "Now, about the duration. Would you be alright with a codicil that gives you the right to have the troops removed with thirty days' notice?"

"That would work, although given our current circumstances, their stay could be quite lengthy."

"Understood. On point two, I wasn't sure how to word it, but the UN is prepared to facilitate whatever level of humanitarian aid that's needed, at no cost. At least until you can get your oil fields back into production."

"Most generous. On point three, I've got no problem with your inspectors having complete freedom to visit any installation we have left."

"A quick question for the ayatollah, if you don't mind?" General Appleby asked.

"Shoot."

"How did you manage to develop the nuclear weapons you used against the fleet without us knowing?"

"I guess there's no reason to keep it a secret. We didn't develop them, we bought them from Pakistan."

"The lying dogs. I asked them directly if they were supplying you with arms," Secretary General Archambault said. "When we're finished here, I'm going to have them removed from the Security Council, and have an embargo placed against them so this doesn't happen again."

"I've got no problem with that," Ayatollah Rostami

said. "Even though they've been selling us weapons for some time, I've never trusted them."

"Sir, I know you asked not to be interrupted, but I thought you needed to see this," Colonel Wilhelm said, as he handed the president a flash message.

"Damn it to hell, I should have known better than to trust him," President Garcia said. "Is the general still on?"

"Yes, sir, and he's standing by for orders. I have him on a video link in the next room, if you'd like to speak with him."

"Can you transfer it in here?"

The colonel hesitated before he asked, "Yes, sir, but are you sure?"

"They'll find out sooner or later, put him through."

"So the shit has hit the fan again," President Garcia said when General Studdard appeared on the screen.

"For sure. The Israelis have launched all-out incursions into Jordan, Palestine, and Syria," General Studdard said.

"Damn. What else?" President Garcia asked.

"They've got two squadrons of F-16s that are about to take off, and the NSA believes they're going to hit the Iranian oil fields."

"Bastards," Ayatollah Rostami said. "I've got to contact my people and warn them."

"No need," President Garcia said. "General, I want you to have Incirlik scramble two squadrons of F-35s."

"What's the mission?"

"I want them to shoot down any Israeli aircraft that leaves their airspace," President Garcia said.

"You want us to fire on the Israelis?"

"I do, and tell the squadron commanders to make damn sure they shoot them all down."

"Understood."

"You know that's going to stir up a hornets' nest with

your congressional partners," Vice President DeMarco said.

"Hell yes, I do. That's all, General, and call me when it's done. Colonel, see if you can get Prime Minister Weizmann for me."

It took Colonel Wilhelm over an hour to make contact. "Sorry it took so long, but I've got the prime minister on video," Colonel Wilhelm said.

"Prime Minister, I see you're up to no good. I thought we'd agreed you'd back off until the Iran situation had stabilized?"

"I never said I'd hold off forever. I didn't take your call right away because I wanted to verify that your forces had shot down thirty of our aircraft."

"I warned you that I wouldn't stand for any bullshit out of you, and now you can see that unlike you, I'm a man of my word."

"You bastard, I'll see that you're impeached."

"Well you might as well add this to your list of grievances. If you don't recall your ground forces, I'll have them destroyed as well."

"You wouldn't dare. You've already committed war crimes by attacking our aircraft, and you'd be committing political suicide if you carry out your threats."

"Not a threat, it's a promise. Stand down immediately, or I'll wipe them off the face of the earth."

"You're not going to bluff me into stopping this time. I told you that I was going to put an end to those scum, and I mean to do it."

"So be it," President Garcia said as he broke the connection. "I need the general again."

"Yes, sir," General Studdard said.

"What's the easiest way to stop the Israeli ground forces?"

"We don't have anything in the area, so air strikes are

about all we could pull off on short notice. Why, are you wanting to send them a message?"

"No, I want you to wipe them out," President Garcia said.

"Everything?"

"Everything, including their air cover."

"What assets can I use?"

"Anything we have."

"Got it. Consider it done," General Studdard said.

"I can't believe you just did that," Ayatollah Rostami said.

"I gave you my word we'd protect you, and besides that, I'd already put Prime Minister Weizmann on notice," President Garcia said.

They went back to work, but a half hour later, Colonel Wilhelm came in. "The Speaker of the House is demanding to speak with you," Colonel Wilhelm said.

"Damn, that was quick," Vice President DeMarco said.

"Good afternoon, Shelby," President Garcia said.

"I've got to admit you've got balls, but you've gone too far this time," Shelby Cohen said. "I'll see that you're impeached, and if possible, sent to jail."

"Do your worst, but I'll not stand by and let Ben Weizmann murder innocents."

"Innocents? They just killed thousands of our men."

"I'm not going to discuss classified matters with you, but my decision stands, and if they keep pushing, I'll hit them again."

"You're done," she said.

"Same old Shelby," Vice President DeMarco said. "But don't doubt for a second that she's going to try to take us all down over this."

"I'm sure you're right," President Garcia said. "Okay, let's get back to it. I'd like to finish this up this afternoon."

* * *

It took them until 8 P.M., but they managed to hammer out the rest of their plan.

"Gentlemen, I think we're done," President Garcia said.

"President Garcia, I can't tell you what this is going to mean to my country," Ayatollah Rostami said. "I wish I could say that I'd have done the same, but I'm not sure I would have."

"I think you're selling yourself short. I wish we could do more, but were in sorry shape ourselves. Colonel Wilhelm, have we received an update from General Studdard yet?"

"No, sir. Would you like me to get him for you?"

"Yes, and just put it on the screen in here."

"General, I need a status update," President Garcia said.

"We've taken care of their air support, but they're tenacious bastards. They've taken heavy casualties, but they've haven't turned back yet. I've got another round of air strikes scheduled, but we've taken significant losses as well."

The president thought for a moment, and said, "General, I'd like for you to hold off on that. I'm going to give the prime minister one last chance."

"I wasn't expecting to hear from you," Prime Minister Weizmann said. "Have you come to your senses?"

"No, I just wanted to give you one last chance to recall your forces."

"Catching heat from your people?" he sneered.

"I need your answer," President Garcia said.

"Hell, no, and if you kill any more of my people, I'm going to make you pay dearly, and I think you know what I'm talking about."

President Garcia muted the call, and asked, "General Appleby, what the hell is he talking about?"

"They have enough nuclear weapons to wipe out our European and Middle Eastern commands."

"Let me guess, they got them from us?"

"Afraid so. It started with Eisenhower, but we've given them several upgrades over the years."

"Great."

The president unmuted the call and said, "This is what I'm going to do. If you don't turn all of your forces around in the next hour, I'm going to have the navy launch a preemptive nuclear strike against your country."

"That would be genocide," Prime Minister Weizmann said.

"Trust me it's not something I'd want to do, but I simply can't allow you to turn the entire Muslim world against us."

After a lengthy pause, Ben Weizmann said, "I'm sending the order, but so help me God, I'm going to make you regret you were ever born."

"Damn, that was intense," Secretary General Archambault said when the call ended.

"I'd hate to play poker with you. That was a hell of a bluff," Ayatollah Rostami said.

"I wasn't bluffing. I want a complete rundown of everything they have, and I mean everything."

"Yes, sir," General Appleby said. "Normally you'd have been briefed, but President Montblanc blocked it, and when he disappeared, we just never got around to it."

"Ayatollah Rostami, considering the circumstances I'd like for you to stay with us for a few more days," President Garcia said.

"Not a problem, but I'll need to be there before the aid starts arriving, to ensure my people don't do anything stupid."

"Understood. Secretary Archambault, it's late, so you might as well stay another night."

"Not a bad idea, and if the ayatollah doesn't mind, we could have dinner together."

"My pleasure, and could we can have them bring us our meals in here?"

"No problem, I'll get it set up for you," Colonel Wilhelm said.

"Great, that will let me spend a little time with Melinda," President Garcia said. "General, how do you want to handle dinner?"

"If it's alright with everyone, I'll eat in my quarters so I can work on my e-mails. After that I've got a call with General Studdard at twenty-two hundred," General Appleby said.

"I'd stay on to visit with you, but I haven't gotten a decent night's sleep in weeks," Vice President DeMarco said.

"No problem. We'll talk tomorrow," President Garcia said.

When the general and the president had gone, the staff brought them their meals.

"This looks good," Secretary General Archambault said.

"It does, but I'm afraid I'm not very hungry," Ayatollah Rostami replied.

"It has been quite a day," Secretary General Archambault said.

"Without a doubt. I had a complete profile done on President Garcia when he took office, but it didn't do him justice," Ayatollah Rostami said.

"I knew he was a tough customer from his military records, but I never expected him to be as perceptive as he is."

"Do you really think he would have nuked the Israelis? I've only known him a short time, but I sense he means exactly what he says."

"Ben was right, history would have judged him harshly," Secretary General Archambault said.

"Probably, but the truth is, he's right. If he'd allowed them to wipe us out, it would have ignited a holy war that would have made World War II look like a skirmish."

When Klaus called Fredericka at 0300, she answered on the first ring. "I thought you'd be asleep," he said.

"Who can sleep with this shit going on?"

"You should try it from my side for a while," Klaus said.

"No, thanks, the stress is getting to me as it is. We're in deep shit. I've done everything I can think of, but he's a tough son of a bitch, and a lot sharper than I gave him credit for."

"Tell me about it. I still don't know for sure if he would have gone through with it, but after everything he's done, I simply couldn't take the chance."

"Trust me, he would have done it."

"It almost sounds like you admire him," Klaus said.

"Admire, no. However, I do respect him for standing firm on what he believes in. At another time, I would have been in his corner. But enough of this, what do we do now?"

"I was hoping you had some sort of plan. Let's do this: you spend a few days exploring any potential options you may have, and I'll huddle with my people and see if they've got any ideas."

"Will do, but I've got a really bad feeling about this," she said.

CHAPTER 47

When President Garcia walked into their suite of rooms, Father Mendoza and Melinda were talking.

"You look terrible," Melinda said.

"Thanks, I love you too," he said. "What are you two up to?"

"Nothing much," Melinda said.

"I'll leave, and give you some time alone," Father Mendoza said.

"You're welcome to stay and eat dinner with us," Melinda said.

"No, thanks. I could use some time alone myself," Father Mendoza said.

"How was your day?" Melinda asked.

"I think most would have considered it a bit stressful."

"That bad? Tell me about it. If you can."

"I'll spare you the details, but it got so bad that I threatened to nuke Ben Weizmann."

"You didn't."

"Afraid so."

"My God, how could you do that? They're one of our closest allies."

"At one time that was true, but I'm not so sure anymore."

"I'm sorry you had such a bad day."

"Don't worry your pretty little head about it. I'll get it figured out," he said as he bent over to give her a kiss.

As they sat eating their evening meal, they both tried to keep the conversation light.

"A fine pair we are," Melinda said. "Afraid to talk about what's really bothering us."

"I know, but what good does it do to talk about it? We'll just end up in tears," Victor said.

"Believe it or not, I'm doing better. Father has gotten me to a good place. I don't know what I would have done without him."

"I'm glad."

"He could help you too, if you'd let him."

"I'm sure you're right, but I simply can't afford the time right now."

For a change they got a good night's sleep, and for the first time since the kids' deaths, they got up in a good mood.

"Can I count on you for dinner again?" Melinda asked as he was finishing his breakfast.

"I hope so."

"You're chipper this morning," Colonel Wilhelm said when President Garcia walked in.

"So far, so good. What's on for today?"

"Nothing too pressing at the moment."

"Have you heard anything out of the rest of the group?" President Garcia asked.

"General Appleby stopped by a few minutes ago, and he said he'd be back in half an hour."

"How about the ayatollah, and the secretary general?"

"I haven't heard from either of them this morning. Would you like some coffee?"

"Sure, if it's fresh."

The colonel set his coffee down, along with the daily briefing folder. President Garcia was about halfway through the material when Ayatollah Rostami came in.

"Good morning, President Garcia," he said.

"How did you and Paul-Henri get along last night?"

"Fine, I think. I've had many conversations with him before, and I thought I had a pretty good perspective of how he thought, but meeting him in person has changed that. He's a much more open person than I'd given him credit for. In retrospect, had the meeting taken place sooner, it could have prevented much of the last years' drama, and potentially saved a lot of innocent lives."

"Damn, that's quite a shift for one evening," President Garcia said.

"It is, and it's the second time in as many days that I've had my opinion of someone changed." Ayatollah Rostami said.

"Is that a good thing?"

"Very much so. I had a much different opinion of you, and your country, before the events that have transpired over the last few days. Seeing a man like John Chambers willingly sacrifice his life to save us, and your willingness to stand your ground against one of your staunchest allies, has caused me to rethink my entire position on your country."

"Good, I was hoping we could finish working out our differences."

"I have every intention of doing just that."

When the team got back together, they spent the rest of the day hammering out the details of a new way forward.

"It's getting late, and we should probably call it a day," President Garcia said.

"If you don't mind, I'd like to go ahead and try to finish up," Ayatollah Rostami said.

"OK, but why the rush?"

"I'd like to see about getting back home."

"Even if we finish polishing the agreements tonight, I'd rather you stay on for a few more days," President Garcia said. "At least until we're comfortable that Prime Minister Weizmann isn't going to pull any more shenanigans."

"I understand your concerns, but what difference does it make whether I'm here or there?"

"Not much, I suppose. I guess I'm getting a little paranoid."

"Understandable, considering everything that's occurred, but my people need me there with them."

"Fine. Let's take a short break while we get your travel arrangements made, and then we'll finish up. Colonel Wilhelm, will you have Special Agent Stubbs come in please?" President Garcia asked. "And General Appleby, I'd like for you to stay as well."

"Yes, sir, what can I do for you?" Special Agent Stubbs asked.

"When we finish up this evening, we're going to take the ayatollah back home."

"I'll make the arrangements."

"Hold on. I want to do this a little differently this time."

"Different in what way?"

"Different in that I don't want someone trying to shoot the aircraft down. His itinerary is to be need-to-know only, and I want his aircraft to have air cover the entire way."

"The general will need to help me out with that," Special Agent Stubbs said.

"That's why he's here. I want the military to handle every aspect of this trip, but I do want a Secret Service detail assigned to accompany him."

When they returned to the meeting, President Garcia said, "There's a helicopter standing by to take you back to Edwards, so you can leave as soon as we're finished."

"Many thanks," Ayatollah Rostami said.

"Tom, would you walk us through what we have down so far?" President Garcia asked.

"Sure. The UN will expand its presence in Iran by a hundred thousand troops by the end of the month. Their mission is to guarantee Iran's security from internal and external forces. The term of the engagement is open-ended, but Iran can have the troops removed with thirty days' notice. Next, the UN will arrange transportation for all of Iran's oil exports and ensure that the funds received are used in accordance with this agreement."

"Would you mind clarifying that last point for me?" Ayatollah Rostami asked.

"No problem. I tried this a couple of ways before I decided it was easier to list the prohibited items, instead of trying to detail all of the items you would be allowed to purchase. Here is the list of prohibited items," Vice President DeMarco said. "As you can see, I've tried to keep it as succinct as possible."

"This is great. I don't have any issues with it," Ayatollah Rostami said.

"The next item is going to take some maneuvering by Secretary General Archambault and President Garcia," Vice President DeMarco said.

"This is quite a commitment," Ayatollah Rostami said. "You've expanded it since we last discussed it."

"At my insistence," President Garcia said. "The United States and our UN partners need to take responsibility for what has happened to your country. Even though everyone involved was duped into many of the actions we've taken, we must bear the responsibility for rebuilding your nation."

"I agree, but this is going to be a hard sell to the UN Security Council," Secretary General Archambault said.

"Then you and I had better get our salesman hats on, because this isn't negotiable," President Garcia said.

"I'm in, but don't think it's going to be easy."

"Great," Vice President DeMarco said. "The rest of the items on the list are fairly trivial, so unless one of you has any questions or concerns, I think we're done."

"It's been an honor to work with all of you, and even though we may have vastly different views on life, I think we've made a start toward a long-lasting peace," Ayatollah Rostami said.

"Let me second those thoughts," Secretary General Archambault said. "And furthermore, I'd like to commend President Garcia for his stellar leadership. I, for one, doubted that something of this magnitude was even possible, but he's shown all of us what a truly dedicated man can achieve."

"I have no doubt that we'll be faced with some difficult decisions as we move forward, but with God's help, we can get this done," President Garcia said. "It's late, so let's get you on your way home. Have a safe trip, and once you get an idea of what else we can do to help out, please feel free to reach out to any of us."

"My thanks to all of you, and may Allah be with each of you as we move forward," Ayatollah Rostami said.

"I hope we get him back without any incidents this time," Vice President DeMarco said.

"That's not going to be an issue," General Appleby said. "The air force is going to provide a fighter escort for the entire trip."

"I hope you're right," Secretary General Archambault said. "It would be catastrophic if something were to happen while he's in our care."

"I agree, that's why I had the general take charge of this trip, and why we've got to get back to work on our little rodent problem."

"Not tonight, I hope," Vice President DeMarco said as he looked at his watch. "It's almost two, and I'm about to fall asleep in my chair."

"It has been a long day. Let's get some rest, and we'll meet back here at say, sixteen hundred hours," President Garcia said. "Paul-Henri, I'll have Special Agent Stubbs's men take you home when you get up."

"Thanks, and again I'd like to say what a monumental thing you've pulled off."

"Um, you're back," Melinda said when she felt him getting into bed.

"Finally. Go back to sleep, and we'll talk in the morning."

CHAPTER 48

"There you are, I thought you were going to sleep all day," Melinda said when Victor came out of the bedroom.

"I left my watch somewhere, what time is it?" Victor asked.

"It's on the end table, and it's almost eleven."

"Damn, I've got things to do. Hasn't anyone come by for me?"

"Colonel Wilhelm came by around ten to see whether you were up yet, but he said not to disturb you."

"That gives me some hope for the day. Have you eaten already?"

"I was waiting to eat with you. Anything special you want for breakfast?"

"No, just something quick."

"Always in a hurry."

"I'm sorry. I know I haven't spent much time with you, but it's been one thing after another."

"I wasn't trying to guilt you. It's just that I miss our quiet time together, and with the kids gone, it's hard some days."

"I know, sweetie. I'll do my best to spend more time with you, but don't be shy, you can come down anytime you want."

"I don't want to get in the way, or be a distraction."

"Distraction? Hell, the thought of you is all that keeps me going most days."

"Thanks for that, maybe I will."

When President Garcia walked in, Colonel Wilhelm came over with the daily briefing folder.

"Anything critical in here?" President Garcia asked.

"I'm still prioritizing the latest batch that came in, but so far I haven't seen anything out of the ordinary," Colonel Wilhelm said. "Are you ready for the vice president to call in?"

"Sure, put him on. Did the ayatollah make it back alright?" President Garcia asked.

"No issues whatsoever," Colonel Wilhelm said as he was finishing the last of the communications. "I may have misspoken. The Chinese have captured Special Agent Collie in Shanghai."

"He's alive?"

"Evidently."

"When can we get our hands on the sorry bastard?"

"After that last debacle, it might be better if we send Leonard there," Vice President DeMarco said.

"I suppose you're right. We'd have to deal with all of the bullshit red tape and lawyers, if we brought him back. Alright, have Leonard Strauss drop whatever he's working on, and have him get to work on that piece of shit."

"He's in Rota, Spain, at the moment, but we can have him in Shanghai by tomorrow night," Colonel Wilhelm said.

"This is great news, even though it brings back all the pain," President Garcia said.

"I can't begin to imagine what you and Melinda have gone through, but maybe this can bring you some closure," Vice President DeMarco said.

"Sorry I'm late," General Appleby said as he sat down.

"I just heard the good news. You should sic Strauss on him."

"Just did," President Garcia said.

"He deserves everything he gets, but I've seen Strauss work, and he'd have been better off if he'd killed himself," General Appleby said.

Since there wasn't anything pressing, they only worked a couple of hours before they quit for the day.

"You're back awfully early," Melinda said.

"Wasn't much going on for a change," Victor said. He'd already decided not to share the news about Collie's capture, so they spent a nice quiet rest of the day together.

Three days later, President Garcia's patience was at an end. "I need an update on Collie," he said as he sat down to start their morning meeting.

"Strauss's report came in at three thirty this morning," Colonel Wilhelm said.

"Hand it over, I'd like to read it before we get started."

"Of course, but he included a video, along with his notes on the interrogation. Would you like to watch it before you read his notes?"

"Sure."

"Mr. President, my apologies for taking so long, but the subject was a tough nut to crack," Leonard Strauss said. "I've included a written synopsis of the notes from the interrogation, but I thought you'd want to see his actual confession for yourself. The footage is pretty graphic, so if you have any civilians in the room, you may want to have them step out."

Colonel Wilhelm paused the footage and asked, "Anyone want to leave?"

"Hell, no," General Appleby said.

"I'm good," Vice President DeMarco said.

"Get on with it," President Garcia said.

As they watched the first segment of the video, Vice President DeMarco found himself cringing a couple of times as Special Agent Collie screamed in agony.

When the first section ended, Leonard came back on. "This next part is where he started spilling his guts. Don't bother writing the names down, I've included them as a separate attachment."

As they listened to Agent Collie recount the names of the people he knew were involved in the plot, they were all growing angrier by the minute. He'd been talking for almost ten minutes when his body contracted and he slumped over in the chair.

"That's all I was able to get out of him before he had a stroke and died," Leonard Strauss said. "I'm terribly sorry, I don't usually have this issue, but he must have had a prior condition."

Damn it to hell, I wanted to kill the bastard myself, President Garcia thought to himself. *But at least the piece of shit won't hurt anybody else.*

"How trustworthy do we think the list of names is?" Vice President DeMarco asked.

"I took the liberty of reading Leonard's notes, and he thought we could trust what he gave up," Colonel Wilhelm said.

"I've always heard that anything gathered via torture was suspect," Vice President DeMarco said.

"Maybe so, but it's a hell of lot more than what we had. Let's get all of this over to NSA, so Randy Gosford can get to work on it," President Garcia said.

That night Victor waited until they were lying in bed to share the news with Melinda. "Honey, I need to tell you something."

"OK, but that doesn't sound like it's going to be good news," Melinda said.

"I'm afraid it's in the bittersweet category. The Chinese captured Special Agent Collie a couple of weeks ago in Shanghai."

"Finally. When do we get to face him?" she asked.

"Unfortunately he's already dead."

"Why did you have him killed?"

"We didn't kill him on purpose, he suffered a stroke during the interrogation."

She didn't say anything for a second or two. "Sorry, I was asking God to forgive me for what I was thinking."

"I'm pretty sure Collie won't be talking with him."

"I should hope not. I'm hoping he burns in hell for eternity."

"I'm sure he's already there."

"You were right. His death doesn't solve a thing, but I'm still glad he can't hurt anyone else," Melinda said. "Did your people get any information out of him before he died?"

"Oh, yes, and we're working on it as we speak."

"Good, I hope you get the ones that put him up to it," Melinda said.

Ten days later, Colonel Wilhelm met the president at the door of the situation room. "I was just coming to get you. As soon as you have an opening, Randy Gosford would like an hour or so."

"What do we have scheduled so far?" President Garcia asked.

"You and the team have a call with Admiral Kenyan at ten, but so far that's it."

"I don't want to cut him short, so let's schedule Gosford for noon."

President Garcia found his mind wandering as they went through the admiral's status update.

When they were finished, Vice President DeMarco said, "You seem distracted. Is there something bothering you?"

"Sorry. I guess I was thinking ahead to our next call," President Garcia said.

"Next call?" General Appleby asked.

"Sorry, I forgot to mention it, we've got an update scheduled with Randy Gosford at noon."

"Good news, I hope," Vice President DeMarco said.

"He didn't say."

"Thank you for working me in," Randy Gosford said.

"Never an issue. We're hoping you've got some good news for us," President Garcia said.

"That depends on your point of view."

"That's rather cryptic, but continue."

"I've followed up on the list of names we got from Collie. However, as I suspected, they were all fairly low level, and their interrogations didn't yield any actionable intelligence. That is, until I got to the last one. He really didn't know much either, but he'd picked up Sara McCluskey's name somewhere, and she turned out to be the key to unraveling this rat's nest. As the old saying goes, follow the money. It turns out that she's handled all of the group's worldwide disbursements. It took us a while to decrypt her computer files, but she kept meticulous records, and the data led us to at least some of the heavy hitters."

"That's great news," Vice President DeMarco said.

"That part is, but as I dug deeper, I've uncovered another set of leads that has taken me down a very disturbing path."

"I can't imagine how it could get worse, but please continue," President Garcia said.

"The trail led straight to Harry Miller."

"Oh shit, no wonder he committed suicide," General Appleby said.

"Randy, I need you to follow this as far as it goes, but the three of us are the only ones who can see the entire list."

"No problem, I've kept my teams compartmentalized," Randy Gosford said. "Assuming I don't run into a dead end, I should be finished by the end of the month."

"Good, that will give us some time to figure out what the hell we can do about it," President Garcia said.

"Well that was a kick in the head," General Appleby said.

"It's bad alright, but I'm assuming that no matter how hard we dig, there's going to be several that we won't discover," President Garcia said. "Unless something changes I don't believe the courts are going to be an option, so I'm afraid we may need to resort to a more direct solution."

"That sounds ominous," Vice President DeMarco said.

"That's because it is," General Appleby said.

"Tom, I'm going to have to ask you to drop off," President Garcia said, after a lengthy pause.

"Why? Don't you trust me?"

"Of course I trust you. I just don't want you involved in this phase. If it goes south on us, the country will need you."

"I don't like it, but I understand," Vice President DeMarco said.

"I hadn't considered that side of it, but that was a good move," General Appleby said.

"I should have discussed it with you first, but I assumed you'd want to help me with this," President Garcia said.

"Hell, yes. We're both soldiers, and what we may have to do would disgust a civilian like Tom. Besides that, the lawyer in him would get in the way."

"I'd forgotten he was once a lawyer. I don't doubt he'd have jumped in with both feet, but I was serious about the country needing him if we go down over this."

"It's a risk I'm willing to take," General Appleby said.

"Have you got any ideas about what we can or should do?"

"Nothing specific yet, but I don't think we're going to be able to avoid getting our hands bloody."

"No issue here, but how about you? You're the president of the United States, and we'll probably end up killing U.S. citizens before we're finished with this."

"To my way of thinking they gave up that right when they started this. I view this challenge to be much like the one Abraham Lincoln faced."

"I sure as hell hope it doesn't get that bad, but if it does, we just need to make sure we don't waver in our commitment."

"Agreed. When it comes down to it, who do you think we can trust to carry through with this? NSA is problematic at best. The CIA has the skills for it, but I'm not sure we can trust them either, particularly with stateside operations."

"General Young is a lifelong friend of mine, and if you don't mind, I'd like to pull him into this discussion."

"Isn't he the head of the United States Special Operations command?"

"He is, and he's got a lot of experience planning and carrying out this sort of mission."

"As long as you trust him, go ahead," President Garcia said.

"I do, and if we're done for today, I'll give him a call right away."

"Yes. I've had about as much of this as I can stand for today. See you in the morning, unless something goes to hell sooner."

"Good afternoon, this is General Appleby. Is General Young available for a short call?"

"Stewart, you old reprobate, how have you been?" General Young said.

"I'm good, Paul. Is there anyone with you?"

"No, why?" General Young asked.

"The information I'm about to divulge can't be shared with anyone, not even your chief of staff."

"Got it, but what the hell are you up to now?"

"You know what, this isn't a good idea. Can you meet me at the Pentagon, at say, eight o'clock tonight?"

"Sure, but why all the drama?"

"I'll fill you in tonight."

"Sorry I'm late, traffic was a bitch," General Young said.

"No problem," General Appleby said. "I'm sorry to put you to all this trouble, but this is a conversation that I can't chance being overheard."

"What's up, Stewart? This isn't like you," General Young said.

"Paul, this is the hardest conversation I've ever had to have, so bear with me. The president and I need your help."

"You know I'll do my part."

"I do, but what I'm about to ask your help with could be construed as treason if we fail."

"Good lord, man, what are you contemplating?"

"The events that have transpired over the last year have all been orchestrated by an as-yet unknown foreign power."

"What are you saying? Iran has been behind all of this. Haven't they?"

"So we thought, until we uncovered information that proved we'd been duped into thinking Iran was behind it all."

"OK, but what does that have to do with committing treason?"

"We've identified a number of U.S. citizens that are involved in this, and some of them hold some pretty high-powered positions in our military, government, and the courts."

General Young didn't say anything for several seconds as he tried to digest what General Appleby was saying. "I'll play along for the moment. What are you asking of me?"

"I need you to put together a team to remove the threats."

"Kill?"

"In some cases, yes. In others, we may just transfer them to Gitmo for processing before we make a final determination."

"You want me to help you kill or illegally detain U.S. citizens?"

"You've got it."

"Have you been smoking crack?"

"I almost wish I had. Unfortunately, I'm deadly serious."

"And the president is alright with this?"

"A hundred percent. Will you help us?"

It took General Young over a minute before he responded.

"I will. Tell me what you need me to do."

"I can't give you specifics yet, but the team will need the skills to assassinate the conspirators, and make it look like either natural causes or an accident. There may even be some circumstances that require us to just kill them in cold blood, and take our chances with the authorities."

"That's it?"

"I'm sorry, but I really can't tell you much more than that at the moment."

"I've never had to task a domestic mission like this, but we do this sort of thing every day, so it won't be a problem."

"Do you have men you can trust to keep their mouths shut?"

"Absolutely, and they all know the repercussions if they don't. Any idea how big the team needs to be?"

"I don't imagine we'll need more than a dozen, but if

my thinking changes, I'll let you know," General Appleby said.

"I can have them ready within the week."

"Thanks, and you'll be hearing from me."

Fredericka shuddered when the phone rang. "Yes?"

"They've captured Special Agent Collie again," Klaus said.

"How? I thought they'd guaranteed no one could get their hands on him."

"They did, but the chairman of the central committee pulled another purge, and our guys got caught up in it."

"What now?"

"I wish I knew. All but one of them was killed when they tried to arrest them, and if we got lucky he didn't spill his guts to those Chinese goons."

"What about Collie?" Fredericka asked.

"Unknown at this time, but he's not aware of anyone important, so he can't hurt us too badly."

"We can only hope. Make sure you let me know if anything changes."

Very early the next morning Vice President DeMarco's satellite phone rang. "Why the hell haven't I heard from you?" Golem asked.

"My damn phone won't work when I'm inside the facility, and there's a protection detail with me when I go outside. I wouldn't be calling now, if I hadn't convinced them I needed a little alone time to gather my thoughts."

"I expect you to keep feeding me the intel we need, no matter what the risk."

"I'll do my best, but I can't promise anything."

CHAPTER 49

"I'm afraid we've hit a dead end," Randy Gosford said. "I just wish they hadn't made us destroy all of the raw data from our phone monitoring programs."

"Boss, I've got something I need to tell you," said Walter Hagan, Randy's best cryptographic analyst.

"Well, spit it out."

"Do you know anything about the wide-band program?"

"A little, but I thought we discontinued that years ago."

"We were supposed to, but some of us thought it was a mistake. So when they disbanded the analytics group, we didn't turn off the automated data gathering systems. No one's looked at the data in years, but it's all there."

"You'll need to put the data in context for me. That initiative was started before my time, and I never had the clearance for it."

"The wide-band program was started up in the early seventies, and as you might guess from the name, it was built to capture virtually anything that was transmitted over the air waves."

"Do you have enough information on our persons of interest to do a search on their activities?"

"You know I do."

"Do you need anything from me?" Randy Gosford asked.

"Access to one of the new supercomputers would help speed it up," Walter Hagan said.

"Use the new clusters they just installed on the lower level. They haven't been tasked to a project yet, so no one will notice that you're using them."

Several weeks passed without any further incidents, but when they made the connection to Cheyenne Mountain for their daily call, Vice President DeMarco said, "You two look like you had a rough night."

"We were on a call with Ayatollah Rostami until midnight, and then we had a follow-up call with Prime Minister Weizmann," President Garcia said.

"You should have told me, I would have joined you," Vice President DeMarco said.

"No need. Once I talked with Ayatollah Rostami, and found out what had happened, it was a simple conversation with Mr. Weizmann."

"What did he do this time?"

"They sent a squadron of F-16s to try to sink the oil tankers carrying the monthly Iranian oil shipments."

"What good did they think that would do?" Vice President DeMarco asked. "Even if they'd succeeded, the UN had already paid them for it."

"Who knows, but we shot them all down before they even got close," General Appleby said. "I guess when we stopped the flyovers, they assumed we weren't still keeping an eye on them."

"I don't think the prime minister will make that mistake again," President Garcia said.

General Appleby chuckled, and said, "I thought he was going to puke when you told him you'd drop a cruise missile on him if he ever did it again."

"It funny how your view of war changes when you think you're the one that's going to be killed," President Garcia said.

"You threatened to kill him?" Vice President DeMarco asked.

"Promised would be closer to the truth," General Appleby said.

"I'd have loved to have seen it," Vice President De-Marco said. "Other than that, how was the ayatollah?"

"Quite well actually. They're starting to make progress with the rebuilding, and now that they have a flow of income to buy what they need, his domestic issues have started to quiet down."

"Sir, I have Randy Gosford on the line, and he'd like to give you an update on what they've found," Colonel Wilhelm said.

"Great. Tom, would you mind dropping off? We'll call you back when we're finished. OK, Colonel, you can conference him in," President Garcia said. "Randy, what have you got?"

"I don't have it tied up as well as you'll need to take action, but I wanted to let you know what we've uncovered."

"Let's hear it."

"There's no doubt that our esteemed Speaker of the House is up to her horns in this."

"Shelby Cohen! No way," General Appleby said. "She's a total bitch, but I've know her for years, and there's no one I can think of that loves this country more."

"As much as I dislike her, I'd have to agree," President Garcia said.

"I'm not saying she hates this country, but she has really strong ties to Israel. After listening to several hours of her conversations, I'm convinced they didn't intend to cause any real damage to the U.S."

"No real damage?" President Garcia said. "My God, man, we have over a million casualties, and they've murdered my children in cold blood. I don't give a shit what they intended, I know what their actions have caused."

"Sorry. I didn't mean to trivialize what's happened."

"I know you didn't, and I'm sorry I yelled at you, but don't think I'm going to cut anyone involved in this any slack."

"Understandable, but given the positions of some of the people involved, it's going to be difficult to hold them accountable."

"I don't care if I have to go all the way to the Supreme Court, I'll see justice done," President Garcia said.

"Which brings me to the worst part of it," Randy Gosford said. "Bradley Lynch, Jeremy Burnsides, and Margaret Gothenburg are involved as well."

"Dear God," General Appleby said. "How is that possible? Those are the justices that Peter named to the court."

"You're right, that's a hell of a problem," President Garcia said. "I apologize for asking, but are you absolutely sure?"

"I can let you listen to some of the intercepts if you'd like, but yes, I'm sure."

"OK, this is what I need you to do. I need a copy of everything you have, and then I want you to stand down. I don't want you implicated in anything that may happen from this point on. Are you clear on that?"

"Yes, sir, but are you sure you don't need my help?"

"I am. You've done a great service to your country, but your part in this is finished."

"Understood. I've already copied the relevant data to portable hard drives, and I'll have one of our couriers run it over."

"Very good, and thanks again."

"Well that little revelation certainly limits your options," General Appleby said.

"It sure does," President Garcia said.

"Colonel, Director Gosford is sending over a courier, and I need the material to come directly to me."

"No problem, I'll have security bring it down as soon as it arrives."

"One other thing. Would you inform the vice president that it could be a couple of hours before we call him back?"

"Got it. You need anything else?"

"No, we're good for now."

The president took a few minutes to organize his thoughts. "Sorry, I wanted to jot down a few things before we continued," President Garcia said.

"No problem, but what now?" General Appleby asked.

"Once we've gone through the rest of Randy's data, we'll lay out the complete plan," President Garcia said. "However, I think it's fairly obvious what comes first."

"Care to enlighten me?"

"Even though we have a list of the coconspirators, there's no way we've gotten them all."

"Probably true, and I doubt that many of them are even aware of the others," General Appleby said.

"That could be true, but we've got to start somewhere, and we're going to start with our esteemed Speaker of the House."

"OK, but how far are you prepared to go?" General Appleby asked.

"I'm going all-in, as the old poker saying goes, and here's what I think we should do," President Garcia said as he slid a sheet of paper over to the general.

"Oh hell, you were serious."

"Damn straight."

"I'll contact General Long as soon as we're done here."

"Great. Let's get Tom back on," President Garcia said.

"Are you going to clue him in?" General Appleby asked.

"No way. He needs to keep his hands clean."

They worked straight through lunch, as they tried to get through the seemingly endless list of issues.

"That's it for me, boys," President Garcia said. "The rest of this crap will still be here tomorrow."

"Good. I've got a meeting at the Pentagon, and this will let me miss the rush hour traffic," General Appleby said.

"Same time tomorrow?" Vice President DeMarco asked.

"If it's alright, I'd like to start at oh-five-hundred," President Garcia said.

"No problem for me," Vice President DeMarco said. "It's not like I have anything else to do."

"I'm sorry you're still cooped up there, but the Secret Service thinks there are still valid threats out there."

"I know. They briefed me yesterday, but it doesn't make it any easier."

"I need to spend a couple of days at the Pentagon. So if it's alright, I'd like to participate by video conference," General Appleby said.

"No problem. See you boys in the morning."

"You look terrible," Melinda said when he walked in.

"Thanks, I love you too," Victor said.

"You know I didn't mean it like that. I just worry about your health, with all of the pressure on you."

"I know you didn't, sweetie."

"What did you do today?"

"Same old crap."

"Do you think we'll ever get back to some sort of normal lives?"

"I wish I knew, and it could get a lot worse before it gets better."

"I don't know how," she said.

That night when they went to bed, Melinda said, "I've been thinking about your earlier comment. What did you mean it could get worse?"

"Sorry, I shouldn't have said that."

"Bull, you've got to tell someone, and it might as well be me. Vent away."

After he'd shared their latest findings, she said, "What are you going to do? It doesn't sound like you have any chance against them."

"That could be true, but I promise you that we're not going down without a hell of a fight. I may be remembered as the man who destroyed the Constitution, but I'm not going to allow this manipulation to continue."

"You do whatever you need to do, and don't worry about me," Melinda said as she laid her head on his chest.

"Sorry to get you out at this time of night, but I wanted to keep this as discreet as possible," General Appleby said.

"At least the traffic has let up by this time of night," General Young said. "I assumed it was a continuation of our last conversation."

"Afraid so. This first task is going to require absolute secrecy, and has to be seen as a horrible tragedy."

"Sounds grim."

"Depends on your point of view. I see it as the first step to eradicating the vermin who have sold out our country."

"Let's hear it," General Young said.

"I can't give you any of the specifics. I've been instructed to handle the details of the operations personally."

"What's that mean?"

"I need you to transfer the team to me, and I'll handle it from there."

"Why the change? Don't you trust me?"

"It's has nothing to do with you. If this goes to hell, the president wants to limit the damage to as few people as possible."

"I appreciate the sentiment, but I'm more than willing to take the risks with you."

"It may come to that, but for now, this is the way it has to be. The president was quite specific."

"Fine."

"What's up?" Klaus asked when he answered the early morning call.

"I couldn't sleep," Fredericka said. "I'm afraid that they're closing in on me."

"What makes you think that?"

"Nothing specific, but several of my best sources have been cut out of the loop, and that kind of shift makes me nervous."

"I'm having similar issues, but even if that's the case, there's not much we can do about it. Just stay the course, and hopefully this will come to an end pretty soon."

"End? Is there something I need to be aware of?" she asked.

"Nothing I can share at the moment. Don't worry; I'll let you know the details when the time's right. Now go back to sleep, and quit fretting over things you can't control."

CHAPTER 50

For the third straight night, Shelby Cohen had great difficulty getting to sleep. Frustrated, she'd taken an extra sleeping pill. When she woke the next morning, and saw what time it was, she mumbled, "Shit, this is a huge day, and I'm going to be late."

Her car had been outside waiting to take her to the Capitol for over an hour by the time she got ready. She'd just grabbed her purse and started toward the door, when her satellite phone rang. She took it out of the hidden pocket in her purse. "You know I don't like you to call me during the day," she said.

"I know, but it couldn't wait. One or more of your teammates have been talking," Klaus said.

"I thought you said not to worry about it," Shelby Cohen said.

"I know, but I've changed my mind. I'm putting the operation we discussed last week in play."

"Don't do it. Haven't we caused enough chaos?"

"Regrettable, but it's far too late to stop."

"I suppose you're right, but why did you call?"

"I'm going to need you to push the impeachment proceedings forward."

"There's no way that's going to succeed."

"I don't expect success, I just need a distraction."

"Whatever you say. I'm past worrying about it," she said.

* * *

"You're running awfully late, Ms. Cohen. Is everything alright?"

"It's fine, Dave. I got a call that I had to take. I know traffic is awful at this time of day, but do what you can to get me there by nine thirty."

"I'll do my best. You'd better buckle up."

The D.C. police knew her car, so they looked the other way as her driver weaved through traffic. When her satellite phone rang again, she slid the window closed that separated her from Dave, and asked, "What do you want now?"

"I'd been hoping it wasn't true, but here we are," he said.

"Who the hell is this?" she asked.

"I would have thought you'd recognize my voice by now."

"President Garcia?"

"I'm afraid so, Shelby. It pains me to know that you've been a party to all of this."

"Party to what, Mr. President?"

"Don't play coy with me. You know damn well what I'm talking about. This phone is your secure link to the bastard who's behind all of this. Look, I'm going to get right to it. I'm going to give you a chance to come clean. If you'll divulge everything you know, and I mean name names, I'll let you retire quietly."

"Or what, you spic bastard?" Shelby Cohen asked.

"So be it."

Shaken, she didn't even notice when her driver opened the window. "Sorry, Ms. Cohen, I didn't make up much time," Dave said as he slowed to a stop near the entrance.

"You're fine. It's not that big of a deal."

"If you'll give me a second, I'll get you right up to the entrance, once those people get out of the way."

As the car crept slowly forward, Dave caught a

movement out of the corner of his eye. "What the hell is that doing here?" he asked when he saw the remote controlled toy monster truck speeding toward them. As it ran up under the car, the C4 it was carrying detonated. The force of the blast shattered the limo, turning it into flying pieces of shrapnel.

"What's on tap for today?" President Garcia asked when he arrived for the morning briefing.

"Since we're getting started later than usual, you've got a full schedule, but you're probably going to put it on hold once you see this," Colonel Wilhelm said as he put the TV broadcast up on the big screen.

"This is James Johansen, WRC-TV, reporting live in front of the Capitol building. Approximately twenty minutes ago there was an explosion near the east entrance, and first indications are that it may have been another terrorist attack. So far first responders have verified three casualties, and at least ten wounded.

"The explosion was massive, and police are telling us it will probably require DNA testing to positively identify some of the victims. Stay tuned to this channel for further details as they become available."

"Shit, I'd hoped we were past all of this," President Garcia said.

"Why the long faces?" General Appleby asked when he called in for their video conference.

"There's been an explosion outside the Capitol building," President Garcia said.

"Casualties?"

"Tentatively three," Colonel Wilhelm said. "However, all we have so far is from a TV news crew. Our rapid response team should be on the scene in five minutes."

"Sorry I'm late," Vice President DeMarco said when he joined them. "I was watching the coverage of the Capitol explosion."

"Us too," President Garcia said. "We're waiting for an update."

"I've got Captain Calloway on the line," Colonel Wilhelm said.

"Good, put him on speaker so everyone can hear," President Garcia said. "What have you got, Captain?" he asked.

"At least six dead and fourteen wounded, three of which are in critical condition."

"Suicide bomber?" Vice President DeMarco asked.

"That's what we expected, however, when we interviewed a few of the witnesses, they all reported seeing a remote controlled toy monster truck running under the car just before the explosion."

"I know it's probably too soon to know, but have you identified any of the victims?"

"The car that was targeted was Shelby Cohen's, the Speaker of the House, and we believe that she and her driver perished in the attack."

"How could you know that?" Vice President DeMarco asked. "From the video I saw, you couldn't even tell what make of car it was."

"We found the rear license plate across the street," Captain Calloway said.

"Damn. I never liked the bitch, but at least we knew where we stood with her," Vice President DeMarco said.

"Very true, but maybe we'll get lucky and her replacement will be a better partner," President Garcia said. "In light of what's going on, let's cancel for today. We'll try again in the morning."

When the vice president dropped off, General Appleby asked, "You want me to hang on?"

"Yes, please. Colonel, would you mind giving us the room?"

* * *

"Was this our work?" President Garcia asked.

"Unfortunately yes. The collateral damage was much worse than we'd anticipated. For some reason she delayed her departure this morning, and there were far more pedestrians than we'd anticipated."

"Is the rest of the operation on track?"

"It is, and I hope to God it goes to plan, because there was already a lot of risk in the next phases."

When the speakerphone rang, President Garcia answered it.

"I'm sorry to interrupt," Colonel Wilhelm said. "There's been another incident."

"You can come back in," President Garcia said. "And please reconnect us with the vice president."

"There's been another incident, and I thought you should be on with us," President Garcia said. When Colonel Wilhelm returned, the president asked, "Where is this one?"

"The Supreme Court chamber."

"I didn't think they were in session," Vice President DeMarco said.

"The full court wasn't, but three of the justices were meeting on their own," Colonel Wilhelm said.

"What happened?" General Appleby asked.

"It's unclear. When one of the interns delivered some research they'd requested, she found them all dead in their chairs."

"That sounds familiar," Vice President DeMarco said.

"It does sound like the sarin gas attack on Roger Heinrich and his team," General Appleby said.

"The Supreme Court building is a secure facility," Colonel Wilhelm said. "They should have surveillance cameras covering the entire facility."

"Let's give them some time to work the situation before we reach out for an update," General Appleby said.

"Since we've got all of this going on, we might get a little work done while we're waiting," President Garcia said.

They had a working lunch, and just as they were finishing, the colonel's cell phone rang. "I've got Tony Fitzgerald, the leader of the FBI team working the case, and he has an update for you."

"Transfer it to the speakerphone," President Garcia said.

"Thank you for taking my call," Tony Fitzgerald said. "Justices Lynch, Burnside, and Gothenburg are confirmed casualties. I've had my team scan the last twenty-four hours of the security footage, but we haven't identified any unauthorized personnel entering the area."

"Was this a gas attack?" Vice President DeMarco asked.

"Unknown at this time. Our forensic team is on site, but we won't have a cause of death until they complete the autopsies."

"Thanks for taking the time to update us, Mr. Fitzgerald. Please don't hesitate to reach out if you need anything from us," President Garcia said.

"This just keeps getting worse," Vice President DeMarco said. "I realize this may seem crass at a time like this, but you need to start working on recommendations for their replacements. Would you like for me to take the lead on that?"

"Thanks for the offer, but I'm going to handle this myself," President Garcia said.

"OK, but don't hesitate to ask if you need help."

"Thanks. I need some time to work through my thoughts, so let's call it a day," President Garcia said.

"Excuse me, sir, I've got a call for you on line one," Representative Jeremiah's aide said.

"Who is it?"

"He said his name was Agent Smith, with the FBI."

"OK, put him through."

"What can I do for the FBI today?" Representative Jeremiah asked.

As the voice on the other end of the line spelled out what they knew, and what he was expected to do, Jeremiah broke out in a cold sweat.

"This is outrageous. I don't know where you got your information, but you're sadly mistaken if you think you can blackmail me into going along with what you're asking."

"Take a quick look in your secret e-mail account."

"Oh, dear God. Why are you targeting me?" he asked after he'd read the detailed accounting of his activities.

"We'll be talking with the others, but I need your answer."

"I'll do it, but you didn't leave me much choice."

"That's the first good decision you've made in a while. We'll keep in touch, and don't even consider tipping off the ones pulling your strings, or we'll be forced to take action."

That night when President Garcia sat down to eat dinner with Melinda, she asked. "Is something troubling you?"

"No, it's fine," Victor said.

"You don't look fine. I hope it's still okay if Father Mendoza eats with us?"

"Absolutely."

President Garcia tried to make light conversation as they ate, but as they were waiting on their dessert and coffee, Father Mendoza said, "I sense there's something troubling you."

"I've been getting a lot of that tonight, but everything is fine."

"Doubtful. I've been at this a long time, and I can tell when someone has something eating at them."

"I'm sorry but it's not something I'd care to get into," President Garcia said.

"There are no secrets from God."

"Don't I know it. But I'm afraid there's not much hope for my soul."

"Please don't say that," Melinda said.

"Sorry, I didn't mean to alarm you, sweetie, and I don't want you worrying about me. It will all work out."

"When you're ready to talk, I'll be there for you, as will God," Father Mendoza said. "He won't give up on you, if you don't give up on him."

"I'm counting on it, Father."

That night as they lay in bed, Melinda asked, "Are you going to tell me about it, or not?"

"I'm sorry, I can't."

"Can't or won't?"

"A little of both, I suppose. It's my burden and you've suffered enough."

"Nothing can bring our children back, but I don't want to lose you too."

"I promise that I'll do what I can to not let that happen, but none of us know the day it will end."

"I know, but you don't need to hurry it along."

Two weeks later, the FBI scheduled an update for the president and his team.

"Mr. Fitzgerald, I hope you've got some answers for us," Vice President DeMarco said impatiently.

"Not many, I'm afraid," Special Agent Fitzgerald said. "I'll start with what we do know. The justices were killed by sarin gas. The canisters were concealed in the bottom of their chairs, and they were activated via a cellular signal. There were nine canisters in all, and had the full court been in session, it would have killed everyone in the room."

"Any leads?" Vice President DeMarco asked.

"We're almost positive they were in the chairs all along. They'd replaced the chairs a few days before, and it looks like they came that way from the factory. We've interviewed everyone in the manufacturing plant, but so far nothing."

"Any progress on the assassins who killed Shelby Cohen?" Vice President DeMarco asked.

"Afraid not. We interviewed twenty witnesses, but none of them saw anything. Obviously we'll continue our investigations, but I wouldn't hold out much hope of us ever finding the perpetrators."

"Thanks for the update," President Garcia said.

"Well that was a complete waste of time," Vice President DeMarco said.

"I'm not that surprised," General Appleby said. "Whoever is behind all of this is quite good."

"They are, but these attacks seemed different," Vice President DeMarco said.

"How so?"

"Up to now they'd been intended to cause widespread panic, but these seemed much more targeted."

"It's a confusing situation for sure. Hell, I've never been comfortable that we even knew what they were trying to achieve," General Appleby said.

"Changing subjects on you," Vice President DeMarco said. "When can I get out of this hell hole?"

"That bad?" President Garcia asked.

"Not really. Everyone here has tried to make me as comfortable as possible, I just miss D.C."

"I don't know that I've ever heard someone admit that," General Appleby said.

"We'll get you back here as soon as the Secret Service

gives the all-clear, but given what's just occurred, I wouldn't think it's going to be anytime soon," President Garcia said.

"It's about time you called," Klaus said.

"I told you it was going to be difficult for me, and this last round of shit you pulled hasn't helped any," Vice President DeMarco said.

"That wasn't us."

"Don't bullshit me, you murderous bastard."

"I swear it wasn't us. Why would I kill them?"

"Who then?"

"I've got no idea, but whoever's behind it has really hurt our cause. Luckily we should be able to replace them rather quickly. When do you anticipate getting out of there?"

"Unclear. Sorry, I've got to go, they're coming back."

Late that night, Special Agent Bowers received an unexpected call on the phone they'd given him. "Hello, this is Jim Bowers."

"I've got a little task I need you to do," Klaus said.

"I'm not doing shit until I know my family is still alive, and that you'll release them when I do whatever it is you want."

"You have my word, and I'll let you speak briefly with your wife."

"Sonja, is that you, honey?" Jim Bowers asked.

"I'm so scared. Please get us out of here," Sonja said.

"I'm doing everything I can. Are you and the kids alright?"

"Yes, but we want to come home."

"I understand, sweetie, I'll—"

"That's enough for now. Did you receive the device we sent you?"

"Yes, but it doesn't seem to work. I tried it out last night, and the damn thing doesn't put out any light."

"It's not supposed to, it's a black light. Now listen carefully.

You need to take the freight elevator at the end of the main hallway. You're going to go to the lowest level of the basement complex, and when you get off the elevator, proceed to the far right corner of the room.

"When you reach the corner, turn on the light we sent, and you'll be able to see the outline of the box that's concealed there. You'll need to bring something with you to break the concrete. It's not very deep so it shouldn't take much. Once you've broken through, you'll see a small metal compartment. Open the lid, and flip the toggle switch inside. The device is on a thirty-minute delay, so that's all the time you'll have to get away. Any questions?"

"I'm going to blow up the White House?"

"Just the basement levels where that mongrel is hiding."

"When am I supposed to do this?"

"It's imperative that you do it no later than ten A.M. tomorrow."

"And you promise you'll let my family go?"

"Yes, as soon as we receive confirmation that you've completed the task."

"I'll do it, but I hope you burn in hell."

"I'm sure you do. Just make sure you hold up your end of the bargain."

CHAPTER 51

As they were starting their morning meeting, President Garcia asked, "Any idea who they're considering to replace Shelby?"

"I'd be shocked if it wasn't Walter Johnson," Vice President DeMarco said.

"I hope not. I'm already having a hard time with Prime Minister Weizmann."

"I understand, but he's definitely the leading candidate in my mind. Speaking of replacements. How are you coming with your Supreme Court nominations?"

"I'm submitting them in the morning."

"That was quick. Did you take a look at the list I sent you?"

"I appreciated the thought, but I didn't take it into consideration."

"I get it, but would you mind if I ask who you've picked?"

"No problem. Catharine Lipscomb, Barbara Thrush, and Cassandra Butts."

"There's no way in hell you can get those broads confirmed," Vice President DeMarco said.

I wonder what brought that on, President Garcia thought to himself. "Why not? They've got stellar judicial records, and they're all open-minded conservatives."

Damn it, I shouldn't have said that, Vice President

DeMarco thought to himself. "My apologies, it's yours to do, and I could be mistaken on their chances."

"I guess time will tell. We'll get started in a minute, but I want to wait until General Appleby calls in."

"Is he still holing up in the Pentagon?"

"He is. The Secret Service protocol doesn't address the chairman of the Joint Chiefs, but I'd hate for the country to have to get by without him."

"Sorry I'm late. Admiral Kenyan and I were checking in with Ayatollah Rostami," General Appleby said.

"Troubles?"

"Not at all. In fact the reconstruction projects are several months ahead of schedule."

"Great news. I'll have to give them a call and congratulate them on a job well done."

"So what's up? You both look like you just lost your last friend."

"I think Tom is upset with my picks for the Supreme Court," President Garcia said.

"I'm sorry about that earlier remark," Vice President DeMarco said. "It just that I thought the names on my list would have been much better suited to the task, and certainly easier to get confirmed."

"I'm glad that shit's in your court, because I'm not much of a political animal," General Appleby said.

"Me neither," President Garcia said, "but I'm learning."

Far faster than I would have believed, Vice President DeMarco thought to himself.

"I won't keep you very long today," President Garcia said. "I just wanted to share some news with you before it hits the press. They've confirmed Dilbert Morrison as the new Speaker of the House."

"What the hell?" Vice President DeMarco said under his breath.

"He's a good guy," General Appleby said. "He'll do a good job."

"I thought so too," President Garcia said. "Unless one

of you has something that can't wait, I've got a couple of things that I need to take care of."

"I'm good," Vice President DeMarco said.

"I have one thing, if you've got a minute," General Appleby said.

"Go."

"I'd like to relocate my family to the Pentagon with me."

"Great minds think alike. Their helicopter took off about half an hour ago. They should be landing at your location in about ten minutes."

"Thanks. I've missed them."

"Anything else?"

"Nope, that's all I had."

"Good. Same time tomorrow then."

As soon as they dropped off the call, President Garcia called Colonel Wilhelm back in. "Colonel, see if you can get Prime Minister Weizmann for me, and I need General Appleby back."

"No problem."

Several minutes later, Colonel Wilhelm returned. "The prime minister's assistant said he wouldn't be available for the rest of the week. Supposedly he's on holiday at the Orchid Hotel and Resort."

"I've been there," General Appleby said. "It's near the Red Sea, and it's quite nice. My wife and I spent our twentieth wedding anniversary there."

"How did you end up there?" President Garcia asked.

"I was in Israel, on an assignment for NATO, so we took the opportunity for a little R and R while we were there."

"I'd hoped to twist Ben's tail a little, but I guess it will have to wait," President Garcia said.

"I'm sorry to disturb you again, but Randy Gosford is demanding to speak with you immediately," Colonel Wilhelm said.

"Put him through.

"Where's the fire?" President Garcia asked.

"Under your ass if you don't get out of there," Randy Gosford said.

"Excuse me?"

"You need to evacuate immediately."

"You can't be serious. I'm a hundred feet underground, in one of the most secure locations in the world."

"If what I've uncovered is true, all it's going to be is the world's deepest tomb."

"I can't believe anyone could penetrate our new security measures."

"We can debate its validity at another time. You need to haul ass, and I mean now."

"Colonel, get Special Agent Stubbs in here," President Garcia said. "General, I'm going to drop off and deal with this."

"Understood. Contact me when you've reached a secure location."

"Mr. President, we need to move," Special Agent Stubbs said.

"How did you know?" President Garcia asked.

"I e-mailed him our assessment of the threat while we were talking," Randy Gosford said. "Now get going."

"Where are we going?" Melinda asked as they entered the elevator to the ground floor.

"No time, I'll brief you later," Special Agent Stubbs said.

When they stepped off the elevator, a dozen heavily armed agents and a special detachment of SEALs met them. "Follow me," the SEAL team leader said.

They kept them in the center of the group as they hustled them across the White House lawn, to where the *Marine One* helicopter was waiting. Its rotors were already turning up as they entered.

President Garcia looked over at Melinda and Father Mendoza, and said, "It's going to be alright. This is simply a precautionary measure."

* * *

Special Agent Bowers had been in a panic by the time he managed to sneak away. As the elevator started down, he glanced at his watch and said, "Damn, it's ten-oh-five."

He'd never been on the lowest level, so he had no idea what to expect. It hadn't been used since the late sixties and had once housed the nuclear reactor that powered the entire facility. When they'd upgraded to a new reactor, they'd installed the new one on the next floor up. Since they were abandoning that level, they'd removed the decommissioned reactor's fuel rods and encased it in cement. What they didn't know was that the workers had secretly hidden a three-kiloton nuclear weapon inside, before they'd sealed it up.

The security lights had long since burned out, so the door opened to pitch black. As Agent Bowers exited the elevator, he tapped the flashlight app on his phone. The light from his phone didn't carry very far in the massive room, and he couldn't help but shiver as he heard his footsteps echoing into the darkness. When he reached the corner he turned on the black light and immediately saw the faint green outline on the floor. He used the small hammer he'd stolen off one of the maintenance carts to break the thin layer of concrete. The lid screeched ominously as he pried it up. He said a quick prayer to ask God to forgive him, and flipped the switch to begin the countdown.

The president's helicopter had just cleared the White House grounds when they heard and felt the explosion. As they all turned to look out the windows, they saw the West Wing of the White House disappear into a plume of smoke and fire.

"Lord save us," Father Mendoza said. "What was that?"

President Garcia didn't answer his question as he picked up the intercom phone and said, "I need to speak with General Appleby immediately."

"Where are you?" General Appleby asked.

"We just left in *Marine One,* and Randy's intelligence was spot-on. There was a massive explosion shortly after we lifted off."

"How bad?"

"It was hard to tell, but it looked like the entire West Wing may be gone, and I suspect all the floors below it."

"Son of a bitch, there were a lot of good people down there," General Appleby said.

"Where are we at with the operation?" President Garcia asked.

"I'd rather not discuss it on this line. Give me a call when you've reached your destination."

"Hell, I don't even know where we're going," President Garcia said.

"We're headed to *Air Force One,*" Special Agent Stubbs said.

"Don't we have another secure location available nearby?"

"Yes, we do, but none that I'm going to trust."

"Where then?"

"I'll let you know when you hang up."

"General, I've got to drop off. I'll call you when we arrive."

"Good, and I'm going to finish this up while you're en route."

"OK. Where are you taking us?" President Garcia asked.

"Nevada."

"Where in Nevada?"

"Area Fifty-one."

"No way," Father Mendoza said. "Are we going to see where the aliens are hidden?"

"I'm afraid that's a myth, but it is one of the most secure locations in the world."

The engines on *Air Force One* were already running

as Special Agent Stubbs and his men escorted them on board.

"Please take your seats and buckle, up, we're leaving," Colonel Tibias, the chief pilot, said as they entered the cabin.

The 747-900 had reached the end of the runway by the time they'd gotten settled in. Colonel Tibias slammed the throttles forward, and in seconds the massive plane was at full acceleration. As soon as the plane lifted off, Colonel Tibias flipped the lever to retract the landing gear and ordered, "Prepare to deploy countermeasures on my command." As the massive plane clawed for altitude, he ordered, "Execute."

As the flares spewed out behind it, a cloud of metal chaff to confuse any possible missile strikes followed. "Stay alert for missile warnings," he ordered.

"*Air Force One,* this is *Guardian One,* we'll be your escort for today," the F-35 squadron commander announced.

"Roger that, *Guardian One.* Glad to have you."

When they landed at the Area 51 airstrip, a second SEAL team and the entire base security force met them.

"Welcome to Area Fifty-one, Mr. President. I'm General Trimble, the base commander."

"Good to meet you, General, although I wish it could have been under better circumstances," President Garcia said. "This is my wife, Melinda, and Father Mendoza."

"We'll talk more when we get you settled in, but right now we need to get you out of the open."

When they entered the massive hangar, there were several strange-looking aircraft parked inside.

"I knew it, alien spaceships," Father Mendoza said.

"Sorry, Father," General Trimble said. "Nothing that sinister. These are some of our prototype next-gen spy planes. Here we are. Please follow me."

"Great, another basement," Melinda said.

"Afraid so," General Trimble said as the elevator started down.

After almost a minute, President Garcia asked, "How deep is this facility?"

"Just over eleven hundred feet. The entire facility is shielded by twenty feet of concrete and ten feet of solid lead, encased in a titanium shell."

"Good lord, isn't that a bit over the top?" President Garcia asked.

"You can never be too careful."

"Don't I know it," President Garcia said. "I need to get back to work. Do you have a secure channel so I can speak with General Appleby?"

"The best money can buy. Much like everything else in this facility."

"Good, you made it," General Appleby said.

"No issues for a change," President Garcia said. "Are you alone?"

"Yes, I am, and the circuit we're using has NSA's newest encryption."

"I sure as hell hope it works. Have you got an update for me?"

"Unfortunately, yes. It may take weeks to get a final tally, but so far we've identified seventy-five military dead."

"Colonel Wilhelm?"

"Unknown. He'd radioed the perimeter security team that he had his wife and were on their way out, but no one has seen or heard from him since."

"That's a shame. He was a good man."

"It's still utter chaos here, so he could still turn up."

"Is that all?"

"The Secret Service has lost forty agents, and we believe there may have been as many as a hundred civilian workers in the building when it went down. The entire

West Wing dropped over sixty feet when the lower levels collapsed, so it's going to take some time to recover the bodies."

"Sixty feet."

"It's rather unbelievable. The scene resembles one of those monster sinkholes you see in Florida."

"Do you have any idea what they used, or how they got it past our security?"

"It had to be an inside job, but from the radiation levels we're seeing, we believe they used a tactical nuclear weapon."

"Bastards. If I still had any doubts about our path forward, this settles it."

"Agreed. I guess that means you're ready to implement the next phase?"

"I hate it, but yes," President Garcia said.

"Very well, I'll contact them as soon as we're finished."

"Actually, unless you have something, I don't have anything else we need to discuss. I'm going to call Vice President DeMarco and let him know where I am, so you don't need to worry about that. We'll talk more later."

"You really screwed the pooch this time."

"What do you mean?" Klaus asked.

"You missed him again," Vice President DeMarco said.

"How could you know that already?"

"I just got off a call with him."

"I'm surrounded by incompetents."

Takes one to know one, he thought to himself. "Whatever, I've got to go, but I thought you should know."

CHAPTER 52

When Father Mendoza sat down to eat breakfast, he said, "This place in unbelievable."

"I agree, but what's got you all worked up?" Melinda asked.

"Have you tried out any of the apps on the iPad in your room?"

"Just the TV and a couple of movies. Why?"

"You've got to try the one marked 'scenic views.' You can select from over a thousand different locations from around the world, and when you make your selection the walls seem to disappear, and whatever scene you picked appears. It looks like it's right outside your windows."

"I'll have to try it out. You're just picking at your food, Victor. Is there something wrong with your meal?" Melinda asked.

"No, it's fine. I was just thinking through a few things," Victor said. "Father, I'm sorry we got you into all of this. I can probably talk the Secret Service into taking you back to Albuquerque if you'd like."

"I appreciate that, but as I told you when I came, I intend to be here for you two until you no longer need me. Besides, as much as I hate to admit it, this has been the adventure of my life."

"Very well, but the offer stands," President Garcia said. "I hate to eat and run, but I've got a full day."

"What's new there?" Melinda said. "Sorry, that sounded like I was trying to guilt you."

"I wouldn't blame you if you were, but I've got to see this through."

"I know, and don't pay any mind to me, I'm just feeling sorry for myself this morning. Father Mendoza and I will entertain each other."

"What have we got this morning, Walter?" President Garcia asked when he entered the situation room. He'd thought the White House situation center was something, but this was far beyond that. There weren't any projectors or screens that you could see, but when needed, the full expanse of the walls morphed into ultra-hi-def monitors. The scenes could be scaled to allow multiple presentations on each wall, or one that used the entire wall. The first time he'd seen it, the view had almost overwhelmed his senses.

"Just the normal crap so far," Air Force Colonel Walter Bushnell said as he tapped the controls to put the reports up on the wall in front of the president. "Where would you like to start?" Colonel Bushnell asked.

"I need to touch base with General Appleby before we get the rest of the team on. I'll need the room for a few minutes," President Garcia said. "I'll call you back in when we're done."

"Good morning," General Appleby said.

"Good morning yourself. How are you coming with the next phase of our little plan?"

"On schedule, and so far so good. I talked to the team leader just before you called, and he thinks they'll be done ahead of schedule."

"Damn, some good news for a change."

"You still going to handle the last part yourself?"

"I am, and one part of me is actually looking forward to it."

"I'm not surprised. You deserve a little payback."

"I'd rather look him in the eye as I choke the life out of him, but I suppose this will have to do," President Garcia said. "You got anything you need to share before we get the rest of the team on?"

"No, I'm good," General Appleby, said.

"That's everybody," Colonel Bushnell said.

"Good morning, everyone," President Garcia said. "It looks like we had a quiet night, so hopefully we can finish before noon. Randy, let's start with you."

"Thanks. I only have one situation that I want to bring to everyone's attention," Randy Gosford said. "When President Garcia got the Israelis to call off their last offensive, they were supposed to pull out of all of the territories they'd occupied, but our sources tell us that they've been consolidating their positions in Gaza, Jordan, and Syria."

"If I remember correctly, the DIA had assured us that they'd removed their troops," General Appleby said.

"They did pull out their army units, but not before they relocated several thousand settlers into the areas they wanted to occupy."

"The miserable little bastard," President Garcia said.

"Do you want me to handle Prime Minister Weizmann?" Vice President DeMarco asked.

"No, leave him to me."

"That's all I've got," Randy Gosford said.

"General, you're up."

"I won't bore the group with the details, but the Iranian reconstruction programs are well ahead of schedule, and significantly under budget. They're now saying they will be finished before Christmas."

"That's outstanding," said Jeremy Scalph, the secretary

of the Treasury. "If it's true, we could reallocate some of that money to start reconstruction in the Portland area."

"A nice thought, but I'm not prepared to bite that off yet," President Garcia said. "Anything else for the group?"

"That's all I had."

"Miss Bannister, what does FEMA have for us today?"

"I have what we're going to call the final casualty list from the White House attack. The final tally puts the death toll at three hundred and one."

"That's higher than you'd projected," Vice President DeMarco said.

"It is. There were more civilians in the building than we'd originally thought."

"I infer from your comment that you're still not convinced we've found everyone," General Appleby said.

"That's correct, and the basement levels are far too radioactive to excavate."

"How's that going to modify the rebuilding efforts?" President Garcia asked.

"We're going to seal the area over with a thirty-foot-thick cement cap. Once that's in place we'll be able to rebuild the aboveground portions of the West Wing complex."

"So we won't be rebuilding the basement levels?" President Garcia asked.

"We're going to place the underground levels on the other side of the complex. When we're done, the public shouldn't see much difference, but this one will be far more secure, because we're going to use the same techniques that were used in your current location."

"How much is that going to cost?" Secretary Scalph asked.

"Our initial estimates put the total reconstruction cost at just over five hundred million, not counting what it takes to finish it out."

"Whoa. That takes care of a big chunk of the Iranian money."

"True enough, but it will be money well spent," President Garcia said.

"What's to stop them from blowing it up again?" Secretary Scalph asked.

"Trust me, that's not going to happen again," General Appleby said.

Everyone on the call thought he was just trying to put up a good front, so no one said anything about his comment.

"Homeland, you're next," President Garcia said.

"I've actually got some good news for a change," said Mary Beth Greider, the director of Homeland Security. "We've gone a full month without any border incursions."

"That's great, but it's probably just a temporary lull," General Appleby said.

"Could be, but I discussed the situation with Mr. Gosford, and he said that the chatter they'd been monitoring has pretty much died away as well."

"God, wouldn't that be great if we're finally seeing the end of this nightmare," said Walter Hagan, the attorney general.

"It would at that," President Garcia said. "I guess we'll have to wait and see what it means. Anyone else got something for the group?

"OK then, we're done for today."

"It looks like our efforts are bearing fruit," General Appleby said when they were alone again.

"It does at that. Hopefully this last push will put it to bed for good."

"We'll see. Speaking of that, I'd better drop off as well. I need to talk to our guy and get him started."

"If you can spare a few more minutes, I'd like to pass something by you."

"Sure."

"I've decided to modify our plan a bit."

"It's a little late for remorse."

"I'm not remorseful, but after I said my nightly prayers, it hit me that I could use this to strengthen the Constitution instead of destroying it."

"How's that possible?"

"Now that the Supreme Court and Congress are trustworthy again, I'm going to involve them in the last portion of the solution."

"What are you thinking?"

"I'm going to ask Congress to appoint a new federal court to deal with the traitors we've identified."

"Can they do that?"

"It's clearly covered under section one, article three of the Constitution. Once the new court is in place, it can hold the trials for the conspirators, and the Supreme Court will handle the appeals."

"Why the change of heart?"

"There are far more people involved than we'd anticipated, and I'd be shocked if we don't uncover even more as the judicial process plays out."

"Are you getting cold feet?"

"Absolutely not. I'm still willing to do whatever it takes, but I don't want to kill any more people than absolutely necessary. Plus I want to make an example of them, so that anyone that's tempted to go down this path in the future, might think about it first."

"Good points. Do I need to modify our current operations?"

"No, we'll stay the course on what we've put in motion."

"Anything else?"

"No, and thanks for listening.

"Colonel Bushnell, would you see if Chief Justice Avery has time for a quick call?"

* * *

"President Garcia, I'm so relieved that you're alright," Chief Justice Avery said.

"Thanks. I know you're up to your ears like the rest of us, but I need your expert opinion on a very sensitive matter."

"Happy to help."

"I know you've personally experienced some of the horrors our country has experienced, so I'm hopeful the court will be sympathetic to what I'm going to propose."

"What do you have in mind?"

"I'm going to ask Congress to declare a new federal court."

"They can certainly do that, but to what end? We have plenty of courts to address whatever it is you're up to."

"The new court will be responsible for trying over fifteen hundred American citizens for treason. Some of whom are very highly placed in business, the judicial system, government, and the military."

"Lord save us."

"I have hopes of that," President Garcia said. "Unlike the normal process, I want the Supreme Court to be the first and only court of appeals."

"That's doable. May I ask a question?"

"Of course."

"Is this a case of domestic terrorism, or is there a foreign power involved?"

"There's definitely a foreign power involved."

"Iran?"

"That's what everyone believes, but it's not them. I'm not ready to divulge who it is, but unfortunately the three justices that died were involved with them."

"I'm not going to ask the question their deaths bring to mind, because I frankly don't care. However, I can promise you the court will carry out its duty during this tragic phase of American history."

"Thank you for that. Now that I know you're on

board, I'll have this same conversation with Dilbert Morrison, Shelby Cohen's replacement, and Harry Bullard."

"I don't know Mr. Bullard, but Dilbert and I go way back, so if you need any help with him, just let me know."

"Will do, and thank you."

"You needn't thank me for doing my job, but while we're on the subject, I must thank you for the job you've done. I have no idea how you've stood up to the pressure, and the tragedy of this last year. You've done a stellar job."

"That means a lot, coming from you."

"I didn't think you were ever going to call," Klaus said.

"It's difficult to get them to give me any privacy. I've got to hurry, but I need to tell you that everyone I've been working with has stopped returning my calls."

"I know. We're having the same problem. I even sent an operative in to try to contact some of them in person, but every one of them refused to meet with her."

"That's not good. It sounds like someone has gotten to them."

"No doubt. I've got a meeting in two days to discuss our next moves, but I'm not sure what we'll come up with. Do you have any thoughts?"

"None that I could actually pull off. Look, I've done everything you've asked, and more. It's time you follow through on your promises."

"You're not in any position to make demands."

"Look, I'm tired of your bullshit," Vice President DeMarco said. "If you don't get my family back to me within the week, I'm going to turn myself in, and spill my guts."

"You're a fool. They'd either execute you for treason, or you'd spend the rest of your life in a super-max prison."

"I don't give a shit. If I can't have my family, I'd rather be dead."

Klaus muted the call for almost a minute while he discussed the situation with his team. "Alright. I'll have them in Virginia by next Saturday. I'll call you with the location when I know where they're going to drop them off. In the meantime don't do anything stupid."

"You just make damn sure you follow through."

When they'd finished, his chief of staff asked, "What the hell? You know damn well they've been dead for months."

"I know, but what else could I say? I know we've lost contact with almost everyone, but do we still have a man inside the facility where he's located?"

"One, but he's not going to do anything extreme."

"Can't you convince him?"

"He's not the kind of man you can threaten, and he has no family, so we don't have any leverage."

"Fine, I'll have to look elsewhere."

CHAPTER 53

"Good morning," General Appleby said.

"It is, isn't it," President Garcia said. "Tom won't be joining us again today, he's still got the flu."

"That sucks, but it's certainly going around. So what's got you so chipper this morning?"

"Things are starting to come together. Congress has authorized the new court, and I've submitted the five names that Chief Justice Avery gave me, and they'll receive fast path confirmations."

"Damn, I've never seen the politicians work that fast."

"Once I briefed the Speaker and the president pro tempore, they understood the urgency."

"What's next?"

"I'm speaking with Paul-Henri in an hour. Once I've gotten his recommendations, I'll know the timing of my next conversation with Prime Minister Weizmann."

"Great. If you don't mind, I need to drop off. I've got a call in half an hour, and I haven't finished my notes yet."

"No problem. We'll talk in the morning."

"Paul-Henri, it's been too long," President Garcia said.

"It has, but I hope the topic is more positive this time."

"That will definitely depend on your perspective."

"Shit. OK, let's hear it."

"I need the name of someone who could take over if Ben Weizmann was suddenly out of the way, and it needs to be someone who we can be sure wasn't part of the plot."

"Adina Gorwitz would be my recommendation, but why do you ask? It's unlikely Ben Weizmann is going anywhere. He's the most powerful man in Israel, and has been for decades."

After President Garcia had shared what they knew of his activities, Paul-Henri said, "My God. I knew he could be ruthless, but if even half of this is true, he's assured himself of a place in hell."

"Trust me, he's got a lock on it. I've never heard of this Gorwitz. What sort of man is he?"

"He's a woman. Adina means delicate, or gentle in Hebrew, but trust me when I tell you, she's anything but that. She was second in command of Mossad until she retired, and she doesn't take shit from anyone."

"Sounds like a woman after my own heart. How can I arrange a discreet conversation with her?"

"I can take care of that for you. When would you like to talk?"

"As soon as possible."

"I'll give her a call as soon as we're done."

"Thanks. I'll be in touch once I have a feel for the timing."

"I'll be ready."

President Garcia decided to write down some of his talking points with Ms. Gorwitz. He'd only been working for a little over an hour when Colonel Burnsides came in.

"I've got an Adina Gorwitz on the video conference. I've got no idea how she knew how to reach us, but she said you're expecting her call."

"I am, put her on."

"President Garcia, thank you for taking my call," Ms. Gorwitz said.

"No, thank you for agreeing to speak with me. I take it you've talked with Paul-Henri?"

"I have. In fact, he's the one that transferred me to your location after we talked."

"My apologies for being direct, but I don't have any time to beat around the bush."

"Never apologize to me for being direct. You'll find I'm the same way."

"Paul-Henri alluded to that. Okay then. Prime Minister Weizmann has been behind the events that have killed millions of people."

"I wish I could say I was shocked, but continue."

President Garcia spent the next forty minutes detailing what they knew of Ben Weizmann's machinations. When he finished, Ms. Gorwitz didn't say anything for almost two minutes.

"Are you alright?" President Garcia asked.

"Sorry. I assume you can prove what you've told me?"

"Absolutely."

"Good. What do you want from me? I haven't held an official position in over five years."

"That's exactly why I wanted to talk with you. I need to know if you'd be willing to assume the role of prime minister. If Weizmann were to step down."

"There's not a chance in hell he'd be willing to do that."

"It will be his choice, but if he doesn't, I'll see that he's tried by an international military tribunal for his crimes, and executed."

"What makes you think he'd fall for that? There hasn't been a military tribunal since the Nuremberg trials."

"I've already got Britain, Russia, and China lined up to sponsor it."

"You've done your homework, but why me?"

"Paul-Henri convinced me that you'll stand by your word, and although your reputation precedes you, he has complete confidence in your integrity."

"He's a good man. Normally I'd want some time to

consider this, but I know you're anxious for an answer. I'll do it, but I'll require your written guarantee that my country won't be punished for his misdeeds."

"You'll have it. So do we have a deal?"

"We do. How do we proceed?"

"Once I have everything in place, I'll contact the prime minister and lay out his options. Once he makes his decision, I'll contact you with the specifics of how you'll assume power."

"I'll be ready."

That night when they sat down to eat, President Garcia was noticeably more upbeat.

"You must have had a good day," Melinda said.

"Is it that obvious?"

"For sure," Father Mendoza said. "It's been weeks since you've looked this relaxed."

"I'm finally starting to make some headway. With any luck we'll be able to put an end to this nightmare before very long much longer."

"Praise God," Father Mendoza said.

"Amen, Father," Melinda said. "Does that mean we can get out of here?"

"Yes, dear. I'll be leaving in a few days, and I hope to send for you two shortly after that."

"You're not leaving without me," she said.

"I'm afraid I'm going to have to. The situation is still very volatile, and I'm not going to take any chances with your life."

"OK, but I don't like it."

The next morning President Garcia left on *Air Force One*.

"President Garcia is on the move," Vice President DeMarco said.

"Where's he headed?" Klaus asked.

"No idea. I don't think I was even supposed to know he was leaving. I've been down with the flu, and I haven't been on our call for a couple of days. Why haven't you contacted me with the location where I can pick up my family?"

There was a long pause before Klaus said, "I'm so sorry. There's been a terrible accident. Their plane went down in a freak thunderstorm, and they're all dead."

He felt like puking, but his rage overcame the feeling. "Bullshit. I thought you'd been lying to me for some time; I just didn't want to admit it. I warned you there would be repercussions, and I promise you there will be," Vice President DeMarco said as he hung up.

When the President landed at Andrews Air Force Base in Maryland, *Marine One* met him. As *Marine One* prepared to land at the White House, President Garcia leaned closer to the window. "The pictures didn't do justice to the devastation," he said as he surveyed what was left of the West Wing. "Is there somewhere I can make a few calls?"

"They've got a temporary situation room set up in the East Garden room," Special Agent Stubbs said. "It's not as secure as I'd like, but given the security measures we've put in place it should be fine."

"Are those drones?" President Garcia asked.

"Yes, sir. We've got ten of them overhead at all times, and they're fully armed."

"No issues with the FAA?"

"No. They've tripled the circumference of the no-fly zone around the White House, so there's no chance of a civilian aircraft interacting with them."

"Welcome back, Mr. President. I'm Colonel Saint James, and I'm your new aide."

"Good to meet you, but becoming my aide hasn't been a life-enriching endeavor of late."

"I'll take my chances. Is there anything you need?"

"I need to make a couple of calls, and I'll require complete privacy."

"No problem. If you'll follow me, we've got a sound-proof, electronically protected room set up down the hall. All of the gear has the latest encryption, and there's audio, as well as video equipment."

"Thanks, Colonel, I'll let you know when I'm done."

"Good to see you again, Mr. President," Vice President DeMarco said.

"You too, Tom. Are you feeling any better?"

"Finally. I didn't think I'd ever kick whatever it was I had. Is General Appleby going to be joining us?"

"Not today. He's busy tying up some loose ends."

"Good, because I've got something I need to tell you."

"That sounds pretty ominous."

"You have no idea. I've been feeding information to the Israelis. I've tried to limit it to stuff that would cause the least amount of harm, but I know damn well some of it has gotten people killed."

"Why in God's name would you do that?"

"They've been holding my family hostage, and said they'd kill them if I didn't go along."

"So why tell me now?"

"They're all dead. I think I've known for a while, I just couldn't bring myself to admit it."

"I can't tell you how sorry I am about your wife and kids, but I know exactly how you feel," President Garcia said.

"Thanks for that. Of course I'll step down, and take whatever punishment you care to mete out."

President Garcia pondered his options for a few seconds, before he said, "Bullshit. I don't know what I'd have done in your situation, but I'm sure as hell not going to blame you for what you did."

"But—"

"No buts. Who else is aware of what's been going on?"

"As far as I know, only Ben Weizmann."

"I was hoping that's what you'd say. Here's what we're going to do." President Garcia spent the next half an hour detailing what he had in mind. "What do you think?"

"I think it could work, but do you think he'll even take the meeting?" Vice President DeMarco asked.

"I believe he will, if Paul-Henri sets it up."

"Then I'm in."

CHAPTER 54

"Thanks for coming on such short notice," President Garcia said.

"No problem, but why the urgency?" Chief Justice Avery asked.

"I needed to discuss the new court with you, and I wanted to do it in person."

"Great, but I thought we were in agreement on the procedures?"

"I wanted to see if you would consider another approach."

"What do you have in mind?"

"I want to hold all of the trials in secret, including any appeals."

"I thought you wanted to make an example of them?"

"I did, but let me explain what's changed."

When President Garcia finished, Chief Justice Avery was at a loss of how to express what he was thinking.

"You alright?" President Garcia finally asked.

"No, I'm not. I would have never believed a nation whose very core is based on a belief in God and His teachings could stoop this low."

"I understand, but I promise you they're behind all of it."

"It will be a minor tweak to the process, so it shouldn't hold up the trials or the appeals, but where are you going to send them if they get jail time?"

"I've worked out an agreement with the British. They're going to house them at Gibraltar. They're converting the World War II tunnels into a high-security prison."

"I wouldn't have thought of that, but it should provide both security and secrecy."

"That's certainly our intent. I'm sure you already realize this, but you can't speak of this to anyone."

"Of course. Just let me know if you need anything else from me or the courts."

On Friday of that week, Prime Minister Weizmann's plane landed at JFK International Airport.

"Your car is waiting, sir," said Hadar Blomstein, his chief of security.

"Thank you. How long to the UN building?"

"It's only seventeen miles, but at this time of day it could be over an hour."

"Damn, I'm going to be late. I'll give them a call from the car."

When Prime Minster Weizmann's car arrived, they hustled him directly to the room where he was going to meet with President Garcia.

"There's coffee and tea on the table, and if you need anything else, just ask," the UN aide said.

"No, this will be fine. Is President Garcia here yet?"

"His car just arrived. He should be with you shortly."

"Sorry I'm late," Vice President DeMarco said.

"What the hell are you doing here?" Prime Minister Weizmann asked.

"I'm going to handle the meeting for the president."

"Unacceptable. I'm not going to deal with you."

"Sit down and shut up, you sorry piece of shit," Vice President DeMarco said.

"How dare you speak to me like that?"

"I'll speak to you in any manner I want, you murdering bastard."

Shaken, Prime Minister Weizmann sat down.

"That's better," Vice President DeMarco said as he walked over to the table to pour a glass of water. "Would you care for something?"

"I'd take a glass of water."

"Here you go," Vice President DeMarco said as he sat down across from the prime minister.

"Thanks. I can't tell you how sorry I am about what happened to your family," Prime Minister Weizmann said.

"You can drop the act. I know you don't give a shit about anything other than your agenda," Vice President DeMarco said.

"Fine, but don't think for a second that you can threaten me. You're nothing but a traitor, and if you're ever found out, you'll be in as much shit as the rest of us."

"You haven't left me anything to live for, so that's not going to work on me anymore."

"Whatever. Didn't the mongrel have enough balls to meet with me?"

"It's probably a good thing he didn't. He'd have ripped your head off, and shit down your throat."

"That's quite enough of that. What is it that you want?" Prime Minister Weizmann asked.

"It's time for this to end. If you'll agree to step down, and let a replacement of our choosing take your place, we won't let the world know what you've done."

As his mind raced through his options, it only took a few seconds for him to decide. "Very well. I took my chances, but my country can't afford to have this come out. The damned Islamists would wipe us off the face of the earth. As soon as I reach Tel Aviv I'll step down. Who do you have in mind to take over?"

"We'll let you know that once you've followed through on your commitment."

"We have an agreement then," Prime Minister Weizmann said.

* * *

"How did your meeting go?" Hadar Blomstein asked.

"Total bullshit. Get me to the airport."

As soon as his aircraft was airborne, Prime Minister Weizmann took out his laptop and started laying out his attack strategy.

"What are you working on so diligently?" his minister of defense, Jacob Grossman, asked.

"The first phase of our offensive."

"What offensive? Are you out of your mind? We've already suffered almost catastrophic losses because of your machinations, and we're in no shape to be starting a war."

"Not a war. I'm going to annihilate them. I'm going to nuke all of their Middle Eastern and European bases. Then we'll see who has to step down."

"They'll wipe us off the map."

"No, they won't. That's the beauty of being surrounded. They can't hit us with much without starting a war with the Arabs."

Crazy bastard, Minister Grossman thought to himself.

"We'll talk more when we land," Prime Minister Weizmann said. "I've got a bit of a headache, and my throat feels horrible. I'm going to lie down for a few minutes."

Jacob Grossman gently shook the prime minister when they landed.

"What is it?" Prime Minister Weizmann asked.

"We've landed."

"Damn, I feel like shit," Prime Minister Weizmann said.

His car was waiting to take him to his office, but shortly after they'd pulled out of the airport, Ben Weizmann lifted the lid to the ice tray and puked in it. "I think I need to go to the hospital."

"Right away, sir," his driver said.

The driver had called ahead, and there was a medical team standing by when they pulled up to the emergency room door.

"What seems to be the problem?" Dr. Dobias asked.

"My throat is on fire, and I'm throwing up," Prime Minister Weizmann said.

"Sounds like the flu, but we'll get you inside and get you checked out."

By the time Dr. Dobias finished his initial exam, Ben's condition had gotten much worse.

"I'm going to admit you so we can run some more tests," Dr. Dobias said.

"I haven't got time for that," Ben Weizmann said as he tried to get up. Before the doctor could tell him to lie back down, he passed out.

"Get him to his room. I need blood drawn, and start a saline IV," Dr. Dobias said.

President Garcia was holding his morning status call, when Colonel Saint James handed him a message.

"Prime Minister Weizmann has been taken to the hospital with an undisclosed ailment," President Garcia said.

"Too damn bad. I hope he drops dead," Vice President DeMarco said.

"Agreed," General Appleby said.

"Back to it," President Garcia said. "Chief Justice Avery is reporting that they should be able to finish the trials by the end of July," President Garcia said.

"That fast?" General Appleby asked.

"Most of them are pleading guilty."

"As they should," General Appleby said.

"What comes after the trials?" Vice President DeMarco asked.

"Once we've resolved the Israeli problem, I'm hoping we can get back to some sense of normalcy."

"Wouldn't that be nice," General Appleby said. "If you don't have anything else for me, I've got a call with the Joint Chiefs that I need to be on."

"Nope. You can drop off," President Garcia said.

"Thank you for not telling the general about my actions," Vice President DeMarco said.

"I told you it would stay between the two of us, and I meant it. You've suffered enough."

Six days later they received the news. "Prime Minister Weizmann has expired," President Garcia said.

"Shit. I doubt he had a chance to lay out our agreement," Vice President DeMarco said.

"What now?" General Appleby asked.

"I've reached out to the Knesset to arrange a meeting when I attend the prime minister's funeral."

"Do you think that's safe?" General Appleby asked. "They've been trying to kill you for some time now."

"I don't think they'd chance taking me out now, but I'll set up a video conference to make sure they know that we're on to them. I've already given Adina Gorwitz a heads-up, and she's ready to go."

"Thank you for taking my call," President Garcia said.

"No problem," Minister Ben Zeev said. "I assume you're calling about the prime minister's death."

"That's one of the things I need to discuss," President Garcia said.

"It's your dime."

"I've just sent you a document that explains the situation and our expectations of your government."

"Expectations?"

"Yes, expectations. Take a moment to read what I've sent you, and then we can proceed."

"This is ludicrous, we're not about to let you name our next prime minister, and what proof do you have of your allegations?"

"I've just sent you a small sample of our proof. Once

you've read it, you should probably delete it, so it doesn't fall into the wrong hands."

A few minutes later Minister Zeev un-muted the call, and said, "We're prepared to agree to your demands, but what assurance do we have that it'll end here?"

"Only my word, but trust me, it's better than your country's track record for truth."

"Point taken. I'll personally contact Adina. I don't know how you selected her, but she's well thought of, so it shouldn't be an issue."

"Excellent. I'll be attending the funeral, and we can talk more while I'm there."

"I wouldn't do that."

"Why not?"

"We'll accede to your demands, but I'm not foolish enough to think that there aren't others that wouldn't."

"You certainly know your people better than I do."

A few hours after Ben Weizmann's funeral, Adina Gorwitz called President Garcia. "Well, he's in the ground," she said.

"Good riddance as far as I'm concerned," President Garcia said.

"I understand. Honestly, if he'd done the things to me that he's done to you and your countrymen, he'd have died a horrible death."

"How's it going with the Knesset?"

"Surprisingly well. I didn't know what to expect, but there are still several members that I'd worked with in the old days, and they've helped me get started."

"Excellent. I look forward to a more beneficial relationship in the future," President Garcia said.

"As long as you follow through on your promises, it will be."

"That isn't going to be an issue."

* * *

"You look like the cat that ate the canary," Melinda said when he walked in.

"Close. Adina is now the head of the Israeli government, and we're wrapping up the last of the trials."

"That is good news," Father Mendoza said. "Does that mean I can go back home?"

"Yes, it does," President Garcia said.

"And I can't begin to tell you what you've meant to me," Melinda said.

"Trust me, child, I know."

"When we finish dinner, I'll arrange for them to take you home," President Garcia said.

After dinner, Melinda went off to take a shower.

"Father?"

"Yes, my son?"

"Would you mind taking my confession?"

"Of course not."

They went down the hall to an empty room so they'd have some privacy. It had been longer than he could remember since his last confession, and the events of the last year had weighed heavily on his mind.

After almost an hour, they were both exhausted. "Thank you, Father, I feel better."

"No problem, that's what I do. However, I sense you're still not at peace."

"Very perceptive. I'm not sure I believe that God could forgive my sins. I've had to do some truly awful things."

"As I told you, if you are truly repentant, God will forgive."

Eight months later, President Garcia was holding his first Security Council meeting in their new briefing center.

"This place is amazing," Mary Beth Greider said.

"It sure is," Randy Gosford said. "How deep are we?"

"Eight hundred feet on this level, although there are three more below this one," President Garcia said.

When they'd finished, President Garcia asked Vice President DeMarco to stay.

"We've never talked about it, but did you get tested like I asked?" President Garcia asked.

"I did, and you were right, I did have some exposure, but the doctor said I'd be fine."

"Weizmann croaked faster than you'd projected."

"I'm afraid it's not an exact science. Alexander Litvinenko lasted almost three weeks, but I must have used a larger dose than they did," Vice President DeMarco said.

"That was some nasty shit you used. I never asked, but why did you pick polonium-210? There are plenty of poisons that would have worked better, and faster."

"I wanted him to suffer as long as possible."

"Understandable."

"Do you think we're done with this?" Vice President DeMarco asked.

"I hope so. NSA hasn't picked up any chatter since Ben Weizmann's death, so maybe we are."

"You going to run for reelection?"

"I haven't decided, but if I do, I want you to run with me."

"Thanks for that, but I think I'm done."

"Honestly I don't blame you, but I feel like there are still things I'd like to accomplish."

"You're a good man, and there are still a great many issues facing us, so I'll back you to the hilt."

"Finally. I was afraid they'd gotten all of you," Golem said.

"No, there are still a few of us in place."

"We're going to lay low for a while. I'll contact you when it cools off."

"We'll be ready."